The Complete Chess Addict

also by Mike Fox

Rolls-Royce
The Complete Works
(with Steve Smith)

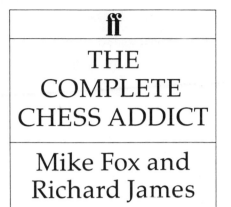

THE
COMPLETE
CHESS ADDICT

Mike Fox and
Richard James

faber and faber

LONDON · BOSTON

First published in 1987
by Faber and Faber Limited
3 Queen Square London WC1N 3AU

Filmset in Sabon by Filmtype Services Limited
Scarborough North Yorkshire
Printed in Great Britain by Redwood Burn Limited
Trowbridge Wiltshire
All rights reserved

British Library Cataloguing in Publication Data

Fox, Mike
The complete chess addict
1. Chess
I. Title   II. James, Richard
794.1   GV1445
ISBN 0–571–14901–4

To Natalie, without whom this book
would have been finished a lot earlier

A problem by Aladdin

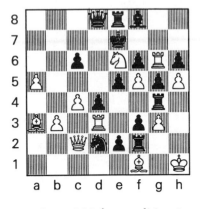

(See p.201 for conditions)

Contents

Acknowledgements

So many people helped it would be too space-consuming to acknowledge everyone, but thanks to: Betty and Howard James for their forbearance and hospitality; Janet and Emma Fox for their useful comments on the style, the spelling, the grammar, the content and even the acknowledgements; B. H. Wood for being so generous with his time, memory and pictures; Peter Gibbs for correcting some of the grosser errors; Steve Smith and the Pope for their encouragement; Colin Loose of Birmingham Chess Club for books; Bill Husselby for Napoleon's silk stocking; Laurie Hall for Haroun al-Rashid; Juliet Cook and Amanda Wilmoth for their patience and co-operation; Amy Fox for help with the title; Graham Storey for a desert island; Bernard Levin, Patrick Moore, Art Buchwald, Steve Davis, Michael Foot, Tony Benn, Edmund Dell, Buckingham Palace, the Archbishop of Canterbury, Steve Ovett, A. J. Ayer, Mike Gatting and numerous others for answering our daft questions; Ken Whyld for his help with some of the facts; Hilary Boszko for being a test-market patzer; Robert Maxwell for a book; Paddy Goldring for a joke; Harry Fox for his omniscience in the world of pop music; Niel Anderson for a bare bottom; Ken and Dinah Norman for reading the manuscript, for hospitality and for the loan of books; George Hill for checking some of the game scores; various members of Richmond Chess Club for books and/or information: Chris Baker, Ben Beake, Ray Cannon, Philip Poyser, Gene Veglio, Gavin Wall; Abraham Neviazsky for his part in Chapter IV; Matthew Evans of Faber and Faber for patience and munificence; the ever helpful staff of Birmingham's terrific Central Library; Mike Sheehan of Caïssa Books; Janet and Dave Allen for massive support when they had so much else on their minds; and especially, all those authors whose work we pillaged in our quest for facts; notably Messrs Murray, Hooper, Whyld, Krabbé, Golombek, Chernev, Knight and Twiss.

For permission to reprint copyright material the publishers gratefully acknowledge the following: extract from *Abinger Harvest* by E. M. Forster, reprinted by permission of Edward Arnold (Publishers) Ltd; extract from *The Art of Coarse Sport* by Michael Green, reprinted by permission of Century Hutchinson Publishing Group Ltd; *The Ballad of Edward Bray* by A. A. Milne, A. A. Milne, reprinted by permission of Curtis Brown Ltd, London.

For permission to reproduce illustrations the publishers gratefully acknowledge the following: Niel Anderson for the chapter heading illustration for Chapter IV; Associated Press Limited for Pope John Paul II; BBC Hulton Picture Library for Paul Morphy, Emanuel Lasker, José Raúl Capablanca, Alexander Alekhine, Aleister Crowley; Denis O'Regan/Idols for Phil Lynott; *Liverpool Post and Echo* for William Wallace; The Mansell Collection for engravings of the First World Chess Championship and Chevalier d'Eon; Raduga Publishers, Moscow (from *The Soviet Chess School* by A. Kotov and M. Yudovich, (1982)) for Tolstoy and Lenin; David Redfern/David Redfern Photography for Dizzy Gillespie; Graham Storey for the chapter heading illustration for Chapter VI; Steve Tynan and *The Sunday Times*, for Ossie Ardiles, Steve Davis, Terry Marsh; Syndication International Limited for Harold Davidson; The Tate Gallery Archive for Walter Sickert (Sickert 3.4 pb), and Marcel Duchamps (John Banting 779.8.127); Tate Gallery for *The Child's Problem* by Richard Dadd; Ken Whyld for the engraving of Philidor; and Naomi Sim for the photograph of George Cole and Alastair Sim.

Faber and Faber apologizes for any errors or omissions in the above list and would be grateful to be notified of any corrections that should be incorporated in the next edition of this volume.

Preface

> 'It's a great game of chess that's being played – all over the world.'
>
> Lewis Carroll, *Through the Looking Glass*

We wanted to call it 'The Monkey's Bum'[1] but Faber thought this lacked *gravitas*. Maybe they were right – but *gravitas* is a commodity you won't find much of in what follows. This is a not deadly serious look at chess.

Our simple intent is to have you say 'Wow!' every couple of pages or so; for *The Complete Chess Addict* is our own private collection of Wow!-inducing facts, anecdotes, legends and quotes about the world's best game.

Somewhere in these pages you'll find: games by Humphrey Bogart, Che Guevara, Yehudi Menuhin, Tolstoy, Patrick Moore, Karl Marx and other notables; Barbra Streisand and Bobby Fischer sharing *MAD* magazine in high school; the awful truth about Pope John Paul II's chess problem; the most depraved team in the history of the universe; the chess master who ate the pieces; the weirdest chess variants; the most difficult problem of all; the world's oldest game of chess; the world's silliest loss by a grandmaster; the state of the art in computer chess; and what 'bra drag' means in some chess circles.

And just in case you're worrying about investing your hard-earned in something utterly frivolous, we've chucked in for free (as it were) a collection of sixty of the best games ever played. This alone is worth the price of admission.

We also give you, for the first time ever, the results of the matches you've dreamed about: Fischer–Alekhine; Capablanca–Kasparov; and Paul Morphy versus Nigel Short.

What you won't find here is yards of in-depth analysis; the authors[2] aren't qualified to give it. But if you are, as they say, game for a laugh – or at least the occasional wry smile – then you're just the chap we're looking for. Welcome to *The Complete Chess Addict*.

[1] see page 181.
[2] a couple of patzers (see Glossary).

Postscript 1

If you're not a regular player, and you don't know about chess notation, a quick look at the next few pages ('Glossary' and 'Notation') will double the enjoyment you get from this book.

Postscript 2

The quotes at the head of each chapter are mostly by chess-players (including that all-time loser, Anon).

Glossary

BCF: British Chess Federation.

Blindfold simul: An expert plays several opponents without sight of the boards.

Blitz: Lightning chess – usually five minutes each on the clock.

Candidates' Tournament/Match: FIDE-organized event to select World Championship challenger.

Cheapo: A tactical trick.

Draughts: English for what the Americans call 'checkers'.

ELO Rating: Measurement of the comparative strength of a chess player (see page 89).

En Prise: Of a piece, able to be captured.

En Passant: A pawn capture in which a pawn on the fifth rank captures an enemy pawn which has just moved two squares as if it had moved one square.

Exchange (the): Advantage of rook for bishop or knight.

FIDE: Fédération Internationale des Échecs, the international governing body of chess.

Fifty-Move Rule: This states that either player may claim a draw after fifty moves have been played by both sides without a pawn move or capture. (This has been extended to 100 moves for certain rare positions.)

Fish: *See* Patzer.

Grandmaster (GM, IGM): Chess title awarded by FIDE to players who have achieved a certain standard in tournaments. (Strictly speaking: International Grandmaster.)

International Master (IM): FIDE-awarded title below that of Grand-master.

Interzonal Tournament: FIDE-organized event to select participants in Candidates' Tournament or Matches (q.v.).

J'adoube: 'I adjust': warning to opponent that you intend to adjust a piece on its square without moving it.

Lemon: A bad move, frequently played by patzers (q.v.).

Patzer: A bad player (also Rabbit, Fish, Woodpusher etc.).

Rabbit: *See* Patzer.

Sac: A sacrifice.

Sealed Move: Move placed in an envelope by the player whose turn it is to move when a game is adjourned.

Simultaneous Display (Simul): Chess display in which an expert plays a number of opponents at once.

Woodpusher: See Patzer.

Zonal Tournament: Tournament within FIDE zone to select participants in Interzonal Tournaments (q.v.).

Zugzwang: Compulsion to move – a term used when the player doesn't want to.

Notation

If you are unfamiliar with chess notation, or are only familiar with the outmoded Descriptive (or English) notation don't be put off. The notation used in this book, Algebraic (or Standard) notation is simple enough to be picked up by young children within five minutes.

Each file (vertical row of squares) is assigned a letter and each rank (horizontal row of squares) a number. Each square has a unique name derived from its file and rank, c.g. a1, e4, h8 (see diagram).

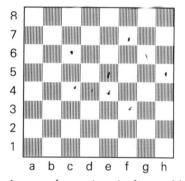

A move by a piece is denoted by the initial letter of the piece (N for knight) followed by the destination square, for instance Qe2, Nf6. For a pawn move only the destination square is given, for example e4 or d5. If two pieces of the same type can move to the same square the starting rank or file of the piece is specified, as in Ngf3.

Other symbols used:

x : Captures. (Nxe5 is a piece capture, dxe5 a pawn capture.)

+ : Check.

O–O : Castles king-side.

O–O–O : Castles queen-side.

! : Good Move

!! : Terrific move.

? : Poor move.

?? : Terrible move.

!? : Interesting move.

?! : Risky move

What is Chess?

Chefs is a nice and abftrufe game in which two fets of men are moved
in oppofition to each other
Dr Samuel Johnson's *Dictionary of the English Language*

Chess is a testy, cholericke game, and very offensive to him that looseth
the mate *Robert Burton*

Chess is ouer-wise and Philosophicke a folly *James I*

Chess is one long regret *Stephen Leacock*

Chess is a sad waste of brains *Sir Walter Scott*

Chess . . . is a foolish expedient for making idle people believe they are
doing something very clever *George Bernard Shaw*

Chess is not a game but a disease *Sir Henry Campbell-Bannerman*

Chess is a cure for diarrhoea and erysipelas
A mistranslation of Herodotus

Chess is a cure for headaches *John Maynard Keynes*

Chess is a beautiful mistress *Bent Larsen*

Chess is as much a mystery as women *Cecil Purdy*

Chess is vanity *Alexander Alekhine*

Chess is one of the sins of pride *John Bromyard*

Chess is life *Bobby Fischer*

Chess is like life *Boris Spassky*

Chess is my life *Viktor Korchnoi*

Chess is my life – but my life isn't just chess *Anatoly Karpov*

Chess is most certainly not my life *Tony Miles*

Chess is life in miniature. Chess is struggle, chess is battles
   Gary Kasparov

Chess is a fight *Emanuel Lasker*

Chess is a fighting game which is purely intellectual and excludes
   chance *Richard Réti*

Chess is a game of war *Anthony Saidy and Norman Lessing*

Chess is a test of wills *Paul Keres*

Chess is the art of battle for the victorious battle of art
   Savielly Tartakower

Chess is the art of analysis *Mikhail Botvinnik*

Chess is the art which expresses the science of logic *Mikhail Botvinnik*

Chess is not only knowledge and logic *Alexander Alekhine*

Chess is an art appearing in the form of a game *Soviet Encyclopaedia*

Chess is an art *Gary Kasparov*

Chess is everything – art, science and sport *Anatoly Karpov*

Chess is a game *Boris Spassky*

Chess is only a game and not to be classed with . . . science . . . or the arts
   Emanuel Lasker

Chess is undoubtedly the same sort of art as painting or sculpture
   José Raúl Capablanca

Chess is too difficult to be a game, and not serious enough to be a science or an art *Attributed to Napoleon*

Chess is not just a game; it bears an international significance *Jeremy Hanley MP*

Chess is not a science *Henri Poincaré*

Chess is beautiful enough to waste your life for *Hans Ree*

Chess is the most exciting game in the world *Irving Chernev*

Chess is the most interesting game that exists *Lothar Schmid*

Chess is the game which reflects most honour on human wit *Voltaire*

Chess is one of the noblest inventions of the human mind *Cyril Edwin Mitchinson Joad*

Chess is the most beautiful and reasonable of all games *Mme de Sévigné*

Chess is the fairest of all games *Isaac Bashevis Singer*

Chess is a fine entertainment *Leo Tolstoy*

Chess is an exercise full of delights *Arthur Saul*

Chess is an earnest exercise of the minde *Thomas Cogan*

Chess is not merely an idle amusement . . . life is a kind of chess *Ben Franklin*

Chess . . . is a forcing house where the fruits of character can ripen more fully than in life *Edward Morgan Forster*

Chess is a sport *Ray Keene*

Chess is a sport. A violent sport *Marcel Duchamp*

Chess is imagination *David Bronstein*

Chess is work *Walter Browne*

Chess is a cold bath for the mind *Andrew Bonar Law*

Chess is a form of intellectual productiveness
  Siegbert Tarrasch

Chess is the touchstone of the intellect *Johann Wolfgang von Goethe*

Chess is not for timid souls *Wilhelm Steinitz*

Chess is a powerful weapon of intellectual culture
  Slogan for 1924 All-Union Congress of Soviet Union

Chess is the struggle against error *Johannes Zukertort*

Chess is a game of bad moves *Andy Soltis*

Chess is a fairy tale of 1001 blunders *Savielly Tartakower*

Chess is the sublimated fight *par excellence*
  Anthony Saidy and Norman Lessing

Chess is . . . a mime of the family romance and of the Ocdipal drama
  Alexander Cockburn

Chess is a contest between two men in which there is considerable ego
  involvement *Reuben Fine*

Chess is a pursuit crammed with tension and emotion
  Anthony Saidy and Norman Lessing

Chess is the movement of pieces eating each other
  Marcel Duchamp

Chess is a dromenon *Frank Vigor Morley*

Chess is an international language *Edward Lasker*

Chess is a sea in which a gnat may drink and an elephant may bathe
  Indian Proverb

Chess is me *Salvador Dali*

Chess is a game of skill for two played with figures or men of different
  kinds which are moved on a chequered board
  Chambers 20th Century Dictionary

I *The Famous*

It will be cheering to know that many people are skilful chess-players, though in many instances their brains, in a general way, compare unfavourably with the cogitative faculties of a rabbit.

James Mortimer

I get my kicks above the waistline, sunshine.

Tim Rice, from Chess, *the musical*

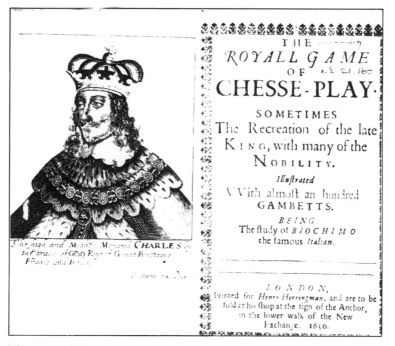

The game of Kings

This is chess from Aladdin to Zatopek. A bouillabaisse of celebrities who made their mark on history as movie stars, musicians, mass murderers, millionaires or marathon runners – and still found time to become adept at the world's best game.

Jostling for your attention you'll find Hollywood's most famous tough guy (he hustled chess on Broadway before becoming a megastar); history's best known transvestite; and the most notorious murderer of modern times.

We've grouped our celebrities by occupation; so if you're interested, you can work out that the musicians have probably the strongest team, followed at a distance by the writers, the holy and the baddies (captained by Britain's most famous defrocked vicar).

After you've read this chapter you can make up your own dream matches. Would big Frank Bruno have beaten Albert Einstein? Very possibly. Einstein loathed the game. Megabrain Bertrand Russell versus John (Britain's most wanted man) McVicar? Almost certainly a win for McVicar. He was an Essex boys' champion. Soccer magician Ossie Ardiles versus George Bernard Shaw? Ardiles would have strolled it. GBS was a self-confessed duffer. And Ardiles, as you'll see, is a classy player.

And Aladdin? If you thought he was just a character played by Paul Daniels[1] on the BBC's Christmas Special, think again. In AD 1387 he was the nearest thing they had to a world champion. For the details read on.

The Royals

It's called the royal game; it was invented, says the myth,[2] to please a king; and practically every king, queen, emperor, maharajah, shah and

[1] a non-player, by the way.
[2] For the myth, see 'The Awesome'.

tsar you've heard of played it. Some of them played it in the grand manner...

The great Mogul emperor Akbar played on a giant board (it still exists, at Fatehpur Sikri) with elephants as pieces, horses as pawns; and Shah Jehan (the chap who built the Taj Mahal) played living chess with thirty-two virgins as pieces. According to some sources, the winner took the thirty-two virgins as prize.[1] The Emperor Ming Huan (712–56) had a similar inspiration – he played living chess against his favourite concubine Yang Kwei-fei, using palace maids. But, for sheer thrill-a-minute stuff we turn to King Muley Hassan of Morocco. His contribution to brighter chess was to use prisoners from the royal dungeons. What made his games prime-time viewing was that captured pieces were beheaded on the spot. And you thought American football was rugged. The prisoners must have taken a keen interest in Muley's opening repertoire. Gruesome (but not necessarily accurate) legend has it that he was particularly fond of the Danish Gambit.[2]

Tamerlane (or Tīmūr the Lame), Emperor of the Mongols, was just as bloodthirsty as Muley, and an even more obsessive chess freak. His favourite occupation was collecting the skulls of his enemies into vast pyramids; but when he wasn't doing that he played chess like an emperor: on a super-board of 112 squares. Tīmūr was so besotted with the game that in 1377 he called one of his sons Knight-fork;[3] but his main claim to a niche in chess history was the fact that he employed Aladdin as his court lawyer. Yes, the same fellow who owned the wonderful lamp.

In the late fourteenth century Aladdin was the best chess-player in the world (his nickname was Ali the chess-player). His speed of play was prodigious; and 400 years before the great Philidor he was wowing the patzers with blindfold chess – four[4] games at a time, while carrying on a conversation with the spectators, *plus* one more game under normal conditions. He was also an early composer of chess problems (see our frontispiece).

[1]The modern equivalent of this would be a year's subscription to the *British Chess Magazine*.

[2]1. e4 e5 2. d4 exd4 3. c3 dxc3 4. Bc4 cxb2, and so bloodily on.

[3]Well, Shah-rukh actually. At the moment his son's birth was announced, Tīmūr managed to attack his opponent's rook and king simultaneously. He immortalized the instant in his son's name. Which event pleased him more we are not told. (All of this happened, say the history books, on 20 August, which we hereby designate International Knight Fork Day.)

[4]Even Philidor only managed three.

♛

Star of the Arabian Nights was Haroun al-Rashid,[1] Caliph of Baghdad, for whom the slave girl Sheherazade was supposed to have created the thousand and one stories. He flourished about 600 years before Aladdin and Tamerlane – but, says legend, was equally keen on the royal game. Haroun had the girls of his famous harem trained in chess, as well as the more exotic skills of the seraglio; and he spent 10,000 gold pieces on acquiring the world's first woman grandmaster – a slave girl famed for her chess skill.

In their first encounter she beat him, three out of three, and as her reward got a royal pardon for her imprisoned boy-friend. Later, according to Sheherazade's 461st story, the slave girl invented one of the best of all variations on the game: strip chess. Playing a court 'expert' in front of Haroun she beat him twice, then challenged him to a game at odds. She played without her queen, king's rook and queen's knight (he can't have been very good). 'If thou beatest me,' she said, 'take my clothes. If I beat thee, I will take thy clothes.'

Thinking he was on to a sure thing he gleefully grabbed the bait; but further deft sacrifices of material allowed her to queen a pawn and checkmate him. A sadder and wiser chess master left the court in his underpants.

♛

Just as embarrassing is the nightmare come true that happened to a nobleman while playing chess against the first of the Bourbons, King Henry IV, at the French court. François de Bassompierre, Marshal of France, and gambling companion of Henry, shocked the court, himself and his king, by breaking wind loudly and involuntarily while making a knight move. His future as a courtier hanging in shreds, the wretched Bassompierre had enough sang-froid left to explain: 'Your majesty, my knight will not move if he does not hear the trumpet call.' The king, it is recorded, smiled a wintry smile. But Bassompierre probably wasn't invited back for a while.

♛

The most crushing put-down in chess comes from a royal. When (around AD 905) court favourite al-Māwardī lost his title to the legendary as-Sūlī (the first 'all-time great' of chess history), he got the royal boot from his ruler, the Caliph al-Muktafī, with a line that has come ringing down the ages: 'Your rose-water has turned to urine.' You may

---

[1]or, more correctly, Harūn ar-Rashīd. His name translates to Haroun the Pusher – a tribute to his exploits in the harem.

be interested to know that this gag is a pun on poor old Māwardī's name: *māward* being ancient Persian for rose-water. Or then again you may not.

♚

If you're a caliph, or a king, whose every whim is law, then losing a game of chess must be a chastening experience. This accounts no doubt for the large number of sore losers in the history of royal chess. There are too many to tell all, but here is a selection of the more interesting.

King Canute, the first king of all England (the one who commanded the tide to stop) was playing Earl Ulf of Denmark, when he blundered away a knight. Imperiously he tried to take the move back, but Ulf wasn't having any. After a vigorous debate, the Earl, fed up at seeing an easy win snatched away, knocked the board over. This was an early example of a fatal chess blunder: Canute had him slain for arguing (the hit-man was called, appropriately, Ivor the White).

♚

William the Conqueror broke a chessboard over a French prince's head when he lost a game. The entente got even less cordiale a generation later: the Dauphin, Louis the Fat,[1] lost a game to William's son Henry, so he threw the pieces at him.

> ... Henry won fo much at Cheffe of Louis the King's eldest fon, as hee growing into Choller, called him the fonne of a Baftard,[2] and threw the cheffe in his face. Henry takes vp the Cheffe-board, and ftrake Louis with that force as drew bloud.
>
> Daniel's *The Collection of the History of England*, 1621.

It all makes Kasparov–Karpov seem rather tame.

For more bad language – and more violence – see Chapter III, 'The Frightful'.

♚

As well as Louis the Fat, there was Pepin the Short. His son, choked at losing to a Bavarian nobleman, killed him with a rook.

♚

A timely reminder of the rules, and a spot of off-the-board violence, was exhibited by the aforementioned Louis. On being seized in battle by an English knight, Louis calmly raised his broadsword, and with the words 'Know ye not, a knight cannot take a king?' bisected the unfortunate chevalier.

[1] He became Louis VI.
[2] Pretty strong stuff, since, according to Murray, the French prince was only nine at the time.

6

♚

The award for the best defensive player in this section goes to Prince Valdemar of Denmark. It seems he was playing with King Knut (the fifth of Denmark if you're interested), when they were attacked by a rival king. Knut was killed; Valdemar escaped by employing an early form of king's-side defence: he used his board as a shield.

♚

The Emperor Charlemagne is said to have played chess – and if you go to the Bibliothèque Nationale in Paris you can see the most splendid chess-piece of all, claimed (but modern scholars don't believe this) to have been a present to the emperor from his great contemporary Haroun al-Rashid.

♚

The classiest homicide in chess happened to Charlemagne's nephew, Berthelot. Renaud de Montauban, a French knight, no doubt fed up with losing, chose as his particular blunt instrument a golden chess-board. He smote Berthelot 'so harde that he cloved him to the teeth', says Caxton.

♚

The only known chess instance of someone putting down a king and getting away with it happened in Louis XIV's reign. Louis is playing a courtier, goes the story. There is a disagreement about the game. It gets heated. The members of the court sit frozen in horrified silence. An old and trusted courtier enters. Angrily Louis asks his opinion. 'You are in the wrong, your majesty,' ventures the old man, without looking at the position. 'How can you possibly know that?' says the outraged monarch. 'If you were in the right, sire, these gentlemen (indicating the silent courtiers) would have been only too eager to tell you so.' He must have been a *very* favourite retainer.

♚

King Conchubair of Ireland seems to have got his priorities about right. According to Irish legend,[1] he divided his day into three: one third for drinking, one third for fighting, and one third for chess.

♚

It is to a king we owe the idea of travelling chess sets. Louis XIII of

[1] There is a fair amount of legend in this section. Many of the early chess stories about the famous and the mighty were written centuries later in the form of medieval romances.

France secures his place in history not merely as the founder of the Académie Française, but as the king whose bright idea it was to travel with a chessboard made of wool, in the form of a cushion. If he wished to play on horseback or in his jolting carriage, he used this board and spiked pieces. Later in history the French nobility used the same idea to play chess on the sand at Dieppe. *Pique-sable* is what they called these pieces and a flourishing business in ivory carving grew up in Dieppe as a result.

♚

King Philip of Spain (the one who sent out the Spanish Armada) organized the first international match, Spain *v.* Italy, at his court. Representing Spain was a priest called Ruy López, after whom they named the opening. To Philip's annoyance, the Italians won easily, but he was big enough to give one of the winners – Leonardo – a thousand crowns.

♚

It's stretching the point a little, but it's conceivable that we owe the discovery of America to chess. According to the world's first chess magazine, *Le Palamède*, when Columbus was making his pitch for funds to discover a new route to the Indies, King Ferdinand was engaged in a game of chess, which he won. So pleased was the king that he granted the intrepid Christopher's request on the spot.[1] (For the story of how Britain *lost* America through chess see below under 'The Soldiers'.)

♚

Atahualpa, king of the Incas, was taught chess by the Spaniards whilst they pillaged his kingdom. He became expert at the game,[2] playing numberless games with his captors until they treacherously garrotted him in 1533. (And King Montezuma learned chess before he was stoned to death in Mexico thirteen years earlier.)

♚

The Tsars nearly all played chess. Next time you're in Leningrad, pop into the Hermitage museum and take a look at the chess-sets of Peter the Great and Catherine the Great.

Ivan the Terrible, the first of all the Tsars, had an ambivalent attitude to the game. In 1551, in the middle of reforming the clergy, he banned

---

[1]Says Edward Lasker in *The Adventure of Chess*.
[2]'He plays chess very well', said Gaspar de Espinosa in a letter to the Emperor Charles V.

it as an invention of Hellenic devilry. And yet he met his death, dramatically, at the chessboard. Here's how the English ambassador of the time told it. Ivan is playing, would you believe, Boris Godunov. He's just set up the pieces, but mysteriously, his king won't stay upright. Then: 'The Emperor in his lose gown, shirtt and lynen hose, faints and falls backward. Great owtcrie and sturr; one sent for Aqua vita, another to the oppatheke for marigold and rose water, and to call his gostlie father and the phizicions.' But it was all useless. The Tsar of All the Russias was 'strangled and stark dead'.

♚

Charles XII of Sweden (d. 1718), said Voltaire, lost his games because he moved his king far more than any other piece.

♚

Most of the kings and queens of England played chess. Richard the Lionheart is reputed to have been taught by his great enemy Saladin whilst in captivity.

♚

King John was playing chess when he was supposed to be relieving the siege of Rouen.

♚

Edward III was the king who founded the Order of the Garter. You may recall that the order (instituted to celebrate the battle of Crécy) came about when one of the ladies of the court dropped a blue garter at a court ball. The lady in question was the devastatingly beautiful Princess Joan of Wales, the Fair Maid of Kent. According to Froissart's chronicles, Edward formed a violent passion for Joan (her husband was, conveniently, in prison in France), and as a means of advancing his suit offered to play chess for a hugely valuable ruby ring. Edward, with some difficulty, contrived to lose. He then made what can only be described as overtures to the princess. She, with great dignity, declined. She also declined the ring, and after a certain amount of to-ing and fro-ing with the expensive bauble, she saved everyone's embarrassment by allowing her lady-in-waiting to keep it.

♚

Among the bizarre jobs handed out by Edward III to his courtiers was a cushy number given to the Lord of the Manor of Kingston Russell in Dorset, which involved 'counting the King's chess-pieces every Christmasse'. This was called a serjeantyh of the King. It wasn't the only serjeantyh. Another involved 'holding the King's head when he was seasicke'. At one time, the same individual held both these onerous posts simultaneously.

♚

Henry V (of Agincourt) suffered a rook checkmate while playing John Walcot of Walcot. That's why the Walcot arms bear 'three chessrooks ermine'.[1]

♚

King Henry VIII had a chess-maker on his staff – and his wardrobe lists included 'one bagge of greene velvette with chessmen' and 'a case of black leather conteynynge chestmen'. He was playing chess with Anne Boleyn when the news of Thomas More's execution arrived.

♚

Roger Ascham taught Queen Elizabeth I chess as well as Latin. One of her boards, inlaid with gold, silver and pearls, became Charles I's property – and was sold off by the Roundheads after the Civil War.

♚

Charles's tragic history had a recurring chess theme. During the Bishops' War with Scotland (caused by Archbishop Laud's interference in Scottish church affairs), Charles was playing chess with the Marquess of Winchester. Charles was contemplating a bishop's move when the marquess observed, 'See, sire, how troublesome these bishops are.' Charles got the point.

♚

There is still a Charles I chessboard at Windsor Castle.

It was made just after the outbreak of the Civil War. Around its base is engraved in Latin the poignant legend: *With these, subject and ruler strive without bloodshed.*

And when the beleaguered Charles received the bad news that the Scots were about to hand him over to the pursuing English, he was in the middle of a game of chess. He was philosophical enough to continue the game.

♚

George III lost the American colonies (see below, 'The Soldiers') but was accounted a strong player by his contemporaries.

[1]If you happen to be called Abelyne, Arthur, Bunbury, Colville, Dawkins, Ormsby-Gore, Pickering, Rockwood, Smart or Walsingham you'll be pleased to know that your family's coat of arms also includes chessrooks (Papworth's *Directory of British Armorials*, 1874, and other sources).

♚

Victoria was perhaps the most addicted of all British monarchs. According to a contemporary report in the *Hereford Times*, chess was the great solace of her widowhood; she seldom travelled without a chess set. Among Eugene Morphy's collection of Paul Morphy[1] memorabilia was a sheepskin chessboard signed by Queen Victoria. Is it possible that the Empress of India had met the greatest player of the nineteenth century? Maybe: the *New Orleans Times Democrat* for 11 July 1884 carries an account of a Morphy loss to Victoria: 'Morphy gallantly permitted Her Majesty to win' – which is more than he did for Napoleon III.

♚

In the twentieth century chess-playing royals are few – but then there aren't too many twentieth-century monarchs. King Farouk played when he wasn't dallying. King Alfonso of Spain played in a chess tournament in the twenties (and was knocked out by one of his colonels). King Abdullah of Jordan played Atomic chess – a pawn on being promoted became an 'atom-bomb' which destroyed all the pieces around it. And Archduke Ferdinand used to carry a pocket set made of silver on state visits. Whether it was with him on that unfortunate day in Sarajevo, we don't know.

♚

Kaiser Wilhelm II carried on the grand old tradition of assault and battery by chess-playing royals. As a boy, when he lost to his tutor, young Wilhelm hit him over the head with the board.

♚

The Duke of Gloucester, according to B. H. Wood, was a keen player as a boy.

♚

Sadly, the chess-playing tradition of English royalty seems to be dying out. Princess Alexandra is reported as saying she finds chess 'too devious', and that she prefers backgammon. The present sovereign, according to Buckingham Palace, currently 'has no interest in the game' – although, they say, she did have Charles, Anne and the other royal children taught in the nursery.

But according to *Chess* magazine (1956) the Queen, being shown

---

[1]See Chapter II. For more on Morphy and Victoria see *Paul Morphy, the Pride and Sorrow of Chess* by David Lawson.

round a working-men's hostel in St Pancras, came across some chess-players. Her comment: 'I play, but I am always losing. I learned my chess the hard way.'

The Holy

A bad scene. Our saints, popes and religious leaders, with a few notable exceptions, have taken a dim view of the noble game. In the twelfth century you could be excommunicated for what in some circles today would be considered normal club-night behaviour (drunkenness and chess-playing). The Muslims banned it (because the pieces were graven images);[1] the Jews banned it in 1322; the Buddha banned it long before chess was invented (he was against games on an eight by eight board);[2] the Christians were always banning it; and, most recently, the Ayatollah Khomeni banned it.

♟

St Bernard of Clairvaux, going right over the top, called chess 'a carnal pleasure'; St Louis went even further; he said it was boring. Both of them banned it.

♟

In 1061 the Bishop of Florence, poor fellow, was caught playing chess in an inn. He got into all kinds of trouble with his archbishop as a result of this abomination ('shameful, senseless and disgusting'). As a penance he had to wash the feet of twelve paupers.

♟

In 1291 the Prior and Canons of Coxford in Norfolk got it in the neck from the Archbishop of Canterbury[3] for playing chess, 'which heinous vice was to be banished, even if it came to three days and nights on bread and water'. Harsh stuff.

♟

[1] Muslim chess freaks got round the ban by carving pieces in abstract designs – echoed in the design, for example, of today's bishop and rooks.
[2] He also banned spillikins and tip-cat.
[3] The present Archbishop of Canterbury feels less strongly about it, but doesn't himself play.

In the fourteenth century John Wycliffe called chess-playing 'ydelnesse and wauntounnesse' and placed it somewhere between lying 'in softe beddis' and 'lecherie' as an example of scandalous behaviour by the priesthood.

♗

During the Inquisition, Savonarola threatened the inhabitants of Florence with eternal damnation if they were caught playing.

♗

There were exceptions though: St Francis Xavier saved a soldier's soul by teaching him chess; St Francis de Sales encouraged it – in moderation; and Thomas à Becket is said to have played chess with Henry II before things turned nasty. But the outstanding chess-player among the saints was a woman: St Teresa of Ávila was keen enough on the game to use it as a means of instruction. She devotes a whole chapter in *The Way of Perfection* to the game, in which she relates the development of the pieces to the development of our faculty for divine love. Her enthusiam for the game led to her being declared the patron saint of chess-players.

One of her habits though, would have got her into trouble with FIDE: apparently she was given to involuntary levitation and had to hang on to iron grids to keep herself off the ceiling. This must have been very off-putting for her opponents. Nevertheless, we nominate St Teresa captain of our holy team.

♗

St Teresa might have a little difficulty getting a full team together, but she'd have a scorcher on board one. He wasn't a saint, or even a pope, just an ordinary Spanish priest; but Ruy López *was* the first world champion of the modern game.

The church never made Ruy a bishop – but chess had its compensations – a pension from Philip II of Spain (plus a gold rook on a gold chain), a stipend of 2,000 gold crowns a year from an Italian duke, and the income from one of history's most successful chess books, meant that Ruy López was, for a while, a good deal more prosperous than most modern grandmasters.

♗

The rest of the divine team has a curious look: two popes, an American priest, and a cluster of nineteenth-century English vicars. Strongest of the popes was indubitably Leo XIII, who made it to the throne of St

Peter in 1878. Here's one of his brilliancies played when he was just plain old Cardinal Pecci:

Revd Fr Guila–Joachim, Cardinal Pecci, Perugia, *c.* 1875.
Giuoco Piano

1. e4 e5	6. e5 d5	11. Nxd4 Bxd4	16. Kxg2 Qg6+
2. Nf3 Nc6	7. exf6 dxc4	12. Qh5 Qf6	17. Kh1 Bd5+
3. Bc4 Bc5	8. Qe2+ Be6	13. O–O Rxg7	18. f3 Bxf3+
4. c3 Nf6	9. fxg7 Rg8	14. Qb5+ c6	19. Rxf3 Qg1
5. d4 exd4	10. cxd4 Nxd4	15. Qxb7 Rxg2+!	mate

Innocent III was another chess-playing pope. How good he was isn't clear, but he's worth a mention for a ruling which even the British Chess Federation would have difficulty making stick – killing after a game of chess is not a crime. '... If any clerk plays at chess and should quarrel in consequence of so playing, and kill his man, such homicide shall be accounted casual and not voluntary ... the reason is: he employeth himself in a lawful work' (quoted by Dr Salvio in 1634).

And now we come to a tale of the most appalling duplicity. Take a look at this:

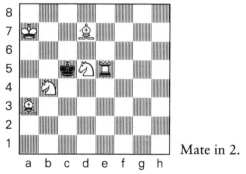

Mate in 2.

It appeared in that respected publication, *The Problemist*, in March 1987. Accompanying it was this astonishing letter:

Dear Sir
You will please forgive the few syntax mistakes that I surely did in this fast written letter.
    My friend the Cardinal Hume claims *The Problemist* is the best international publication devoted to chess problems (contrary to the French ones, narrow minded and sectarian). Consequently, I would like to take out a subscription. Could you either send me a specimen of your review or specify me the price of a yearly subscription.

I still happen to compose some problems, from time to time, and I believe it is a kind of healthy relaxation. I send to you three of my recent and unpublished problems, because until today the Polish specialised review never edited them (my pontifical duty must embarrass them ...) If you are interested, please be kind enough when they are published, to signed them Karol Wojtyła instead of John Paul II.

Please accept all my thanks. I send you my fatherly benediction if you are a Roman Catholic. If you are part of the Anglican Church, believe in my brotherly feelings of

Joannes Paulus P.P. II

P.S. John Nunn's *Solving in Style* was my bedside book the whole last summer. Teaching how to resolve, the author reveals in a remarkable way the art of composing.

The authors got very excited about all this. Hitherto there had only been rumours about the chess-playing ability of God's supreme representative on earth. Could it be that John Paul II (one of the few popes who has also been a soccer goalie) was a demon on the chessboard? Alas, a phone call to *The Problemist* revealed that the whole thing was a hoax on Vatican City notepaper. Our maledictions on the perpetrator (a Frenchman). Chess-players have been excommunicated for less.[1]

A very strong board two for the holy team is the American priest, William Lombardy. Father William is an international grandmaster, has twice been US Open Champion and in 1972 he was Bobby Fischer's second in his match against Boris Spassky.

In 1957 Lombardy won the World Junior Championship with a 100 per cent score, a feat which may never be equalled. Here's how he demolished the West German representative.

M. Gerusel–W. Lombardy, Toronto, 1957. Nimzo-Indian Defence

1. d4 Nf6	6. a3 Bxc3+	11. Be3 d4	16. Qb3 Nc5
2. c4 e6	7. Qxc3 Ne4	12. Rd1 dxe3	17. Qc3 Na5
3. Nc3 Bb4	8. Qc2 e5	13. Rxd8 exf2+	18. e4 Nab3+
4. Qc2 Nc6	9. dxe5 Bf5	14. Kd1 Rfxd8+	White resigns
5. Nf3 d5	10. Qa4 O–O	15. Kc1 a6	

[1]We wrote to the Pope asking for enlightenment. He blessed us and our work, but didn't add to our knowledge.

♟

The English parsons were a talented mob; presumably quiet country parishes in the nineteenth century gave one the leisure needed to become a star. Most of them played under an alias so that their parishioners couldn't know what they were up to on those long weekends in London. They're too numerous to mention all, but here are a few.

The Reverend George Alcock MacDonnell[1] played under the name 'Hiber' and was perhaps the strongest Revd of the lot. The following game was dubbed the 'Koh-i-Noor' of chess.

G. A. MacDonnell–S. S. Boden, London, 1861 (Casual game?).
Evans Gambit Declined

1. e4 e5	9. Be3 Nxb4	17. f4 Nd5	25. Re2 Qxd1
2. Nf3 Nc6	10. Ne2 Nc6	18. Qh5 f6	26. Nh5 Rg8
3. Bc4 Bc5	11. Ng3 d5	19. Ng6 Qe3+	27. Nxg8 Rxg8
4. b4 Bb6	12. Bb5 dxe4	20. Kh2 Rd8	28. Re8 Black
5. O–O d6	13. Bxc6 bxc6	21. Rfe1 Qxd3	resigns
6. h3 Nf6	14. Nxe5 exd3	22. Rad1 Qc2	
7. d3 O–O	15. cxd3 Qe8	23. Ne7+ Kh8	
8. Nc3 h6	16. Bxb6 axb6	24. Qf7 Bxh3	

MacDonnell caused a flutter in clerical circles in 1872 by carrying out the marriage ceremony for a divorcee, so they took his curacy off him. This did wonders for his chess; he achieved his best result six months later: third equal at London.

♟

The Revd John Owen played as 'Alter'. He was strong enough to play matches with Morphy and Zukertort, and to beat Anderssen in their game at London, 1862. Owen's Defence (1. . . .b6), which was trendy a few years ago, was named after him.

♟

The Revd C. E. Ranken[2] was a friend of Winston Churchill's father, Randolph, with whom he founded Oxford University Chess Club (of which Ranken was the first president). Not as strong as the other two, his best result was first at Malvern in 1872 (followed by the Revd Thorold and the Revd Wayte).

---

[1] He seems to have been the John Virgo of chess: he was celebrated for his impressions of other famous players.
[2] His claim to chess fame was *Chess Openings Ancient and Modern* – a nineteenth-century precursor of *Modern Chess Openings*.

♟

For the record (and because it's so impressive) here is the most devout team of all time. If there is anything in the efficacy of prayer they'd be tough to stop:

1. Fr Ruy López
2. Fr William Lombardy
3. Revd G. A. MacDonnell
4. Revd J. Owen
5. His Holiness Pope Leo XIII
6. His Holiness Pope Innocent III
7. St Teresa of Ávila (capt.)
8. St Thomas à Becket

Among the reserves would be: Luther (M) (his recurring dream was of owning an ornate gold and silver chess-set); Cardinal Richelieu (an enthusiastic player); two more popes, Gregory VI and Leo X; Archbishop Cranmer (who played chess every day after dinner); Sir Thomas More, who said chess would be played in Utopia; Cardinal Wolsey, who had a cake made in the shape of a chessboard for the French ambassador; and, when he is not saving souls, Billy Graham.

♟

Somewhere in there would be a Dominican monk who had the sinister task of running the Inquisition in Genoa. Jacopo da Cessole found time to spare from the rack and the stake to write the first of all European chess books. William Caxton published a translation in 1481–the second book printed in English. Cessole called his book *Liber de moribus Hominum et officiis Nobilium ac Popularium super ludo scacchorum*. Caxton gave it a snappier title: *The Game and Playe of the Chesse*.

♟

St Charles Borromeo, a leader of the Counter-Reformation, had the right idea. As a cardinal he was rebuked for his devotion to chess: 'What would you do if you were playing and the world came to an end?' 'Carry on playing', replied Charles. He deserved to be canonized.

♟

If you go to the Musée de Cluny in Paris you can see one of the most beautiful chess-sets ever made. It's in rock crystal and smoky topaz set in gold, and it is said to have been a gift from the legendary Rashīd al-Din as-Sinān, the Old Man of the Mountains (leader of the Assassins) to King (later Saint) Louis IX in the thirteenth century. (Not everyone agrees—Murray says the set is at least fourteenth century.)[1]

♟

Solution to papal problem: 1. Bb5

The Sinners

One of the strongest of all teams and a threat to anyone (including as it does four of Britain's best-known murderers, a g.b.h. specialist, the most famous assassin of all time and a magician in league with the devil).

As captain we select the late, great, Harold Davidson, one of the most colourful characters in a section teeming with them. Harold was the rector who became a geek.[2] In 1932, the year of the yo-yo, he cheered up Britain and pushed the rise of Hitler off the front pages with headlines like 'Rector's midnight call on waitress', 'The rector and the nude model' and 'Rector's black eye'. To tell it briefly, Harold went to the quiet parish of Stiffkey in Norfolk as rector in the late twenties. Finding rural life a little slow, he spent his weekends in Soho, saving young girls from sin. At his trial the prosecution maintained that what he was saving them for was himself. Anyway, after much eloquence from Harold and a number of salacious photographs in evidence, he was defrocked.

The scene shifts (uneasily, as S. J. Perelman once said) to Blackpool's Golden Mile where the Rector of Stiffkey became a star attraction, exhibited in a barrel (with a chimney for his cigar smoke) to crowds of Lancashire holidaymakers.

As a variation, he also appeared before the pleasure-seekers in a glass oven while a mechanical demon prodded his bottom with a pitchfork. For a while, Harold was in the big money, easily the most popular spectacle on the Golden Mile (completely eclipsing such contemporary attractions as the Starving Woman of Haslingden, and the Genuine Pacific Mermaid). He was also a master of showbiz. On emerging from gaol (for non-payment of rent) he made a triumphant ride along Blackpool's promenade in a horse-drawn carriage, attended by two

---

[1]And we know that St Louis is supposed to have banned the game (see above).
[2]A geek (US slang): a side-show exhibit in fairgrounds; originally one who performed bizarre acts such as biting the heads off live animals. With Harold, as you'll see, almost the reverse happened.

statuesque African girls who threw flowers to the enthusiastic crowds.

Our story stops abruptly on 28 July 1937, in Skegness Amusement Park. The ex-pillar of the church was now appearing in a cage with Toto and Freddy, two hitherto docile lions. Freddy didn't take kindly to this intrusion (presumably feeling that his new companion lowered the tone somewhat) and after a little injudicious whip cracking, there was a growl, a gulp, and one of the more fascinating footnotes in British social history came to a messy end.

What, you are patiently wondering, has all this to do with chess? Well, the surprising Harold, in the early years of the century, was one of the strongest young players in the country. He was President of Oxford Chess Club and captain of the Combined Universities team that beat American Universities in 1903. In that year, Harold was cheered by the onlookers for a spectacular win on top board that decided the match; and after he'd come down from university he was strong enough to take on five opponents simultaneously, blindfold.

(Freddy, incidentally, achieved fleeting celebrity, drawing thousands as 'the Lion that ate the Rector'. He didn't, as far as we know, play chess.)

Just as strange was the career of bad old Aleister Crowley a.k.a. the wickedest man in the world; the King of Depravity; Alastor the Destroyer; the Wanderer of the Wasteland; the ipsissimus; the Great Beast; 666; Brother Perdurabo; Master Thereon et cetera. In view of his proclivities, we nominate Aleister Vice-captain.

Crowley was hell-bent from an early age. As a youth he poisoned, gassed, hanged, drowned, bashed, chloroformed, defenestrated and sliced up a family moggy to check the theory that cats have nine lives (they don't, it transpired). He went on to become the most notorious practitioner of black magic of the twentieth century, a prolific author on the subject, and the greatest poet since Shakespeare (according to Aleister). Shocking stories of his life-style filtered into the popular press: nameless orgies in a Sicilian abbey; his habit of filing his teeth to a point so he could give women the mark of the beast on their wrists on being introduced (most didn't like it—but enough did to make it seem a good idea); the mountaineering expedition from which his companions inexplicably failed to return; and his watchword: 'Do what thou wilt shall be the whole of the Law.'

Between the cat episode and the Sicilian orgies, Aleister found time to become at least as strong a player as Davidson. Around 1896 he represented Trinity College, Cambridge, and the combined Oxford/

Cambridge team, and he rarely lost. (The exception: an Oxford–Cambridge match when Spencer Churchill beat him on top board in a Petroff Defence.)

In this position in the 1896 inter-varsity match, *v.* Robbins, Aleister (black) was clearly dead lost, yet won. Witchcraft? Possibly. The fact that his opponent ran out of time probably helped.

More interestingly, a Crowley problem. White (it should perhaps, since it's Crowley, be black[1]) to play and mate in 3:

British Chess Magazine, 1894, (Solution at end of section)

♜

We turn (with a slight moue of distaste) from witchcraft to mucky books, and another colourful member of our sinners' team. John Mansfield is the name on the passport; he is currently a resident of Amsterdam, and he's a keen chess-player. He's better known to the police however, as Porny John, the prince of European porn. In May 1986 he

---

[1]In all problems in this book it is white to move.

appeared on Central TV fondling a rather splendid marble chess-set.

♜

Depressingly, the ringleader of the unspeakable Chelsea Headhunters, a gang of soccer hooligans, is a chess-player. He had a BCF grade of 128 and played in the London Legal League before he was put away for ten years in May 1987 for causing an affray. We don't want to give him further publicity, so we shan't publish his name.

♜

One of the strongest sinners of all was Norman Tweed Whitaker, the lawyer who became a conman. Whitaker reached international master strength in the twenties. He was placed well in several American tournaments (1st, San Francisco 1923, 1st Kalamazoo 1927) and he beat former American champ Jackson Showalter in a match (+4, =3, −1). But neither chess nor law provided the kind of income Norman needed—so he turned to crime. His most famous scam was extracting $100,000 from the Lindbergh parents on a promise that he could return the kidnapped Lindbergh infant. Needless to say, Whitaker had never set eyes on the child. The cops caught up with him, Norm was sent down for a five-stretch, but the $100,000 was never seen again.

Norman had a long (eighty-five years) and interesting life. In the latter half of it he supplemented his precarious income by the skilful use of a screwdriver on car odometers. He made enough money from this and other confidence tricks to finance several tours of Europe. But it all concluded rather shabbily: the one-time high-flyer ended his days in a disused army hut on some waste ground. We make him board two for the sinners.

Here's a game between International Master Norm and the Sportsmen's board two. For once Norman's swindling ability failed him.

N. T. Whitaker–Sir G. A. Thomas, USA–GB Cable Match, 1930. Evans Gambit Declined

1. e4 e5	7. d4 d6	13. Nc3 cxd4	19. Kf1 Nd2+
2. Nf3 Nc6	8. Bxh6 dxe5	14. Nd5 Qe8	20. Qxd2 Qxb5+
3. Bc4 Bc5	9. Bxg7 Rg8	15. Qg3 Nc4	21. Kg1 Bxd2
4. b4 Bb6	10. Bxf7+ Kxf7	16. Qf4+ Ke6	22. Nc7+ Kxe5
5. b5 Na5	11. Bxe5 Bg4	17. h3 Ba5+	23. Nxb5 Bf3
6. Nxe5 Nh6	12. Qd3 c5	18. c3 Bxc3+	White resigns

♜

Next, the murderers. If you believe the Warren Report (we do), The Man Who Killed Kennedy was a keen player. In *The Trial of Lee*

Harvey Oswald, shown on British TV in 1986, Nelson Delgado, Oswald's squad leader in the Marines, said, 'Chess was Lee's favourite game.'

♖

Board one for the sinners would be Raymond Weinstein, currently doing life in an American gaol for an axe murder. He was an International Master and an opponent of Bobby Fischer. According to an article in the *British Chess Magazine*, *before* the crime, he 'had a ruthless killer instinct' for the game.

♖

The euphoniously named Claude Bloodgood wrote a well-known openings textbook, *The Tactical Grob*, while in the Virginia State slammer for matricide. Prison did not dull his tactical brilliance: in the course of a chess match he improvised a successful escape; but was subsequently recaptured.

Here's Claude using his favourite opening to blitz a patzer.

C. Bloodgood–J. Boothe, Correspondence, 1972. Grob's Opening

1. g4 d5	4. Qb3 Qc7	7. Nb5 Qb6	10. Qxb7
2. Bg2 Bxg4	5. cxd5 cxd5	8. Bxb7 Qxb7??	Black resigns
3. c4 c6	6. Nc3 d4?	9. Nd6+ exd6	

For another game with this opening turn to 'The Artists' where we reveal the identity of the eponymous Grob.

♖

Patrick Magee, the Brighton bomber, a keen player, is now looking for opponents in Wandsworth prison; and the infamous Moors Murderer, Ian Brady, played chess during his stay at Wormwood Scrubs. Among his opponents was former Postmaster-General John Stonehouse (see below).

♖

If he did it (and the pundits can't agree) then William Herbert Wallace was much better at murder than chess. William was at the centre of what Raymond Chandler and many others called the most fascinating murder case of all. The story is too well documented to retell in detail, but *en bref*: in January 1931, Wallace, an insurance agent and chess-player, was telephoned at Liverpool Central Chess Club about a business appointment. He didn't take the call himself, and his appointment turned out to be a hoax to lure him to a distant part of Liverpool. While he was out, someone eliminated his wife. Wallace was held on a murder charge (the prosecution's case being that he made the call himself to establish an alibi). Much was made at the trial of Wallace's 'scheming chess-player's mind'. In fact, his fellow club-members said he was a really awful player.[1] His solicitor however, Hector Munro, was a strong county player – and Wallace was acquitted.[2]

♜

John Reginald Halliday Christie was a goodish chess-player—and the most celebrated mass murderer of the forties. Whilst awaiting the ultimate punishment in Brixton, he passed the time thrashing his warders at chess (Chris the chess champion, they nicknamed him).

♜

The last on our roster of murderers is the most famous of all. According to a well-argued book by Stephen Knight,[3] Jack the Ripper (who gave London an autumn of terror in 1888) was in fact the painter Walter Sickert as part of a three-man team. One of the things we know about Sickert was that he was a keen chess-player. If Knight's theory is correct, then we must place Jack on a high board in our macabre team, if only for his ability to scare the hell out of the opposition.

♜

Rounding off this section: three men who've paid their debt to society.

H.R. Haldeman was the most senior of that frightful bunch of (expletives deleted) who fouled up American history by assisting President Nixon in the Watergate episode. His hobby when he wasn't organizing dirty tricks was chess.

John McVicar, gang boss and for a while Britain's most wanted man, was an Essex boy champion before he turned to crime and subsequent stardom. He resumed his chess career in HM prisons, where it is said he met another strong player: John Stonehouse, ex-MP, ex-Postmaster-General and (following a financial imbroglio) mastermind of a well-publicized fake suicide disappearing act. After the Old Bill caught up with John in Australia, he and McVicar were finalists, legend has it, in the Wormwood Scrubs chess championships. Certainly (because one of

---

[1] One of them said: 'The murder of his wife apart, I think Wallace ought to be hanged for being such a bad chess-player.'
[2] For more on this fascinating case see a very good book: *The Killing of Julia Wallace* by Jonathan Goodman (Harrap, 1969).
[3] *Jack the Ripper: The Final Solution.*

the authors played there) the Scrubs had a flourishing and strong chess team in the sixties. So did Broadmoor and Wandsworth prison incidentally.

Postscript

If he were available for selection, an excellent addition to the sinners' team would be the devil himself. A good friend of Aleister Crowley, he is currently endorsing a well-known make of chess computer.[1] According to legend and several short stories Old Nick is practically unbeatable. Club secretaries willing to stake their soul on an infernally strong top board could try lighting thirteen candles and reciting the Lord's Prayer backwards while looking in a mirror...

(For more sinners, see 'The Politicians'.)

Solution to Crowley problem: Qb6.

The Musicians

In the championship of the professions, the musicians beat most other teams out of sight. Indeed if the players below could be reincarnated, they'd look pretty good in the European club championship (and even better at the post-match concert).

No argument about board one: the French composer François-André Danican Philidor (1726–95). When he wasn't composing (twenty-one musical comedies and a grand opera that netted him a pension from Louis XV), Philidor found time to become the strongest player of the eighteenth century, the wonder of the age at blindfold play, and author of the most successful chess textbook in history. Grandmaster Larsen rated him as all-time number one. We think this is pushing it a bit, but Phil was certainly world championship standard. As a musician, his compositions lasted less well than his chess, but in 1976 there was a 250th anniversary performance of one of his operas (*Blaise le Savetier*) in London. Here's a Philidor game:

[1] The Mephisto.

Capt. Smith–Philidor, London, 1790. Bishop's Opening

1. e4 e5	9. Nf3 d6	17. f3 Nf8	26. Qxg3 Qxg3+
2. Bc4 Nf6	10. Qd2 Be6	18. Ne2 Ng6	27. Nxg3 Nf4+
3. d3 c6	11. Bxe6 fxe6	19. c3 Rag8	28. Kh1 Rxh3
4. Bg5 h6	12. O–O g5	20. d4 Bb6	29. Rg1 Rxh2+
5. Bxf6 Qxf6	13. h3 Nd7	21. dxe5 Qxe5	30. Kxh2 Rh8+
6. Nc3 b5	14. Nh2 h5	22. Nd4 Kd7	31. Nh5 Rxh5+
7. Bb3 a5	15. g3 Ke7	23. Rae1 h4	32. Kg3 Nh3+
8. a3 Bc5	16. Kg2 d5	24. Qf2 Bc7	33. Kg4 Rh4
		25. Ne2 hxg3	mate.

♚

Board two, the Viennese concert pianist Moriz Rosenthal, the last surviving pupil of Liszt, and the strongest musician that US master Ed Lasker (who also played our boards four and five) ever met.

♚

Fighting it out for board three, below the pianist, would be composer Serge Prokofiev and violin virtuosi Mischa Elman and David Oistrakh. Prokofiev was chess crazy, and played well enough to beat Lasker, Capablanca and Rubinstein in simultaneous exhibitions. Here's a game against grandmaster Tartakower:

Tartakower–Prokofiev, Paris, February 1934. Evans Gambit Declined

1. e4 e5	9. Bxa1 Nb8	17. Rd1 Qg4+	25. Bxd7+ Bxd7
2. Nf3 Nc6	10. d4 f6	18. Kxf2 Nd7	26. Qxd7+ Rxd7
3. Bc4 Bc5	11. dxe5 dxe5	19. Qxc7 Ke7	27. Rxh5 Rd2
4. b4 Bb6	12. Qe2 Nh6	20. Nc3 Rf8+	28. Rd5 Rxc2
5. a4 a6	13. Nxe5 fxe5	21. Kg1 Rd8	29. Nd1
6. Bb2 d6	14. Qh5+ Kf8	22. Qd6+ Ke8	Black resigns
7. b5 axb5	15. Qxe5 Bxf2+	23. Be6 Qh5	
8. axb5 Rxa1	16. Ke2 Qd7	24. Rd5 Nf7	

This was a friendly game. Tarta describes his opponent as being of master strength.

♚

In 1937 a match Prokofiev v. Oistrakh was arranged in the USSR. The violinist beat the composer: four draws and a win (so we'll make Oistrakh board three). Oistrakh was rated a USSR category one player – approximately a 190–200 grading. Here's how he fiddled a draw when two pawns down to Prokofiev:

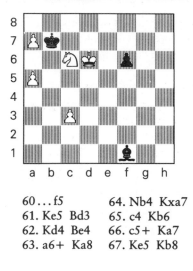

60...f5	64. Nb4 Kxa7	68. Nd5 Bd3!	72. Nxc6 Kb7
61. Ke5 Bd3	65. c4 Kb6	69. Nb4 Be4	Draw
62. Kd4 Be4	66. c5+ Ka7	70. c6 Kc7	
63. a6+ Ka8	67. Ke5 Kb8	71. a7 Bxc6!	

Mischa Elman (board five) played in style: with a hundred-year-old Staunton pattern set handed down from world champion Paul Morphy. Elman was strong enough to play regularly with US master Edward Lasker, who rated him 'very good'. While Prokofiev was in the USA, Lasker arranged a couple of Prokofiev–Elman games. The result: a win apiece.

A very strong board six (and maybe higher) would be a former Master of the King's Musick:[1] Sir Walter Parratt, organist at St George's Chapel Windsor, who won on top board for Oxford in the first Oxford–Cambridge match, 1873. Well after his eightieth birthday, Sir Walter was still good enough to beat Bonar Law (easily the strongest of British prime ministers) while the latter was staying at Windsor Castle. Parratt's party trick was to play Bach fugues while conducting two games simultaneously, blindfold.

On board seven, another master of the violin: Yehudi Menuhin. Yehudi was a strong child player (after a recital at the Paris Opera, the twelve-

---

[1]A master of the Queen's Musick, Sir Arthur Bliss, composed the music for the chess ballet, *Checkmate*.

year-old Menuhin surprised journalists by giving interviews while playing chess). In later life (1944) he played this casual game on a train
against Aird Thomson, who was Scottish champion in 1951:

Y. Menuhin–A.A. Thomson, 1944. Four Knights Game

1. e4 e5	12. h3 Rg8	23. Bxf5 Ne7	34. Kd5 Bg3
2. Nf3 Nc6	13. c3 Bxh3	24. g4 Nxf5	35. c4 h3
3. Nc3 Nf6	14. Nh4 f5	25. gxf5 Kd7	36. c5 dxc5
4. Bc4 Bb4	15. Qh5 Qg5	26. Kg2 Rf8	37. Kxc5+ Ke7
5. Nd5 Nxe4	16. Nxc7+ Bxc7	27. Kf3 Rxf5+	38. a4 Bf2+
6. a3 Bc5	17. Qxf7+ Kd8	28. Ke3 Bb6+	39. Kb5 h2
7. O–O d6	18. Qxg8+ Qxg8	29. Kd3 Bxf2	40. a5 Bgl
8. d3 Nf6	19. Bxg8 Bg4	30. Re4 h5	White resigns
9. Bg5 h6	20. Be6 Be2	31. Rd1 h4	
10. Bxf6 gxf6	21. Rfel Bxd3	32. Kc4 Rf4	
11. b4 Bb6	22. Nxf5 Bxf5	33. Rxf4 exf4	

♚

And board eight, a good player and phenomenal violinist: Fritz Kreis-
ler. Once, while he was staying with some musical friends, dinner interrupted his game. When he returned, the pianist Paderewski had set up
the adjourned position on the chequered floor of the drawing-room,
with human pieces instead of chessmen.

♚

Jostling for a place among the reserves would be Schumann, who took
a chess book as solace into the asylum at Endenich; Mendelssohn (a
strong player), Richard Strauss (who also played against Ed Lasker),
Mussorgsky, Shostakovich, Rimsky-Korsakov, Verdi, Borodin, Villa-
Lobos, Dvořák, Rossini, Arthur Rubinstein, Sviatoslav Richter, Sir
Thomas Beecham,[1] Adolf Brodsky (first to perform the Tchaikovsky
violin concerto, and a strong player), Isaac Stern, Ruggiero Ricci, Pablo
Casals, Gregor Piatigorsky (the cellist, whose wife sponsored two legendary tournaments in the sixties), John Lill (the classical pianist in
psychic communication with Beethoven – he picked *Modern Chess
Openings* as his book to take with him on *Desert Island Discs*), Aaron
Copland and John Cage, the modern musician responsible for *4'33"*
(which, if you haven't not heard it consists of four minutes and thirty-

---

[1] Described by the lady manager of the Berlin Philharmonic as 'a passionate
player'.

three seconds of absolute silence[1]). And, according to the *Polish History of Chess*, Chopin and Beethoven.

♚

One composer who might be surprised to find himself in the above company is Johnny Marks, a member of the board of governors of New York's Marshall Chess Club. His claim to musical immortality: 'Rudolph the Red-Nosed Reindeer'.

♚

From the great vocal virtuosi, we can only track down Feodor Chaliapin and Paul Robeson, who used to play with his son.

♚

Among jazz musicians we have the doyen of British jazz and master of the one-liner,[2] Ronnie Scott; Dizzy Gillespie (who played against Ronnie on a British gig); and drumming phenomenon Gene Krupa (if you haven't heard his drum solo on Benny Goodman's 'Sing, sing, sing' you haven't lived).

♚

Rudolf Willmers, concert pianist (1821–78), was pretty obsessive about chess problems: in the middle of a recital in Copenhagen he stopped to write down on his cuff the solution to a problem that had been troubling him.

Postscript

Not that the musicians need it, but if we stretched a point, we could considerably strengthen even the above team by adding in a few musicians (Smyslov, Taimanov, du Mont) who are more famous to us for their chess than their music. (After his terrible 6–0 defeat by Fischer, Taimanov consoled himself: 'At least I still have my music.') See chapter VI for more on chess-playing musicians; and 'The Entertainers' for pop musicians.

---

[1] It's in three movements. Cage also composed a piece, 'Imaginary Landscape No.4' in which 24 performers randomly twiddle the knobs on 12 radios. He played 3–D chess (of which more in chapter VII). One of his disciples, Anna Lockwood, wrote a piece called 'Piano Burning' which is exactly that.
[2] Addressing a more than usually small audience: 'I should've stayed in bed – there were more people there.'

The Artists

Not as strong as the musicians, but on the top two boards players of master strength. Captain and board two is one of the most influential artists of the twentieth century: Marcel Duchamp.

Duchamp was one of the founders of Dadaism, surrealism and cubism, but became so obsessed with chess he gave up art.[1] He won tournaments in Paris (1932, ahead of Znosko-Borovsky) and New York, played for France in four Olympiads, and co-authored one of the most obscure of all books on the endgame: *L'Opposition et les Cases conjugées sont réconciliées*. ('The positions discussed in it will occur about once a lifetime,' he said proudly.)

High spot of Duchamp's chess career was probably Hamburg 1930 when, Alekhine being indisposed, he had to face one of the all-time greats, Frank Marshall, in a France–USA match. To France's surprise and delight, Duchamp snatched a draw from the grand master.

Marcel's passion for the game was overwhelming. On his honeymoon in 1927, he spent the days studying chess problems and most of the nights sleeping off his chess jags. After a week of disappointment, his enraged bride, Lydie, crept downstairs one night and glued all the pieces to the board.[2] Surprisingly, the marriage lasted three months.[3]

Here is one of Marcel's games:

J.J. O'Hanlon–M. Duchamp, Nice, 1930. Caro–Kann Defence

1. e4 c6	10. Nd2 Ne7	19. Kf2 Bh4	28. Bf1 Rhe8
2. d4 d5	11. Be2 Nc6	20. Rhe1 b5	29. Re2 g5
3. exd5 cxd5	12. Bg3 Be7	21. Re2 Bxg3+	30. Ke1 Nd3+
4. c3 Nc6	13. Nf3 f6	22. hxg3 e5	31. Rxd3 Rxe2+
5. Nf3 Bf5	14. Nh4 Be4	23. dxe5 Qa7+	32. Qxe2 Rxe2+
6. Bf4 e6	15. f3 Bg6	24. Re3 Nxe5	33. Bxe2 Ke5
7. Qb3 Qd7	16. Nxg6 hxg6	25. Qd2 Rae8	34. Rd4 Qc5
8. Ne5 Nxe5	17. Bd3 Kf7	26. Re1 Re6	White resigns
9. Bxe5 a6	18. Qc2 f5	27. b3 Kf6	

'When you play a game of chess. it is like designing something or

---

[1] 'My attention is so completely absorbed by chess. I play night and day...I like painting less and less.' Duchamp in a letter, 1919.

[2] Another glue gag: German master Carl Carls was famous for never playing anything but 1. c4 for white. Some jokester once glued his c-pawn to the board.

[3] 'He needs a good game of chess like a baby needs a bottle' – Roche (a friend of his).

constructing some mechanism of some kind by which you win or lose. The competitive side of it has no importance. The thing itself is very very plastic. That is probably what attracted me to the game.'

&

Just beating Duchamp for board one: Henry Grob, portrait painter and International Master. He won the Swiss Championship twice, beat Grandmaster Mieses in a match (1934), and at Ostend 1937 he won games from two of the strongest players in the world, Keres and Fine (and shared first place with them). His artistic works include portraits of Alekhine and Fischer. Here's a strange game with the obscure opening he made his own.

H. Grob–H. Sperling Correspondence. Grob's Opening

1. g4 d5
2. Bg2 c6
3. g5 e5
4. h4 Bc5
5. d3 d4
6. Nf3 Qd6
7. Nbd2 Be6
8. Ne4 Qd5
9. Nfd2 (threat: Nf6+) Ke7
10. Kf1 Bb6
11. Nc4 Nd7
12. Ned6 Black resigns (if 12... Qc5 13. b4 Qxb4 14. c3 dxc3 15. Ba3)

&

The exotically named Maximilian Mopp[1] was, like Duchamp, one of the founders of Dadaism, and was reckoned to be in the Duchamp class as a chess-player, so we put him on board three. As for the rest, you choose.

Max Ernst and Man Ray both played chess with Duchamp: but they were more famous for their chess-set designs than for the quality of their play.

&

If you go to the Tate you can see a very strange painting by artist/chess-player Richard Dadd. It's called *The Child's Problem*. The chess problem is indeed simple; what makes the painting disturbing is the sinister expression on the child's face – and the knowledge that Dadd killed his own father. In his journals he raved about the Ruy López.

&

Other chess-playing artists: Rembrandt (who, according to one biographer, learned from Ruy López's textbook), Gustav Doré (he played against Ajeeb the automaton – see Chapter VIII), Paul Klee,

[1] né Max Oppenheim.

René Magritte, Georges Braque, Vicky the cartoonist,[1] Yves Tanguy (he designed a set from broom handles); Maurice Vlaminck, Walter Sickert (see 'The Sinners') and Salvador Dali, who designed a surreal set made up of solid silver fingers and thumbs, and whose only known dictum on the game is the characteristic: 'Les échecs, c'est moi' (in a book on Duchamp).

The Writers

This is the biggest, and one of the strongest teams of all (with, as we shall see, an extraordinary number of Nobel Prize winners).

Here, first, are the top ten in ascending order of strength.

♟

The best excuse anyone ever had for losing a chess game happened to the writers' board ten, William Golding. In 1983 the author of *Lord of the Flies* was in the middle of a difficult Evans Gambit with the Literary Editor of the *Financial Times* when the news of his Nobel Prize came through. Understandably agitated, the author mailed off an inaccuracy. The Nobel Prize cost him the game. You win some, you lose some. Here's the disaster:

William Golding–Anthony Curtis. Evans Gambit

1. e4 e5	5. c3 Bc5	9. Bxf7+ Kf8	13. Ng5+ Ke8
2. Nf3 Nc6	6. d4 exd4	10. Ba3+ d6	14. Qf4 Qf6
3. Bc4 Bc5	7. cxd4 Bb4+	11. Rc1 Bxd2+	15. Qxf6 Nxf6
4. b4 Bxb4	8. Nbd2 Bc3	12. Qxd2 Kxf7	16. d5 Nd4

At this point, the good news from Sweden came through, followed by a Golding blunder:

---

[1] Here's a fragment from a game against British champion Alexander in a simultaneous display:

Alexander–Vicky. French Defence.

1. e4 e6	5. a3 Bxc3+	9. Qf4 Qc7	13. Nxh7 Nxg4
2. d4 d5	6. bx3 Nc6	10. Qf6 Rg8	14. Qh4 Rg7
3. Nc3 Bb4	7. Qg4 g6	11. Ng5 Nf5	and White
4. e5 c5	8. Nf3 Nge7	12. g4 Nh6	won

17. Rxc7?? Nb5   18. Rxg7

(Golding's annotation, according to Curtis: 'Fork it')

A few moves later the 1983 Nobel Laureate resigned. Golding, incidentally, also plays correspondence chess against Richard Adams of *Watership Down* fame. Who usually wins we don't know.

♟

On board nine, a biggie. Count Leo Nikolaievich Tolstoy learned chess as a boy. When he was fifteen he played against Turgenev, about whom more in a minute. Tolstoy must have been pretty keen: as a young officer he was gaoled for playing chess when he should have been on guard duty; but he wasted the early part of his life losing money at cards and writing *War and Peace*. Later on he took up the game again, most enthusiastically, and according to *Z Szachami Przez Wieki I Kraje*[1] became an ingenious tactical player. In his diary, he gave himself a piece of bad advice: 'One's main concern should be not to win at all costs, but to go in for interesting combinations.'

Tolstoy's skill at the game was honed in games with a really outstanding player: Prince Sergei S. Urusov (for *his* exploits, see 'The Aristocrats'). During the siege of Sebastopol, when he wasn't losing most of his roubles at cards with his fellow officers, he had dozens of games against the prince, one of the strongest Russian players of the nineteenth century.

♟

Here's a Tolstoy game (played in his eighties!)[2] against his biographer:

Count L. Tolstoy–Aylmer Maude, Yasnaya Polyana, 1906. King's Gambit

1. e4 e5	6. Kf1 d5	11. Rg1 Qh4+	16. Qe1 Qe7
2. f4 exf4	7. Bxd5 f3	12. Ke2 Nh6	17. Nc3 f6
3. Nf3 g5	8. gxf3 Qh3+	13. Rxg2 c6	18. Nxd5 Qd6
4. Bc4 g4	9. Ke1 g3	14. Bxh6 cxd5	19. Qg3
5. Nc5 Qh4+	10. d4 g2	15. Bxf8 Kxf8	Black resigns

♟

Art Buchwald is our board eight. Art, long-time columnist for the *New York Herald Tribune* and one of America's funniest writers, was good

---

[1] A Polish history of chess by Jerzy Gizycki, translated by Wojciechowski, Ronowicz and Bartoszewski. (We read the translation.)

[2] Sprightly is the word to describe old Tolstoy: at sixty-seven he learned to ride the bicycle.

enough to beat Humphrey Bogart (see below 'The Entertainers')
regularly. In Paris, Art lost to Marcel Duchamp ('he was broke, so I
bought one of his famous cigar boxes for $250') but then he moved to
Washington and knocked over a string of celebrity chess players: Henry
Kissinger ('I used the Kremlin defense'), Secretary of Defense Zbigniew
Brzezinski ('Very tough. He won't let you smoke cigars in his office')
and Vice-President Spiro T. Agnew, when he was governor of Maryland
(a pretty good player, but Buchwald reckons he had the better of him).

Board seven is one of the best-loved of all children's authors. Arthur
Ransome was a good player and gets a place in chess history for a weird
juxtaposition: the author of *Swallows and Amazons* once played chess
with Lenin, not to mention a number of other Russian notables.

Next, the French romanticist, Alfred de Musset, a strong café player. He
would have been placed higher than board six were it not for his determined attempts to combine chess with absinthe-drinking. When he
wasn't falling off his chair, Alfred was pretty good: you can get some
idea of his powers from this, his most famous contribution to chess. It's
a clever demonstration of the impossible: you can't force mate with two
knights.

A. de Musset, La Régence, 1849

Mate in 3. (Solution at end
of this section.)

Board five is yet another Nobel Laureate: Samuel Beckett. The author
of *Waiting for Godot* played for Trinity College Dublin as a student;
later, in Paris, he met Marcel Duchamp with whom he played many
games (lost forever, unfortunately). They were both obsessed with endings and the Beckett–Duchamp encounters ('some of the most stimulat-

ing of Beckett's life,' says his biographer) are supposed to have inspired the Beckett play *Endgame*.

This 'game' is from Beckett's *Murphy*, annotations translated by Ken Whyld.

Murphy—Endon. Opening: Affense Endon, or Zweispringerspott

1. e4 (*The basic cause of White's subsequent problems*) 1...Nh6 2. Nh3 Rg8 3. Rg1 Nc6 4. Nc3 Ne5 5. Nd5 (*Bad, but there seems to be nothing better*) 5...Rh8 6. Rh1 Nc6 7. Nc3 Ng8 8. Nb1 Nb8 (*Fine and ingenious opening, sometimes called* bol d'air) 9. Ng1 e6 10. g3 (*Ill-judged*) 10...Ne7 11. Ne2 Ng6 12. g4 Be7 13. Ng3 d6 14. Be2 Qd7 15. d3 Kd8 (*Never seen at the Café de la Régence, rarely at Simpson's Divan*) 16. Qd2 Qe8 17. Kd1 Nd7 18. Nc3 (*Distress signal*) 18...Rb8 19. Rb1 Nb6 20. Na4 Bd7 21. b3 Rg8 22. Rg1 Kc8 (*Exquisitely played*) 23. Bb2 Qf8 24. Kc1 Be8 25. Bc3 (*It is hard to imagine a more deplorable situation than that of the unhappy White here*) 25...Nh8 26. b4 Bd8 27. Qh6 (*The ingenuity of desperation*) 27... Na8 (*Black now has an irresistible game*) 28. Qf6 Ng6 29. Be5 Be7 30. Nc5 (*The obstinacy with which White is set on losing a piece merits all praise*) 30...Kd8 (*At this point, without even taking the trouble to say 'J'adoube'. M. Endon turned his king and queen's rook upside down, and tried to maintain them thus until the end of the game*) 31. Nh1 (*Somewhat late waiting move*) 31...Bd7 32. Kb2!! Rh8 33. Kb3 Bc8 34. Ka4 Qe8 (*M. Endon not giving check aloud, or otherwise showing the least sign of knowing he was attacking the king of his adversary, or rather opposite, Murphy, in accordance with law 18. was spared from bothering about it. But that would be to admit the escape was adventitious*) 35. Ka5 Nb6 36. Bf4 Nd7 37. Qc3 Ra8 38. Na6 (*The written word is unable to express the anguish of the soul that inspired in White this abject attack*)38...Bf8 39. Kb5 Ne7 40. Ka5 Nb8 41. Qc6 Ng8 42. Kb5 Ke7 (*This brilliancy's ending is admirably played by M. Endon*) 43. Ka5 Qd8 (*To persist further would be frivolous and vexatious and Murphy resigned*).
White resigns.

♟

One of the great short-story writers, Lord Dunsany[1] is board four. Dunsany was a strong player (he played in the Irish championship), an ingenious problemist, and was elected president of the Irish Chess Union and the Kent County Chess Association. In this game from a simultaneous display Dunsany holds the great Capa to a draw.

J.R.Capablanca–Lord Dunsany, London, 1929. Ruy López.

1. e4 e5	9. dxc7 Qxc7	17. Re1 Qd6	25. Nd4 Rc5
2. Nf3 Nc6	10. Nc3 Bb7	18. Ne4 Qc6	26. Nb3 Rd5
3. Bb5 a6	11. a4 b4	19. Bg5 Bxg5	27. Rae1 Nd7
4. Ba4 b5	12. Nxd5 Bxd5	20. Nxg5 Rac8	28. Re4 Nb6
5. Bb3 Nf6	13. Bxd5 Nxd5	21. Qf3 Nf6	29. Re5 Rfd8
6. Ng5 d5	14. O–O Be7	22. Re2 h6	30. Rxd5 Rxd5
7. exd5 Ne7	15. d4 O–O	23. Qxc6 Rxc6	31. Kf1 Nxa4
8. d6 Ned5	16. dxe5 Qxe5	24. Nf3 a5	Draw agreed

This Dunsany problem is as strange as some of his stories.

Mate in 4. (Solution at end of this section.)

♟

Board three belongs to Sir Richard Burton (no, not *that* one), explorer, soldier, author and, the way the Victorians saw it, pornographer (he translated the much banned *Arabian Nights Entertainment*[2] from the Persian). Burton played chess, like he did most things, pretty well. He

---

[1] If you can get your hands on it, try the collection *Jorkens has a Large Whiskey*. Brilliant. Or if you like chess stories, 'The Three Sailors' Gambit'. And see Chapter VII for a Dunsany chess variant.

[2] Plus that positional masterpiece the *Kama Sutra*; and the *The Perfumed Garden* (which recommends monkey dung as an aphrodisiac. The authors cannot endorse this).

could manage two games simultaneously, blindfold. Whilst an intelligence officer in Sind, he disguised himself as a native and played chess with likely sources of information.

♟

Board two on the writers' team is the Russian novelist Ivan Sergeyevitch Turgenev. He was strong enough to play a match in Paris against a Polish professional, Maczuski (+1, =2, −3) in 1861. A year later he finished second of sixty in a tournament at the Café de la Régence (Rivière, a strong French master, won it). In 1870 he was elected vice-chairman of the Baden-Baden tournament. Here's a game extract:

Conclusion of a game Maczuski–Turgenev, Paris, 1861.

33. ...Rg8	37. h4 Rff2	41. exd5 Rxd5	45. Ka4 Rc7
34. Bc3 Ba4	38. Kc3 Rxd2	42. h6 Bf5	46. Kb3 Rb5+
35. Qd4 Rg2	39. Qh8+ Kb7	43. Qf6 Rc2+	47. Ka4 Bd7! and
36. Bd2 Bd7!	40. h5 exd5	44. Kb4 a5+	White resigns

♟

A tremendous number one for the writers is the polyglot[1] Henry Buckle, author of the influential masterwork *The History of Civilisation in England*. Buckle was one of the strongest players of the mid-ninetenth century (he won the first modern chess tournament: London 1849). Two world-class players, Anderssen and Steinitz, rated him as among the best they'd ever met. Certainly he would thrash most of the other top boards in this chapter. Here's a brief sample of his skill from 1847. He's giving the other chap the odds of queen's rook (i.e. remove White's QR from the initial line-up):

[1]He spoke or wrote nineteen languages.

Buckle–Brown. London 1849. Petroff's Defence

1. e4 e5	5. Bd3 Nc5	9. exd6 Qxd6	13. Nd6+ Kf8
2. Nf3 Nf6	6. O–O Nxd3	10. Na3 c5	14. Ng5 Qd8
3. d4 exd4	7. Qxd3 d6	11. Nb5 Qb6	15. Qc4 Be6
4. e5 Ne4	8. Re1 Be7	12. Bf4 Na6	

16. Rxe6! Bxd6 17. Nxf7! Qd7   18. Bxd6+ Kg8   19. Nh6+! gxh6
                                                  20. Rg6 mate

Buckle died of fever in Damascus; his famous last words are appropriate for the writers' top board: 'My book, my book! I shall never finish my book!' We know the feeling.

♟

The remaining chess-playing writers are numerous enough to make up a second team. Among the contenders for a place is another Nobel Prize winner (1981), Elias Canetti. Canetti is a keen player, and, according to Anthony Curtis, an expert problem composer. He is especially interesting because of his novel *Auto da Fé*. One of the characters in *Auto da Fé* is an obsessive chess-player called Fischerle (which he shortens to Fischer). Like the great Bobby, Canetti's Fischer is a chess phenomenon: like Bobby, he lives, sleeps, breathes the game; like Bobby, he dreams of the day when chess will bring him enough money to buy hundreds of hand-made suits, and to live in a chess palace modelled on the pieces (a Bobby fantasy, see Chapter VI); and he imagines making (like Bobby) huge financial demands for his services. The spooky thing is that *Auto da Fé* was published eight years before the real Bobby Fischer was born.

♟

Yet more Nobel Prize winners: Sinclair Lewis, who took lessons in chess from US star Al Horowitz; W. B. Yeats who, a member of the same weird circle as Aleister Crowley (see 'The Sinners'), played chess against a ghost at a house in Paris;[1] Henryk Sienkiewicz (who wrote *Quo Vadis* and played a lot of café chess in Warsaw); Gabriel García Márquez (who wrote a true short story, 'The Long Chess Night of Paul Badura-Škoda'); Isaac Bashevis Singer ('I consider chess the fairest of games because the opponents can hide nothing from each other'); and Boris Pasternak. Bertrand Russell was a Nobel Laureate too, but we've put him in with the philosophers who need all the help they can get. And so was Churchill – he's in with the politicians.

♟

One Nobel Prize winner who would never be picked is George Bernard Shaw. He deserves a FIDE life ban for his acid observation, 'Chess . . . is a foolish expedient for making idle people believe they are doing something very clever, when they are only wasting their time.' GBS was a rotten player anyway: 'I am hopeless . . . my genius did not point in that direction,' he once said. Sir Walter Scott, who played as a boy, was on Shaw's side: 'Surely chess is a sad waste of brains.' A ban in perpetuity too, for the king of hard-boiled fiction (and a chess-player), Raymond Chandler, for: '. . . as elaborate a waste of human intelligence as you could find anywhere outside an advertising agency' (*The Long Goodbye*).

♟

Apart from Tolstoy, Turgenev and Pasternak some other Russians are worth a mention. The Russian national poet Alexander Pushkin (*Eugene Onegin* and *Boris Godunov*) was a chess fanatic. He wrote to his beautiful wife Natalia, 'Thank you darling, for learning to play chess. It is an absolute necessity in any well-organized family' (and quite right too). But chess wasn't enough to occupy Natalia; as a result of her flirtations, poor old Pushkin got involved in a fatal duel; the night before he met his doom he passed the time playing chess.[2]

Dostoevsky was a member of the St Petersburg chess club; Maxim Gorky was a chess addict; so was Lermontov – and he too met his end in a duel.

♟

[1] It was four-sided chess, Yeats and a Mrs Mathers versus Mr Mathers and a spirit partner. Mr Mathers would 'shade his eyes and gaze earnestly at the spirit's empty chair' when it was its move.
[2] When his rival, d'Anthès, appeared, Pushkin removed a knight from the board, saying, 'This officer threatens to checkmate me. I shall have to kill him.' Unfortunately for literature (and chess) it didn't work out like that.

Vladimir Nabokov might well make the first team; apart from writing one of the best novels about chess (*The Defence*) he was apparently quite a good player and a published problemist.

Nabokov considered this his best problem and discussed its composition in his autobiography, *Speak, Memory*. It's mate in 2.

(Solution at end of this section.)

One man who deserves an entry into the 'not a lot of people know that' section is Peter Mark Roget, the writers' friend. Most writers in English owe him a debt for devising the thesaurus; the bit you didn't know is that chess-players also owe him a debt for inventing the truly pocket[1] chess-set (1845). He called it 'The Economic Chess Board'.[2]

King James II gave Samuel Pepys a magnificent chess-table and men for his services to the Crown.

Some short stories about the remaining British writers/players:

Lord Tennyson was President of the British Chess Association; Charles Dickens loved social chess, and was especially fond of problems – he called them, facetiously, 'chess-nuts'; Lord Alfred Douglas (or 'Bosie'), friend of Oscar Wilde, was a Muzio Gambit player; Guy Bellamy, author of the novel *The Secret Lemonade Drinker* is a self-confessed lousy player – the book itself contains a pretty awful chess game that he himself played; David Benedictus, contemporary author

---

[1] i.e. two-dimensional
[2] And doubtless told his friends it was ingenious, imaginative, brilliant, clever, felicitous, apt, slick, well contrived. He also published solutions to the Knight's Tour. See our section on 'Desert Island Chess'.

39

(*The Fourth of June* was his first novel) plays for Richmond (Surrey); the author of *A Passage to India*, E. M. Forster, gave the best-ever analysis of the Evans Gambit;[1] and R. D. Blackmore of *Lorna Doone* fame was a friend of world champion Steinitz: ('the only game worth playing', Blackmore said, 'think of the genius who invented the knight's move'). Dr Johnson called chessmen 'puppets' in his dictionary and wrote the dedication to the first English textbook on draughts.

George Eliot, Oliver Goldsmith, Robert Louis Stevenson, A. A. Milne, H. G. Wells, John Ruskin (a life-long patzer), Lewis Carroll (who solved chess problems as a cure for insomnia), Enid Blyton, A. P. Herbert, Evelyn Waugh, Martin Amis, Malcolm Muggeridge (who has been playing chess with his wife for sixty years), and Bernard Levin, were, or are, all addicts. Levin, a self-confessed woodpusher, has lost to some stars: Michael Foot; former *New Statesman* editor Kingsley Martin (a strong Cambridge University player); Captain Liddell Hart (see 'The Soldiers'); and *The Times* former editor, William Rees-Mogg. Levin's most painful loss though, was to fellow journalist Tim Jones, who 'not only beat me but broke one of my Sheraton chairs while doing so'.

Harold Evans, former editor of *The Times*, lists chess amongst his recreations in *Who's Who*.

The best poem about chess by a patzer:

The Ballad of Edward Bray

'The author cannot lay claim to any technical knowledge of chess,[2] but he fancies that he understands the spirit of the game. He feels that, after the many poems on the Boat Race, a few bracing lines on the Inter-University Chess Match would be a welcome change'. (A. A. Milne)

[1] 'I play the Evans.
'The invention of a naval officer, the Evans Gambit is noted for its liquidity. A heavy current rapidly sets in from the South-West and laps against the foundations of Black's King's Bishop's Pawn. The whole surface of the board breaks into whirlpools. But sooner or later out of this marine display there rises a familiar corpse. It is mine. Oh, what have I been doing, what have I been doing? The usual thing. Premature attack, followed by timidity. Oh, why didn't I move out my Rook's Pawn? Because as always I was misled by superficial emotion. No, not as always. It must be that the Evans doesn't suit my style. Henceforward I play Old Stodge.' (*The Game of Life*)
[2] Milne was too modest. He was champion of his house at school.

THIS IS THE BALLAD of Edward Bray.
   Captain of Catherine's, Cambridge Blue –
Oh, no one ever had just his way
   Of huffing a bishop with KB2.

The day breaks fine, and the evening brings
   A worthy foe in the Oxford man –
A great finesser with pawns and things,
   But quick in the loose when the game began.

The board was set, and the rivals tossed,
   But Fortune (alas!) was Oxford's friend,
'Tail' cried Edward, and Edward lost:
   So Oxford played from the fireplace end.

We hold our breath, for the game's begun –
   Oh, who so gallant as Edward Bray!
He's taken a bishop from KQ1
   And ruffed it just in the Cambridge way!

Then Oxford castles his QBKnight
   (He follows the old, old Oxford groove;
Though never a gambit saw the light
   That's able to cope with Edward's move.)

The game went on, and the game was fast,
   Oh, Oxford huffed and his King was crowned,
The exchange was lost, and a pawn was passed,
   And under the table a knight was found!

Then Oxford chuckled; but Edward swore,
   A horrible, horrible oath swore he;
And landed him one on the QB4,
   And followed it up with an RQ3.

Time was called; with an air of pride
   Up to his feet rose Edward Bray.
'Marker, what of the score?' he cried,
   'What of the battle I've won this day?'

The score was counted; and Bray had won
   By two in honours, and four by tricks,
And half of a bishop that came undone,
   And all of a bishop on KQ6.

         . . .

Then here's to Chess: and a cheer again
   For the man who fought on an April day
With never a thought of sordid gain!
   England's proud of you, Edward Bray!   A.A. Milne

The best bit of chess analysis by a patzer:

> ... a hoarse voice called from the corner of the lounge.
> 'Pssst!' cried the voice. 'Honoured Grand Master
> Mr Green!'
> I turned and saw the gnome-like figure of Globovitch,
> the world chess champion, crouched malevolently at a
> table.
> 'Just one game,' he begged. 'Just one game, before you
> go to bed. I have never forgiven you for that thrashing
> in Moscow.'
> I strolled over and pushing aside the Russian's hand,
> casually moved forward my King's Pawn. Sweat broke out
> on the Russian's forehead. Half an hour later he
> desperately moved his own King's Pawn. I shrugged and
> brought out my Knight. He gave an hysterical cry and
> buried his face in his hands.
> 'I resign,' he sobbed. 'In thirteen moves your Queen
> will take my undefended Rook on the back line and all
> will be lost.'
> 'That's the way the cookie crumbles, Globovitch.'
> I grinned and moved away. He bored me.
> Slowly I walked up the broad central staircase of the
> hotel. Behind me came the sound of a shot. Poor fellow.
> These Russians can't stand being beaten.

Michael Green, *The Art of Coarse Sport*

♟

The remaining Americans include Walter Tevis (*The Hustler* and *The Queen's Gambit*); James (*From Here to Eternity*) Jones, a keen student of the game; Edgar Allan Poe (who preferred draughts because he thought it was deeper); L. Frank Baum (*The Wizard of Oz*); Charles MacArthur (co-author of that terrific play *The Front Page*); John Steinbeck; O. Henry, master of the short story, who played against Ajeeb (see chapter VIII); the Canadian humorist and economics professor, Stephen Leacock; and the great Argentinian author, Jorge Luis Borges (he wrote a poem about the game).

♟

Among the Europeans we haven't yet mentioned are: Rabelais (probably the first great writer to play modern chess; his scatological master-piece *Gargantua and Pantagruel* contains – book five – the first description in literature of castling), Balzac, Goethe ('Chess is the touchstone of the intellect'), Ionesco,[1] Joseph Conrad, Henrik Ibsen, Tristan Tzara (he was one of the founders of Dadaism and might well, like Arthur Ransome, have played with Lenin), Boccaccio, Cervantes, half the brothers Grimm (Jakob), Verlaine, Bertolt Brecht – who tried to invent a chess variant in which the pieces changed their powers during the game, and Stefan Zweig, who wrote the best-ever story about chess: *The Royal Game*.

♟

Omar Khayyám played Shatranj (see Chapter VII) and gave us (via Edward FitzGerald) the best known lines about the game.[2]

♟

One name that hasn't come up yet is that of William Shakespeare (or as US boxing impresario Don King recently and unnecessarily dubbed him: 'the late, great, William Shakespeare').

Nobody knows for sure whether the Swan of Avon played chess. The only evidence we have is a painting by Karel van Mander of him (we think) launching a queen's-side attack against Ben Jonson. It is *circa* 1603. This is around the time he wrote *King Lear*, which contains one of only four[3] references to the game in his plays.

Our bet is that as an educated Elizabethan he probably knew the moves, but the scant number of references to the game in his oeuvre suggest he wasn't addicted. So, regrettably, the Bard doesn't make our dream team.

♟

A strong player who would have been chucked off the writers' team by a unanimous vote of its members is the infamous Dr Thomas Bowdler, the expletive-deleter of Shakespeare. Bowdler's *Family Shakespeare* was the Bard without the dirty bits – or as Bowdler expressed it, a version of Shakespeare which would 'no longer raise a blush on the cheek of modest innocence' for Dr Thomas had expunged all those passages 'which cannot with propriety be read aloud to the family'. The result was abysmal. He did the same thing to Gibbon's *Decline and Fall*

---

[1] See 'Desert Island Chess' for more about him, Sartre and others.
[2] 'Tis all a chequer board of Nights and Days
Where Destiny with Men for Pieces plays;
Hither and thither moves and mates and slays,
And one by one back in the closet lays.
[3] If you care to track them down they are: *The Tempest*, Act V Scene 1; *King John*, Act II Scene 1; *King Lear*, Act I Scene 1; *The Taming of the Shrew*, Act 1 Scene 1

of the Roman Empire, to similar effect. (Gibbon, by the way, was a chess-player.) Still, his chess was sparkling enough. Here's Bowdler, with the first double rook sacrifice on record, beating the daylights out of a member of parliament:

Bowdler–General Conway, London, 1796. Bishop's Opening

1. e4 e5	7. Qf3 Qxb2	13. Qg4+ Kc7	19. d4 b4
2. Bc4 Bc5	8. Bxf7+ Kd7	14. Qxg7 Nd7	20. Bxb4 Kb5
3. d3 c6	9. Ne2 Qxa1	15. Qg3 b6	21. c4+ Kxb4
4. Qe2 d6	10. Kd2 Bb4+	16. Nb5+! cxb5	22. Qb3+ Ka5
5. f4 exf4	11. Nbc3 Bxc3+	17. Bxd6+ Kb7	23. Qb5
6. Bxf4 Qb6	12. Nxc3 Qxh1	18. Bd5+ Ka6	mate

Dr Bowdler also beat the great Philidor[1] (but he had a pawn and two moves start).

To balance the Bowdler entry, we conclude with a quotation from a terrific writer whose work must have the good Dr Bowdler spinning in his grave:

> During the Baroque period of chess the practice of harrying your opponent with some annoying mannerism came into general use. Some players used dental floss, others cracked their joints or blew saliva bubbles. The method was constantly developed. In the 1917 match at Baghdad, the Arab Arachnid Khayam defeated the German master Kurt Schlemiel by humming 'I'll Be Around When You're Gone' forty thousand times, and each time reaching his hand towards the board as if he intended to make a move. Schlemiel went into convulsions finally.
>
> *Queer,* William Burroughs

Solution to Dunsany problem: the position as it stands is impossible so rotate the board by 180 degrees. Then

1. Nc6 Nf3	2. Nb4 Ne5	3. Qxe5 and	4. Nd3 mate.

Solution to Alfred de Musset problem:

1. Rd7 Nxd7	2. Nc6 and	3. Nf6 mate.

Solution to Nabokov problem:

1. Bc2 (not b8 = N? c2!)

[1]See 'The Musicians'. And for much more on literature and chess, see Norman Knight's superb books (Bibliography).

The Entertainers

The movie buffs amongst you will recall that in *Casablanca*, our first view of Rick (Humphrey Bogart) shows him playing solitaire chess.[1] The scene was suggested to the director, Mike Curtiz, by the actor himself, for Bogie was an addict.

Probably the strongest of all the major movie stars, Bogart was obsessed by the game from his student days onwards; and in the depths of the great depression, when struggling young actors were earning even less than they do in normal years, he found a novel way of adding to the family income. Bogart lived near a New York chess café, with a resident 'expert' who hustled customers for dimes. The actor beat the expert so often that the café owner offered him the job. Humphrey declined, but chess hustling up and down Broadway made an appreciable difference to the Bogarts' standard of living.

Decades later, when he'd become box-office magic, he still hustled chess, in Hollywood and for much larger sums. One of his biographers says he rated his friends on their ability to play chess and hold liquor. Bogart was adept at both. Unfortunately the only Bogie games we have are losses against masters. Here's Humphrey (black), on location for *The African Queen*, losing to Belgian master Limbos, watched by Lauren Bacall and Katharine Hepburn:

P. Limbos–H. Bogart, Stanleyville, 1951. French Defence

1. e4 e6	7. O–O c6	13. Rfe1 Nb6	19. Re1 Qd6
2. d4 d5	8. Bg5 Nbd7	14. Re2 Bd7	20. g4 Rd8
3. Nc3 Bb4	9. Ng3 Qc7	15. Be7 Bxe7	21. f4 g5
4. exd5 exd5	10. Nh5 Nxh5	16. Rxe7 Rf7	22. h4 Black
5. Bd3 Nf6	11. Qxh5 g6	17. Rxf7 Kxf7	resigns
6. Ne2 O–O	12. Qh6 f5	18. Qxh7+ Kf6	

The star of *Casablanca* didn't have it all his own way. Art Buchwald (columnist for the *Herald Tribune* – you read of him above, under 'The Writers') beat Bogie regularly. And so did Hollywood's most famous restaurateur – Mike Romanoff. Indeed so one-sided were the matches that Romanoff once bet Bogart $100 that he could win twenty consecutive games. Humphrey lost – and planned a terrible revenge. He called up Romanoff and challenged him to just one more game, by phone, for a similar stake. Mike jumped at the easy money and was

---

[1] Movie buffs will also recall that Ronald Reagan was the first choice for the part. Just imagine.

thunderstruck when the actor blitzed him in twenty moves. What he didn't know was that sitting at Bogart's elbow was Herman Steiner, US chess champion (and organizer of the Hollywood Chess Club).

♖

Marlon Brando played chess on the set of *Julius Caesar*. Whilst filming, he gave an interview to a Hollywood reporter on condition they played chess. The reporter thrashed him. Brando's comment: 'That was the worse interview I ever gave.'

♖

John Wayne – you wouldn't have thought it – was a chess player, too. According to his agent Wayne was 'a good country player', whatever that means. He did play a series of games against William Windom, a lesser-known actor (*To Kill a Mockingbird*) who was rated about 1600 US. Big John, showing true grit, lost the match 5–0.

♖

Charles Boyer, the archetypal French lover, was in the Bogart league as a chess player.

♖

Al Jolson, after he became the first movie actor of the talkies, was keen enough to form a chess club of radio stars called Knight Riders of the Air.

♖

And more recently, Nigel Havers, on the set of *A Passage to India*, played chess pretty incessantly. He, being a kind-hearted chap, decided to teach some Indian children the game. Annoyingly for Nigel, they beat him easily.

♖

Other chess-playing film stars were and are: Shirley Temple, Marlene Dietrich, Lionel Barrymore, Charlie Chaplin (who was taught by the ten-year-old wonderkid Sammy Reshevsky), Douglas Fairbanks Jnr, Errol Flynn (when he wasn't raising hell), Leo Genn, Peter Lorre (another star of *Casablanca*), Belinda Lee (British sex symbol of the fifties), Ray Milland, Yves Montand (with Simone Signoret), Anthony (*Zorba*) Quinn, Walter Pidgeon, George Peppard, George C. Scott, and Alastair Sim. Ralph Morgan (*Charlie Chan's Last Chance, The Power and the Glory*) had one of the world's smallest chess-sets: carved from date stones, the kings were less than half an inch high (but if the *Guinness Book of Records* is reading this, the smallest ever is probably that made by five engineering students from Geneva. The board dimensions are 8mm by 8mm, the pawns are 1.5mm high and the king is 2.5mm, says *Chess Notes*).[1]

♖

Bing Crosby didn't[2] ('I have worries enough already,' he said in one of his films), but Sinatra does, occasionally. Bob Hope played once, and memorably. On a TV spectacular in 1972 he became one of the handful of people who have beaten Bobby Fischer. It is just possible that Bobby, for once in his life, wasn't entirely serious.

♖

A nicely balanced match would be movie stars versus directors. The directors team: Stanley Kubrick (who featured HAL, a chess-playing robot in *2001*,[3] and who likes to play his stars before filming); Roger 'Mr Bardot' Vadim who chose a computer chess-set as his one luxury on *Desert Island Discs*; Ingmar Bergman; John Huston; Milos Forman; Roberto Rossellini; Sergei Bondarchuk, Eisenstein, and Vsevolod Pudovkin (who made *Chess Fever*, a film starring Capablanca). In Rome's Cinecittà in the fifties, Vadim played against Rossellini and Bondarchuk. The Frenchman won both games.

♖

The ten best films with chess scenes

1.	*A Matter of Life and Death*	Michael Powell and Emeric Pressburger
2.	*The Seventh Seal*	Ingmar Bergman
3.	*Casablanca*	Michael Curtiz
4.	*2001*	Stanley Kubrick
5.	*Ivan the Terrible*	Sergei Eisenstein
6.	*The Chess Players*	Satyajit Ray
7.	*Blazing Saddles*	Mel Brooks
8.	*Blade Runner*	Ridley Scott
9.	*The Thomas Crown Affair*	Norman Jewison
10.	*From Russia with Love*	Terence Young

(plus some very soft porn: a *Betty Boop* cartoon in which Betty is captured by a black king and rescued by white pawns).

♖

[1] Another contender — a chess set on sale in Ciudadela, Menorca in 1987 was small enough to fit into a match box.
[2] One of the authors asked him, on Turnberry Golf Course.
[3] And a Russian called Smyslov.

47

In the film *8×8* by the Dadaist Hans Richter, Jean Cocteau plays a pawn that is promoted to a queen.

♖

Of stage actors, we know that Sarah Bernhardt played; and from the BBC TV programme *My Favourite Things* that the divine Felicity Kendal likes playing with her son; Jessie Matthews (Mrs Dale) played; Patrick McGoohan (star of that terrific TV series *The Prisoner*) is a keen player; so is Anthony Andrews, of *Brideshead Revisited*; and ballet star Mikhail Baryshnikov, who with Milos Forman, was a keen spectator at the USSR v. Rest of World match (1984).

♖

Kate Jackson of *Charlie's Angels* said in a TV interview she would rather play with her Sargon chess computer than watch television.

♖

One of the funniest men on TV, Stephen Fry, of *Blackadder* and *Saturday Night Live*, is a chess freak. He has a superb board of bird's-eye maple and Moluccan ebony, edged in sycamore, an 1871 boxwood and ebony Staunton set, plus a chess clock by Grant's of Stamford. Dolefully he confesses that what he brings to this wonderful equipment is the playing talent of a dead rat.

♖

Magicians seem particularly addicted to chess. Houdini, the wizard of escape played (how well we don't know). And David Nixon, the TV star, was a keen and capable player. One of the authors helped him beat an early chess computer at an Islington chess congress in the seventies. But the prize for chess cheek goes to magician, hypnotist and showman, The Great Romark. Towards the end of the Fischer–Spassky 'Match of the Century', a cable arrived from Romark challenging the two superstars to a simultaneous match. Romark, blindfold, would take on Boris and Bobby together for a $50,000 stake. Spassky declined, but Fischer expressed enough interest in it to have Romark's financial status checked out. Nothing came of it though.

How it's done

If you'd like to do a Romark, and play, say Kasparov and Karpov (or merely two of your club stars) together and guarantee to come out even, here's how. After agreeing suitably high stakes, and after placing the boards some distance apart, you take white against Kasparov and, generously, black against Karpov. You then await Karpov's first move.

'd4' says the wizard of Zlatoust. 'd4' you say to Kasparov. 'Nf6' replies the world champion; which of course is your reply to Anatoly. And so on. If you can pull it off before they tumble, it should do wonders for your grading.

The last we read of Romark was in the *Book of Heroic Failures*. In a memorable demonstration of blindfold driving he, eyes tightly bandaged, blundered along the main street of Ilford and wrecked a police van.

♖

Another magician, The Amazing Kreskin, whilst appearing in a mental magic act at Reno, Nevada, went one further. He (having played less than a dozen games in his life) challenged Fischer, Karpov or Korchnoi to play him for $50,000. The Amazing K. would be blindfold, and the grandmasters needn't announce their moves. Larry Evans (not quite in the Karpov class, although still a grandmaster) took up the challenge but Kreskin, pleading a hectic business schedule, chickened out.

♖

Alistair Cooke, doyen of British broadcasters from America (who might also represent the writers) lists chess amongst his hobbies in *Who's Who*.

♖

From the world of pop we have the following (maybe they should be among the musicians, but the classical virtuosi have a strong enough team already): Bobby Darin; one quarter of Abba (Björn Ulvaeus); Phil Lynott of Thin Lizzy; Country and Western star Willie Nelson; Adam Faith; Sting (of The Police); Dr Robert of the Blow Monkeys; and at least two of the Fab Four—John Lennon, who on the promo film accompanying the song 'Imagine' played chess with Yoko (they both used white pieces to symbolize peace and love); and Ringo, who after the split-up, designed a chess-set in the shape of human hands. The royal jewellers made two copies of it in gold and silver. In the sixties Jefferson Airplane had a song about getting stoned which included the line (sung by Grace Slick) '. . . when the chess pieces start to tell you where to go'. We don't know if they themselves played.

♖

Apart from Ulvaeus, other people involved with the musical *Chess* play; Tim Rice is an addict; and last time we heard, Elaine Paige was learning.

♖

49

Our showbiz allstars team is:

1. Humphrey Bogart
2. Al Jolson
3. John Wayne
4. Sir Charles Chaplin
5. John Lennon
6. Frank Sinatra
7. Harry Houdini
8. Marlon Brando

This lot would pull in the crowds like no other chess team in the history of the universe. But if you're looking for board strength make room for: William Windom[1] whom we mentioned earlier; Fritz Feld (dapper cameo actor of dozens of films[2] and organizer of the Hollywood Chess Club in the forties); Mike Romanoff (almost an entertainer in his own right); Roger Vadim; and Stanley Kubrick (who beat George C. Scott on the set of *Dr Strangelove*).

The Sportsmen

If you watched Norwegian second-division football more often than you do, you might be aware of a talented young midfield player called Simen Agdestein. He's also the world's youngest grandmaster and top board for our sportsmen's team. The multi-faceted Simen played under-21 football for his country around the same time he was becoming Nordic chess champion, and heads a formidable line-up for the athletes.

On board two, the Daley Thompson of ball games, the amazing Sir

---

[1] Here's Windom beating a Greek master in a simul:
    Windom–Kourkounakis, 1972. Queen's Pawn Game

1. Nf3 d5	5. d4 Bd6	9. Bxh7+ Kxh7	13. Nf3 Be7
2. e3 Nf6	6. Bd3 O-O	10. Qh5+ Kg8	14. Qh8+ Kf7
3. Ne5 Nbd7	7. Nd2 Ne8	11. Ng6 c5	
4. f4 e6	8. O-O f6	12. c3 f5	

Now Nfe5+ is mate in 4, but instead Windom played Nxf8 and won on move 58.

[2] *The Secret Life of Walter Mitty, Hello Dolly, Silent Movie, The Sunshine Boys,* et cetera.

George Thomas. Sir George played hockey for Hampshire, tennis for England (he reached the last eight at Wimbledon) and was All-England badminton champion in 1920, 21, 22 and 23. In this last year he scored a remarkable double: he was also British chess champion. (Another unique double: he captained England at badminton and chess.)

Sir George did pretty well for an amateur; at the Hastings Tournament of 1934–5 he came ahead of two all-time greats (Capablanca and Botvinnik) and first equal with a future world champion (Euwe). He played for England in seven Olympiads, and at his best approached grandmaster strength. Here's a sample of his play – a lightning (ten minutes) game against a master when he was nearly seventy.

Sir G. A. Thomas–E. Klein, London, 1946. Ruy López

1. e4 e5	7. Bb3 d5	13. Nd4! Nxd4	19. f6 g6
2. Nf3 Nc6	8. dxe5 Be6	14. cxd4 Ng5	20. Qh6 Ne6
3. Bb5 a6	9. c3 Bc5	15. f3 Bc8	21. Bc2 Kh8
4. Ba4 Nf6	10. Qe2 Bg4	16. Nd2 c6	22. Rf5 Rg8
5. O–O Nxe4	11. Be3 Bxe3	17. f4 Ne6	23. Qxh7+ Black
6. d4 b5	12. Qxe3 O–O	18. f5 Nc7	resigns

On board three another soccer star. Time's ever-rolling stream has wiped out most people's memory of C. Wreford Brown, but in the early part of the century he played for the all-conquering Corinthian Casuals. He was rated by C.B. Fry as the best centre-half of his day, playing until he was fifty-nine; and he was good enough to represent England at chess. He also played in the British championships, 1933, scored a win and a draw, then withdrew through illness. His claim to immortality: he coined the word 'soccer'.

C. Wreford Brown–P. R. Gibbs, London, 1918 (Casual Game). Giuoco Piano (Max Lange Attack)

1. e4 e5	5. d4 exd4	9. Bg5 gxf6	13. Qe2 Ne5
2. Nf3 Nc6	6. e5 d5	10. Bh6+ Kg8	14. Nxe5 Bxe2
3. Bc4 Bc5	7. exf6 dxc4	11. Nc3 Bb6	15. Nd7
4. O–O Nf6	8. Re1+ Kf8	12. Ne4 Bg4	Black resigns

Board four goes to bridge pro Alan Truscott. Alan now makes a living out of bridge in the USA, but before taking the wrong path, he was a strong Cambridge University player.

If you're not American you may not have heard of our board five, Ron Guidry. If you have, you'll know he's the pitcher with the second highest lifetime winning percentage in major league baseball. 'Rapid' Ron is a strong player–good enough to take US master Bruce Pandolfini to the end game before losing.

Board six is a surprise: the current world light welterweight boxing champion, Terry Marsh. Before he took up boxing Terry was a chess star: at eleven, he was a London schools champion. He now plays computer chess. He likens boxing to chess: 'It's all about nullifying your opponent's strengths, and exploiting their weakness.'

Board seven, yet another footballer, and a very famous one: Ossie Ardiles, world cup wizard and Spurs idol, has played correspondence chess with former England international Michael Franklin. He is also a friend of G.M. Quinteros. Ossie says he devotes ten to twelve hours a week to studying or playing chess: 'I'm probably more competitive in chess than in football.'

On board eight, another world champion and (according to the TV series *The Greatest*) the greatest snooker player who ever drew breath: Steve Davis. Steve gave up Space Invaders to concentrate on the more difficult game, and is now a dedicated computer chess player (he's currently on his fifth computer, a Conchess).

Steve learned to play chess before he could play snooker (his father taught him when he was three years old); and one of his early opponents was chess expert and author, Jimmy Adams.

'I know I'm bad, but by most standards I'm OK,' he says about his prowess. A couple of years ago he threw out a chess challenge to his fellow snooker stars, but there were no takers.

Steve's proudest chess moment: after he won the world title in 1987, he received a telegram of congratulations from Anatoly Karpov. (Karpov, you'll be surprised to hear, is a snooker fan. When he was in London in 1982 for the Phillips and Drew tournament, someone tried to arrange a chess/snooker match between Davis and Karpov: they were both keen but their tournament schedules didn't allow it. Pity.)

We agonized for a long time about first reserve; in the end world heavyweight title contender Frank Bruno got the nod. He listed chess among his hobbies in his autobiography and on a TV interview. How good he is we're not sure, but the mere sight of him standing in the wings should be worth a couple of points. Know what I mean, Harry?

Competing for (but not quite catching) the judge's eye for big Frank's place were such superstars as:

— World heavyweight contender Joe Bugner (perhaps they could settle it over twelve rounds). Joe chose a chess set for his luxury on *Desert Island Discs*;

— Prince of milers and Olympic hero, Steve Ovett, who takes a chess computer with him on those long flights between meets (Seb Coe doesn't play, incidentally);

— the first sub-3.50 miler, John Walker, a frequent Ovett opponent on the track;

— Chris Bonnington, Britain's most famous climber, who played chess four miles up a Himalayan mountain called Changabang;

— the formidable father of English cricket, W. G. Grace; the *British Chess Magazine* once published a poem celebrating his chess-playing ability;

— Tennis ace, Ivan Lendl, a keen player and son of a Czech junior chess champion;

— Winter sports champ, Tony Kastner, who swapped ski lessons for chess lessons with Bobby Fischer;

— the most cultured former heavyweight champion of the world, Gene Tunney, who was rumoured to have played George Bernard Shaw;

— the robust (to put it mildly) Rugby Union international Gareth Chilcott (England's answer to The Refrigerator) who claims to thrash all his Oxbridge-educated team mates (at chess, that is);

— the greatest bridge publicist of all time, Ely Culbertson, friend of world champion Emanuel Lasker, and a grateful recipient of chess master Janowski's money over the card table;

— Jimmy Greaves, soccer wizard and TV sage, who challenged Terry Marsh to a game on *This is Your Life*;

— another multi-talented sportsman, Lord Brabazon of Tara — first Englishman down the Cresta run, first Briton to hold a pilot's licence, and a county standard chess-player (there's now a Brabazon trophy for chess);

— someone else who, like Agdestein and Thomas, scored a strange double is Othmar Eggar — he was champion of Birmingham at wrestling and chess in the early part of the century;

— and England's cricket captain, the man who brought back the Ashes, Mike Gatting, is a chess-player.

Plus Alfredo di Stefano (football); Wally Hammond (cricket); Bobby Jones (golf); Emil Zatopek and Lord Burleigh (track); Willi Trepp (cycling); Terence Reese and Tobias Stone (bridge); and the whole of the Zurich football team in the sixties, for whom chess was made a compulsory part of their training. (It didn't catch on.)

Of the commentators, BBC's Mr Boxing, Harry Carpenter, is currently engaged in a World Series of games against his computer. The computer is winning. Desmond Lynam was a keen schoolboy player and taught his son to play by the time he was four.

Postscript

An outstanding challenger for a high board among the sportsmen is the astonishing Newell M. Banks.

Banks was a draughts (checkers) champion, but embarrassed several chess stars in his career, among them grandmaster Frank Marshall (US champion), and Isaac Kashdan, one of the world's ten best grandmasters in the thirties. Banks was also pretty stunning in simultaneous displays. A typical effort would be 25 games of chess, plus 25 games of draughts, plus 6 blindfold games of draughts.[1] And occasionally he'd have a game of billiards on the side.

But since he was a professional board-games player, we think it wouldn't be fair to include him. The athletes' team is good enough without Banks anyway.[2]

♞

As we went to press, we discovered that international master Béla Soos was a Romanian international footballer.

The Thinkers

Surprisingly the thinkers (philosophers and mathematicians) have one of the weakest teams of all. Presumably if you spend your time thinking up the General Theory of Relativity or writing *Principia Mathematica* you don't have much time left for rook and pawn endgames.

Certainly Einstein for one was a self-confessed duffer: 'I am no chess-player...indeed I have to confess I have always disliked the fierce competitive spirit embodied in that highly intellectual game.' Bertrand Russell gave up chess at eighteen, the better to concentrate on whatever mathematical philosophers concentrate on. Henri Poincaré (1854–1912), one of the most brilliant of all mathematicians, confessed himself a hopeless chess-player.

The father of computer chess and pioneer of machine intelligence, Alan Turing, was so bad that Harry Golombek used to give him a queen start and still beat him.[3] And Ken Thompson, the brain who programmed BELLE, the outstanding chess computer of the early eighties, confessed (shock, horror) he doesn't play chess at all!

[1] It's nothing to do with chess but in a *45-day* blindfold splurge he took on 1,187 draughts games without sight of the board, and lost only two.
[2] For similar reasons, we exclude that prodigious whist-player, billiards champ and gardener, A. L. H. L. Deschapelles (see p. 191).
[3] Turing merits a place in Chapter VII for his invention 'round-the-houses' chess, which he played with David Champernowne (an expert on the computer composition of music). After you've made your move, run around the house; if you get back before your opponent has moved, you get another move. Turing was a better runner than a chess-player.

Nor, as far as we know, were the great philosophers of history much better. The men whose brains helped bring about the French Revolution for example, were rabbits.

Jean-Jacques Rousseau (who played in a fur hat and cape) determined to master the game by hard study. After months of solitary toil he returned to his favourite café – and one of the finest minds of eighteenth-century France was slaughtered by a humble patzer. It is said that when Jean-Jacques played at the Café de la Régence, crowds used to press up against the windows to watch. It certainly wasn't the quality of his games that attracted them (perhaps it was the fur hat).[1]

Rousseau's fellow encyclopaedist, Denis Diderot, gave up playing and took up watching when he figured he'd never master the game; and Voltaire (who played correspondence chess with Frederick the Great) complained when a 'donkey' called Father Adam beat him ceaselessly. (Voltaire gets on our long list of people who used to knock the pieces over when they lost – see Chapter IV).

So, to boost this sorry lot, we've chucked in the scientists. This makes the thinkers' team respectable, though not unbeatable.

Board one: good old Karl Marx, the strongest philosopher. He played a lot of his chess in London (Holborn and Covent Garden) while writing *Das Kapital*. He was a bad loser (Liebknecht, the German revolutionary, tells how Karl tried to detain him by force when Liebknecht wanted to quit while he was winning) but a good player. Here's a sample:

Karl Marx–Meyer. King's Gambit

1. e4 e5	9. Nc3 Ne7	17. Qe4 d6	25. Qxe6 Ra6
2. f4 exf4	10. Bd2 Nbc6	18. h4 Qg4	26. Rf1 Qg7
3. Nf3 g5	11. Rae1 Qf5	19. Bxf7 Rf8	27. Bg4 Nb8
4. Bc4 g4	12. Nd5 Kd8	20. Bh5 Qg7	28. Rf7
5. O–O gxf3	13. Bc3 Rg8	21. d4 N5c6	Black resigns
6. Qxf3 Qf6	14. Bf6 Bg5	22. c3 a5	
7. e5 Qxe5	15. Bxg5 Qxg5	23. Ne6+ Bxe6	
8. d3 Bh6	16. Nxf4 Ne5	24. Rxf8+ Qxf8	

[1] A frequently published brilliancy by Rousseau against the Prince de Conti is believed to be a fake.

Next a couple of Nobel Prize winners for chemistry.

Board two, Professor John Cornforth,[1] who in his youth was one of the strongest players in Australia. He held (and may still hold) the Australian blindfold simultaneous record (twelve). When he moved to England he was on the strong Hampstead team of the sixties (with British champ Jonathan Penrose) and regularly played for Middlesex. Here's one of the games from the simul:

J. W. Cornforth–F. F. Kelly, Perth, 1937. Damiano's Defence

1. e4 e5	7. dxe4 Qxe4	13. Bxe8 Kxe8	19. Nxd6+ cxd6
2. Nf3 f6	8. O–O Bd6	14. Nc3 a6	20. Qxd6
3. Nxe5 Qe7	9. Bb5+ Kf8	15. Qd5 Bc8	Black resigns
4. Nf3 d5	10. Re1 Qg4	16. Bd2 Ne7	
5. d3 Bf5	11. h3 Qh5	17. Re1 Nd7	
6. Be2 dxc4	12. Re8+ Qxe8	18. Ne4 Rf8	

♗

Board three, Sir Robert Robinson, Nobel Prize winner in 1947, Order of Merit 1949, and one of Britain's greatest scientists: Sir Robert was also a chess author, twice Oxfordshire champion and the man who taught Professor Cornforth.

♗

Board four – television star Jacob Bronowski. Bronowski was Yorkshire champion (1936), a published problemist, and a noted player in the London Commercial League. His name is commemorated in the Bronowski Cup, an inter-league competition. Here's Jacob in action:

Dr J. Bronowski–E.W. Harrison, London Commercial League, 1962. Réti Opening

1. Nf3 Nf6	11. Nd5 Nxd5	22. Qxd7+ Kxd7	33. Bg7 Rc8
2. c4 d6	12. cxd5 Nb8	23. dxc6+ bxc6	34. Bc4 Bd2
3. b3 e5	13. Qe3 a6	24. Rxc6 a5	35. d4 Bc3
4. Bb2 Bg4	14. Rc1 Qb5	25. Ra6 Rc8	36. e5 Ke8
5. h3 Bh5	15. O–O f5	26. Ra7+ Rc7	37. d5 Rd8
6. g4 Bg6	16. gxf5 Bxf5	27. Rxc7+ Kxc7	38. Bf6 Rb8
7. Bg2 Nc6	17. Nxe5 dxe5	28. Bd5 Rd8	39. d6
8. Nc3 Be7	18. Qxe5 Qd7	29. e4 g6	Black resigns
9. d3 Qd7	19. Rxc7+ Qxc7	30. f4 Rf8	
10. Qd2	20. Rc1 Nc6	31. Kg2 Kd7	
O–O–O	21. Qxf5+ Qd7	32. Kg3 Bb4	

[1] His Nobel Prize, if you're interested, was for work on the stereo-chemistry of enzyme-catalysed reactions.

♗

Professor Lionel Penrose, who gets in at board five, played board one for Cambridge University and on a high board for Essex and was a skilled problemist. To scientists he's the world-famous geneticist: but chess-players know him best as the father of Jonathan Penrose, ten times British champion.

♗

The only pure mathematician to make the thinkers' team goes in at board six. Abraham de Moivre was a seventeenth-century pioneer in probability theory, and the man called in to settle the Leibniz–Newton squabble about who invented differential calculus. But mathematics didn't pay enough; so de Moivre became a chess professional.[1] Like Roget, and that much greater mathematician, Leonard Euler, he published solutions to the Knight's Tour (see our section, 'Desert Island Chess').

♗

Erich Ernest Zepler arrived in England with practically nothing in 1935, a refugee from the Nazis. By 1949 he had become a leading international expert on electronics, and Britain's first professor of electronics (at Southampton). He also found time to become one of the world's most eminent problemists (International Master of Composition, 1973). We don't know how good he was as a player, but we'll take a chance on him at board seven.

♗

On board eight, another problemist. Wolfgang Pauly was one of the greatest problem composers who ever lived. In private life he was an actuary and an astronomer (he discovered comet 1898VII). If you're feeling sharp, have a go at this:

---

[1] Irrelevant but interesting is how de Moivre met his death. He vowed to sleep a quarter of an hour more each successive night. This worked fine until he'd got up to 23¾ hours – after which, you guessed it, he died in his sleep.

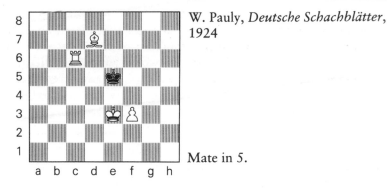

W. Pauly, *Deutsche Schachblätter,*
1924

Mate in 5.

See end of section for solution.

⚜

That's the thinkers' team. You may be thinking we've put Karl Marx on too high a board – but we imagine the thinkers would be cute enough to juggle the board order to give them wins over stronger teams.

⚜

First reserve might well be TV supernova, starwatcher Patrick Moore. Not a lot of people know it, but Patrick was a founder of the East Grinstead Chess Club and represented Sussex at chess. Here's a game:

Revd C. Dinwoodie–P. Moore, 1960. Nimzo-Larsen Attack

1. b3 e5	10. e3 Qe5	19. Kg3 Be2	28. a4 Re4
2. Bb2 Nc6	11. d4 Bxc3+	20. Bxe2 Qxe2	29. Rf3 Rhe8
3. Nf3 e4	12. Ke2 Qb5+	21. Rh3 Qg4+	30. f5 Rxh4+
4. Nd4 Nxd4	13. Kf3 Qf5+	22. Kh2 O–O–O	31. Kg3 g5
5. Bxd4 Nf6	14. Ke2 Bxa1	23. Qc3 Qd7	32. f6 Rhe4
6. Nc3 c6	15. Qxa1 Qxc2+	24. Qc5 Qd6+	33. Kf2 g4
7. Bxf6 Qxf6	16. Kf3 d5	25. f4 Qxc5	34. Rf5 h4
8. Nxe4 Qd4	17. a3 h5	26. dxc5 Rde8	White resigns
9. Nc3 Bb4	18. h4 Bg4+	27. Rg3 g6	

⚜

Alongside Patrick, we place one of Russia's greatest scientists. Dmitri Mendeleyev, when he wasn't busy discovering the periodicity of the elements, was an avid player and student of the game. He claimed it refreshed his mind after hard study.

⚜

Among the other reserves we have: astronomer Fred Hoyle (he played for Cambridge in the inter-varsity match – maybe he should be on the team); Erasmus (who played chess while standing up and wisecracking); Newton; Gauss; Machiavelli (after he was banished by the Medici, chess was his solace); Girolamo Cardano, gambler and founder of probability theory; Wittgenstein (his writings are spattered with chess analogies); Lord Keynes (his father was a strong Cambridge player); Francis Bacon; the great mathematicians Leibniz ('People's ingenuity is best revealed at chess') and Euler; philosopher A.J. Ayer (who once won a friendly match with Tony Benn); Professor C.E.M. Joad, nationally famous in the forties on the BBC's *Brains Trust* was a county player, and once won a game of living chess against a bus conductor; and one of the men who first split the atom, another Nobel Prize winner: Sir Frederick Soddy. Soddy played in the Oxford–Cambridge match around the same time as those two reprobates Aleister Crowley and Harold Davidson (see 'The Sinners'). Finally, Professor Robin Matthews, Master of Clare College and economic guru of the SDP, is one of the world's leading three-move problemists.

Solution to Pauly problem:

1. Bc8 Kd5	3. Rg6 Kf5	5. f4 mate
2. Bb7 Ke5	4. Be4+ Ke5	

The Politicians

The squabbling over board order would be endless, but if you could get them to stop talking and start playing, the politicians would have a pretty good team.

Here's a future British prime minister (playing white) knocking off a sparkling miniature against the chess editor of the *Observer*:

11 Downing Street, c.1920. Ruy López

1. e4 e5	5. d4 exd4	9. Qxd4 Nxb5	13. Qxf7 Kd6
2. Nf3 Nc6	6. Nxd4 Nd6	10. Qxg7 Rf8	14. Rxe7 Black
3. Bb5 Nf6	7. Re1+ Be7	11. Bh6 d5	resigns (if
4. O–O Nxe4	8. Qg4 Nxd4	12. Qxf8+ Kd7	Qxe7
			15. Bf8)

That was Andrew Bonar Law, throwing off the cares of office, against Brian Harley. Bonar Law was easily the best of our prime ministers. Mrs

Thatcher doesn't play at all (though she opened the Kasparov–Karpov world championship in 1986), but Jim Callaghan (who closed it) does. The Marquess of Rockingham, Sir Robert Peel, the younger Pitt, Gladstone, Disraeli, Balfour, Asquith, Churchill and Attlee all did. Prime Minister Campbell-Bannerman called chess 'not a game, but a disease'.

♖

Churchill is one of the great might-have-beens of chess. He learned at prep school in Hove: 'Dear Mamma ... do not forget to get the set of chess for me. I should like the board to be red and white, not black and white ...' said a letter from the twelve-year-old Winston. By the time he was twenty-one he was beginning to show signs of addiction. A letter from Bombay told how he'd reached the semi-finals of a shipboard tournament and continued ... 'I shall try and get really good when I am in India.' But other distractions occupied the great man and he never fulfilled his early promise. The only later record we have is of a game with Asquith before which Churchill gave vent to his bizarre battle cry: 'Marshal your Baldwins!' (Churchillian slang for pawns.)

♖

The American presidents are less well represented. Jefferson and Washington both played. The fifth president, James Monroe, kept an English fine bone china set on display in his office. President Harding played a bit (but preferred draughts) and Teddy Roosevelt played the automaton, Ajeeb. Abe Lincoln (according to the *American Chess Magazine*, 1898) was 'a really skilful devotee'. Evidence of Abe's superhuman good nature is that when, in the middle of a serious game with a judge, his young son, Tad, kicked the board over, Lincoln calmly remarked, 'I guess that's Tad's game.' More recently, Rosalynn and Amy Carter, wife and daughter of the former president, were said to be players. Whether Jimmy was, we don't know.

♖

Lenin, like Marx, was a keen player, but a bad loser.[1] He didn't play much after the Revolution but whilst in exile he was so preoccupied with correspondence chess that he raved about it in his sleep. If you're in Paris, check Metro Alésia – that's where Lenin used to play, at a café on the corner of the Avenue d'Orléans and the Place Montrouge.

♖

---

[1] Maxim Gorky records, 'He got peeved and depressed when he lost.' Don't we all?

Here's our team. We elect J. Stalin (a non-player[1] but a world-class disciplinarian) captain of an ill-assorted bunch in which the forces of the left have the edge over those of the right:

Board one, one of the strongest players of the 1850s, Marmaduke Wyvill, Tory MP for Richmond, Yorkshire. He was good enough to take two games off the great Adolf Anderssen in the London 1851 tournament (Wyvill was second to Adolf). Here he is, carving up the world's best player:

A. Anderssen–M. Wyvill, London, 1851. Sicilian Defence

1. e4 c5	11. f4 f5	21. Qf2 Bb7	31. Kf2 Nd5
2. d4 cxd4	12. Rf3 c5	22. Bf1 Ng4	32. Rgd3 Qc6
3. Nf3 Nc6	13. Rh3 Rf7	23. Qh4 Qd7	33. Rd2 Qb6
4. Nxd4 e6	14. b3 g6	24. Rd1 Rc8	34. Bc4 Rc2
5. Be3 Nf6	15. Nf3 Nb6	25. Be2 h5	35. Ke1 Rxd2
6. Bd3 Be7	16. Bf2 d4	26. Rg3 Qe8	36. Rxd2 Qg1+
7. O–O O–O	17. Bh4 Nd5	27. Rd2 Rg7	37. Bf1 Rc7
8. Nd2 d5	18. Qd2 a5	28. c3 Ne3	38. Rd1 Rc2
9. Nxc6 bxc6	19. Bxe7 Rxe7	29. cxd4 cxd4	39. Qg3 Ba6
10. e5 Nd7	20. Ng5 Ne3	30. Rxd4 Rc1+	40. Qf3 Bxf1
			White resigns

♜

Board two, Josip Broz Tito. Tito learned chess as a boy, and found time, whilst raising hell against the Nazis as a Yugoslav partisan, to play the occasional game. He rose to Yugoslav candidate master standard. When the Russians queried his prowess at chess, he offered to take on the whole of the Soviet Praesidium in a simul. Nothing further was heard from the USSR. At the 1950 Dubrovnik Olympiad, the Marshal played a game *hors concours*.

♜

Board three, János Kádár, leader of the Hungarian Communist Party, and also a candidate master.

♜

Board four, Bonar Law, an example of whose play we saw above. Law was good at most indoor games but brilliant at chess. Grandmaster Mieses rated him as one of the best amateur players he'd met. (But we

---

[1] A Stalin game featured in various publications is a hoax. 'Comrade Stalin is a very busy man, but if he ever found time to play he would reveal strategic judgement of the very highest order' was what Soviet diplomats used to say of their boss.

saw in 'The Musicians' how he met his match against old Walter Parratt.)

𝕀

Board five, at the opposite end of the political spectrum: Che Guevara. Che and Fidel Castro played together in the mountains during the revolution, but Che was by far the better player. He played in Cuban tournaments and had a number of casual games against British IM Bob Wade. Bob rates him highly: 'about 180 to 200 grading' he says – which would get him into most English county sides. This is Che drawing a simultaneous game against Grandmaster Najdorf:

M. Najdorf–Che Guevara, Havana, 1962. Ruy López

1. e4 e5	6. Re1 b5	11. Nbd2 Bf8	16. Be3 Be6
2. Nf3 Nc6	7. Bb3 d6	12. d5 Ne7	Draw agreed
3. Bb5 a6	8. c3 O–O	13. c4 bxc4	(but Ba4 is
4. Ba4 Nf6	9. h3 h6	14. Nxc4 c6	winning for
5. O–O Be7	10. d4 Re8	15. dxc6 Nxc6	White)

𝕀

Board six (and perhaps deserving a higher place), former Birmingham MP Julius Silverman. Julius, the man who carried out the investigations into the Birmingham riots, was for many years the strongest chess-playing MP. He played in international tournaments in the thirties and won (among others) a spectacular game against Eliskases, who at the time was one of the world's best players:

J. Silverman–E. Eliskases, Birmingham, 1937. King's Gambit

1. e4 e5	7. Bb3 Bd6	13. Qe2 d4	19. Bxf7+ Kh8
2. f4 exf4	8. O–O O–O	14. Nd5 Bxd5	20. Qxh7+
3. Bc4 Nf6	9. d4 Be6	15. Bxd5 Ne3	Black resigns
4. Nc3 c6	10. Ne5 Bxe5	16. Bxe3 dxe3	
5. Nf3 d5	11. dxe5 Qb6+	17. Rxf4 Nc6	
6. exd5 cxd5	12. Kh1 Ng4	18. Qh5 Qxb2	

𝕀

Board seven, Edmund Dell, Secretary of State for Trade and Industry under Harold Wilson, chairman of Channel Four at the time of writing and 1937 London under-eighteen champion (at fifteen). Dell played individual games against Grandmaster Tartakower, and drew a game in a twenty-five board simul against Grandmaster Reshevsky (the other twenty-four lost). After beating the University of Oxford captain 2–0 Dell quit chess until, in 1977, he was challenged to a game whilst leading a British government trade delegation in Moscow. His opponent: Deputy Prime Minister Kirillin, Head of the Soviet Academy of Sciences and a friend of Smyslov and Petrosian. The result, an honourable 1–1 draw. Here's the young Dell *en route* to the London under-eighteen title:

E. Dell–N. A. Phillips, 1937. Queen's Gambit Declined

1. d4 e6	14. b4 Nxb4	27. h3 Rd8	40. Rc6 Qb1+
2. c4 Nf6	15. O–O Nxd3	28. Rc7 Rdd7	41. Kh2 Qe4
3. Nc3 c6	16. Rxd3 Bd7	29. Rc8 Rd6	42. Qxe4
4. Bg5 d5	17. Rb1 b5	30. h4 e5	and White
5. e3 Be7	18. Qc2 O–O	31. h5 e4	won
6. Nf3 h6	19. Ne5 Be8	32. Qd1 Rd5	
7. Bh4 Bb4	20. Rc3 f6	33. R1c7 Rdd7	
8. Rc1 Bxc3+	21. Nxc6 Bxc6	34. Rxd7 Rxd7	
9. Rxc3 Nbd7	22. Rxc6 Rfe8	35. Qg4 Re7	
10. Bd3 Qa5	23. Qb3 Kf7	36. Qg6+ Ke6	
11. Bxf6 Nxf6	24. Qxb5 Rab8	37. Qxe4+ Kf7	
12. Qb3 dxc4	25. Qd3 Qxa2	38. Qg6+ Ke6	
13. Qxc4 Nd5	26. Rbc1 Re7	39. Qg4+ Kf7	

♜

Board eight, the man who's probably done more for world chess than anyone: Nikolai Krylenko, first Bolshevik Commissar for War. A much feared man, his one contribution to civilization was to persuade the new Soviet state to popularize chess. He once played a game against Arthur Ransome—we don't know who won—and wrote a book on the 1935 Moscow tournament.

♜

Other political contenders: Michael Foot, one of the strongest players in the House of Commons, Charles James Fox (like Lenin he couldn't sleep for thinking about chess), Willy Brandt, Jan Masaryk, Robespierre, Rowland Hill (who gave us the penny post), Ho Chi Minh (who wrote a poem about chess and played in the jungle when he wasn't fighting the Americans), four times Mayor of New York Fiorello La Guardia (he played Tito, but said 'I am absolutely the worst player in the world. Nobody approaches me.'), Ben Franklin (who wasn't all that good, but wrote a book about chess morals), Leon Trotsky, Vice-President Spiro T. Agnew (not a bad player apparently), Henry Kissinger, Clement Freud, Valéry Giscard d'Estaing, Gamal Abdul Nasser, Fidel Castro (to whom grandmaster Petrosian ceded a diplomatic draw); and President Marcos of the Philippines (ditto against Bobby

Fischer). Tony Benn once won a game off philosopher A. J. Ayer (but lost several more). Harold Lever, Cabinet Minister under Wilson played Korchnoi in a simul. Enoch Powell went to the same school as British champions Hugh Alexander and Tony Miles, but it didn't catch—he played as a boy, then gave up. Here's an unimpressive Castro game:

Filiberto Terrazas–Fidel Castro, Havana, 1966. King's Gambit

1. e4 e5	6. c3 Ba5	11. Qa4+ Nc6	16. c7+ Bd7
2. f4 exf4	7. Bxf4 g5	12. d5 Bd8	17. c8=Q Rxc8
3. Nf3 Bd6	8. Bg3 Qe7	13. dxc6 b5	18. Qd4 gxf3
4. d4 h6	9. Be2 d6	14. Qxb5 a6	19. Qxh8 Qxe2
5. e5 Bb4+	10. exd6 cxd6	15. Qa4 g4	mate

For coolness under fire, we give a special mention to Israeli prime minister Menachem Begin. In September 1940 he was playing chess with his wife, when Russian soldiers burst into his house to arrest him. As they dragged him away, he shouted back to Mrs Begin: 'I resign! I resign!'

Currently the strongest player in the House of Commons, says Raymond Keene, is Jeremy Hanley, Tory MP for Richmond and Barnes. But that was before the June 1987 General Election. It would be interesting to see a Foot–Hanley match.

We couldn't find much about the leading Nazi politicians and chess. Hitler made a reference to 'dog lovers and members of chess clubs' in a 1933 speech: and in 1941 he was presented with a chess set, filched from the Croat National History Museum, by Ante Pavelić, the Croat Quisling. We know Adolf was a dog-lover; was he perhaps a chess-player?

The unspeakable Hans Frank, Governor General of Poland after 1939, was a chess player. He founded a chess college, and in 1941 played four games against former world championship contender Bogoljubow and a partner. We don't know how good Frank's chess was, but he certainly knew how to pick allies: *his* consultation partner was the world champion, Alekhine.

Bogoljubow and Stolzyk (?)–Alekhine & Frank, Warsaw 1941.
Queen's Gambit Declined.

1. d4 d5	13. dxe5 Ne4	25. gxf5 dxe3	37. Bd3 g5
2. c4 e6	14. Bxe7 Qxe7	26. Bh5 b5	38. Kc3 h5
3. Nf3 Nf6	15. f4 Nxc3	27. Kf1 Be4	39. Kd4 h4
4. Bg5 Nbd7	16. bxc3 f6	28. Ke2 Bxf5	40. Ke3 Kf8
5. e3 Be7	17. Qh5 fxe5	29. a3 a5	41. Kd4 Kg7
6. Nc3 O–O	18. fxe5 Rxf1+	30. Kxe3 b4	42. Kc3 Be6
7. Rc1 h6	19. Rxf1 Rf8	31. axb4 axb4	43. Kd4 g4
8. Bh4 b6	20. Rxf8+ Kxf8	32. Kd4 Be6	44. Kc3 Kh6
9. cxd5 exd5	21. Bg6 Qe6	33. Bg6 Ke7	45. Kd4 Kg5
10. Bd3 Bb7	22. g4 d4	34. Kc5 b3	46. Be4 Bf5
11. O–O c5	23. cxd4 cxd4	35. Kb4 Bf7	White resigns
12. Ne5 Nxe5	24. Qf5+ Qxf5	36. Bf5 g6	

♟

The traitor William Joyce (Lord Haw-Haw) played chess in his cell in Wandsworth to take his mind off his impending execution. 'He concentrated on his moves without the least sign of strain', said an observer.

Postscript

For a century, the only game permitted in the Palace of Westminster was chess. But, alas, on 17 April 1987, *The Times* reported that 'because of the diminishing number of MPs with the time or inclination for chess' the hallowed chess room was to be thrown open for games of chance 'from mah-jong to poker'. Ghastly.

The Soldiers

In the Café de la Régence, for a hundred years, there was a table with a brass plaque saying 'Napoleon Bonaparte used to play chess at this table'. What it didn't say is that the greatest military tactician in history was a pretty rotten player. George Walker, the chess historian, reckons he could have given Bonaparte a rook start (and George was no grandmaster). His contemporaries said Napoleon was too impatient, too given to impetuous attacks. But he did love the game. Even at the height of his great campaigns, when he was making mincemeat of the best generals in Europe, he took time off to get thrashed by his own generals[1] over the chessboard.

Later, after his coronation, he started to win more games. But that's because his opponents had become, shall we say, more tactful;[2] the Emperor was getting a reputation as a bad-tempered loser. Walker reports that he was 'sore and irritable' after a defeat; and as you'll see in Chapter VIII, when Maelzel's automaton beat him, Napoleon knocked the pieces to the floor.

Another annoying habit he picked up around this time was a rabid insistence on the touch and move rule—for his opponents only. When *he* wanted to take a move back, Napoleon acted like an emperor.

Here's a game that Napoleon is supposed to have won against a good player, the beautiful Madame de Rémusat. The historically minded will be interested to know that the game happened the night before the young Duc d'Enghien was executed.

'Mme de Rémusat'–'Napoleon Bonaparte', Paris, 1802.

1. e4 Nf6	5. Nc3 Nfg4	9. Ke2 Nxd4+	13. Kd5 Qd6
2. d3 Nc6	6. d4 Qh4+	10. Kd3 Ne5+	mate
3. f4 e5	7. g3 Qf6	11. Kxd4 Bc5+	
4. fxe5 Nxe5	8. Nh3 Nf3+	12. Kxc5 Qb6+	

You will have noticed the use of the word 'supposed' in the above paragraph: modern authorities reckon that all published Napoleon games are fakes.

After Waterloo, Bonaparte continued his chessboard battles in exile; and his loyal staff still continued to let the ex-emperor win.

What neither he nor they knew was that his chess pieces may have hidden a most poignant secret. According to an article in the London *Morning Post* of 1928 (about an exhibition of Napoleonic relics) a French officer was despatched to St Helena with a chess-set in ivory and mother-of-pearl. He was to tell Napoleon that inside some of the pieces were secret compartments containing an escape plan. The officer was killed by a falling spar on board ship; Napoleon accepted the set, played with it to the end of his days—but never discovered the plans.

♚

[1] Murat, Berthier, Beauharnais.
[2] All except his foreign minister Talleyrand. He regularly beat the emperor. Perhaps that's why Napoleon once described him as a silk stocking full of dung.

The next most famous chess-playing general was the hero of Alamein, Viscount Montgomery. He gave up the game on being beaten by his nine-year-old son. Another World War Two hero, General Sir Claude Auchinleck was also a keen player.

♚

The British colonel Rall, played chess. Perhaps it cost us the American colonies.

On Christmas Day, 1776, George Washington was preparing his troops to attack the British at Trenton across the Delaware River. An Englishman who lived nearby sent his son with a note to Colonel Rall, warning him of the danger. Rall, immersed in a game of chess, took the note and put it, unopened, in his pocket.

Next day Washington attacked, and the Americans won their first great victory. Colonel Rall was killed, and the note discovered in his pocket. His game of chess marked the turning in the tide of the colonists' fortunes.

♚

That brilliant tactician Robert E. Lee, commander of the Confederate armies, had his own travelling chess-set and was an enthusiastic player. So was one of his most formidable opponents, General McClellan.

♚

America's General Pershing carried a pocket chess-set with him during the First World War.

♚

Captain Sir Basil Liddell Hart was perhaps Britain's greatest military historian and strategist; his chess strategy was poor though. Arthur Ransome said of him, 'He dashes into attack in a Churchill manner with insufficient concentration of forces.' Another of his opponents (and a friend of Montgomery) was Bernard Levin (see 'The Writers').

♚

Not a soldier, but a chess-playing sailor was the unfortunate[1] Admiral Byng. All we know of his prowess is a loss to the exquisitely named Don Scipione del Grotto, champion of the Naples Academy.

---

[1] He was the chap who got shot, *'pour encourager les autres'*, for failing to take Minorca in 1756.

The Aristocrats

Sergei Semyenevich Urusov was a Russian prince and one of the strongest players of the mid-nineteenth century. He invented a gambit (1. e4 e5 2. Bc4 Nf6 3. d4 exd4 4. Nf3), played innumerable games with Tolstoy, and during the siege of Sebastopol tried to win a battle by chess. The Russians and the English had been disputing the same ridge of ground for weeks with great losses and no result. Prince Sergei went to his commanding officer with a novel suggestion: let the English pick their best player and the two of them would play for the ridge. The general was entranced by the romantic idea (someone should try it on Reagan and Gorbachev)[1] but turned it down on the reasonable grounds that even if Urusov won, they couldn't be sure the English would keep their bargain.

♛

There are lots more aristocrats in early chess history.[2] But since most of them got famous for aggro with a chessboard, and since you read enough about that under 'The Royals', we'll mention just a few more.

The Duke of Brunswick and Count Isouard de Vauvenargue get into the history books for just one game – and that they lost. It's the best-known game in all chess history, and it was played against the tragic American genius Paul Morphy in 1858. The conditions of play were unusual: Morphy had been invited to the Paris Opera to see a performance (*Norma*, say most authorities).[3] The game was played in a box. Whether the opera was being performed at the time is not clear, but the game itself is a sizzler. It's in every collection of great games, but just in case you've missed it, see our Chapter II.

♛

Duke Huon of Bordeaux played for one night of love with a princess. Huon was a guest at the court of a Muslim ruler (King Ivoryn), and, boasting of his prowess at chess and love-making, was challenged to play the king's daughter. If he won he got the daughter for a night, plus a hundred marks. If he lost, he lost his head. The game must have been pretty exciting, although the princess seems not to have been trying too hard ('I wolde this game were at an end, so that I were in bed with him all nyght'). Huon won the game, and chivalrously declined the girl – much to her intense annoyance ('Yf I had knowne that thou woldest a refused my

---

[1] Our money's on Gorbachev.
[2] E.g. Charles d'Orléans, who spent twenty-five years after the Battle of Agincourt in captivity, playing chess and writing poetry about it.
[3] But not all. *The Barber of Seville* is another contender.

company, I wold have mated the'). (From a thirteenth century French romance).

The Businessmen

You'd think life was too short for anyone to become both a chessmaster and a millionaire, but a couple of bright sparks managed it.

Ignac Kolisch, one of the best players in the world in the 1860s, always had an eye peeled for the green stuff; when he won the great Paris tournament of 1867, his prize, from Napoleon III, was a magnificent Sèvres vase; he sold it instantly for 4,000 francs which he invested in property. The year after that he met Baron Albert Rothschild – himself a strong player.[1] Rothschild, impressed with Ignac's financial wizardry, found a novel way of helping him. The baron played the chessmaster a match for a thousand pounds. Kolisch won of course, and was off on a dazzling financial career. Helped by the Rothschilds, he set up as a banker. Within nine years he'd made his first million, and a year after that became a baron. Perhaps the moral is, if you want to become a millionaire, give up chess.[2] Here's Kolisch beating the writers' board two, Turgenev:

Turgenev–Kolisch, *c.* 1870. Two Knights Defence

1. e4 e5	7. Nf3 e4	13. Kd1 Re8	19. Bc1 Qxg2
2. Nf3 Nc6	8. Qe2 Nxc4	14. Qf3 Bxd2	20. Rf1 and Black
3. Bc4 Nf6	9. dxc4 Bc5	15. Nxd2 c6	mates in 2
4. Ng5 d5	10. Nfd2 O–O	16. b3 cxd5	
5. exd5 Na5	11. h3 e3	17. Bb2 Ne4	
6. d3 h6	12. fxe3 Bxe3	18. c5 Qg5	

♟

[1]He was a pupil of world champion Steinitz. Here's a Rothschild game against a player of master strength:

A. Clerc-Rothschild, Paris, (Casual Game) 1884. King's Gambit

1. e4 e5	8. h4 g4	15. Kh3 g2	21. Qxf6+ Ne7
2. f4 exf4	9. Nh2 f3	16. Rg1 h5	22. Be3 Rxh6+!
3. Nf3 g5	10. gxf3 g3	17. g5 Nh6!!	23. Qxh6 Qh1+
4. Bc4 Bg7	11. Ng4 Qxh4	18. gxh6 Bf6	24. Kg3 Qxh6
5. d4 d6	12. Kg2 Bxg4	19. Qxh5? Qxg1	25. Bxh6 g1=Q+
6. O–O h6	13. Rh1 Qf6	20. Qxf7+ Kd8	White resigns
7. c3 Nc6	14. fxg4 Qf2+		

[2]Kolisch didn't quite give up; he was a generous patron of many tournaments – and hence gave much financial assistance to impoverished former colleagues.

Someone who didn't give up chess and managed nevertheless to be a millionaire is German grandmaster Lothar Schmid. Lothar was chief arbiter at the Fischer–Spassky match (1972) and at the 1986 Kasparov–Karpov match. Herr Schmid made a fortune in publishing[1] and yet managed to become one of Western Europe's best players in the sixties. He used his money to create the largest private chess library in the world.

Here's a Lothar brevity against a player from Hong Kong: the shortest game in the 1968 Olympics.

Gibbs–L. Schmid, Lugano 1968. Alekhine's Defence

1. e4 Nf6	4. Nge2 Nc6	7. Bxd5 Qxd5!
2. Nc3 d5	5. g3? Bg4	8. f3 (if Nxd5 it's mate) Qxf3
3. exd5 Nxd5	6. Bg2 Nd4	9. Rf1 Qg2 White resigns

♟

Jim Slater, the financier and children's author, was a strong schoolboy player. He gave up chess for finance. This turned out a very good thing for chess, since he was able to tempt Bobby Fischer (with a £50,000 increase in stake-money) into playing Boris Spassky for the world title in 1972. Here's what the young Slater was capable of:

J. D. Slater–P. C. Tomlin, West London Chess Club, 1947. Orang Utan opening

1. b4 Nf6	8. h4 d6	15. Nb5! cxb5	22. Rg1 Rc8
2. Bb2 g6	9. Nc3 Be6	16. Bxa8 bxc4	23. Rb3 Nf5
3. g4 Bg7	10. d3 Qb6	17. e4 c3	24. Rxc3 Nd4!
4. g5 Nh5	11. Qd2 Bf5	18. Qc2 O–O	Draw agreed
5. Bxg7 Nxg7	12. Rb1 Nbd7	19. exf5 Rxa8	
6. Bg2 c6	13. b5 Qc7	20. fxg6 hxg6	
7. c4 e5	14. bxc6 bxc6	21. Ne2 Qc6	

♟

John Spedan Lewis founded the John Lewis chain of stores and was a great benefactor of British chess:

L. Vine–J. S. Lewis, Philidor's Defence

1. e4 e5	5. Bc4 Nh6	9. f5 gxf5	13. Rxf6 Bxg4
2. Nf3 d6	6. O–O Ng4	10. Qxg4 Qf6	14. Nxg4 Bxb2
3. d4 exd4	7. f4 Bh6	11. Nxf5 Bxc1	White resigns
4. Nxd4 g6	8. Bxf7+ Kxf7	12. Nh6+ Ke7	

[1] His speciality: Westerns

Sir Jeremy Morse, chairman of Lloyds Bank (who do much for chess), is an accomplished problemist. A sample of his work:

First Prize, the *Observer*, 1964

Mate in 2. Solution at end of section.

Other chess-playing businessmen: Charles Saatchi[1] (head of the world's largest advertising agency and according to *Chess* magazine, a garrulous lunchtime player); Rosser Reeves (former chairman of the Ted Bates agency, founder of the USP[2] school of advertising and non-playing captain of the US Olympic chess team); Robert Maxwell, chairman of Mirror Group Newspapers (Maxwell was a keen player in his youth. In his office he keeps an elegant marble chess set; unfortunately, last time we saw it, the board was the wrong way round); Cecil King, another newspaper magnate ('I have always felt that chess should be a part of every business executive's training') and Leslie Waddington, managing director of London's most influential private art dealers (who was, as a young man, an enthusiastic and good player).

Solution to the Morse problem: Qc4

The Rest

First, some twentieth-century names who don't quite fit into any of the above teams; and then a collection of exotica who defy categorization.

Brian Walden[3] said he was giving up TV to become a chess master.

---

[1] According to the *Observer*, he rarely takes longer than ten seconds over a move. This doesn't necessarily mean he's any good.

[2] Unique Selling Proposition.

[3] We couldn't make our minds up whether he was a writer, politician or entertainer – hence his inclusion here.

We think he was joking – but he was once strong enough to play in the British Boys' Championship (1948), and in the Junior World Championship Qualifying Tournament (1951). He was equal fifth.

♟

Ninth in the same tournament was Walter Marshall, now Lord Marshall of the Central Electricity Generating Board, a Welsh Junior International who won a brilliancy prize on top board for his country in 1949. He scored 50 per cent in a Junior International Tournament (Birmingham 1950), including a draw with future World Championship Candidate, Fridrik Olafsson. Nowadays all he has time for is computer chess. He generally wins.

♟

From the world of espionage and counter-espionage, Graham Mitchell who was deputy director of MI5,[1] He was also an international master of correspondence chess, and in the time he wasn't dealing with real-life James Bonds, he found the time for such entertaining games as this:

Mitchell–Riley, Correspondence, 1964–5. Sicilian Defence

1. e4 c5	8. Qd2 Qxb2	15. Bxe6 Bxd4	22. Bh6 Rfd8
2. Nf3 d6	9. Rb1 Qa3	16. Bxd7+ Nxd7	23. Rxg6 fxg6
3. d4 cxd4	10. e5 dxe5	17. Qxd4 O-O	24. Bxg7+ Kxg7
4. Nxd4 Nf6	11. fxe5 Nfd7	18. O-O Nxe5	25. Ne8+ Kh6
5. Nc3 a6	12. Bc4 Bb4	19. Ne4 Be6	26. Qf4+ Black
6. Bg5 e6	13. Rb3 Qa5	20. Rg3 Kh8	resigns
7. f4 Qb6	14. a3 Bc5	21. Nf6 Ng6	

There has been recent speculation that Mitchell may have been the mysterious 'fifth man'; it was suggested (inanely) that he used his correspondence games as a code to communicate with the Eastern bloc.

♟

Captain Robert Falcon Scott, the explorer, was an addict. According to Edward Wilson's diaries Scott played every evening on one of his Antarctic expeditions; and got 'in a cantanker' if he lost.

♟

The cosmonaut Vitaly Sevastianov became head of the Soviet Chess Federation. He played in the first game between space and earth (Soyuz-9, represented by Sevastianov and A. Nikolayev; earth by Air Force Colonel General N. Kamanin and cosmonaut V. Gorbatko).

---

[1] Another spymaster/chess-player was Fouché, head of Napoleon's secret police.

Soyuz-9–Earth, 1970. Queen's Gambit Accepted

1. d4 d5	10. h3 Bf5	19. bxc3 Be4	28. g5 Qd6
2. c4 dxc4	11. Nh4 Qd7	20. Qg3 c6	29. Nxd5 cxd5
3. e3 e5	12. Qf3 Ne7	21. f3 Bd5	30. Bf4 Qd8
4. Bxc4 exd4	13. g4 Bg6	22. Bd3 b5	31. Be5+ f6
5. exd4 Nc6	14. Rae1 Kh8	23. Qh4 g6	32. gxf6 Nxf6
6. Be3 Bd6	15. Bg5 Neg8!	24. Nf4 Bc4!	33. Bxf6+ Rxf6
7. Nc3 Nf6	16. Ng2 Rae8	25. Bxc4 bxc4	34. Re8+ Qxe8
8. Nf3 O–O	17. Be3 Bb4	26. Bd2 Rxe1	35. Qxf6+ Kg8
9. O–O Bg4	18. a3 Bxc3	27. Rxe1 Nd5	Draw

♟

The Chevalier d'Éon was history's most famous transvestite. Charles Geneviève Louis Auguste André Timothée d'Éon de Beaumont (1728–1810) had a most colourful career as a diplomat, swordsman, chess-player, nun and Lady-in-Waiting to the Empress of Russia. He disguised himself as a woman when acting as a spy for Louis XV, became attached to the idea, and spent half his life dressed as a woman (the rest of the time he masqueraded as her – or rather his – own brother). So convincing was he that when he showed up at the court of Versailles dressed as a man, he was ordered to change into women's clothes; and became Lady-in-Waiting to Marie Antoinette.

Later on he spent several years in London, where he became a noted chess-player (a member of the St George's Club), good enough to beat Philidor in a simul.

The Chevalier was a celebrity – mainly on account of the large wagers placed on the question of his gender. In 1810 all bets were settled when the gallant Chevalier died, and a post-mortem established his masculinity.

♟

Dr Charles Stanley Hunter of Rochdale was joint British Correspondence Chess Champion in 1961. What gets him into this collection of oddballs is that in 1968 he became the world's fastest speaker (Hamlet's best-known soliloquy in forty-one seconds. His fastest burst was fifty words in 7.2 seconds).

♟

General Tom Thumb – star attraction of Barnum's American Museum – was born Charles S. Stratton. A normal baby, he stopped growing at twenty-five inches. At this point fate, in the shape of the great showman, Phineas T. Barnum, stepped in, and Charles became the most famous midget of all time. First New York, then Europe went wild about the little chap. He was granted an audience with Queen Victoria, swapped jokes with President Lincoln, and was Barnum's greatest ever crowd-puller.[1]

Tom was, according to contemporary reports 'an excellent chess player for his size', and won many games from his fans (because, it was said, his opponents couldn't distinguish between him and the pieces). This game was attributed to him:

Scotch Gambit

1. e4 e5	3. d4 exd4	5. Ng5 d5	7. Nxf7 Kxf7
2. Nf3 Nc6	4. Bc4 Nf6	6. exd5 Nxd5	8. Qf3+ Kg8,

and the world's smallest adult chess-player announced mate in three.

But it was probably all a Barnum publicity stunt.

This has nothing to do with chess, but you may be interested to know that Tom Thumb was married to Mercy Bumpus, over whom he came to blows with the equally diminutive Commodore Nutt.[2]

♟

Madame Tussaud was a chess-player: among her possessions, a chess-set in green and white ivory.

♟

Casanova played chess – but not well. We learn from his memoirs that he played a girl called Pauline as part of the process of seduction. He lost the first game in four moves, the second in five. But almost certainly his mind was on lower things.

♟

Finally, if you believe fifteenth-century French romances, we have the great Merlin. In addition to all that stuff with the sword and the stone, King Arthur's wizard was a whizz at chess: he found time to build the world's first chess computer – a wonderful board of gold and ivory that, without so much as a silicon chip to help it, could beat any opponent in the world. (Incidentally, Merlin was not the only member of King Arthur's court to play chess: Lancelot used the game as a cover when he wooed Guinevere.)

---

[1] When the crowds stayed too long for profit, the ingenious Barnum had a sign erected saying, accurately, 'This way to the Giant Egress!' It worked like a charm.

[2] Freaky footnote: Alekhine once won two consultation games off an American player, W. K. Wimsatt Jnr, who, said the press, stood seven foot in his stockinged feet.

II *The Greatest*

Genius is pain   *John Lennon*

The Greatest

American Chess Bulletin

(ISSUED BI-MONTHLY: $2.00 A YEAR)

ESTABLISHED IN 1904

150 NASSAU STREET

Telephone: BEekman 3-3763

CHESS PARAPHERNALIA
OF EVERY DESCRIPTION

Cable Address: CHESS, New York
Publisher: H. HELMS

New York 7, N. Y.

January 13, 1951

Mrs. R. Fischer,
1059 Union St.,
Brooklyn, N. Y.

Dear Madam:

Your postcard of Nov. 14th, mislaid in The Eagle
office, has just reached me.

If you can bring your little chess-playing boy to
the Brooklyn Public Library, Grand Army Plaza, next Wednesday
evening at eight o'clock, he might find someone there about
his own age. If he should care to take a board and play against
Mr. Pavey, who is to give an exhibition of simultaneous play at
that time, just have him bring along his own set of chessmen with
which to play. The boards, I understand, are to be provided.

I will also bring your request to the attention of Mr.
Henry Spinner, secretary of the Brooklyn Chess Club, which meets
Tuesday, Friday and Saturday evenings on the third floor of the
Brooklyn Academy of Music. It is quite possible that Mr. Spinner
may know a boy or two of that age.

Yours respectfully,

H. Helms,

Chess Editor.

This is chess at the summit. The strongest grandmasters, the most gifted prodigies, the most formidable geriatrics, the most phenomenal blind-fold performances, the toughest tournaments – and our modest attempt to answer the unanswerables: would Capa have beaten Kasparov? Or Fischer, Alekhine? Who *was* the greatest?

Here too, is our favourite section: a shot at the sixty greatest games ever played. It would be unbecoming for players of our modest attain-ments to add notes to such masterworks; but we suggest that if you, dear reader, were to devote your leisure hours to annotating them yourself, it would do your grading no harm whatsoever.

The Great Prodigies

Meet first the megabrats of the chequered board: the kids who made the headlines by duffing up their elders and (supposedly) betters at an age when most of us preferred ludo or Lego to bad bishops and smothered mates.

♚

A January 1987 report in *The Times* featured ten-year-old Adragon Eastwood DeMello (distantly related to Clint), from (where else?) California. Modestly described by his father as 'probably the most gifted scholar this century has ever seen', Adragon had, we are told, mastered chess by the age of two and a half. To the best of our know-ledge he has now abandoned chess in favour of nuclear physics, brain surgery or whatever it is ten-year-old geniuses study. But Adragon wins our nomination for the world's strongest-ever two-year-old chess-player.

♚

With the world's best four-year-old we reach one of the all-time greats. José Raúl Capablanca learned chess, so he told us, at the age of four by watching his father play. Having thrashed his astonished father, Capa was taken along to Havana Chess Club where an unsuspecting opponent offered him queen odds. This is what happened:

R. Iglesias–J. R. Capablanca, Havana, 1893 (Remove White's Queen).
Petroff's Defence

1. e4 e5	11. O–O–O Bd7	21. Bxc4 Bxg4	31. Rcg2 Rxg2
2. Nf3 Nf6	12. Kb1 Na5	22. Bd3 Bf3	32. Rxg2 Qf6
3. Nxe5 Nxe4	13. Rc1 Nb3	23. Rh3 Bxd5	33. Bg7+ Qxg7
4. d4 d6	14. Rc2 c5	24. h5 Be6	34. Rxg7 Kxg7
5. Nf3 Be7	15. d5 Re8	25. Rg3 g6	35. Kc2 Kf6
6. Bd3 Nf6	16. h4 b5	26. f4 Bh4	36. Kd3 Ke5
7. c4 O–O	17. g4 Nd4	27. Rg1 Kh8	37. h6 f4
8. Nc3 Nc6	18. Nxd4 cxd4	28. f5 Bxf5	38. Ke2 White
9. a3 a6	19. Ne4 bxc4	29. Bxf5 gxf5	resigns
10. Bd2 b6	20. Nxf6+ Bxf6	30. Bh6 Rg8	

The infant Capa hardly needed the queen start.

♚

The next few awards all go to the same player. Sammy Reshevsky, the boy wonder of the early 1920s, was wowing the crowds with simuls and blindfold games across two continents between the ages of six and eleven. Here's an example of his play, from a simul in Hanover when he was eight years old.

S. Reshevsky–Dr H. Traube, Hanover, 1920. Bird's Opening

1. f4 e6	6. Ne5 Ne7	11. b4 f6	16. Qg6+ Ke7
2. Nf3 d5	7. Be3 c6	12. Nxc6 Nxc6	17. Qf7
3. g3 Nf6	8. a3 h6	13. cxd5 exd5	mate
4. Bg2 Bd6	9. Nd2 Nd7	14. Bxd5 Bb7	
5. d4 Nc6	10. c4 b6	15. Qc2 Rc8	

Sammy is also the youngest player to have beaten a grandmaster in a tournament game. At the age of ten he took a game off David Janowski, who had been good enough to play a World Championship match against Lasker twelve years earlier. Shortly afterwards, Reshevsky all but gave up chess for nearly ten years to pursue a more conventional education. Here's the historic game:

D. Janowski–S. Reshevsky, New York, 1922. Queens Gambit Declined

1. d4 Nf6	6. e3 c6	11. Bxe7 Qxe7	16. Qc2 h6
2. Nf3 d5	7. Bd3 a6	12. Qd2 Nxc3	17. Rfe1 b6
3. c4 e6	8. O–O dxc4	13. bxc3 c5	18. Rb2 Rb8
4. Nc3 Nbd7	9. Bxc4 Nb6	14. Rab1 Nd7	19. Reb1 Qd6
5. Bg5 Be7	10. Bd3 Nfd5	15. a4 O–O	20. Qe2 a5

21. Bb5 Rd8	34. c4 Qf7	45. Kxh3 Rh8+	led to a draw)
22. h3 Qc7	35. Kh2 Ng6	46. Kg3 Qxa4	Qd2
23. e4 Nf8	36. Rbg1 Rg8	47. Qf3 f4+	57. Rh1 Qd3+
24. Qe3 Bd7	37. d6 Qb7	48. Kg4 Qc2	58. Kg2 Qxg6+
25. Ne5 Be8	38. h4 (Ng5+	49. Qxf4 Qe2+	59. Kf2 Qf5+
26. Bxe8 Rxe8	would have	50. Kg3 Qd3+	60. Kg2 Qg4+
27. f4 f6	won) Qc6	51. Kg2 Qe2+	61. Kh2 Qe2+
28. Nf3 Nd7	39. h5 Nh8	52. Kg3 Qh2	62. Kh3 Qd3+
29. e5 f5	40. Ng5+ hxg5	53. Kf3 Rf8	63. Kh4 Qxd7
30. g4 g6	41. fxg5 Ng6	54. Qf6+ Kg8	64. Rg1+ Kf8
31. gxf5 gxf5	42. Rg3 Kg7	55. d7 Rxf6+	65. Kg5 Qd4
32. d5 Nf8	43. Rh3 Rh8	56. gxf6 (exf6	White resigns
33. Rg2+ Kh7	44. hxg6 Rxh3+	would have	

♚

For the strongest twelve-year-old of all time we turn the clock back to
1850. The location: New Orleans, where young Paul Morphy had
already proved himself the best player around. Johann Löwenthal, a
political refugee from Hungary and one of the world's strongest players
was in town and condescended to play the young lad. Paul won twice
and generously agreed a draw in the third game following a Löwenthal
lemon.

Here's an example of Morphy at the age of twelve, surprising local
champ Eugène Rousseau.

P. Morphy–E. Rousseau, New Orleans, 1849. King's Gambit

1. e4 e5	6. Nxf7 Kxf7	11. Kd1 Kd8	16. Nxd5+ Kd6
2. f4 exf4	7. Qxg4 Qf6	12. Re1 Qc5	17. Qc7
3. Nf3 g5	8. Bc4+ Ke7	13. Bxg8 d5	mate
4. h4 g4	9. Nc3 c6	14. Re8+ Kxe8	
5. Ng5 h6	10. e5 Qxe5+	15. Qxc8+ Ke7	

♚

For the world's strongest fifteen-year-old we turn yet again to the New
World, and the supreme megabrat of chess, Bobby Fischer. US Junior
Champion at thirteen, US Open and Closed Champion at fourteen,
grandmaster and World Championship candidate at fifteen – truly
phenomenal achievements. At only thirteen he played one of the
greatest games of all time (against Donald Byrne), dubbed 'The Game
of the Century'. You'll find it later in this chapter.

♚

But Bobby can no longer claim to have been the World's Strongest
Teenager. That honour now rests with Gary Kasparov, who reached the

Number Two spot in the International Rating List at the age of nineteen.

♛

And what, you may ask, about the girls? Well, there was Elaine Saunders (now Pritchard), from England, British and International Girls' Champion at ten and British Ladies Champion at thirteen. And Jutta Hempel, born in West Germany in 1960, was a female Reshevsky. She learned the moves at three, and two years later she was giving simuls. She beat the local champion at the age of six, and scored 1–1 against Danish International Master Jens Enevoldsen at nine. She gave up chess on leaving school at eighteen.

But the most remarkable girl prodigies are the Polgár sisters from Budapest. Zsuzsa (Susan), born in 1969, won the Budapest Under-Eleven Championship at the age of four and a half with a 100 per cent score. At the age of fourteen, only Fischer was significantly stronger. Progress since then has been slightly slower, but at seventeen she is still ranked above all the boys of her age. Her younger sisters Sofia and Judith are both stronger than Zsuzsa was at their ages. In 1986 they took second and third places in the World Under-Fourteen Championship at the ages of eleven and nine. And – an amazing stop-press note: at Adelaide 1986/7 Judith, now aged ten, beat Romanian international master Drimer and missed a win against Yugoslav grandmaster Djurić. Here's the win:

J. Polgár–D. Drimer, Adelaide, 1986/7. Sicilian Defence

1. e4 c5	17. Bc4 Be7	34. Qd2 Rc4	50. Re8+ Kd6
2. Nf3 e6	18. O–O Bg5	35. c3 Rxe4	51. Rxe6+ Bxe6
3. d4 cxd4	19. b5 axb5	36. Kh1 Be6	52. Qd1+ Ke7
4. Nxd4 Nf6	20. Rxb5 O–O	37. Nc2 Bxa2	53. Qf3 Ra4
5. Nc3 Nc6	21. Bd3 Bxe3	38. Qd3 f5	54. Qb7+ Kf6
6. Ndb5 d6	22. fxe3 Qg5	39. Qa6 Bc4	55. exf4 Rxf4
7. Bf4 e5	23. Rxb7 Rb8	40. Qc8+ Kh7	56. g3 Rf1+
8. Be3 a6	24. Rxb8 Nxb8	41. Rd8 Qf6	57. Kg2 Rc1
9. Na3 Be6	25. Bb5 Nd7	42. Rf8 Qe6	58. Ne3 Rxc3
10. Nc4 Rb8	26. Bxd7 Bxd7	43. Qd8 f4	59. Qf3+ Kg6
11. Nb6 Ng4	27. Qd2 Bc6	44. h3 Kg6	60. Qe4+ Kf6
12. Nbd5 Nxe3	28. Rb1 h5	45. h4 Kh7	61. g4 Rc5
13. Nxe3 Qb6	29. Rb6 Rc8	46. Rh8+ Kg6	62. Qb4 Rc8
14. Rb1 Rc8	30. Qc3 Bb7	47. Qg5+ Kf7	and Black
15. Ncd5	31. Qd3 Bc6	48. Qxh5+ Kf6	resigns (not
Qa5+	32. Nb4 Bd7	49. Rf8+ Ke7	before time)
16. b4 Qd8	33. Rxd6 Bh3		

♔

Over the last few years, considerable effort has gone into developing junior chess in Britain; so it is not surprising that many contemporary prodigies are British.

The best known and most successful (so far) of the new generation of English boy wonders is Nigel Short. Nigel rocketed to megastardom in 1976 when he took a simul game off Viktor (The Leningrad Lip) Korchnoi. He qualified for the British Championship three days before his twelfth birthday, and at the age of fourteen shared first place in the same event, becoming the youngest player to attain an international master norm.

♔

In 1986 no less than three English prodigies made their mark in the record books. Michael Adams scored two international master norms at the age of fourteen. Twelve-year-old Matthew Sadler drew with four international masters in succession in the Lloyds Bank Masters. And young Jack Rudd, at the age of seven, became, to the best of our knowledge, the youngest player to win an adult tournament. Jack, who has already been billed by National Junior Squad Manager Leonard Barden as the next Nigel Short, is said to have an IQ of over 200 and reads maths books between moves.

♔

Briefly, a couple of other kiddie records. The youngest player to beat a master – Evan Turtel, who, at the age of nine, beat US Master Alan Williams in 1982. And the youngest national champion is Niaz Murshed, champion of Bangladesh in 1982 at the age of twelve. To prove it was no fluke he did it again at thirteen and fourteen.

The Golden Oldies

Now we pay our respects to those who achieved excellence at chess in their sixties or above.

First, we have two candidates for the best performance by players in their sixties. Vasily Smyslov, World Champion 1957/8, celebrated his sixty-third birthday during his Candidates' Final match against Gary Kasparov. For a delightful game from his semi-final match against Hungarian GM Zoltán Ribli, see the Games Section at the end of this chapter.

Smyslov's only rival in the over-sixties stakes was the great Emanuel Lasker. Driven by financial hardship to make a come-back in his mid-sixties, nine years after his retirement, his best result in later years was at Moscow in 1935. At the age of sixty-six he finished third, half a point behind the coming men Botvinnik and Flohr, and the same distance in front of no less a player than Capablanca.

♔

Our nomination for the strongest septuagenarian is a familiar name – the amazing Sammy Reshevsky. Yes, the same player who won our vote as the strongest six-year-old. In his mid-seventies, and after two heart attacks, the indomitable Sammy is still beating young grandmasters (first equal, Reykjavik Open 1984 at seventy-two; second equal, Lugano Open 1985 at seventy-three; fifth equal, ½ point behind the leaders, Holon Open 1987 at seventy-five. Astonishing.)

S. Kudrin–S. Reshevsky, Lugano, 1985. Sicilian Defence

1. e4 c5	10. Bf2 Be6	19. Bd3 h6	28. Rb1 Qe5
2. Nf3 d6	11. O–O–O Rc8	20. Qc7 dxe4	29. Rbe1 Qa5+
3. d4 cxd4	12. Qe1 Be7	21. Qxe7 Rxd4	30. c3 Bc4
4. Nxd4 Nf6	13. g4 Qa5	22. fxc4 Nxe4	31. Qc2 Rf4
5. Nc3 Nc6	14. Kb1 Rxc3	23. Qe8+ Kh7	32. Kd1 Qa1+
6. f3 a6	15. Qxc3 Qxa2+	24. Bxe4+ Rxe4	33. Qc1 Qa4+
7. Be3 e6	16. Kc1 d5	25. Qd8 Qa1+	34. Kd2 Qa2+
8. Qe2 Nxd4	17. Qxe5 O–O	26. Kd2 Qxb2	White resigns
9. Bxd4 e5	18. Bd4 Rd8	27. Qd3 f5	

♔

Here's a simple question that's sure to win you a lot of bets at your local club. Who was the first English grandmaster? The surprising answer is Jacques Mieses, a German Jew born in 1865. He fled his homeland in the thirties and settled in England, becoming a naturalized British citizen shortly before being chosen as one of the first FIDE grandmasters in 1950. He played in his last grandmaster event in 1948, gaining our nomination as the strongest octogenarian. Here's the sprightly veteran in action at the age of eighty-three:

J. Mieses–Dr H. G. Schenk, Oxford, 1948. Nimzowitsch Defence

1. e4 Nc6	6. Be3 Bg4	11. dxe5 Nh6	16. c3 axb5
2. d4 d5	7. Be2 O–O–O	12. Nb5 a6	17. cxb4 Qa6
3. exd5 Qxd5	8. O–O Qa5	13. a4 Be7	18. a5 Nf5
4. Nf3 e5	9. Nxe5 Bxe2	14. b4 Bxb4	19. Bb6 Rd5
5. Nc3 Bb4	10. Qxe2 Nxe5	15. Rfb1 c6	20. Rd1 Ne7

21. Qg4+ Kb8	23. Qf6 Rxd1+	25. Qd6+ Ka8	27. g3 Black
22. Qxg7 Rc8	24. Rxd1 Nd5	26. Rxd5 cxd5	resigns

♛

We have three candidates for the nonagenarian award. For quality of play, though, the vote goes to Edward Lasker (1885–1981), a very distant relation of Emanuel, who at the age of ninety in 1976 played for New York on the Board of Honour in a telex match against London. His game lasted nine hours! Here's how he played a year earlier, at eighty-nine, against another veteran master:

Ed Lasker–S. Bernstein, New York, 1975. Ruy López

1. e4 e5	16. Ng4 Ng6	31. Qd5 Qf7	46. Rd5 Rd7
2. Nf3 Nc6	17. g3 Be7	32. Qd4 Nd7	47. Rxd7 Ne5+
3. Bb5 a6	18. d4 f6	33. Ng5 Qc4	48. Ke4 Nxd7
4. Ba4 Nf6	19. Ne3 Qe8	34. Ne6 Qxd4	49. Bc3 b4
5. O–O Be7	20. Nf5 Bd8	35. cxd4 Nb6	50. Bd4 Bb6
6. Re1 b5	21. h4 Rf7	36. Rac1 Nd5	51. f4 Bxd4
7. Bb3 O–O	22. a4 Rb8	37. Kg2 Ra8	52. Kxd4 Ra1
8. h3 d6	23. axb5 axb5	38. Kf3 Rd7	53. Kc4 Rg1
9. c3 Be6	24. Be3 Ne7	39. Rh1 Ne7	54. g5 fxg5
10. d3 Bxb3	25. Qb3 Nxf5	40. g4 Nd5	55. fxg5 Rg4+
11. Qxb3 Nd7	26. exf5 Nf8	41. Bh6 Nb4	56. Kb3 Ne5
12. Nbd2 Nc5	27. h5 Kh8	42. Rh5 c5	57. Rh6 Nf7
13. Qc2 Bf6	28. Qd1 Re7	43. dxc5 dxc5	58. Rf6 and
14. Nf1 Ne6	29. dxe5 Qxh5	44. Rxc5 Rb7	White soon
15. Ne3 Ne7	30. exf6 gxf6	45. Bd2 Nd3	won

♛

We must also mention Joseph Blake, who achieved his lifetime best result at Weston-super-Mare at sixty-three and was champion of Kingston, Surrey, at the grand age of 90.

Finally, spare a thought for G.A. Peck, champion of Rugby (the place, not the game) in 1967 when a mere ninety-seven years of age.

We have still to come across a centenarian active in tournament or match chess. If you know of, or are, one we'd love to hear from you.

♛

Our award for the best female geriatric achievement goes to Edith Price, British Ladies' Champion in 1946 at seventy-six. A close runner-up is Mary Houlding, seventy-eight years old when champion of Newport, Monmouthshire in 1928.

♛

Lady Jane Carew ('a strong player' says Whyld) lived in three centuries, from 1797 to 1901. We don't know how long she carried on playing.

The Greats

Before we examine the achievements of the all-time greats, let us mention briefly a player who, though not quite reaching that level, was perhaps the most phenomenal of all Grandmasters. His name was Mir Sultan Khan and he was born in the Punjab in 1905. As a boy he learned the Indian form of chess and by the age of twenty-one was the best player in the state. In 1926 he was discovered by Sir Umar Hayat Khan, who took the young man into his household, taught him the Western game and brought him to England in 1929. That year he won the British Championship, a feat which he repeated in 1932 and 1933, and in other tournaments proved himself not far short of the world's best. And this despite the handicap of being unable to read Western chess literature and suffering frequent bouts of malaria. At the end of 1933 he returned to his homeland and retired from chess, apart from a match against another Indian player in 1935. He died of tuberculosis in 1966. To see how he beat the chess machine Capablanca turn to the end of the chapter.

Unofficial World Champions

(You may be interested to know that history's first Number One – according to our list – was black; the third, Chinese. Don't write and complain if you disagree with what follows; it is highly speculative.)

a) Shaṭranj Champions

Name	Dates	Nationality	Champion
Sa'id bin Jubair	665–714	Africa/Persia	*c.*700–714
Jābīr al-Kūfī		Persia	Early 9th C.
Rabrab Khatā'ī		China/Persia	Early 9th C.
Abū'n Na'ām		Persia	Early 9th C.
al-'Adlī ar-Rumi		Turkey/Persia	*c.*835–*c.*848
ar-Rāzī		Persia	*c.*848–?
al-Māwardī		Persia	?–*c.*905
as-Sūlī[1]	*c.*880–946	Turkey/Persia	*c.*905–*c.*940
al-Lajlāj[2] (The Stammerer)	d. *c.*970	Persia	*c.*940–*c.*970
Abū 'l-Fath Ahmad		Persia	11th/12th C.
'Alā'Addin at-Tabrīzī (Aladdin)		Persia	late 14th C.

[1] His full name was Abū-Bakr Muhammed Ben Yahyā as-Sūlī.
[2] In full, Abu'l-Faraj bin al-Muzaffar bin Sa'-īd al-Lajlāj. See Chapter VI for some equally impressive names.

b) Chess Champions

Name	Dates	Nationality	Champion
Ruy López	*c*.1530–*c*.80	Spain	*c*.1560–75
Giovanni Leonardo di Bona da Cutri	1542–87	Italy	1575–87
Paolo Boi	1528–98	Italy	1575–98
Alessandro Salvio	*c*.1570–*c*.1640	Italy	1598–*c*.1621 *c*.1634–40
Gioacchino Greco	*c*.1600–*c*.34	Italy	*c*1621–34
Legall de Kermeur[1]	1702–92	France	*c*.1730–47
François-André Philidor	1726–95	France	1747–95
Alexandre Deschapelles	1780–1847	France	*c*.1798–1824
Louis de la Bourdonnais	1795–1840	France	*c*.1824–40
Howard Staunton	1810–74	England	1843–51
Adolf Anderssen	1818–79	Germany	1851–58 1859–66
Paul Morphy	1837–84	USA	1858–59
Wilhelm Steinitz	1836–1900	Bohemia/USA	1866–86

The Official World Champions

Name	Dates	Nationality	Champion
1. Wilhelm Steinitz	1836–1900	Bohemia/USA	1886–94
2. Emanuel Lasker	1868–1941	Germany	1894–1921
3. José Raúl Capablanca	1888–1942	Cuba	1921–27
4. Alexander Alekhine	1892–1946	Russia/France	1927–35 1937–46
5. Machgielis (Max) Euwe	1901–81	Holland	1935–37
6. Mikhail Botvinnik	1911–	USSR	1948–57 1958–60 1961–63
7. Vasily Smyslov	1921–	USSR	1957–58
8. Mikhail Tal	1936–	USSR	1960–61
9. Tigran Petrosian	1929–84	USSR	1963–69
10. Boris Spassky	1937–	USSR (now France)	1969–72
11. Robert (Bobby) Fischer	1943–	USA	1972–75
12. Anatoly Karpov	1951–	USSR	1975–85
13. Gary Kasparov	1963–	USSR	1985–

[1] His only surviving game runs as follows: Legall–St Brie, Paris 1750. Philidor's Defence. 1. e4 e5 2. Bc4 d6 3. Nf3 Bg4 4. Nc3 g6 5. Nxe5 Bxd1 6. Bxf7+ Ke7 7. Nd5 mate: the famous Legall's Mate.

The World Championship Matches

Champion	Challenger	+	=	−	Date
1. Steinitz	Zukertort	10	5	5	1886
2. Steinitz	Chigorin	10	1	6	1889
3. Steinitz	Gunsberg	6	9	4	1890/91
4. Steinitz	Chigorin	10	5	8	1892
5. Steinitz	Lasker	5	4	10	1894
6. Lasker	Steinitz	10	5	2	1896/7
7. Lasker	Marshall	8	7	0	1907
8. Lasker	Tarrasch	8	5	3	1908
9. Lasker	Schlechter	1	8	1	1910
10. Lasker	Janowski	8	3	0	1910
11. Lasker	Capablanca	0	10	4	1921
12. Capablanca	Alekhine	3	25	6	1927
13. Alekhine	Bogoljubow	11	9	5	1929
14. Alekhine	Bogoljubow	8	15	3	1934
15. Alekhine	Euwe	8	13	9	1935
16. Euwe	Alekhine	4	11	10	1937

World Championship Match-Tournament 1948:
Botvinnik 14, Smyslov 11, Keres & Reshevsky 10½, Euwe 4

Champion	Challenger	+	=	−	Date
17. Botvinnik	Bronstein	5	14	5	1951
18. Botvinnik	Smyslov	7	10	7	1954
19. Botvinnik	Smyslov	3	13	6	1957
20. Smyslov	Botvinnik	5	11	7	1958
21. Botvinnik	Tal	2	13	6	1960
22. Tal	Botvinnik	5	6	10	1961
23. Botvinnik	Petrosian	2	15	5	1963
24. Petrosian	Spassky	4	17	3	1966
25. Petrosian	Spassky	4	13	6	1969
26. Spassky	Fischer[1]	3	11	7	1972

Karpov became champion in 1975, Fischer refusing to defend his title

Champion	Challenger	+	=	−	Date
27. Karpov	Korchnoi	6	21	5	1978
28. Karpov	Korchnoi	6	10	2	1981
29. Karpov	Kasparov	5	40	3	1984/5

Match abandoned with no decision

Champion	Challenger	+	=	−	Date
30. Karpov	Kasparov	3	16	5	1985
31. Kasparov	Karpov	5	15	4	1986

---

[1] 'This little thing between me and Spassky is bigger than Frazier and Ali. It's the free world against the lying, cheating, hypocritical Russians,' said Bobby.

The sixty strongest players

Since 1972 FIDE has published a regular rating list, first annually, now twice a year. Two attempts have been made to grade retrospectively tournament and match results before 1972, one by Professor Elo, inventor of the FIDE rating system, and one by English civil servant and grading expert Sir Richard Clarke. These two, in many cases, produced very different results.

The following lists are largely subjective and make no claim to statistical accuracy. For a few young players, their rating at 1 January 1987 has been used, for players who have reached their peak since 1972 their best five-year average, and for earlier players a combination of Elo's and Clarke's figures.

All the players on the first list have achieved a rating of 2600, equivalent to that of a credible challenger for the world title.[1]

Grade	Name	Dates	Nationality
1. 2785	Robert Fischer	1943–	USA
2. 2765	José Raúl Capablanca	1888–1942	Cuba
3. 2745	Emanuel Lasker	1868–1941	Germany
4. 2735	Gary Kasparov	1963–	USSR
	Alexander Alekhine	1892–1946	Russia/France
6. 2730	Mikhail Botvinnik	1911–	USSR
7. 2715	Anatoly Karpov	1951–	USSR
8. 2710	Mikhail Tal	1936–	USSR
9. 2700	Vasily Smyslov	1921–	USSR
10. 2690	Paul Morphy	1837–84	USA
	Tigran Petrosian	1929–84	USSR
12. 2685	Paul Keres	1916–75	Estonia/USSR
13. 2680	Viktor Korchnoi	1931–	USSR/Switzerland
	Samuel Reshevsky	1911–	USA
	Boris Spassky	1937–	USSR/France
16. 2670	David Bronstein	1924–	USSR
17. 2665	Akiba Rubinstein	1882–1961	Poland
	Siegbert Tarrasch	1862–1934	Germany
19. 2660	Reuben Fine	1914–	USA
	Harry Pillsbury	1872–1906	USA
	Wilhelm Steinitz	1836–1900	Bohemia/USA
22. 2655	Max Euwe	1901–81	Holland
	Efim Geller	1925–	USSR

[1] As a guide, a good club player would have a rating of 1800–2000. To convert to BCF grading subtract 600 and divide by 8.

Grade	Name	Dates	Nationality
24. 2650	Efim Bogoljubow	1889–1952	USSR/Germany
	Isaak Boleslavsky	1919–77	USSR
	Géza Maróczy	1870–1951	Hungary
	Aron Nimzowitsch	1886–1935	Latvia/Denmark
28. 2645	Andrei Sokolov	1963–	USSR
	Artur Yusupov	1960–	USSR
30. 2640	Bent Larsen	1935–	Denmark
	Lajos Portisch	1937–	Hungary
	Leonid Stein	1934–73	USSR
33. 2635	Salomon Flohr	1908–83	Czech/USSR
	Miguel Najdorf	1910–	Poland/Argentina
	Lev Polugayevsky	1934–	USSR
36. 2630	Jan Timman	1951–	Holland
37. 2625	Robert Hübner	1948–	West Germany
	Alexander Kotov	1913–81	USSR
	Johannes Zukertort	1842–88	Prussia/England
40. 2620	Mikhail Chigorin	1850–1908	Russia
	Svetozar Gligorić	1923–	Yugoslavia
	Ratmir Kholmov	1925–	USSR
	Milan Vidmar	1885–1962	Yugoslavia
44. 2615	Yuri Averbakh	1922–	USSR
	Ljubomir Ljubojević	1950-	Yugoslavia
	Henrique Mecking	1952–	Brazil
	Nigel Short	1965–	England
48. 2610	Ulf Andersson	1951–	Sweden
	Carl Schlechter	1874–1918	Austria
	Gideon Ståhlberg	1908–67	Sweden
	László Szabó	1917–	Hungary
53. 2605	Rafael Vaganian	1951–	USSR
54. 2600	Adolf Anderssen	1818–79	Germany
	Alexander Belyavsky	1953–	USSR
	Vlastimil Hort	1944–	Czechoslovakia
	David Janowski	1868–1927	Poland/France
	Isaac Kashdan	1905–85	USA
	Tassilo von der Lasa[1]	1818–99	Germany
	Mark Taimanov	1926–	USSR

Notable absentees are Marshall, Tartakower, Réti and Spielmann, whom Elo rated between 2550 and 2570. Clarke's figures are higher.

[1] For his full name see Chapter VI.

The dream matches

According to the ELO system, our ratings suggest the following dream match scores:

Fischer	17,	Alekhine	13;	
Capablanca	16,	Kasparov[1]	14;	
Lasker	15½,	Botvinnik	14½;	
Morphy	16,	Steinitz	14;	
Morphy	18,	Short	12;	

If only they could...

The Top British Players

1.	2615	Nigel Short	1965–
2.	2590	John Nunn	1955–
3.	2580	Tony Miles	1955–
4.	2570	Joseph Blackburne	1841–1924
5.	2560	Murray Chandler	1960–
		Isidor Gunsberg	1854–1930
7.	2540	Henry Atkins	1872–1955
		Jonathan Speelman	1956–
9.	2530	Amos Burn	1848–1925
		Mir Sultan Khan	1905–66
11.	2525	Jonathan Mestel	1957–
12.	2520	Howard Staunton	1810–74
		Michael Stean	1953–

Two other outstanding British players were C.H.O'D Alexander (2475), who beat, amongst others, Botvinnik and Bronstein; and Jonathan Penrose (2470), ten times British Champion in the fifties and sixties. These ELO ratings seem rather low to us.

The Top Women (at 1 January 1987)

1.	2530	Maia Chiburdanidze	USSR
2.	2495	Zsuzsa Polgár	Hungary
3.	2475	Nona Gaprindashvili	USSR
4.	2455	Pia Cramling	Sweden
5.	2435	Elena Akhmilovskaya	USSR
		Nana Ioseliani	USSR

[1] This is on his January 1987 rating – he is still improving. Stop press: his rating on 1 July 1987 was 2740.

Vera Menchik-Stevenson (1906–44), Russian-born but a representative of England, who dominated women's chess in the thirties, had a best five-year average of 2350.

Stop press: Chiburdanidze was 2550 on 1 July 1987, the highest female rating of all time, and level with, say, Réti.

The world's strongest tournaments

The FIDE rating system categorizes tournaments according to the average ELO rating of the participants. The highest category is sixteen (average ELO 2626–50), and thereon down in bands of twenty-five points.

The two strongest tournaments held up to the end of 1986 were undoubtedly the AVRO tournament held in Holland in 1938, consisting of the eight strongest players in the world at the time, and the 1948 World Championship Tournament (The Hague and Moscow) to decide the World Championship which had fallen vacant on Alekhine's death. The former event had an average rating of about 2644 and the latter a phenomenal 2664 (category 17?)

The following table gives the winners of all tournaments of category fifteen or higher (2600+).

Category 16+

AVRO	1938	Fine	8½/14	61%
		Keres		
World Championship	1948	Botvinnik	14/20	70%
Candidates' Tournament	1950	Boleslavsky	12/18	67%
		Bronstein		
Candidates' Tournament	1953	Smyslov	18/28	64%
Candidates' Tournament	1962	Petrosian	17½/27	65%
Johannesburg	1981	Andersson	7/12	58%
Turin	1982	Karpov	6/11[1]	55%
		Andersson		
Bugojno	1986	Karpov	8½/14	61%
OHRA Brussels	1986	Kasparov	7½/10	75%
Amsterdam	1987	Karpov	4/6	67%
		Timman		

[1] Plus one win by default.

Category 15

St Petersburg	1895/6	Lasker	11½/18 64%
St Petersburg Final	1914	Lasker	7/8 88%
New York	1927	Capablanca	14/20 70%
Nauheim, Stuttgart, Garmisch	1937	Euwe	4/6 67%
USSR Absolute Championship	1941	Botvinnik	13½/20 68%
Candidates' Tournament	1956	Smyslov	11½/18 64%
Candidates' Tournament	1959	Tal	20/28 71%
Piatigorsky Cup (Los Angeles)	1963	Keres Petrosian	8½/14 61%
USSR Zonal Tournament	1964	Spassky	7/12 58%
Piatigorsky Cup (Santa Monica)	1966	Spassky	11½/18 64%
Leiden	1970	Spassky	7/12 58%
Milan (Preliminary)	1975	Portisch	7/11 64%
Montreal	1979	Karpov Tal	12/18 67%
Waddinxveen	1979	Karpov	5/6 83%
Tilburg	1979	Karpov	7½/11 68%
Bad Kissingen	1980	Karpov	4½/6 75%
Bugojno	1980	Karpov	8/11 73%
Tilburg	1980	Karpov	7½/11 68%
Moscow	1981	Karpov	9/13 69%
Tilburg	1981	Belyavsky	7½/11 68%
Tilburg	1983	Karpov	7/11 64%
Tilburg	1985	Hübner Miles Korchnoi	8½/14 61%
Tilburg	1986	Belyavsky	8½/14 61%

Other Major Tournaments

Baden-Baden	1870	Anderssen	11/16	69%	Cat. 9
Vienna	1882	Steinitz Winawer	24/34	71%	Cat. 10
London	1883	Zukertort	24½/32	77%	Cat. 10
Hastings	1895	Pillsbury	16½/21	79%	Cat. 10
Nuremburg	1896	Lasker	13½/18	75%	Cat. 11

Budapest	1896	Charousek	8½/12	71%	Cat. 11
		Chigorin			
London	1899	Lasker	21½/26	83%	Cat. 11
San Sebastián	1911	Capablanca	9½/14	68%	Cat. 13
San Sebastián	1912	Rubinstein	12½/19	66%	Cat. 13
St Petersburg	1914	Lasker	13½/18	75%	Cat. 13
New York	1924	Lasker	16/20	80%	Cat. 13
Berlin	1928	Capablanca	8½/12	71%	Cat. 14
Bled	1931	Alekhine	20½/26	79%	Cat. 13
Moscow	1936	Capablanca	13/18	72%	Cat. 13
Nottingham	1936	Botvinnik	10/14	71%	Cat. 14
		Capablanca			
Semmering-Baden	1937	Keres	9/14	64%	Cat. 14
Saltsjöbaden	1948	Bronstein	13½/19	71%	Cat. 14

Notes:
1. Games won by default are not included.
2. At London 1883 the first two drawn games played between opponents were discounted and replayed. These drawn games are included in Zukertort's result.

♚

The longest winning run of all time is held by the first World Champion, Wilhelm Steinitz. He won his last 14 games at Vienna 1873, beat Blackburne 2–0 in the play-off, blitzed the same opponent 7–0 in an 1876 match and won his first two games at Vienna 1882, making a total of 25 consecutive wins in just under nine years.

♚

You might think that in the highly competitive world of modern chess such a performance would be unrepeatable, but Bobby Fischer came pretty close in 1970–1. A run of 20 wins included the last seven rounds of the 1970 Interzonal, 6–0 shutouts of Mark Taimanov and Bent Larsen in the 1971 Candidates' Matches and the first game of the Candidates' Final match against Tigran Petrosian. (Turn to Chapter III for Bobby's win against Panno from the last round of the Interzonal, and to Chapter IV for how Taimanov qualified for the Candidates' Matches.)

♚

Capablanca was undefeated over 63 games (+40, =23) between 10 February 1916 and 21 March 1924.

♚

But the longest unbeaten run in terms of number of games is, surprisingly, held by that combinational genius Mikhail Tal. He played 86 games without defeat between 15 July 1972 and 26 April 1973 (+47, =39).[1]

♚

A 100 per cent score in a tournament is a rather special achievement attained by only a select few at master level. Pride of place here must go to Gustav Neumann, with 34/34 at Berlin back in 1885.

♚

Other 100 per cent scores include:

- *New York 1893:* Emanuel Lasker wins all his 13 games.

- *Amsterdam 1899:* Englishman Henry Atkins scores 15/15.

- *New York 1913:* 13 straight wins for the young Capablanca (including one by default).

- *New York 1963/4:* Bobby Fischer's greatest ever result. 11/11 against some pretty formidable opposition.

♚

The best tournament result of all is Alekhine's 14/15 at San Remo 1930, a category 11 tournament including such superstars as Nimzowitsch, Rubinstein, Bogoljubow, Vidmar and Maróczy, estimated as about a 2900 performance. (Fischer's 1971 Candidates' Matches work out at an astronomical 2950.)

The greatest of all

Faced with this barrage of information we now have to think the unthinkable: who was (or is) the greatest of them all?

[1] But compare:
Sugar Ray Robinson (USA) 91 consecutive fights without a loss;
Ed Moses (USA): 122 400 metre hurdles wins in a row;
Iolande Balas (Romania): 140 high jump wins in a row;
Osamu Watanabe (Japan): unbeaten in 187 consecutive free-style wrestling bouts;
Jahangir Khan (Pakistan): over 500 consecutive wins at squash;
Heather McKay (Australia): unbeaten from 1962–80 in innumerable squash games.

— 'Philidor,' said Larsen back in 1967, 'because he was so far ahead of his peers.'
— 'Morphy,' wrote Bobby Fischer in 1964. 'In a set match he would beat anyone alive today.'
— 'Morphy,' said Max Euwe, the author of several books about the all-time greats.
— 'Morphy,' said Gligorić, who has beaten more world champions than most.

Then we come to the three players who between them dominated chess for the first forty years of the century: Lasker, Capablanca and Alekhine.

— Lasker's opinion: 'I have known many chess players but only one genius, Capablanca.'
— Alekhine on Capa: 'The greatest genius of chess.'
— Botvinnik on Capa: 'I think Capablanca had the greatest natural talent.'
— Spassky on Capa: 'Personally, I think the best chess-player of all time was Capablanca.'

Tartakower, when asked who was the greatest, replied: 'If chess is an art, Alekhine, if chess is a science, Capablanca, if chess is a struggle, Lasker.' But this was before Fischer, not to mention Karpov and Kasparov.

In our search for the greatest player of all time we must regretfully disqualify Philidor and Morphy on the grounds of insufficient evidence, but we feel that a valid case could be made for any of the top seven[1] on our grading list. The word 'greatest', we feel, implies rather more than simply 'strongest', so we choose to award accolades in a number of categories.

The strongest player: Fischer.

The greatest natural genius: Capablanca[2]

The greatest practical player: Lasker.

The greatest tournament players: Lasker and Karpov.

---

[1] The phenomenal Tal would have been a contender were it not for ill health.
[2] Paul Morphy rivals even Capa in this category. By the age of twenty-one (1858) he was streets ahead of his contemporaries. Tragically, he gave it all up after two years at the top. His rating at this point was about the same as the twenty-two-year-old Fischer's. (And see, above, Sultan Khan.)

The greatest match players: Steinitz[1] and Fischer.

The greatest positional player: Capablanca.

The greatest strategist: Botvinnik.

The greatest attacking players: Alekhine, Tal and Kasparov.

The greatest player of all time? Well ...

Botvinnik's overall record is perhaps not quite as good as the others. Kasparov has not yet had time to prove himself over a long enough period. Alekhine's overall record suffers slightly when compared with Capa or Lasker. Karpov's record over the past dozen years has been tremendous but he lacks something in popular appeal and has twice been bested by Kasparov. Capablanca, towering genius though he was, was too lazy to make full use of his talent. Fischer, though the strongest player ever according to the ratings, ruled himself out of contention for the title of 'the greatest' by abdicating. This leaves us with Lasker, who, if you discount his loss to Capa in 1921,[2] did virtually nothing wrong in a career spanning over forty years. Tentatively, then, we nominate Emanuel Lasker (see illustration) as the greatest player of all time. But we have a sneaking feeling that we may one day have to modify that judgement in favour of Kasparov. Or Gata Kamsky, who in 1987 sensationally won the Soviet Junior (under eighteen) championship at twelve (the only other prodigy to do this: Gary Kasparov). Or maybe Judith Polgár. Or perhaps another name will emerge – that of HITECH. If you haven't heard of HITECH, turn to chapter VIII.

♚

A popular diversion amongst the chess fraternity is the simultaneous display (or simul), in which a master or expert takes on a number of players at the same time. Here are our claims for record simultaneous displays:

The largest display: Havana 1966 (during the Chess Olympics). 6840 boards with over 300 experts taking on 20 players each. One of the participants was Fidel Castro, who scored a diplomatic draw against World Champion Tigran Petrosian. The display was held outdoors. The final result: rain stopped play after two hours.

---

[1] Steinitz was only nineteenth on our rating list – but he was world number one for over twenty years. His match record was terrific.
[2] After the match he spent several months in hospital.

The most impressive performance[1]: Capablanca at Cleveland, Ohio 4 February 1922. Played 103, + 102 =1. This was his first chess event for fourteen months and his opponents included the State Champion amongst other strong players. This display lasted seven hours without a break.

The greatest number of opponents: Vlastimil Hort, at Seltjarnes, Iceland, 23–24 April 1977. Played 550, including 201 simultaneously. +477, =63, −10. This event took place immediately after what he described as 'the blackest day of my life', for which see the next chapter.

The greatest number of games: also held by Hort. 663 games over 32.5 hours at Porz, West Germany, 5–6 October 1984. He played between 60 and 100 games at a time, winning over 80 per cent of the games.

The greatest number of games at one time: this one's held by Yugoslav chess journalist Dimitrije Bjelica, who took on 301 opponents at Sarajevo on 18 September 1982. The display lasted nine hours and the final score was +258, =36, −7.

The largest number of games played simultaneously blindfold: a controversial one, this. The Hungarian János Flesch played 52 games blindfold at Budapest in 1960 (+31, =18, −3), but rumour has it that some of his opponents were persuaded to resign after only a few moves. This takes us back to Miguel Najdorf, who took on 45 opponents with a score of +39, =4, −2, in 1947. It is claimed, however, that his moves were written down for him, which disqualifies him from the record books. So the record is still held by George Koltanowski (then Belgium, now USA) who played 34 games, winning 24 and drawing 10, back in 1934.

---

[1] Other contenders: George Koltanowski, the Belgian–American wizard of blindfold play, is reputed to have beaten the rest of the Belgian national team in a simul. Capablanca (again) beat a Swedish team 5–2 in a clock simul in 1928. Kasparov did the same (5 1/2–1/2!) to the Swiss Olympic team in 1987.

The most remarkable simultaneous player: this must be the great American Harry Nelson Pillsbury. Pillsbury would play up to 22 simultaneous games of chess and draughts blindfold while taking part in a game of whist. Before the display he would ask the audience for lists of words or objects, and repeat them at the end of the display. On one famous occasion in London two professors came up with the following curious list of words:

Antiphlogistine	micrococcus	Etchenberg	Bangmanvate
periosteum	plasmodium	American	Schlechter's Nek
takadiastase	Mississippi	Russian	Manzinyama
plasmon	Freiheit	philosophy	theosophy
ambrosia	Philadelphia	Piet Potgelter's	catechism
Threlkeld	Cincinnati	Rost	Madjesoomalops
streptococcus	athletics	Salamagundi	
staphylococcus	no war	Oomisellecootsi	

Pillsbury looked at the list, repeated the words, and then again in reverse order. The next day he recited them again. Here's Pillsbury doing his scintillating stuff. The game was one of twelve chess and four draughts simultaneously *blindfold*, plus a game of whist on the side!

H.N. Pillsbury–Amateur, Toronto, 1899. Queen's Pawn Game.

1. d4 d5	7. e4 dxe4	13. Rfe1 Rc6	19. Rxe6+ fxe6
2. Nf3 e6	8. Nxe4 Bb7	14. Ba3 a5	20. Qg6+ hxg6
3. e3 Nf6	9. Nxd6+ cxd6	15. c4 Ne4	21. Bxg6 mate
4. Bd3 Nbd7	10. Bf4 Bxf3	16. cxd5 Ng5	Wow!
5. O–O b6	11. Qxf3 d5	17. Qg3 Rc8	
6. Nbd2 Bd6	12. Bd6 Rc8	18. dxe6 Nxe6	

♚

The individual chess marathon record (a 75 per cent score against opponents with an average rating of at least 1800 is required) is currently held by Dutchman Erik Knoppert, who, in London between 9.19 on 13 September and 5.17 on 16 September 1985 scored 82.6 per cent in 500 games against opponents averaging ELO 2000.

The chess marathon record as authorized by *The Guinness Book of Records* stands to Roger Long and Graham Croft, who played for 200 hours at Dingles, Bristol between 11 and 19 May 1984.

The sixty greatest games

To conclude this chapter we offer the reader a selection of sixty of the best, most famous and most significant games of all time. The games have been chosen to include specimens of the play of all the official World Champions, the other players in our All-Time Top Twenty, and the top three British players. To those of our readers who have seen them all before we can only apologize and suggest they amuse themselves by compiling their own list. For the rest of you, stand by to be amazed, thrilled, and, dare we say it, educated.

♔

1. Bourdonnais–McDonnell, 50th Match Game, 1834.
Queen's Gambit Accepted
From a series of games between the two best players of their day, the beginnings of modern international chess.

1. d4 d5	11. Rd1 Bg4	21. Bxb5 Bxf3	31. Qa2 Nc4+
2. c4 dxc4	12. d6 cxd6	22. gxf3 Nd4	32. Kg4 Rg8
3. e4 e5	13. Nd5 Nxd5	23. Bc4 Nxf3+	33. Rxb6 axb6
4. d5 f5	14. Bxe7 Ne3+	24. Kf2 Nxd2	34. Kh4 Kf6
5. Nc3 Nf6	15. Ke1 Kxe7	25. Rxg7+ Kf6	35. Qe2 Rg6
6. Bxc4 Bc5	16. Qd3 Rd8	26. Rf7+ Kg6	36. Qh5 Ne3
7. Nf3 Qe7	17. Rd2 Nc6	27. Rb7 Ndxc4	White resigns
8. Bg5 Bxf2+	18. b3 Ba5	28. bxc4 Rxc4	
9. Kf1 Bb6	19. a3 Rac8	29. Qb1 Bb6	
10. Qe2 f4	20. Rg1 b5	30. Kf3 Rc3	

2. McDonnell–Bourdonnais, 62nd Match Game, 1834.
Sicilian Defence
The Frenchman's most famous win in the match (really a series of six matches) in which he came out ahead of his Irish opponent by a score believed to be +45, =13, −27.

1. e4 c5	11. O–O a5	21. Qc4+ Kh8	31. Qc8 Bd8
2. Nf3 Nc6	12. exd5 cxd5	22. Ba4 Qh6	32. Qc4 Qe1
3. d4 cxd4	13. Rd1 d4	23. Bxe8 fxe4	33. Rc1 d2
4. Nxd4 e5	14. c4 Qb6	24. c6 exf3	34. Qc5 Rg8
5. Nxc6 bxc6	15. Bc2 Bb7	25. Rc2 Qe3+	35. Rd1 e3
6. Bc4 Nf6	16. Nd2 Rae8	26. Kh1 Bc8	36. Qc3 Qxd1
7. Bg5 Be7	17. Ne4 Bd8	27. Bd7 f2	37. Rxd1 e2
8. Qe2 d5	18. c5 Qc6	28. Rf1 d3	White resigns
9. Bxf6 Bxf6	19. f3 Be7	29. Rc3 Bxd7	
10. Bb3 O–O	20. Rac1 f5	30. cxd7 e4	

Final position

3. Anderssen–Kieseritzky, Casual Game, London, 1851. King's Gambit
Nicknamed the 'Immortal Game', a classic example of sacrificial attack
against an opponent who neglects his development.

1. e4 e5	7: d3 Nh5	13. h5 Qg5	19. Ke2 Bxg1
2. f4 exf4	8. Nh4 Qg5	14. Qf3 Ng8	20. e5 Na6
3. Bc4 Qh4+	9. Nf5 c6	15. Bxf4 Qf6	21. Nxg7+ Kd8
4. Kf1 b5	10. Rg1 cxb5	16. Nc3 Bc5	22. Qf6+ Nxf6
5. Bxb5 Nf6	11. g4 Nf6	17. Nd5 Qxb2	23. Be7
6. Nf3 Qh6	12. h4 Qg6	18. Bd6 Qxa1+	mate

4. Anderssen–Dufresne, Casual Game, Berlin, 1852. Evans Gambit
Anderssen's other legendary masterpiece, the 'Evergreen Game'. Note
particularly White's nineteenth move, described by Lasker as one of the
most subtle on record.

1. e4 e5	8. Qb3 Qf6	15. Ne4 Qf5	22. Bf5+ Ke8
2. Nf3 Nc6	9. e5 Qg6	16. Bxd3 Qh5	23. Bd7+ Kf8
3. Bc4 Bc5	10. Re1 Nge7	17. Nf6+ gxf6	24. Bxe7
4. b4 Bxb4	11. Ba3 b5	18. exf6 Rg8	mate
5. c3 Ba5	12. Qxb5 Rb8	19. Rad1 Qxf3	
6. d4 exd4	13. Qa4 Bb6	20. Rxe7+ Nxe7	
7. O–O d3	14. Nbd2 Bb7	21. Qxd7+ Kxd7	

5. L. Paulsen–Morphy, New York, 1857. Four Knights Game
From Morphy's only tournament, featuring a stunning queen sacrifice.

1. e4 e5	8. Bc4 b5	15. Qxa4 Bd7	22. Kf1 Bg2+
2. Nf3 Nc6	9. Be2 Nxe4	16. Ra2 Rae8	23. Kg1 Bh3+
3. Nc3 Nf6	10. Nxe4 Rxe4	17. Qa6 Qxf3	24. Kh1 Bxf2
4. Bb5 Bc5	11. Bf3 Re6	18. gxf3 Rg6+	25. Qf1 Bxf1
5. O–O O–O	12. c3 Qd3	19. Kh1 Bh3	26. Rxf1 Re2
6. Nxe5 Re8	13. b4 Bb6	20. Rd1 Bg2+	27. Ra1 Rh6
7. Nxc6 dxc6	14. a4 bxa4	21. Kg1 Bxf3+	28. d4 Be3
			White resigns

6. Morphy–Duke of Brunswick and Count Isouard, Paris Opera House, 1858. Philidor's Defence

Perhaps the most famous, most published game of all time, frequently used by chess teachers to exemplify the value of rapid development.

1. e4 e5	6. Bc4 Nf6	11. Bxb5+ Nbd7 16. Qb8+ Nxb8
2. Nf3 d6	7. Qb3 Qe7	12. O–O–O Rd8 17. Rd8
3. d4 Bg4	8. Nc3 c6	13. Rxd7 Rxd7 mate
4. dxe5 Bxf3	9. Bg5 b5	14. Rd1 Qe6
5. Qxf3 dxe5	10. Nxb5 cxb5	15. Bxd7+ Nxd7

7. Zukertort–Blackburne, London, 1883. Queen's Gambit Declined (by transposition)

A combination by a man who, with better health, might conceivably have become World Champion; it was said to have 'literally electrified the lookers-on'.

1. c4 e6	8. b3 Nbd7	15. Bxc4 d5	22. exf6 Nxf6
2. e3 Nf6	9. Bb2 Qe7	16. Bd3 Rfc8	23. f5 Ne4
3. Nf3 b6	10. Nb5 Ne4	17. Rae1 Rc7	24. Bxe4 dxe4
4. Be2 Bb7	11. Nxd6 cxd6	18. e4 Rac8	25. fxg6 Rc2
5. O–O d5	12. Nd2 Ndf6	19. e5 Ne8	26. gxh7+ Kh8
6. d4 Bd6	13. f3 Nxd2	20. f4 g6	27. d5+
7. Nc3 O–O	14. Qxd2 dxc4	21. Re3 f5	

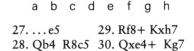

27. ....e5	29. Rf8+ Kxh7	31. Bxe5+ Kxf8	33 Qxe7 Black
28. Qb4 R8c5	30. Qxe4+ Kg7	32. Bg7+ Kg8	resigns

8. Em Lasker–Bauer, Amsterdam, 1889. Bird's Opening
The first example of the famous double bishop sacrifice.

1. f4 d5	10. Ng3 Qc7	19. Rf3 e5	28. e6 Rb7
2. Nf3 e6	11. Ne5 Nxe5	20. Rh3+ Qh6	29. Qg6 f6
3. e3 Nf6	12. Bxe5 Qc6	21. Rxh6+ Kxh6	30. Rxf6+ Bxf6
4. b3 Be7	13. Qe2 a6	22. Qd7 Bf6	31. Qxf6+ Ke8
5. Bb2 b6	14. Nh5 Nxh5	23. Qxb7 Kg7	32. Qh8+ Ke7
6. Bd3 Bb7	15. Bxh7+ Kxh7	24. Rf1 Rab8	33. Qg7+ Black
7. Nc3 O–O	16. Qxh5+ Kg8	25. Qd7 Rfd8	resigns
8. O–O Nbd7	17. Bxg7 Kxg7	26. Qg4+ Kf8	
9. Ne2 c5	18. Qg4+ Kh7	27. fxe5 Bg7	

9. Pillsbury–Tarrasch, Hastings, 1895. Queen's Gambit Declined
A tremendous struggle which signalled the emergence of the previously unknown Pillsbury as a great master.

1. d4 d5	15. Qf3 Nf8	29. Ng4 Nd7	43. Rxg7 Kxg7
2. c4 e6	16. Ne2 Ne4	30. R4f2 Kg8	44. Qg3+ Kxh6
3. Nc3 Nf6	17. Bxe7 Rxe7	31. Nc1 c3	45. Kh1 Qd5
4. Bg5 Be7	18. Bxe4 dxe4	32. b3 Qc6	46. Rg1 Qxf5
5. Nf3 Nbd7	19. Qg3 f6	33. h3 a5	47. Qh4+ Qh5
6. Rc1 O–O	20. Ng4 Kh8	34. Nh2 a4	48. Qf4+ Qg5
7. e3 b6	21. f5 Qd7	35. g4 axb3	49. Rxg5 fxg5
8. cxd5 exd5	22. Rf1 Rd8	36. axb3 Ra8	50. Qd6+ Kh5
9. Bd3 Bb7	23. Rf4 Qd6	37. g5 Ra3	51. Qxd7 c2
10. O–O c5	24. Qh4 Rde8	38. Ng4 Bxb3	52. Qxh7
11. Re1 c4	25. Nc3 Bd5	39. Rg2 Kh8	mate
12. Bb1 a6	26. Nf2 Qc6	40. gxf6 gxf6	
13. Ne5 b5	27. Rf1 b4	41. Nxb3 Rxb3	
14. f4 Re8	28. Ne2 Qa4	42. Nh6 Rg7	

10. Steinitz–Von Bardeleben, Hastings, 1895. Giuoco Piano
From the same tournament, Steinitz's immortal game.

1. e4 e5	8. exd5 Nxd5	15. Qe2 Qd7	22. Rxe7+ Kf8
2. Nf3 Nc6	9. O–O Be6	16. Rac1 c6	23. Rf7+ Kg8
3. Bc4 Bc5	10. Bg5 Be7	17. d5 cxd5	24. Rg7+ Kh8
4. c3 Nf6	11. Bxd5 Bxd5	18. Nd4 Kf7	25. Rxh7+
5. d4 exd4	12. Nxd5 Qxd5	19. Ne6 Rhc8	Black resigns
6. cxd4 Bb4+	13. Bxe7 Nxe7	20. Qg4 g6	
7. Nc3 d5	14. Re1 f6	21. Ng5+ Ke8	

11. Pillsbury–Em Lasker, St Petersburg, 1895–6.
Queen's Gambit Declined
Every one of the games between these two players is full of interest, this one featuring a superb Lasker attack.

1. d4 d5	9. e3 Bd7	18. fxe6 Ra3	27. Qe6+ Kh7
2. c4 e6	10. Kb1 h6	19. exf7+ Rxf7	28. Kxa3 Qc3+
3. Nc3 Nf6	11. cxd5 exd5	20. bxa3 Qb6+	29. Ka4 b5+
4. Nf3 c5	12. Nd4 O–O	21. Bb5 Qxb5+	30. Kxb5 Qc4+
5. Bg5 cxd4	13. Bxf6 Bxf6	22. Ka1 Rc7	31. Ka5 Bd8+
6. Qxd4 Nc6	14. Qh5 Nxd4	23. Rd2 Rc4	32. Qb6 axb6
7. Qh4 Be7	15. exd4 Be6	24. Rhd1 Rc3	mate
8. O–O–O	16. f4 Rac8	25. Qf5 Qc4	
Qa5	17. f5 Rxc3	26. Kb2 Rxa3	

12. Capablanca–Corzo, 11th Match Game, Havana, 1901.
Queen's Pawn Game

Capa at the age of thirteen: the decisive game in a match against the Cuban champion and one of the best ever played by a prodigy.

1. d4 d5	17. h3 Nh6	33. Rxf1 Rxf7	49. Kc3 g3
2. Nf3 c5	18. Qf2 Nf7	34. Rxf5 Rxf5	50. Bh4 g2
3. e3 Nc6	19. Kg2 g5	35. Nxf5+ Kh7	51. Bf2 a5
4. b3 e6	20. g4 Ne7	36. Ne7 Rf8	52. b4 Ke4
5. Bb2 Nf6	21. Qe3 Rg8	37. Kg2 h5	53. Bb6 Kd5
6. Nbd2 cxd4	22. Rae1 Ng6	38. d6 g4	54. Kd3 Kc6
7. exd4 Bd6	23. gxf5 Nf4+	39. hxg4 hxg4	55. Bg1 Kd5
8. Bd3 O–O	24. Kh2 Nxd3	40. Be5 Kh6	56. Bh2 Kc6
9. O–O Nh5	25. Qxd3 exf5	41. d7 Rd8	57. Kd4 a4
10. g3 f5	26. c4 Qe6	42. Ng8+ Rxg8	58. Ke5 Kb6
11. Ne5 Nf6	27. cxd5 Qxd5	43. Bf6 Kg6	59. Kd5 Ka6
12. f4 Bxe5	28. e6 Bb5	44. d8=Q Rxd8	60. Kc5
13. fxe5 Ng4	29. Qxb5 Qxb5	45. Bxd8 b5	Black resigns
14. Qe2 Qb6	30. d5+ Rg7	46. Kf2 Kf5	
15. Nf3 Bd7	31. exf7 h6	47. Ke3 Ke5	
16. a3 Kh8	32. Nd4 Qxf1	48. Kd3 Kd5	

13. Em Lasker–Napier, Cambridge Springs, 1904. Sicilian Defence
A terrific slugfest which the loser rated his best-ever game.

1. e4 c5	11. f4 e5	21. Bxf7 Ne4	31. Kf3 Ra6
2. Nc3 Nc6	12. Nde2 d5	22. Bxe8 Bxb2	32. Kxf4 Ne2+
3. Nf3 g6	13. exd5 Nd4	23. Rb1 Bc3+	33. Kf5 Nc3
4. d4 cxd4	14. Nxd4 Nxd5	24. Kf1 Bg4	34. a3 Na4
5. Nxd4 Bg7	15. Nf5 Nxc3	25. Bxh5 Bxh5	35. Be3
6. Be3 d6	16. Qxd8 Rxd8	26. Rxh5 Ng3+	Black resigns
7. f3 Nf6	17. Ne7+ Kh8	27. Kg2 Nxh5	
8. g4 O–O	18. h5 Re8	28. Rxb7 a5	
9. g5 Ne8	19. Bc5 gxh5	29. Rb3 Bg7	
10. h4 Nc7	20. Bc4 exf4	30. Rh3 Ng3	

The greatest

Philidor   Morphy   Lasker

Capablanca   Alekhine

Botvinnik   Fischer

Karpov   Kasparov

'By most standards I'm OK.'
Steve Davis

Pot Black for reds
(Karpov *v.* Sevastianov)

Boris signs for the Blues
(Spassky in Chelsea strip)

Ardiles attacking down the right wing

The Stars Swap Sports

World champs Tal and Petrosian
(note the pawn in Tal's hand – he was
playing a chess and table tennis simul!)

Britain's best-known fireman leads with
his right (Terry Marsh)

'You can always hear the King's call.'
Phil Lynott

The King of bop blows it (D. Gillespie)

Was he or wasn't he?
(W. Sickert)

Did he or didn't he?
(W. H. Wallace)

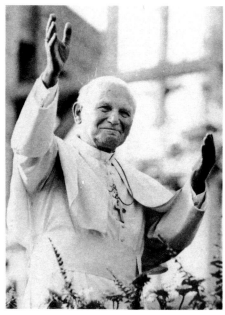

Does he or doesn't he?
(K. Wojtyła)

Was he or was she?
(C.G.L.A.A.T. D'Éon)

Vera Menchik

Pia Cramling

The Polgárs

Maya Chiburdanidze

The monstrous regiment

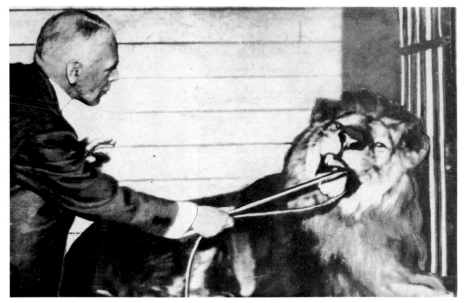

Freddy eyes his lunch (H. Davidson on 28 July 1937)

The Great Beast; vice-captain of the sinners A. Crowley

Arthur Daley *v*. Inspector Cockrill (The young George Cole plays Alastair Sim)

Tolstoy (l.) unwinds after the Tour de France

Maxim Gorky watching Lenin getting
peeved and depressed

Tito, in his mountain hideout, takes a
break from beating up the Nazis

The Child's Problem by R. Dadd (Position: white king h1, queen a8, rook e5, pawns f4, b6; black king d6, knight d7, pawn e6. Solution: Qd8.)

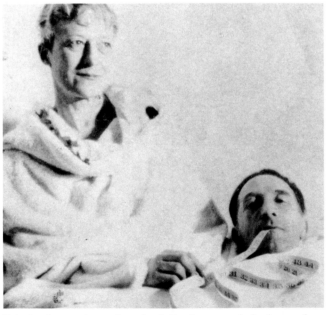

Painting by numbers: chess freak Duchamp and a bad case of tape worm

14. Rotlewi–Rubinstein, Łódź, 1907. Queen's Gambit Declined
Rubinstein's most famous game – another all-time great combination.

1. d4 d5	9. Bb2 O–O	17. f4 Bc7	25. Qg2 Rh3
2. Nf3 e6	10. Qd2 Qe7	18. e4 Rac8	26. Bd4 Bxd4
3. e3 c5	11. Bd3 dxc4	19. e5 Bb6+	27. Rf2 Bxf2
4. c4 Nc6	12. Bxc4 b5	20. Kh1 Ng4	and mate next
5. Nc3 Nf6	13. Bd3 Rd8	21. Be4 Qh4	move
6. dxc5 Bxc5	14. Qe2 Bb7	22. g3 Rxc3	
7. a3 a6	15. O–O Ne5	23. gxh4 Rd2	
8. b4 Bd6	16. Nxe5 Bxe5	24. Qxd2 Bxe4+	

15. Levitsky–Marshall, Brelau, 1912. French Defence
The brilliant American's last move has been described as the most beautiful ever–Marshall said that the spectators showered the board with gold coins[1] after he played it; and we're not surprised.

1. e4 e6	7. O–O Be7	13. Bh3 Rae8	19. Rxd5 Nd4
2. d4 d5	8. Bg5 O–O	14. Qd2 Bb4	20. Qh5 Ref8
3. Nc3 c5	9. dxc5 Be6	15. Bxf6 Rxf6	21. Rc5 Rh6
4. Nf3 Nc6	10. Nd4 Bxc5	16. Rad1 Qc5	22. Qg5 Rxh3
5. exd5 exd5	11. Nxe6 fxe6	17. Qe2 Bxc3	23. Rc5 Qg3
6. Be2 Nf6	12. Bg4 Qd6	18. bxc3 Qxc3	White resigns

16. Bernstein–Capablanca, Exhibition Game, Moscow, 1914. Queen's Gambit Declined

Capa's last move is one of the most famous in chess history.

1. d4 d5	9. Qa4 Bb7	17. Nd4 Bb4	25. Nd4 Rc7
2. c4 e6	10. Ba6 Bxa6	18. b3 Rac8	26. Nb5 Rc5
3. Nc3 Nf6	11. Qxa6 c5	19. bxc4 dxc4	27. Nxc3 Nxc3
4. Nf3 Be7	12. Bxf6 Nxf6	20. Rc2 Bxc3	28. Rxc3 Rxc3
5. Bg5 O–O	13. dxc5 bxc5	21. Rxc3 Nd5	29. Rxc3 Qb2
6. e3 Nbd7	14. O–O Qb6	22. Rc2 c3	White resigns
7. Rc1 b6	15. Qe2 c4	23. Rdc1 Rc5	
8. cxd5 exd5	16. Rfd1 Rfd8	24. Nb3 Rc6	

17. Em Lasker–Capablanca, St Petersburg, 1914. Ruy López
A much-quoted example of Lasker's psychological approach: needing to win at all costs he chooses a drawish variation and his opponent drops his guard.

[1] According to Walter Korn, these were payoffs by Russians who'd backed Levitsky with gold roubles, marks and Austrian crowns.

1. e4 e5	12. f5 b6	23. g4 h6	34. Rdh1 Bb7
2. Nf3 Nc6	13. Bf4 Bb7	24. Rd3 a5	35. e5 dxe5
3. Bb5 a6	14. Bxd6 cxd6	25. h4 axb4	36. Ne4 Nd5
4. Bxc6 dxc6	15. Nd4 Rad8	26. axb4 Rae7	37. N6c5 Bc8
5. d4 exd4	16. Ne6 Rd7	27. Kf3 Rg8	38. Nxd7 Bxd7
6. Qxd4 Qxd4	17. Rad1 Nc8	28. Kf4 g6	39. Rh7 Rf8
7. Nxd4 Bd6	18. Rf2 b5	29. Rg3 g5+	40. Ra1 Kd8
8. Nc3 Ne7	19. Rfd2 Rde7	30. Kf3 Nb6	42. Ra8+ Bc8
9. O–O O–O	20. b4 Kf7	31. hxg5 hxg5	42. Nc5
10. f4 Re8	21. a3 Ba8	32. Rh3 Rd7	Black resigns
11. Nb3 f6	22. Kf2 Ra7	33. Kg3 Ke8	

18. Nimzowitsch–Tarrasch, St. Petersburg, 1914.
Queen's Gambit Declined
Perhaps Tarrasch's best-known game, and another example of the double bishop sacrifice.

1. d4 d5	10. Rc1 Qe7	19. exd4 Bxh2+	28. fxe4 f4+
2. Nf3 c5	11. cxd5 exd5	20. Kxh2 Qh4+	29. Kxf4 Rf8+
3. c4 e6	12. Nh4 g6	21. Kg1 Bxg2	30. Ke5 Qh2+
4. e3 Nf6	13. Nhf3 Rad8	22. f3 Rfe8	31. Ke6 Re8+
5. Bd3 Nc6	14. dxc5 bxc5	23. Ne4 Qh1+	32. Kd7 Bb5
6. O–O Bd6	15. Bb5 Ne4	24. Kf2 Bxf1	mate
7. b3 O–O	16. Bxc6 Bxc6	25. d5 f5	
8. Bb2 b6	17. Qc2 Nxd2	26. Qc3 Qg2+	
9. Nbd2 Bb7	18. Nxd2 d4	27. Ke3 Rxe4+	

19. Bogoljubow–Alekhine, Hastings, 1922. Dutch Defence
'The greatest masterpiece ever created on a chessboard,' according to Irving Chernev.

1. d4 f5	15. Ng5 Bd7	29. Rxa5 b4	43. e4 Nxe4
2. c4 Nf6	16. f3 Nf6	30. Rxa8 dxc3	44. Nxe4 Qxe4
3. g3 e6	17. f4 e4	31. Rxe8 c2	45. d6 cxd6
4. Bg2 Bb4+	18. Rfd1 h6	32. Rxf8+ Kh7	46. f6 gxf6
5. Bd2 Bxd2+	19. Nh3 d5	33. Nf2 c1=Q+	47. Rd2 Qe2
6. Nxd2 Nc6	20. Nf1 Ne7	34. Nf1 Ne1	48. Rxe2 fxe2
7. Ngf3 O–O	21. a4 Nc6	35. Rh2 Qxc4	49. Kf2
8. O–O d6	22. Rd2 Nb4	36. Rb8 Bb5	exf1=Q+
9. Qb3 Kh8	23. Bh1 Qe8	37. Rxb5 Qxb5	50. Kxf1 Kg7
10. Qc3 e5	24. Rg2 dxc4	38. g4 Nf3+	51. Kf2 Kf7
11. e3 a5	25. bxc4 Bxa4	39. Bxf3 exf3	52. Ke3 Ke6
12. b3 Qe8	26. Nf2 Bd7	40. gxf5 Qe2	53. Ke4 d5+
13. a3 Qh5	27. Nd2 b5	41. d5 Kg8	White resigns
14. h4 Ng4	28. Nd1 Nd3	42. h5 Kh7	

20. Alekhine–Yates, London, 1922. Queen's Gambit Declined
Alekhine in positional style: seize the open file, rooks on the seventh rank and wham!

1. d4 Nf6	12. Bxe7 Qxe7	23. a3 h6	34. Rcc7 Rg8
2. c4 e6	13. Ned2 b5	24. Kf2 Kh7	35. Nd7 Kh8
3. Nf3 d5	14. Bxd5 cxd5	25. h4 Rf8	36. Nf6 Rgf8
4. Nc3 Be7	15. O–O a5	26. Kg3 Rfb8	37. Rxg7 Rxf6
5. Bg5 O–O	16. Nb3 a4	27. Rc7 Bb5	38. Ke5
6. e3 Nbd7	17. Nc5 Nxc5	28. R1c5 Ba6	Black resigns
7. Rc1 c6	18. Qxc5 Qxc5	29. R5c6 Re8	
8. Qc2 Re8	19. Rxc5 b4	30. Kf4 Kg8	
9. Bd3 dxc4	20. Rfc1 Ba6	31. h5 Bf1	
10. Bxc4 Nd5	21. Ne5 Reb8	32. g3 Ba6	
11. Ne4 f5	22. f3 b3	33. Rf7 Kh7	

21. Maróczy–Tartakower, Teplitz-Schönau, 1922. Dutch Defence
A marvellous intuitive sacrifice by one of the most imaginative players of his time.

1. d4 c6	11. Bb2 Rf6	21. Nb1 Nh5	31. Bxg3 Nxg3
2. c4 f5	12. Rfe1 Rh6	22. Qd2 Bd7	32. Re1 Nf5
3. Nc3 Nf6	13. g3 Qf6	23. Rf2 Qh4+	33. Qf2 Qg5
4. a3 Be7	14. Bf1 g5	24. Kg1 Bg3	34. dxe5 Bf3+
5. e3 O–O	15. Rad1 g4	25. Bc3 Bxf2+	35. Kf1 Ng3+
6. Bd3 d5	16. Nxe4 fxe4	26. Qxf2 g3	White resigns
7. Nf3 c6	17. Nd2 Rxh2	27. Qg2 Rf8	
8. O–O Ne4	18. Kxh2 Qxf2+	28. Be1 Rxf1+	
9. Qc2 Bd6	19. Kh1 Nf6	29. Kxf1 e5	
10. b3 Nd7	20. Re2 Qxg3	30. Kg1 Bg4	

22. Grünfeld–Alekhine, Carlsbad, 1923. Queen's Gambit Declined
Another Alekhine special, concluding with a great combination.

1. d4 Nf6	11. Bd3 dxc4	21. Qe2 Nc4	31. fxe4 Nf4
2. c4 e6	12. Bxc4 b5	22. Be4 Bg7	32. exf4 Qc4
3. Nf3 d5	13. Ba2 c5	23. Bxb7 Qxb7	33. Qxc4 Rxd1+
4. Nc3 Be7	14. Rd1 cxd4	24. Rc1 e5	34. Qf1 Bd4+
5. Bg5 Nbd7	15. Nxd4 Qb6	25. Nb3 e4	and mate next
6. e3 O–O	16. Bb1 Bb7	26. Nd4 Red8	move
7. Rc1 c6	17. O–O Rac8	27. Rfd1 Ne5	
8. Qc2 a6	18. Qd2 Ne5	28. Na2 Nd3	
9. a3 h6	19. Bxf6 Bxf6	29. Rxc8 Qxc8	
10. Bh4 Re8	20. Qc2 g6	30. f3 Rxd4	

23. Sämisch–Nimzowitsch, Copenhagen, 1923.
Queen's Indian Defence

'The Immortal Zugzwang Game' – a modest pawn move reduces White to complete impotence: he has only a few pawn moves that do not lose material.

1. d4 Nf6	8. Ne5 c6	15. Kh2 Nh5
2. c4 e6	9. cxd5 cxd5	16. Bd2 f5
3. Nf3 b6	10. Bf4 a6	17. Qd1 b4
4. g3 Bb7	11. Rc1 b5	18. Nb1 Bb5
5. Bg2 Be7	12. Qb3 Nc6	19. Rg1 Bd6
6. Nc3 O–O	13. Nxc6 Bxc6	20. e4 fxe4
7. O–O d5	14. h3 Qd7	21. Qxh5 Rxf2

22. Qg5 Raf8
23. Kh1 R8f5
24. Qe3 Bd3
25. Rce1 h6
White resigns

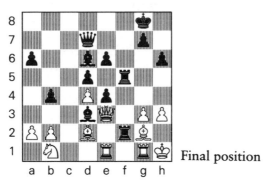

Final position

24. Capablanca–Tartakower, New York, 1924. *Dutch Defence*

Capa's most famous ending, a classic example of a rook and pawn endgame.

1. d4 f5	15. Qh3 Rf6	29. Rh1 Kf8
2. Nf3 e6	16. f4 Na5	30. Rh7 Rc6
3. c4 Nf6	17. Qf3 d6	31. g4 Nc4
4. Bg5 Be7	18. Re1 Qd7	32. g5 Ne3+
5. Nc3 O–O	19. e4 fxe4	33. Kf3 Nf5
6. e3 b6	20. Qxe4 g6	34. Bxf5 gxf5
7. Bd3 Bb7	21. g3 Kf8	35. Kg3 Rxc3+
8. O–O Qe8	22. Kg2 Rf7	36. Kh4 Rf3
9. Qe2 Ne4	23. h4 d5	37. g6 Rxf4+
10. Bxe7 Nxc3	24. cxd5 exd5	38. Kg5 Re4
11. bxc3 Qxe7	25. Qxe8+ Qxe8	39. Kf6 Kg8
12. a4 Bxf3	26. Rxe8+ Kxe8	40. Rg7+ Kh8
13. Qxf3 Nc6	27. h5 Rf6	41. Rxc7 Re8
14. Rfb1 Rae8	28. hxg6 hxg6	42. Kxf5 Re4

43. Kf6 Rf4+
44. Ke5 Rg4
45. g7+ Kg8
46. Rxa7 Rg1
47. Kxd5 Rc1
48. Kd6 Rc2
49. d5 Rc1
50. Rc7 Ra1
51. Kc6 Rxa4
52. d6
Black resigns

A footnote to this game: in 1987, Capa's widow, Olga Capablanca Clark, offered for sale the manuscript of a hitherto unpublished Capablanca – Tartakower game. The reserve price, a very reasonable $10,000.

25. Réti–Bogoljubow, New York, 1924. *Réti Opening*
The first brilliancy prize game in one of the greatest tournaments of all time, and voted top of the pops by BCM readers twenty years ago.

1. Nf3 Nf6	8. d4 c6	15. e4 e5	22. Qxf5 Rxd4
2. c4 e6	9. Nbd2 Ne4	16. c5 Bf8	23. Rf1 Rd8
3. g3 d5	10. Nxe4 dxe4	17. Qc2 exd4	24. Bf7+ Kh8
4. Bg2 Bd6	11. Ne5 f5	18. exf5 Rad8	25. Be8
5. O–O O–O	12. f3 exf3	19. Bh5 Re5	Black resigns
6. b3 Re8	13. Bxf3 Qc7	20. Bxd4 Rxf5	
7. Bb2 Nbd7	14. Nxd7 Bxd7	21. Rxf5 Bxf5	

26. Réti–Alekhine, Baden-Baden, 1925. *King's Fianchetto*
One of the most remarkable combinations of all time, lasting from Black's twenty-sixth move to the end of the game.

1. g3 e5	8. Nxd2 O–O	15. Rd2 Qc8	22. Rc1 h4
2. Nf3 e4	9. c4 Na6	16. Nc5 Bh3	23. a4 hxg3
3. Nd4 d5	10. cxd5 Nb4	17. Bf3 Bg4	24. hxg3 Qc7
4. d3 exd3	11. Qc4 Nbxd5	18. Bg2 Bh3	25. b5 axb5
5. Qxd3 Nf6	12. N2b3 c6	19. Bf3 Bg4	26. axb5
6. Bg2 Bb4+	13. O–O Re8	20. Bh1 h5	
7. Bd2 Bxd2+	14. Rfd1 Bg4	21. b4 a6	

26. ...Re3	30. Nxb7 Nxe2+	35. Kh3 Ne5+	40. Bxf3 Nd4
27. Nf3 cxb5	31. Kh2 Ne4	36. Kh2 Rxf3	White resigns
28. Qxb5 Nc3	32. Rc4 Nxf2	37. Rxe2 Ng4+	
29. Qxb7 Qxb7	33. Bg2 Be6	38. Kh3 Ne3+	
	34. Rcc2 Ng4+	39. Kh2 Nxc2	

27. C. Torre–Em Lasker, Moscow, 1925. Torre Attack

Lasker's most famous loss—his Mexican opponent, whose career was tragically cut short by a mental breakdown, wins with an amusing 'windmill' combination.

1. d4 Nf6	12. Rfe1 Rfe8	23. Nc4 Qd5	34. Rxh6+ Kg5
2. Nf3 e6	13. Rad1 Nf8	24. Ne3 Qb5	35. Rh3 Reb8
3. Bg5 c5	14. Bc1 Nd5	25. Bf6 Qxh5	36. Rg3+ Kf6
4. e3 cxd4	15. Ng5 b5	26. Rxg7+ Kh8	37. Rf3+ Kg6
5. exd4 Be7	16. Na3 b4	27. Rxf7+ Kg8	38. a3 a5
6. Nbd2 d6	17. cxb4 Nxb4	28. Rg7+ Kh8	39. bxa5 Rxa5
7. c3 Nbd7	18. Qh5 Bxg5	29. Rxb7+ Kg8	40. Nc4 Rd5
8. Bd3 b6	19. Bxg5 Nxd3	30. Rg7+ Kh8	41. Rf4 Nd7
9. Nc4 Bb7	20. Rxd3 Qa5	31. Rg5+ Kh7	42. Rxe6+ Kg5
10. Qe2 Qc7	21. b4 Qf5	32. Rxh5 Kg6	43. g3
11. O–O O–O	22. Rg3 h6	33. Rh3 Kxf6	Black resigns

28. P. Johner–Nimzowitsch, Dresden, 1926. Nimzo-Indian Defence

Another profound effort by one of the leaders of the Hypermodern School, providing a practical illustration of his theory of the blockade.

1. d4 Nf6	12. Be2 Qd7	23. Nd2 Rg8	34. Bxe4 Bf5
2. c4 e6	13. h3 Ne7	24. Bg2 g5	35. Bxf5 Nxf5
3. Nc3 Bb4	14. Qe1 h5	25. Nf1 Rg7	36. Re2 h4
4. e3 O–O	15. Bd2 Qf5	26. Ra2 Nf5	37. Rgg2 hxg3+
5. Bd3 c5	16. Kh2 Qh7	27. Bh1 Rcg8	38. Kg1 Qh3
6. Nf3 Nc6	17. a4 Nf5	28. Qd1 gxf4	39. Ne3 Nh4
7. O–O Bxc3	18. g3 a5	29. exf4 Bc8	40. Kf1 Re8
8. bxc3 d6	19. Rg1 Nh6	30. Qb3 Ba6	White resigns
9. Nd2 b6	20. Bf1 Bd7	31. Re2 Nh4	
10. Nb3 e5	21. Bc1 Rac8	32. Re3 Bc8	
11. f4 e4	22. d5 Kh8	33. Qc2 Bxh3	

29. Nimzowitsch–Capablanca, New York, 1927. Caro-Kann Defence

Capablanca wins in the style of Nimzowitsch(!) by running his opponent out of moves.

1. e4 c6	8. dxc5 Bxc5	15. Rad1 g6	22. Rd3 Na5
2. d4 d5	9. O–O Ne7	16. g4 Nxe3	23. Re2 Re8
3. e5 Bf5	10. Na4 Qc6	17. Qxe3 h5	24. Kg2 Nc6
4. Bd3 Bxd3	11. Nxc5 Qxc5	18. g5 O–O	25. Red2 Rec8
5. Qxd3 e6	12. Be3 Qc7	19. Nd4 Qb6	26. Re2 Ne7
6. Nc3 Qb6	13. f4 Nf5	20. Rf2 Rfc8	27. Red2 Rc4
7. Nge2 c5	14. c3 Nc6	21. a3 Rc7	28. Qh3 Kg7

29. Rf2 a5	34. Rd4 Rc4	39. Kg1 b4	44. Rf3 Rd1
30. Re2 Nf5	35. Qf2 Qb5	40. axb4 axb4	45. b3 Rc1
31. Nxf5+ gxf5	36. Kg3 Rcxd4	41. Kg2 Qc1	46. Re3 Rf1
32. Qf3 Kg6	37. cxd4 Qc4	42. Kg3 Qh1	White resigns
33. Red2 Re4	38. Kg2 b5	43. Rd3 Re1	

30. Sultan Khan–Capablanca, Hastings, 1930–31.
Queens Indian Defence
The extraordinary Indian genius inexorably manoeuvres his way to victory–and what an opponent!

1. Nf3 Nf6	18. Be2 Rc6	35. R1c2 Qh3	52. Rg1 Bc8
2. d4 b6	19. g4 Rfc8	36. Kc1 Qh4	53. Rc6 Qh4
3. c4 Bb7	20. g5 Ne8	37. Kb2 Qh3	54. Rgc1 Bg4
4. Nc3 e6	21. Bg4 Rc1+	38. Rc1 Qh4	55. Bf1 Qh5
5. a3 d5	22. Kd2 R8c2+	39. R3c2 Qh3	56. Re1 Qh1
6. cxd5 exd5	23. Qxc2 Rxc2+	40. a4 Qh4	57. Rec1 Qh5
7. Bg5 Be7	24. Kxc2 Qc7+	41. Ka3 Qh3	58. Kc3 Qh4
8. e3 O–O	25. Kd2 Qc4	42. Bg3 Qf5	59. Bg3 Qxg5
9. Bd3 Ne4	26. Be2 Qb3	43. Bh4 g6	60. Kd2 Qf5
10. Bf4 Nd7	27. Rab1 Kf7	44. h6 Qd7	61. Rxb6 Ke7
11. Qc2 f5	28. Rhc1 Ke7	45. b5 a5	62. Rb7+ Ke6
12. Nb5 Bd6	29. Rc3 Qa4	46. Bg3 Qf5	63. b6 Nf6
13. Nxd6 cxd6	30. b4 Qd7	47. Bf4 Qh3	64. Bb5 Qf3
14. h4 Rc8	31. Rbc1 a6	48. Kb2 Qg2	65. Rb1
15. Qb3 Qe7	32. Rg1 Qh3	49. Kb1 Qh3	Black resigns
16. Nd2 Ndf6	33. Rgc1 Qd7	50. Ka1 Qg2	
17. Nxe4 fxe4	34. h5 Kd8	51. Kb2 Qh3	

31. Botvinnik–Chekover, Moscow, 1935. Réti Opening
A stirring if untypical, king hunt from the first great Soviet player.

1. Nf3 d5	12. Nf3 Rd8	23. fxg5 N8d7	34. Re1 Be5
2. c4 e6	13. Qc2 Ncd7	24. Nxf7 Kxf7	35. Qh8+ Ke7
3. b3 Nf6	14. d4 c5	25. g6+ Kg8	36. Qxg7+ Kd6
4. Bb2 Be7	15. Ne5 b6	26. Qxe6+ Kh8	37. Qxe5+ Kd7
5. e3 O-O	16. Bd3 cxd4	27. Qh3+ Kg8	38. Qf5+ Kc6
6. Be2 c6	17. exd4 Bb7	28. Bf5 Nf8	39. d5+ Kc5
7. O-O Nbd7	18. Qe2 Nf8	29. Be6+ Nxe6	40. Ba3+ Kxc4
8. Nc3 a6	19. Nd1 Ra7	30. Qxe6+ Kh8	41. Qe4+ Kc3
9. Nd4 dxc4	20. Nf2 Qb8	31. Qh3+ Kg8	42. Bb4+ Kb2
10. bxc4 Nc5	21. Nh3 h6	32. Rxf6 Bxf6	43. Qb1
11. f4 Qc7	22. Ng5 hxg5	33. Qh7+ Kf8	mate

32. Euwe–Alekhine, 26th Game, World Championship Match, 1935. Dutch Defence

The popular Dutchman's most famous game, 'The Pearl of Zandvoort', which helped him towards a sensational match victory.

1. d4 e6	13. d5 d6	25. e4 gxf4	37. fxe5 Rf5
2. c4 f5	14. Nd3 e5	26. gxf4 Bd4	38. Re1 h6
3. g3 Bb4+	15. Kh1 c6	27. e5 Qe8	39. Nd8 Rf2
4. Bd2 Be7	16. Qb3 Kh8	28. e6 Rg8	40. e6 Rd2
5. Bg2 Nf6	17. f4 e4	29. Nf3 Qg6	41. Nc6 Re8
6. Nc3 O–O	18. Nb4 c5	30. Rg1 Bxg1	42. e7 b5
7. Nf3 Ne4	19. Nc2 Nd7	31. Rxg1 Qf6	43. Nd8 Kg7
8. O–O b6	20. Ne3 Bf6	32. Ng5 Rg7	44. Nb7 Kf6
9. Qc2 Bb7	21. Nxf5 Bxc3	33. exd7 Rxd7	45. Re6+ Kg5
10. Ne5 Nxc3	22. Nxd6 Qb8	34. Qe3 Re7	46. Nd6 Rxe7
11. Bxc3 Bxg2	23. Nxe4 Bf6	35. Ne6 Rf8	47. Ne4+
12. Kxg2 Qc8	24. Nd2 g5	36. Qe5 Qxe5	Black resigns

33. Keres–Alekhine, Margate, 1937. Ruy López

A miniature against a formidable opponent demonstrates why the young Estonian was considered a future World Champion.

1. e4 e5	8. Be3 Nf6	15. Bxf8 Rxf8	22. Rhe1 Qb4
2. Nf3 Nc6	9. dxe5 dxe5	16. O–O–O Qe7	23. Qxd7+
3. Bb5 a6	10. Bc5 Nh5	17. Bxc6 Bxc6	Black resigns
4. Ba4 d6	11. Nd5 Nf4	18. Qd3 Bd7	
5. c4 Bd7	12. Nxf4 exf4	19. Nxg5 O–O–O	
6. Nc3 g6	13. e5 g5	20. Nf3 f6	
7. d4 Bg7	14. Qd5 Bf8	21. exf6 Rxf6	

34. Fine–Flohr, AVRO, 1938. French Defence

Reuben Fine gave up chess for a career in psychoanalysis, but he showed what he was capable of by sharing first place in one of the strongest tournaments of all time.

1. e4 e6	10. Re1 h6	19. Nc3 Nf5	28. Be4+
2. d4 d5	11. Na4 Bf8	20. Nb5 Qb6	Black resigns
3. Nc3 Bb4	12. Rc1 Bd7	21. Rxd7 Kxd7	
4. e5 c5	13. Nxh4 Qxh4	22. g4 Nh4	
5. Bd2 Ne7	14. c4 dxc4	23. Qxf7+ Be7	
6. Nf3 Nf5	15. Rxc4 Qd8	24. Bb4 Rae8	
7. dxc5 Bxc5	16. Qh5 Ne7	25. Bxe7 Rxe7	
8. Bd3 Nh4	17. Rd4 g6	26. Qf6 a6	
9. O–O Nc6	18. Qf3 Qc7	27. Rd1 axb5	

35. Botvinnik–Capablanca, AVRO, 1938. Nimzo-Indian Defence
Botvinnik's greatest, and a popular choice for the best game of all: a strategic masterpiece crowned with a fine combination.

1. d4 Nf6	9. Ne2 b6	17. Ng3 Na5	25. Rxe1 Re8
2. c4 e6	10. O–O Ba6	18. f3 Nb3	26. Re6 Rxe6
3. Nc3 Bb4	11. Bxa6 Nxa6	19. e4 Qxa4	27. fxe6 Kg7
4. e3 d5	12. Bb2 Qd7	20. e5 Nd7	28. Qf4 Qe8
5. a3 Bxc3+	13. a4 Rfe8	21. Qf2 g6	29. Qe5 Qe7
6. bxc3 c5	14. Qd3 c4	22. f4 f5	
7. cxd5 exd5	15. Qc2 Nb8	23. exf6 Nxf6	
8. Bd3 O–O	16. Rae1 Nc6	24. f5 Rxe1	

30. Ba3 Qxa3	33. Qxf6+ Kg8	36. Kg3 Qd3+	39. Kh4 Qe4+
31. Nh5+ gxh5	34. e7 Qc1+	37. Kh4 Qe4+	40. g4 Qe1+
32. Qg5+ Kf8	35. Kf2 Qc2+	38. Kxh5 Qe2+	41. Kh5
			Black resigns

36. Botvinnik–Reshevsky, World Championship Tournament, 1948. Nimzo-Indian Defence
The former prodigy, here shown defeating the tournament winner in excellent style, was perhaps the world's strongest player in the early fifties.

1. d4 Nf6	12. Ng3 Ba6	23. Ne3 Qa4	34. Red1 h4
2. c4 e6	13. Qe2 Qd7	24. Qa2 Nxg3	35. Ke1 Nb3
3. Nc3 Bb4	14. f4 f5	25. hxg3 h5	36. Nd5+ exd5
4. e3 c5	15. Rae1 g6	26. Be2 Kf7	37. Bxf5 Nxd2
5. a3 Bxc3+	16. Rd1 Qf7	27. Kf2 Qb3	38. Rxd2 dxc4
6. bxc3 Nc6	17. e5 Rc8	28. Qxb3 Nxb3	39. Bxd7 Rxd7
7. Bd3 O–O	18. Rfe1 dxe5	29. Bd3 Ke7	40. Rf2 Ke6
8. Ne2 b6	19. dxe5 Ng7	30. Ke2 Na5	41. Rf3 Rd3
9. e4 Ne8	20. Nf1 Rfd8	31. Rd2 Rc7	42. Ke2 and
10. Be3 d6	21. Bf2 Nh5	32. g4 Rcd7	White resigns
11. O–O Na5	22. Bg3 Qe8	33. gxf5 gxf5	

37. Averbakh–Kotov, Candidates' Tournament, Neuhausen/Zurich, 1953. Old Indian Defence

An amazing queen sacrifice wins the first brilliancy prize in a tournament immortalized by Bronstein's superb tournament book.

1. d4 Nf6	14. Rbc1 g6	27. gxf5 gxf5	40. Kf5 Ng8+
2. c4 d6	15. Nd2 Rab8	28. Rg2 f4	41. Kg4 Nf6+
3. Nf3 Nbd7	16. Nb3 Nxb3	29. Bf2 Rf6	42. Kf5 Ng8+
4. Nc3 e5	17. Qxb3 c5	30. Ne2 Qxh3+	43. Kg4 Bxg5
5. e4 Be7	18. Kh2 Kh8	31. Kxh3 Rh6+	44. Kxg5 Rf7
6. Be2 O–O	19. Qc2 Ng8	32. Kg4 Nf6+	45. Bh4 Rg6+
7. O–O c6	20. Bg4 Nh6	33. Kf5 Nd7	46. Kh5 Rfg7
8. Qc2 Re8	21. Bxd7 Qxd7	34. Rg5 Rf8+	47. Bg5 Rxg5+
9. Rd1 Bf8	22. Qd2 Ng8	35. Kg4 Nf6+	48. Kh4 Nf6
10. Rb1 a5	23. g4 f5	36. Kf5 Ng8+	49. Ng3 Rxg3
11. d5 Nc5	24. f3 Be7	37. Kg4 Nf6+	50. Qxd6 R3g6
12. Be3 Qc7	25. Rg1 Rf8	38. Kf5 Nxd5+	51. Qb8+ Rg8
13. h3 Bd7	26. Rcf1 Rf7	39. Kg4 Nf6+	White resigns

38. Bronstein–Keres, Interzonal Tournament, Göteborg, 1955. Nimzo-Indian Defence

A modern masterpiece, considered one of the most profound games ever played.

1. d4 Nf6	11. Nb5 exd5	21. Nd6 Bc6	31. h3 Qe2
2. c4 e6	12. a3 Be7	22. Qg4 Kh8	32. Ng3 Qe3+
3. Nc3 Bb4	13. Ng3 dxc4	23. Be4 Bh6	33. Kh2 Nd4
4. e3 c5	14. Bxh6 gxh6	24. Bxc6 dxc6	34. Qd5 Re8
5. Bd3 b6	15. Qd2 Nh7	25. Qxc4 Nc5	35. Nh5 Ne2
6. Ne2 Bb7	16. Qxh6 f5	26. b4 Ne6	36. Nxg7 Qg3+
7. O–O cxd4	17. Nxf5 Rxf5	27. Qxc6 Rb8	37. Kh1 Nxf4
8. exd4 O–O	18. Bxf5 Nf8	28. Ne4 Qg6	38. Qf3 Ne2
9. d5 h6	19. Rad1 Bg5	29. Rd6 Bg7	39. Rh6+
10. Bc2 Na6	20. Qh5 Qf6	30. f4 Qg4	Black resigns

39. D. Byrne–Fischer, Rosenwald Tournament, New York, 1956. Grünfeld Defence

Billed as 'The Game of the Century', in which the thirteen-year-old boy wonder hits the world's headlines for the first time with a remarkable queen sacrifice.

1. Nf3 Nf6	6. Qb3 dxc4	11. Bg5 Na4	16. Bc5 Rfe8+
2. c4 g6	7. Qxc4 c6	12. Qa3 Nxc3	17. Kf1
3. Nc3 Bg7	8. e4 Nbd7	13. bxc3 Nxe4	
4. d4 O–O	9. Rd1 Nb6	14. Bxe7 Qb6	
5. Bf4 d5	10. Qc5 Bg4	15. Bc4 Nxc3	

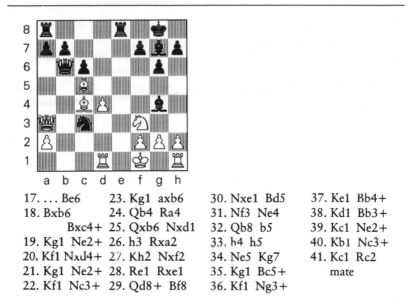

17. ... Be6	23. Kg1 axb6	30. Nxe1 Bd5	37. Ke1 Bb4+
18. Bxb6	24. Qb4 Ra4	31. Nf3 Ne4	38. Kd1 Bb3+
Bxc4+	25. Qxb6 Nxd1	32. Qb8 b5	39. Kc1 Ne2+
19. Kg1 Ne2+	26. h3 Rxa2	33. h4 h5	40. Kb1 Nc3+
20. Kf1 Nxd4+	27. Kh2 Nxf2	34. Ne5 Kg7	41. Kc1 Rc2
21. Kg1 Ne2+	28. Re1 Rxe1	35. Kg1 Bc5+	mate
22. Kf1 Nc3+	29. Qd8+ Bf8	36. Kf1 Ng3+	

40. Spassky–Bronstein, Leningrad, 1959. King's Gambit

In one sense *the* most famous game of all – the final position was used in the film *From Russia With Love* – and just look at white's fifteenth move.

1. e4 e5	8. O–O h6	15. Nd6 Nf8	21. Bb3 Bxe5
2. f4 exf4	9. Ne4 Nxd5	16. Nxf7	22. Nxe5+ Kh7
3. Nf3 d5	10. c4 Ne3	exf1=Q+	23. Qe4+
4. exd5 Bd6	11. Bxe3 fxe3	17. Rxf1 Bf5	Black resigns
5. Nc3 Ne7	12. c5 Be7	18. Qxf5 Qd7	
6. d4 O–O	13. Bc2 Re8	19. Qf4 Bf6	
7. Bd3 Nd7	14. Qd3 e2	20. N3e5 Qe7	

41. Tal–Smyslov, Candidates' Tournament, Bled, 1959. Caro-Kann Defence

The Latvian genius in sparkling form on his way to an appointment with Botvinnik.

1. e4 c6	8. Bg5 Be7	15. Qg5 Nh5	22. Rxa1 Kxf7
2. d3 d5	9. O–O–O O–O	16. Nh6+ Kh8	23. Ne5+ Ke6
3. Nd2 e5	10. Nd6 Qa5	17. Qxh5 Qxa2	24. Nxc6 Ne4+
4. Ngf3 Nd7	11. Bc4 b5	18. Bc3 Nf6	25. Ke3 Bb6+
5. d4 dxe4	12. Bd2 Qa6	19. Qxf7 Qa1+	26. Bd4 Black
6. Nxe4 exd4	13. Nf5 Bd8	20. Kd2 Rxf7	resigns
7. Qxd4 Ngf6	14. Qh4 bxc4	21. Nxf7+ Kg8	

42. Tal–Botvinnik, 1st Game, World Championship Match, 1960. French Defence

Highly original and imaginative play gives Tal a great start in the world title match.

1. e4 e6	10. Qxh7 cxd4	19. Rh3 Qf7	28. fxe3 Kc7
2. d4 d5	11. Kd1 Bd7	20. dxe5 Ncxe5	29. c4 dxc4
3. Nc3 Bb4	12. Qh5+ Ng6	21. Re3 Kd7	30. Bxc4 Qg7
4. e5 c5	13. Ne2 d3	22. Rb1 b6	31. Bxg8 Qxg8
5. a3 Bxc3+	14. cxd3 Ba4+	23. Nf4 Rae8	32. h5 Black
6. bxc3 Qc7	15. Ke1 Qxe5	24. Rb4 Bc6	resigns
7. Qg4 f5	16. Bg5 Nc6	25. Qd1 Nxf4	
8. Qg3 Ne7	17. d4 Qc7	26. Rxf4 Ng6	
9. Qxg7 Rg8	18. h4 e5	27. Rd4 Rxe3+	

43. Korchnoi–Tal, USSR Championship, 1962. Modern Benoni

One of Korchnoi's greatest games, his defusion of his opponent's favourite defence bears the hallmark of true mastery.

1. d4 Nf6	15. a4 a6	29. Bc4 Bc8	43. g4 a5
2. c4 c5	16. Bf1 Qe7	30. Rf1 Rb4	44. Kg3 Rb8
3. d5 e6	17. Nd2 Nc7	31. Bxe6 Bxe6	45. Kh4 Qf7
4. Nc3 exd5	18. f4 b5	32. Bh6 Re8	46. Kg5 fxg4
5. cxd5 d6	19. e5 dxe5	33. Qg5 Re4	47. hxg4 Bd7
6. Nf3 g6	20. Nde4 Qd8	34. Rf2 f5	48. Rc4 a4
7. g3 Bg7	21. Nxf6+ Nxf6	35. Qf6 Qd7	49. Rc7 a3
8. Bg2 O–O	22. d6 Ne6	36. Rxc5 Rc4	50. Rxd7 Qxd7
9. O–O Na6	23. fxe5 b4	37. Rxc4 Bxc4	51. e6 Qa7
10. h3 Nc7	24. Nd5 Nxd5	38. Rd2 Be6	52. Qe5 axb2
11. e4 Nd7	25. Qxd5 Bb7	39. Rd1 Qa7	53. e7 Kf7
12. Re1 Ne8	26. Qd2 Qd7	40. Rd2 Qd7	54. d7 Black
13. Bg5 Bf6	27. Kh2 b3	41. Rd1 Qa7	resigns
14. Be3 Rb8	28. Rac1 Qxa4	42. Rd4 Qd7	

44. R. Byrne–Fischer, US Championship, 1963–4. Grünfeld Defence

A masterpiece in miniature from Bobby's 100 per cent tournament leaves the spectators astonished.

1. d4 Nf6	7. e3 O–O	13. dxe5 Nxe5	19. Kxg2 d4
2. c4 g6	8. Nge2 Nc6	14. Rfd1 Nd3	20. Nxd4 Bb7+
3. g3 c6	9. O–O b6	15. Qc2 Nxf2	21. Kf1 Qd7
4. Bg2 d5	10. b3 Ba6	16. Kxf2 Ng4+	White resigns
5. cxd5 cxd5	11. Ba3 Re8	17. Kg1 Nxe3	
6. Nc3 Bg7	12. Qd2 e5	18. Qd2 Nxg2	

45. Petrosian–Spassky, 10th Game, World Championship Match, 1966. King's Indian Defence
Exchange sacrifices are often said to be the trademark of Soviet players–here Petrosian does it twice.

1. Nf3 Nf6	9. Nd2 c5	17. Bxf3 Bxb2	25. Be6+ Rf7
2. g3 g6	10. Qc2 e5	18. Qxb2 Ne5	26. Ne4 Qh4
3. c4 Bg7	11. b3 Ng4	19. Be2 f4	27. Nxd6 Qg5+
4. Bg2 O–O	12. e4 f5	20. gxf4 Bh3	28. Kh1 Ra7
5. O–O Nc6	13. exf5 gxf5	21. Ne3 Bxf1	29. Bxf7+ Rxf7
6. Nc3 d6	14. Nd1 b5	22. Rxf1 Ng6	30. Qh8+ Black
7. d4 a6	15. f3 e4	23. Bg4 Nxf4	resigns
8. d5 Na5	16. Bb2 exf3	24. Rxf4 Rxf4	

46. Botvinnik–Portisch, Monte Carlo, 1968. English Opening
Even in his late fifties Botvinnik could still play with youthful vigour, here producing one of the games of the decade.

1. c4 e5	8. d3 Be7	15. Rac1 Nb8	22. Ng6+ Kh7
2. Nc3 Nf6	9. a3 a5	16. Rxc7 Bc6	23. Be4 Bd6
3. g3 d5	10. Be3 O–O	17. R1xc6 bxc6	24. Nxe5+ g6
4. cxd5 Nxd5	11. Na4 Nxa4	18. Rxf7 h6	25. Bxg6+ Kg7
5. Bg2 Be6	12. Qxa4 Bd5	19. Rb7 Qc8	26. Bxh6+ Black
6. Nf3 Nc6	13. Rfc1 Re8	20. Qc4+ Kh8	resigns
7. O–O Nb6	14. Rc2 Bf8	21. Nh4 Qxb7	

47. Larsen–Spassky, USSR v. Rest of World, 1969. Larsen's Opening
A scintillating quickie from the 'Match of the Century' and one of the best-known games of recent years.

1. b3 e5	6. Nxc6 dxc6	11. g3 h5	16. Rf1 Qh4+
2. Bb2 Nc6	7. e3 Bf5	12. h3 h4	17. Kd1
3. c4 Nf6	8. Qc2 Qe7	13. hxg4 hxg3	gxf1=Q+
4. Nf3 e4	9. Be2 O–O–O	14. Rg1 Rh1	White resigns
5. Nd4 Bc5	10. f4 Ng4	15. Rxh1 g2	

48. *Fischer–Petrosian, 7th Game, Candidates' Final Match, 1971.*
Sicilian Defence
An instructive positional masterpiece against a redoubtable opponent.

1. e4 c5	10. exd5 exd5	19. Nc5 Bc8	28. Kf3 f5
2. Nf3 e6	11. Nc3 Be7	20. f3 Rea7	29. Ke3 d4+
3. d4 cxd4	12. Qa4+ Qd7	21. Re5 Bd7	30. Kd2 Nb6
4. Nxd4 a6	13. Re1 Qxa4	22. Nxd7+ Rxd7	31. Rce7 Nd5
5. Bd3 Nc6	14. Nxa4 Be6	23. Rc1 Rd6	32. Rf7+ Ke8
6. Nxc6 bxc6	15. Be3 O–O	24. Rc7 Nd7	33. Rb7 Nxb4
7. O–O d5	16. Bc5 Rfe8	25. Re2 g6	34. Bc4 Black
8. c4 Nf6	17. Bxe7 Rxe7	26. Kf2 h5	resigns
9. cxd5 cxd5	18. b4 Kf8	27. f4 h4	

49. *Fischer–Spassky, 6th Game, World Championship Match, 1972.*
Queen's Gambit Declined
Perhaps the best game of the now legendary Fischer–Spassky match,
Bobby proving that e4 is not the only way he knows to start a game.

1. c4 e6	12. Qa4 c5	23. Bc4 Kh8	34. R1f2 Qe8
2. Nf3 d5	13. Qa3 Rc8	24. Qh3 Nf8	35. R2f3 Qd8
3. d4 Nf6	14. Bb5 a6	25. b3 a5	36. Bd3 Qe8
4. Nc3 Be7	15. dxc5 bxc5	26. f5 exf5	37. Qe4 Nf6
5. Bg5 O–O	16. O–O Ra7	27. Rxf5 Nh7	38. Rxf6 gxf6
6. e3 h6	17. Be2 Nd7	28. Rcf1 Qd8	39. Rxf6 Kg8
7. Bh4 b6	18. Nd4 Qf8	29. Qg3 Re7	40. Bc4 Kh8
8. cxd5 Nxd5	19. Nxe6 fxe6	30. h4 Rbb7	41. Qf4 Black
9. Bxe7 Qxe7	20. e4 d4	31. e6 Rbc7	resigns
10. Nxd5 exd5	21. f4 Qe7	32. Qe5 Qe8	
11. Rc1 Be6	22. e5 Rb8	33. a4 Qd8	

50. *Karpov–Spassky, 9th Game, Candidates' Semi-Final, 1974.*
Sicilian Defence
Look out for Karpov's twenty-fourth, the sort of move that only a truly
great player would find, quiet yet deadly.

1. e4 c5	7. O–O O–O	13. Nd4 g6	19. Bg4 h5
2. Nf3 e6	8. f4 Nc6	14. Rf2 e5	20. Bxd7 Qxd7
3. d4 cxd4	9. Be3 Bd7	15. Nxc6 bxc6	21. Qc4 Bh4
4. Nxd4 Nf6	10. Nb3 a5	16. fxe5 dxe5	22. Rd2 Qe7
5. Nc3 d6	11. a4 Nb4	17. Qf1 Qc8	23. Rf1 Rfd8
6. Be2 Be7	12. Bf3 Bc6	18. h3 Nd7	

24. Nb1 Qb7	28. Nd2 Bd8	32. Rxd8 Bxd8
25. Kh2 Kg7	29. Nf3 f6	33. Rd1 Nb8
26. c3 Na6	30. Rd2 Be7	34. Bc5 Rh8
27. Re2 Rf8	31. Qe6 Rad8	35. Rxd8 Black resigns

51. Karpov–Korchnoi, 2nd Game, Candidates' Final, 1974.
Sicilian Defence
Superior opening preparation helps Karpov on his way to a brilliant victory and, by default, the World Championship.

1. e4 c5	9. Bc4 Bd7	17. Bh6 Bxh6	25. exf6 exf6
2. Nf3 d6	10. h4 Rc8	18. Qxh6 Rfc8	26. Qxh7+ Kf8
3. d4 cxd4	11. Bb3 Ne5	19. Rd3 R4c5	27. Qh8+ Black
4. Nxd4 Nf6	12. O-O-O Nc4	20. g5 Rxg5	resigns
5. Nc3 g6	13. Bxc4 Rxc4	21. Rd5 Rxd5	
6. Be3 Bg7	14. h5 Nxh5	22. Nxd5 Re8	
7. f3 Nc6	15. g4 Nf6	23. Nef4 Bc6	
8. Qd2 O-O	16. Nde2 Qa5	24. e5 Bxd5	

52. Karpov–Dorfman, Soviet Championship, Moscow, 1976.
Sicilian Defence
One of Karpov's best games, a long-term piece sacrifice belies his reputation for dull play.

1. e4 c5	8. h4 Nc6	15. Bxg7 Rg8	22. fxe5 Qc4
2. Nf3 d6	9. Be3 a6	16. exd5 Qc7	23. R1d3 Qf4+
3. d4 cxd4	10. Qe2 Qc7	17. Bf6 Ne5	24. Kb1 Rc4
4. Nxd4 Nf6	11. O-O-O b5	18. Bxe5 dxe5	25. d6 Re4
5. Nc3 e6	12. Nxc6 Qxc6	19. f4 Bf5	26. Rhe3 Rxe3
6. g4 Be7	13. Bd4 b4	20. Bh3 Bxh3	27. Rxe3 Qxh4
7. g5 Nfd7	14. Nd5 exd5	21. Rxh3 Rc8	

28. Qf3 Qxg5	34. Qh4+ Ke8	40. Rg1 Rxe5	46. Qd8+ Ke6
29. Re1 Qg2	35. Qxh7 Qf3	41. Rg8+ Ke7	47. Kb2 f6
30. Qf5 Rg6	36. Qh8+ Ke7	42. Qh4+ Kd7	48. Rf8 Qg7
31. Rf1 Qd5	37. Qh4+ Ke8	43. Qf6 Re7	49. Qc8+ Kd5
32. dxe7 Kxe7	38. Qc4 Qb7	44. Qf5+ Kd6	50. Qc4+ Black
33. Qf4 a5	39. b3 Re6	45. Qxa5 Re5	resigns

53. Karpov–Miles, European Team Championship, Skara, 1980.
St George's Defence

England's Number One bamboozles the champ with an eccentric choice of opening.

1. e4 a6	15. Bxc3 Nb4	29. Nc3 Rc8	43. Rg8 Rg2
2. d4 b5	16. Bxb4 Bxb4	30. Ne2 g5	44. Ke1 Bxe2
3. Nf3 Bb7	17. Rac1 Qb6	31. h4 Kg7	45. Bxe2 Rxg3
4. Bd3 Nf6	18. Be4 O–O	32. hxg5 hxg5	46. Ra8 and
5. Qe2 e6	19. Ng5 h6	33. Bd3 a5	White resigns
6. a4 c5	20. Bh7+ Kh8	34. Rg3 Kf6	
7. dxc5 Bxc5	21. Bb1 Be7	35. Rg4 Bd6	
8. Nbd2 b4	22. Ne4 Rac8	36. Kf1 Be5	
9. e5 Nd5	23. Qd3 Rxc1	37. Ke1 Rh8	
10. Ne4 Be7	24. Rxc1 Qxb2	38. f4 gxf4	
11. O–O Nc6	25. Re1 Qxe5	39. Nxf4 Bc6	
12. Bd2 Qc7	26. Qxd7 Bb4	40. Ne2 Rh1+	
13. c4 bxc3	27. Re3 Qd5	41. Kd2 Rh2	
14. Nxc3 Nxc3	28. Qxd5 Bxd5	42. g3 Bf3	

54. Korchnoi–Kasparov, Lucerne Olympiad, 1982. Modern Benoni

Kasparov is prepared to risk unfathomable complications on his way to the full point in a headline-grabbing encounter.

1. d4 Nf6	12. h3 Rb8	23. Bd2 Qxb2	34. Ra8+ Kf7
2. c4 g6	13. Nc4 Ne5	24. fxe5 Bxe5	35. Rh8 Kf6
3. g3 Bg7	14. Na3 Nh5	25. Nc4 Nxg3	36. Kf3 Qxh3+
4. Bg2 c5	15. e4 Rf8	26. Rxf8+ Rxf8	White resigns
5. d5 d6	16. Kh2 f5	27. Qe1 Nxe4+	
6. Nc3 O–O	17. f4 b5	28. Kg2 Qc2	
7. Nf3 e6	18. axb5 axb5	29. Nxe5 Rf2+	
8. O–O exd5	19. Naxb5 fxe4	30. Qxf2 Nxf2	
9. cxd5 a6	20. Bxe4 Bd7	31. Ra2 Qf5	
10. a4 Re8	21. Qe2 Qb6	32. Nxd7 Nd3	
11. Nd2 Nbd7	22. Na3 Rbe8	33. Bh6 Qxd7	

55. Kasparov–Portisch, Nikšić, 1983. Queen's Indian Defence
Regicide in 1980s style–Kasparov produces one of the most brilliant
games of recent years.

1. d4 Nf6	10. Bd3 c5	19. Bxh7+ Kxh7	28. Qh8+ Kf7
2. c4 e6	11. O–O Nc6	20. Rxd5 Kg8	29. Rd3 Nc4
3. Nf3 b6	12. Bb2 Rc8	21. Bxg7 Kxg7	30. Rfd1 Ne5
4. Nc3 Bb7	13. Qe2 O–O	22. Ne5 Rfd8	31. Qh7+ Ke6
5. a3 d5	14. Rad1 Qc7	23. Qg4+ Kf8	32. Qg8+ Kf5
6. cxd5 Nxd5	15. c4 cxd4	24. Qf5 f6	33. g4+ Kf4
7. e3 Nxc3	16. exd4 Na5	25. Nd7+ Rxd7	34. Rd4+ Kf3
8. bxc3 Be7	17. d5 exd5	26. Rxd7 Qc5	35. Qb3+ Black
9. Bb5+ c6	18. cxd5 Bxd5	27. Qh7 Rc7	resigns

56. Smyslov–Ribli, Candidates' Semi-Final, 1983.
Queen's Gambit Declined
The veteran unleashes a cascade of sacrifices *en route* to a showdown
with Kasparov.

1. d4 Nf6	7. Bd3 Be7	13. Bc4 Rd8	19. Bxb5 Qxb5
2. Nf3 e6	8. O–O O–O	14. Ne2 Bd7	20. Ng3 Ng6
3. c4 d5	9. a3 cxd4	15. Qe4 Nce7	21. Ne5 Nde7
4. Nc3 c5	10. exd4 Bf6	16. Bd3 Ba4	
5. cxd5 Nxd5	11. Qc2 h6	17. Qh7+ Kf8	
6. e3 Nc6	12. Rd1 Qb6	18. Re1 Bb5	

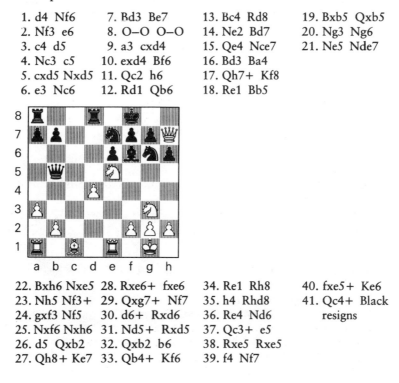

22. Bxh6 Nxe5	28. Rxe6+ fxe6	34. Re1 Rh8	40. fxe5+ Ke6
23. Nh5 Nf3+	29. Qxg7+ Nf7	35. h4 Rhd8	41. Qc4+ Black
24. gxf3 Nf5	30. d6+ Rxd6	36. Re4 Nd6	resigns
25. Nxf6 Nxh6	31. Nd5+ Rxd5	37. Qc3+ e5	
26. d5 Qxb2	32. Qxb2 b6	38. Rxe5 Rxe5	
27. Qh8+ Ke7	33. Qb4+ Kf6	39. f4 Nf7	

57. Belyavsky–Nunn, Wijk-an-Zee, 1985. King's Indian Defence
England's John Nunn plays imaginative, aggressive chess, as portrayed
here in one of his best games.

1. d4 Nf6	8. d5 Ne5	15. Qc2 Qf4	22. Bg2 Nxc4
2. c4 g6	9. h3 Nh5	16. Ne2 Rxf2	23. Qf2 Ne3+
3. Nc3 Bg7	10. Bf2 f5	17. Nxf2 Nf3+	24. Ke2 Qc4
4. e4 d6	11. exf5 Rxf5	18. Kd1 Qh4	25. Bf3 Rf8
5. f3 O–O	12. g4 Rxf3	19. Nd3 Bf5	26. Rg1 Nc2
6. Be3 Nbd7	13. gxh5 Qf8	20. Nec1 Nd2	27. Kd1 Bxd3
7. Qd2 c5	14. Ne4 Bh6	21. hxg6 hxg6	White resigns

*58. Karpov–Kasparov, 16th Game, World Championship Match,
1985. Sicilian Defence*
A stunning (but maybe unsound) pawn sacrifice on move 8 produces a
game destined for the anthologies as Gary reduces his opponent to
complete helplessness.

1. e4 c5	12. O–O O–O	23. g3 Nd7	34. Qxd3 Nf2+
2. Nf3 e6	13. Bf3 Bf5	24. Bg2 Qf6	35. Rxf2 Bxd3
3. d4 cxd4	14. Bg5 Re8	25. a3 a5	36. Rfd2 Qe3
4. Nxd4 Nc6	15. Qd2 b5	26. axb4 axb4	37. Rxd3 Rc1
5. Nb5 d6	16. Rad1 Nd3	27. Qa2 Bg6	38. Nb2 Qf2
6. c4 Nf6	17. Nab1 h6	28. d6 g4	39. Nd2 Rxd1+
7. N1c3 a6	18. Bh4 b4	29. Qd2 Kg7	40. Nxd1 Re1+
8. Na3 d5	19. Na4 Bd6	30. f3 Qxd6	White resigns
9. cxd5 exd5	20. Bg3 Rc8	31. fxg4 Qd4+	
10. exd5 Nb4	21. b3 g5	32. Kh1 Nf6	
11. Be2 Bc5	22. Bxd6 Qxd6	33. Rf4 Ne4	

*59. Kasparov–Karpov, 16th Game, World Championship Match,
1986. Ruy López*
The best game of the 1986 match, according to Kasparov – the commentators were sceptical but Gary claims he had it all worked out from
move 32.

1. e4 e5	9. h3 Bb7	17. Ra3 c4	25. Nxe5 Nbd3
2. Nf3 Nc6	10. d4 Re8	18. Nd4 Qf6	26. Ng4 Qb6
3. Bb5 a6	11. Nbd2 Bf8	19. N2f3 Nc5	27. Rg3 g6
4. Ba4 Nf6	12. a4 h6	20. axb5 axb5	28. Bxh6 Qxb2
5. O–O Be7	13. Bc2 exd4	21. Nxb5 Rxa3	29. Qf3 Nd7
6. Re1 b5	14. cxd4 Nb4	22. Nxa3 Ba6	30. Bxf8 Kxf8
7. Bb3 d6	15. Bb1 c5	23. Re3 Rb8	31. Kh2 Rb3
8. c3 O–O	16. d5 Nd7	24. e5 dxe5	

32. Bxd3 cxd3	35. Rxg6 Qe5	38. Re8+ Kd5	41. Nxf7
33. Qf4 Qxa3	36. Rg8+ Ke7	39. Rxe5+ Nxe5	Black resigns
34. Nh6 Qe7	37. d6+ Ke6	40. d7 Rb8	

60. Short–Kasparov, Brussels (OHRA), 1986. Sicilian Defence

Nigel scores a sensational win over the World Champion – will it prove portentous?

1. e4 c5	12. Rhe1 Rc8	24. Nc2 a5	36. Qxb7 Qxd3+
2. Nf3 d6	13. Kb1 Be7	25. Ba7 Kf8	37. Nc2 Rh2
3. d4 cxd4	14. h4 b4	26. Ne3 Qe6	38. Qc8+ Nf8
4. Nxd4 Nf6	15. Na4 Qa5	27. Nc4 Kg8	39. Rxe5 Rh1+
5. Nc3 a6	16. b3 Nfd7	28. Nxd6 Qxd6	40. Kb2 Qd2
6. Be3 e6	17. g5 g6	29. Nb2 Rc3	41. Re8 Qd6
7. Qd2 b5	18. f4 Nxd3	30. Nc4 Qd5	42. Rd8 Qe5+
8. f3 Nbd7	19. cxd3 hxg5	31. Ne3 Qe6	43. Ka3 Kh7
9. g4 h6	20. hxg5 d5	32. Rc1 Qa6	44. Rxf8 Qd6+
10. O–O–O	21. f5 e5	33. Rxc3 bxc3	45. b4
Bb7	22. exd5 Qxd5	34. Qxc3 Qxa7	Black resigns
11. Bd3 Ne5	23. f6 Bd6	35. Qc7 Qd4	

(only the fourth time this century a British player has beaten the world champion.)

Nov. 29/927.

Dr. A. Alekhine

Cher monsieur Alekhine:
    J'abandonne la partie.
Vous êtes donc le champion
du monde et je vous félicite
pour votre succès.
    Mes compliments à Mme Alekhine
    Sincèrement à vous
        J. R. Capablanca

Dear Mr. Alekhine,
I resign the game.
You are hence the Word Champion.
I congratulate you on your success.
Best regards to Mrs. Alekhine.
Yours sincerely
J. R. Capablanca

III *The Frightful*

We might escape, ah me! how many a pain,
Could we recall bad moves and play again.
Goethe

'Tell me, how long did it take you to learn to play chess so badly?'
  'Sir, it's been nights of study and self-denial'
Apocryphal

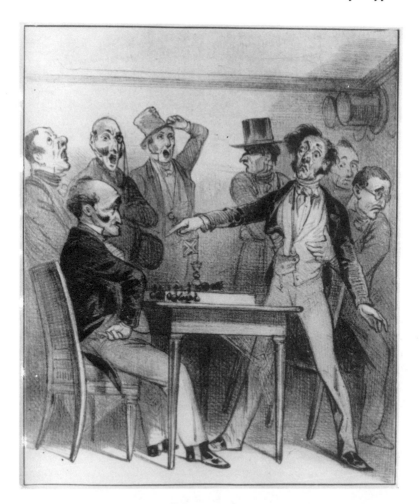

This is the pits. The worst blunders, the quickest losses, the least successful team, the most ghastly tournament results. And as a bonus, the silliest advice ever given, the worst chess commentary, the rottenest chess opening ever devised, and a dozen other assorted clangers. It's the chapter to cheer you up after yet one more disaster. Lost on time? Read how a grandmaster did it thirteen times in the same tournament. Left a knight *en prise* to the club idiot? See how a future world champion left a whole queen dangling. Sealed a stinker? One world-class player forgot to put his move in the envelope. As the man said: 'The mistakes are all there, waiting to be made.' And here they are.

♜

Picking the worst player of all time is even more difficult than picking the best. In 1958, one of the authors, after playing ten minutes of what he thought was a serious game, was jolted by a query from his Italian opponent: 'Excuse me sir, which is the queen?'

♜

Or there's the strange case, reported in *Chess* 1937, of the Sheffield v. Stocksbridge match. Both teams, unbeknownst to the other, were a man short. Both resorted to the last desperate expedient of a team captain: rather than lose a game by default they each picked up a stranger in a pub, gave him a quick refresher course in the moves and stuck him on bottom board. At the end of the match the teams gathered round to gaze in awe at a position unique in 1400 years of chess: both sides were in checkmate.

♜

And Alekhine is said to have watched amused as two café players carried on playing with only kings left on the board. He leaves them to discover the error of their ways; returns to find one jubilant, one crestfallen. 'Draw?' asks the grandmaster. 'No,' he's told. 'I got my king to the eighth rank and made it a queen.'

But we all have to learn, so maybe these don't count.

♜

Of players who've entered chess history, perhaps the strongest claimant for the all-time grandpatzer title is George Hatfeild Dingley Gossip (1841–1907). George had a worse record in major tournaments than anyone in history (last at Breslau 1889, London 1889, Manchester 1890, London 1892, and New York 1893: a total of just 4 wins, 52 losses and 21 draws). This didn't prevent him from promoting himself as a great player; nor did it inhibit him from writing a series of instructional books on the game. These contained a number of flashy (and entirely fictitious) wins he'd scored against famous players; and in one of them he proudly published the summit of his achievement: third prize in the Melbourne Chess Club Handicap Tournament 1885.

♜

Isolating the worst tournament performances of all time is a little easier than picking the world's worst player. We'll announce our finalists, Miss World fashion, in reverse order.[1]

In third spot, an Irishman and part-time magician: Bartholomew O'Sullivan. At the 1947 Zonal Tournament in Hilversum, Mr O'Sullivan managed twelve zeros. A solitary draw spoiled his bid for perfection. What clinches the bronze medal, though, was chess sage Harry Golombek's post-tournament epitaph on the Irishman's chess ability: 'O'Sullivan's play was rather worse than his score.'

Here's O'Sullivan up against a grandmaster and judo brown belt, Rossolimo (France):

B. O'Sullivan–N. Rossolimo, Hilversum, 1947.   Queen's Indian Defence

1. d4 Nf6	4. Bg2 e6	7. Nc3 Ne4	10. Qxe2 Bxg2
2. Nf3 b6	5. O–O Be7	8. Qc2 Nxc3	Resigns
3. g3 Bb7	6. c4 O–O	9. Ng5 Nxe2+	

♜

In the silver-medal position comes Nicholas Menelaus MacLeod, who at the New York tournament of 1889 fought like a tiger to set a mark that will last for ages. Despite a few thoughtless wins (two against, guess who, G. H. D. Gossip) and a draw along the way, he still managed to earn his place in the books with a world record – thirty-one losses in a single tournament: particularly gutsy considering he had to sit there each day and watch Chigorin, on board one, score the *most* tournament wins ever in a major tournament: twenty-seven. MacLeod had plenty of time to reflect on his performance: he died seventy-six years later, aged ninety-five, his record still intact (1965)

[1] Among the contenders were: Breyev, 0/18, Kiev, 1903; McCord, 0/17, US Open, 1944; Didier, who after a 1/16 in Paris 1900, sank to a unique score of ¼/13 in Monte Carlo 1901 (they had a weird scoring system that year); and Trenchard who collected 27 zeros at Vienna, 1898 (but kept himself out of the records with one win and eight draws).

But for sheer perfection, the gold goes to the gallant Colonel Moreau. At the 1903 Monte Carlo tournament, Moreau racked up an achievement so magnificent, we reproduce it here in full:

C. Moreau : 000000000000000000000000000.

Twenty-six games, twenty-six duck eggs; a world record. For dogged persistence, it's a landmark; you or I would have feigned a headache or beriberi or a sick uncle after maybe ten of those noughts. So Colonel Moreau gets our palm for the gamest of good losers.

F. J. Marshall–C. Moreau, Monte Carlo, 1903. King's Gambit

1. e4 e5	10. Kh1 Bh6	19. Na3 Kd7	25. Qd6+ Ke8
2. f4 exf4	11. Bd2 Qg7	20. Nc4 f3 and	26. Re1+ Kf7
3. Nf3 g5	12. Bb3 Nc6	Marshall	27. Ne5+ Ke8
4. Bc4 g4	13. Bc3 Ne5	announced	28. Ng6+ Be3
5. O–O gxf3	14. Qd5 d6	mate in 11:	29. Rxe3+ Qe6
6. Qxf3 Qf6	15. Rd1 Bd7	21. Rxd6+ cxd6	30. Qxe6+ Kd8
7. e5 Qxe5	16. Ba4 Bc6	22. Qxd6+ Kc8	31. Ba5 mate
8. Bxf7+ Kd8	17. Bxc6 bxc6	23. Qxc6+ Kd8	
9. d4 Qxd4+	18. Qxe5 Qg4	24. Rd1+ Ke7	

♖

Worse even than what happened to Colonel Moreau was the fate of Geoffrey Hosking, an English student at Moscow University in 1965. A beginner at chess, he played a game against a Russian fellow student while they were both legless on vodka. The Russian, a candidate master, was perhaps the more susceptible to alcohol, for he lost. Shortly after, the Soviet Chess Federation cabled Moscow University, asking them to send a foreign master to a tournament at Baku. Geoffrey was asked, protested, but was eventually persuaded to go (doubtless he fancied a free trip to Baku). What he found when he got there was a dozen international masters out for blood. Geoffrey's was spilled in considerable quantities. He scored a creditable (given his zero rating) nought out of twelve. (Third Programme talk.)

♖

The worst-ever performance by a chess team? You'd have to go a long way to beat the Cypriot team's effort in the 1962 Olympiad. Twenty matches, twenty losses. Sixteen matches they lost by the maximum: four–nil. And out of eighty individual games they scored just three points. Their third board Ioannidis put himself alongside Colonel Moreau with an unbeatable Olympic record of twenty games, twenty zeros. (In the next Olympiad, Ioannidis was at it again: four noughts in his first four games. At this point the Cypriot team selectors decided they'd had enough, and Ioannidis was dropped for ever.)

In this game (from Cyprus v Bulgaria B 1962), Ioannidis, in his customary self-destruct mode, runs into a Chipev cheapo.

Chipev–Ioannidis, Varna, 1962. Pirc Defence

1. e4 d6	6. f3 O–O	11. O–O–O Qc7 16. Rxh7+
2. d4 g6	7. g4 c5	12. Ng3 a6 Black resigns
3. Nc3 Bg7	8. Nge2 b6	13. g5 Nd7
4. Be3 Nd7	9. h4 Ne8	14. hxg6 fxg6
5. Qd2 Ngf6	10. h5 Ndf6	15. Bc4+ Kh8

♜

Messrs O'Sullivan, MacLeod, Moreau and Ioannidis were, to put it kindly, not first-class players. What about the worst performance by the masters? Here are four to cheer you up, starting with an if-at-first-you-don't-succeed story for the fainthearted. At the Vienna tournament of 1908, Richard Réti put himself in the O'Sullivan class with sixteen zeros and just three draws. Undeterred he went on to become one of the most famous chessmasters in history. (He was the chap who broke Capablanca's eight-year no-loss spell.)

♜

British IM Bob Wade has done more for British chess than most, so it seems a little harsh to publish his most embarrassing moment; but while in Moscow in 1951, he took on a simultaneous display against thirty Russian schoolboys. The result – twenty losses, ten draws, no wins. It couldn't have happened to a nicer guy. (This isn't a record by any means, as you'll see later in this chapter.)

♜

The worst tournament performance by an international master (with a contender for the Worst Game Prize thrown in as a bonus) was perpetrated by Kamran Shirazi in the US championships, 1984. He managed just half a point out of seventeen games; *en route* he tossed off this shambles:

Shirazi–Peters. Sicilian Defence

1. e4 c5	3. a3 d5	5. axb4 Qe5+ and
2. b4 cxb4	4. exd5 Qxd5	White resigns

There's hope for us all.

♖

Another one for the record books happened at the Linköping tournament of 1969. A German player scored zero out of thirteen. Not in the Moreau class, you're saying – but what puts it on a pinnacle of awfulness is this: all thirteen were lost by exceeding the time limit. The hero of this exploit wasn't a patzer either: Fritz Sämisch was a noted German grandmaster. He also set the record for the briefest-ever loss on time: after just twelve thoughtful moves, his flag fell. Fritz (who once thought for an hour about his fourth (!) move) had one of the longest thinks on first move too. His opponent played 1. d4. *Twenty-seven* minutes later, after apparently deep thought, Sämisch came up with the unoriginal Nf6.[1] On another occasion, he thought for forty-five minutes on his first move with white.

♖

All of which brings us to the subject of brevities.

Still pursuing the theme of how the mighty occasionally tread on banana skins, here's what happened when the great Boris Spassky's brain went into neutral against an unknown in Munich in 1979:

Lieb–Spassky. Vienna Game

1. e4 e5	3. Bc4 Nc6	5. f4 d6	7. Rxg1 Ng4
2. Nc3 Nf6	4. d3 Bc5	6. Na4 Bxg1	8. g3 exf4

9. Bxf4 Nxh2?? (a move your granny would be ashamed of)
10. Qh5 and if White wishes to stop the most ancient checkmate of them all, the knight goes. So the former world champion sheepishly resigned.

♖

Just as bad was what happened to a world champion in 1924. Capablanca (the chess machine) was giving a simul in Brooklyn when one of the rabbits bit him on the ankle:

Capablanca–Kevitz. Orang Utan

1. b4 d5	5. Nf3 Bxb4	9. h3 Nc5	12. Qf3 Nxe3
2. Bb2 Bf5	6. Nc3 Nbd7	(threatening mate)	13. Qf2 Nxf1
3. e3 e6	7. Ne2 Ng4	10. Ng3 Bh4	and
4. f4 Nf6	8. c3 Be7	11. Nxh4 Qxh4	White resigns

---

[1] Grandmaster Bronstein was similarly relaxed about the clock: he sometimes took up to thirty minutes over his first move.

One of Capa's quickest losses[1] (though to be fair to him and his opponent, Kevitz was a good deal better than your average simul fodder).

♜

The shortest loss in a proper game between world-class players is the horrible:

Marshall–Chigorin, Monte Carlo, 1903. Queen's Gambit Chigorin's Defence

1. d4 d5	4. d5 Na5	6. e4 e6	8. Qh5+(winning
2. c4 Nc6	5. Bf4 Bd7	7. dxe6 fxe6??	a knight) Black
3. Nc3 dxc4			resigns

♜

Even more embarrassing was a world championship contender's knightmare against an unknown.

Borochow–Fine. Pasadena, 1932. Alekhine's Defence

1. e4 Nf6	3. c4 Nb6	5. d5 Nxe5	7. f4
2. e5 Nd5	4. d4 Nc6?	6. c5 Nbc4	Black resigns

This is how most authorities quote the game. According to Andy Soltis, Fine staggered on with 7. ... e6 8. Qd4! Qh4+ 9. g3 Qh6 10. Nc3 exd5 11. fxe5 Black resigns.)

♜

Of course, in postal play you have oodles of time to make sure disasters like the above never happen. Well, mostly never. Here is an Irish correspondence player in action:

Warren–Selman, correspondence game, 1930. Budapest Defence

1. d4 Nf6	4. a3 d6	6. g3 Nxf2	7. Kxf2 Bxg3+
2. c4 e5	5. exd6 Bxd6	and White	(the queen is a
3. dxe5 Ne4		resigns after	goner.)

An even shorter correspondence game from *Chess*, 1944:

Ellinger–Revd Durrant. Sicilian Defence.

1. e4 c5	3. e5 Nd5	5. Nbc3 Nd3
2. Ne2 Nf6	4. c4 Nb4	mate

[1]The record for beating Capablanca in a simul seems to belong to Mary Bain (USA) who nailed the greatest natural player the game has ever seen in just eleven moves (according to *Chess Notes*). We don't have the game score. This *may* have been Capablanca's well-known chivalry – but Mary was quite a strong player (1937 Women's World Championship challenger).

♜

And there's worse. B. H. Wood tells of this débâcle in a postal tournament. After 1. e4, Black replied: '... b6. 2. Any, Bb7.' Now 'any' is a useful postal chess time-saver; it's shorthand for 'any move you care to make'. So White replied with the diabolical '2. Ba6, Bb7 3. Bxb7' (and wins the rook as well).

♜

For five centuries, bright schoolkids have been zapping their elders with variations on this sucker punch:

1. e4 e5	3. Bc4 Nf6??
2. Qh5 Nc6 (if White's lucky, 2. ... g6	4. Qxf7 mate
losing a rook, is often played)	

The Scholar's Mate; certainly the most played quickie[1] of all time. See any under-tens tournament for half a dozen examples. But does anyone ever try it in an adult tournament? And worse, does anyone fall for it? Watch:

Amillano–Loeffler, Mar del Plata, 1972

1. e4 e5	3. Bc4 g6	5. Qxf7 mate
2. Qh5 Nc6	4. Qf3 Nd4	

♜

The shortest loss by a master was, for decades, supposed to be this much publicized gem played at a café in Paris in 1924. A waiter is said to have dropped a tray of plates when Lazard made his winning move.

Gibaud–Lazard

1. d4 Nf6	2. Nd2 e5	3. de Ng4	4. h3?...

and now, if you haven't seen it before, try to spot the crusher.

What made the history books was 4. .. Ne3! If the knight is taken, it's mate by Qh4+.

Sadly, Gibaud later denied it ever happened like that (well, he would, wouldn't he?).[2] So into the record book went a much less diverting game. It happened to a tired future British champion, in the Chess Olympiad, 1933. Robert Combe, playing for Scotland, had had a tough

[1] Another much played quickie is worth knowing: the Blackburne Shilling Gambit, presumably so named because Blackburne used to win shillings with it. Try it on the next sucker you meet. 1. e4 e5 2. Nf3 Nc6 3. Bc4 Nd4?! 4. Nxe5 Qg5 5. Nxf7? Qxg2 6. Rf1 Qxe4+ 7. Be2 Nf3 mate. This came off twice in successive rounds in a Blackpool tournament in 1987.

[2] To be fair, modern authorities accept his denial.

twelve-hour game the day before, and doubtless sat down hoping for something shorter against a Latvian. That's exactly what he got:

Combe–Hasenfuss, Folkestone, 1933

1. d4 c5	4. Nxe5? Qa5+
2. c4 cxd4	(forking king and
3. Nf3 e5	knight) White resigns[1]

Combe's pained comment: 'The positional layout was perfect: it was unfortunately spoiled by a tactical circumstance.' (Some sources say e4 was white's second move.)

♜

Topping even Combe's effort is this modern version of the same lemon:

Z. Djordjević–M. Kovačević, Bela Crkva, 1984

1. d4 Nf6	3. e3? Qa5+
2. Bg5 c6	and White resigns

♜

There is, of course, a still shorter possibility:

Fool's mate: 1. f3 e5   2. g4?? Qh4 mate

But nobody ever played that in a real game, did they? Probably. Look, for example, at this gem (Masefield–Trinka, 1959 US Open Championships): 1. e4 g5 2. Nc3 f5 3. Qh5 mate.

♜

And still we haven't reached the limits. Here are two that come close.

Blackburne, in a simultaneous display, was confronted by an old gentleman who replied 1. ... e6 to Blackburne's 1. e4. Blackburne, the strongest British player for decades, said jokingly, 'I resign.' The oldie held him to it.

♜

And shorter still: Bobby Fischer, just before he became world champion, played 1. c4 against grandmaster Panno. Panno's reply was original: Resigns.

[1] The Olympiads seem to bring out the worst in people. Here's the Dutch Antilles versus Wales. White should have quit on move 3, but struggled on for two more moves to avoid erasing Combe's name from the record books:

Rigaud–Cooper, Nice, 1974

1. e4 e5	3. fxe5 Qh4+	5. Kf2 Bc5+
2. f4 d5	4. g3 Qxe4+	White resigns

John Watson's analysis of Panno's move in his 'English: Franco, Slav and Flank Defences' is worthy of record:

1. c4 Resigns

... fails to further black's development, but does have a certain surprise value; and one may argue further that you can save a lot of energy by employing the demure approach ... Those disinclined to the rigors of tournament play may find much of interest here.

♖

Opening theoreticians may be interested in an improvement on Panno's idea found by Ken Rogoff, a US master, against grandmaster Hübner. It goes:

Hübner–Rogoff, World Student Team Championship, Graz, 1972

1. c4 Draw

♖

But R. J. Fischer (who else?) holds the ultimate, unsurpassable record. Many others share it; nobody but Bobby played it at such a stratospheric level. In the second game of his world-title match against Spassky, Bobby, with White, just didn't play any moves at all. In effect, the game went:

Fischer–Spassky, Reykjavik, 1972

1. Resigns[1]

♖

Here too, midnight oil has produced improvements even on Fischer's play. Miles v. Reuben, Luton, 1975 (don't blink or you'll miss it):

1. Draw

A more arduous path to the same idea was taken by Van der Sterren and Povah in the Lloyds Bank Masters, 1978:

1. e4 e5   2. Draw

♖

Losing an important game in five moves or less is pretty depressing – but it's not the worst thing in the world. Imagine how Grandmaster Vlastimil Hort (Czechoslovakia) must have felt at Reykjavik in 1977. It's the World Championship Quarter-Finals. Hort has been trying for a decade to get this far. He's level with the great Spassky and only two more games to go. He (black) has this position:

[1] To be strictly accurate, Bobby just didn't show up.

—and less than a minute to make five moves. Tough, but no problem for Vlastimil, for he's seen a sure win. 35. ... Qg4. If 36. g3 Qh3 37. Rf2 Rd1+ and wins. Then, inexplicably, the Czech goes into a trance; completely forgetting his clock, he fails to make any moves at all. His flag falls—and ten years of sweat go down the drain. No wonder he called it 'the blackest day of my life'.

♜

You think that's bad? Look what happened to David Bronstein in even more elevated company. It's Moscow, 1951. He's playing world champion Botvinnik for the title. He has oodles of time; and he has white in this position:

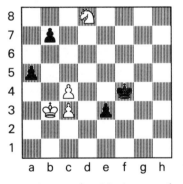

Bronstein sees that Ne6+ gets the draw. Fine; but then he slides off into a daydream about how he should have played the opening. After *forty-five* minutes of irrelevant musing he absent-mindedly picks up his king – and after 57. Kc2?? and Black's 57....Kg3, bang goes the draw.[1]

[1] After 57. ... Kg3 the e pawn queens. But if 57. Ne6 + and Nd4, Black is fighting for the draw.

'Blunder of the century' is what he called it. (Mind you, even the iron man of chess—Mikhail Botvinnik—once proved he was human. In a winning position aganst Smyslov in the World Championship Match of 1958, the most disciplined player in chess history forgot to press his clock.)

Five years after his Moscow débâcle, Bronstein was involved in another supershocker. He's black, playing Tigran (the Tiger) Petrosian, a future world champion, and he's in terrible trouble. He also has practically no time left on his clock.

Desperately, he's just banged a knight on f5, but his game is falling apart. Petrosian, with lots more time, calmly plays the awesome 36. Ng5?? and it's thank you and good-night as the incredulous Bronstein takes off the queen.

Then there's the gruesome thing that befell a Yugoslavian grandmaster in Havana.

It's the summer of 1965, and Borislav Ivkov is on top of the world: he's beaten two all-time greats (Smyslov and Fischer) and he's leading a very strong field in the Capablanca Memorial Tournament. If he wins, it'll be the best result of his life. With two rounds to go, Boris is expected to clinch first place with an easy win against a tail-ender, the Cuban Gilberto García – a relative unknown.

True to form, Ivkov (black) crushes the local boy in the middle game and reaches a position in which García should resign. But, as they say, you never win a game by resigning...

What would you play? Boris chose the move that is still waking him up in the middle of the night: 36. ... d3??; and after 37. Bc3, it was the ashen-faced Ivkov who had to resign.[1] (Doubtless shattered by this horror story, Ivkov blew his last game too – and finished, a sadder and wiser grandmaster, equal fourth.)

♟

Tarrasch (a doctor) called it *amaurosis schacchistica*.[2] It struck several times in the 1977 Korchnoi–Spassky match. The worst example happened, appropriately enough, in game 13. Korchnoi (white) has outplayed Spassky and has just missed an easy win to reach this position:

Then he plays two world-class blunders in a row:

32. Bxf5??   Rxf5   33. Qxf5?? and loses his queen

♟

[1] Anthony Glyn uses this disaster as part of the plot in his absorbing novel *The Dragon Variation* (1969).
[2] Chess blindness

But none of this is as agonizing as what happened to one of the greatest players of all time. It's Chigorin versus Steinitz for the world title. The result of the whole match depends on the outcome of one game. Chigorin (white) has this against the World Champion:

Pick a move for Chigorin. It probably wasn't as bad as what happened: imagine his feelings after Bb4?? and it's mate in two.

✗

There are quite a few examples of grandmasters missing mates in two, but here's one of the best players in the world doing what you'd have thought impossible: missing a mate in *one*.[1] We'll leave you to find it. It was at Saltsjöbaden 1948 in a World Championship qualifying tournament: (Gligorić–Böök.)

While the spectators reeled back in astonishment, Gligo played Rd1+. Fortunately for his sanity, he went on to win eighteen moves later.

[1] Other world-class players who missed a mate in one: Smyslov (v. Florian), Moscow v. Budapest 1950 (Smyslov picked a mate in three instead). Bronstein (v. Gligorić!) Moscow 1967. (From *Chess Notes*)

More annoying still was this (Beverwijk, 1963), one of the most famous blunders of the sixties. The world's leading endgame analyst, Averbakh, is Black against Ståhlberg.

Averbakh, feeling good, threatens a queen and bishop mate with ... Bh3. Seconds later, he's poleaxed, after Qxh6 and mate, next move.

When an ordinary mortal beats a grandmaster, that's news; when he misses a chance to whup an immortal, he spends the rest of his life kicking himself. Here's how Victor Buerger blew a chance against Dr Alekhine (Margate, 1937):

Alekhine plays ... .Qxf4?? How would you have replied? Buerger played: Nxe4??, instead of what any bright chimpanzee would have spotted: Nh5+. (Happily, Buerger eventually *did* win the game.)

Even worse is what an obscure Argentinian, Jaime Emma, missed against a great Soviet grandmaster, Leonid Stein at Mar del Plata, 1966.

Leonid (black), incomprehensibly, and after a twenty-minute think, put his queen *en prise* (34 ... Qc2??). Señor Emma, to his everlasting regret, didn't spot it (35. Rd7??). The game was drawn.

You read above about the blunder of the century. Here's what Bronstein (an expert on such things) called the blunder of five centuries. Once again we're in the chess stratosphere: the 1973 Interzonal Tournament at Petropolis, Brazil. A good result in this means you qualify for the final stages of the world championship.

American grandmaster Sammy Reshevsky has white against the Soviet star Savon.

He has half a minute on his clock; he has one move to make before the time control; and he also has a forced win. Instead of playing it, Sammy, the wizard of time trouble, chose what he thought was checkmate: 40. Qxg6+??? (mate) Bxg6 and white resigns. (40. g5+ would have been mate in three.)

Poor Reshevsky played his shocker in time trouble. Given enough time, a grandmaster would never make the kind of blunders we make, would he? Well, Bogoljubow, world title contender of the twenties, broke the world record for long thinks by taking one hour fifty-seven minutes over a move. After all that sweat he played something that wouldn't look good on board six of your club second team. (It lost a whole knight.)[1]

Instances of masters resigning won games are not unknown. Here's Marco doing it against von Popiel in perhaps the best-known blunder of all:

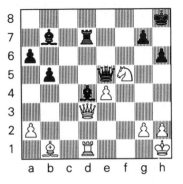

As is well known, Marco delighted generations of chess-players with the unenterprising ... Resigns, instead of winning with ... Bg1.

More recent, and more entertaining, was what happened between Sztern and Lundquist in Australia, 1983. Sztern was offered a draw; he chose instead: Resigns. It happened like this:

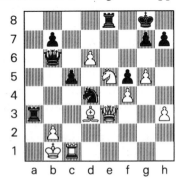

[1] For a longer think, see Chapter V.

Black offers the draw. White asks him to make a move first. Black plays 28. . . . Qxb2+, to which White, stunned, replies 29. Resigns?? This was considered ingenious enough to be awarded the 1983–4 Blunder of the Year award by seven assorted masters and grandmasters. (Legally of course, he could still have taken the draw.)

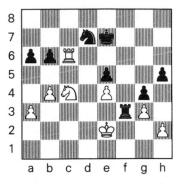

Just to demonstrate that nobody's perfect, here's Kasparov in a world title match missing something any run-of-the-mill computer would have leapt on in seconds.

It's 1986, London, and Kasparov is once again battling with Karpov for the world title. Gary, White in the second game, has miraculously squeezed something from nothing to reach this:

He played 39. Ne3? and a dozen moves later regretfully accepted a draw. But what Kasparov and some masters on the spot missed was the winning 39. Rc7 (threatening Rxd7+ or Nxe5).

You can of course chuck away the win without making a bad move. Such was the horrid fate of Tringov in the Chess Olympiad of 1972. In a quite respectable position, against Korchnoi, the Bulgarian grandmaster sealed (he thought) his move, and adjourned for a night of analysis. Next day he found what he'd got was an empty envelope. The day after, after an agonizing search, he found the errant score sheet tucked in a jacket pocket. Understandably, he was too embarrassed to tell his team mates.

Woman grandmaster Marta Shul blew a key game in the Soviet championship with the same trick. Result, in both cases: a possible win turned into a zero.

Up to now the booboos have all been committed under the tension of match play. For a change, here's a most respected master tripping up in the quiet of his study. It's the Grand Old Man of British chess, Harry Golombek, annotating an Alekhine quickie, back in 1956.

Alekhine–Evensson, Kiev 1918. Vienna Game

1. e4 e5	3. Bc4 Bb4	5. dxc3 Nxe4	7. Qd5+ Ke8
2. Nc3 Nf6	4. f4 Bxc3	6. Bxf7+ Kxf7	8. Qxe4 Nc6

(at which point Golombek's note in *British Chess Magazine* says 'Even more vigorous is 8. ... Castles') (?)

9. fxe5 Qe7	11. Bg5 Qe6	13. Nxe5 a6?
10. Nf3 d6	12. O-O-O dxe5	

and Harry (a world championship arbiter) repeats the blunder: 'Correct was 13. ... Castles' (??)

14. Qxc6+ Black resigns

As scores of delighted readers pointed out – you can't castle if you've moved the king.

♜

Next, the worst display of ignorance by a grandmaster.

At world championship level, you figure that both players know the rules of chess. Imagine umpire O'Kelly's[1] emotions in the Korchnoi–Karpov match (Moscow, 1974) when Korchnoi strolled over to him in one game and posed a beginner's query: can I castle if my rook is attacked? Answer: Yes. Korchnoi's explanation: 'It had never come up before.'

♜

Two nominations for most astounding unconscious breach of the rules (castling again). In the France–Hungary match, 1983, Kouatly (France), against Sax played 24. ... O–O–O, although fourteen moves earlier he'd moved his rook to d8 and then back to a8. No one noticed until the game was published.

♜

And in Ireland in 1973, a player castled twice in the same game – and got away with it. Heidenfeld (a strong player), playing Kerins in a club match, castled king-side. Subsequently, under attack, he moved his king back to the king's square; then, forgetfully, he castled queen-side. No one noticed. (He lost the game, but entered the record books.)

♜

[1] See Chapter VI for his full name.

More worsts:

Worst simultaneous performances on record:

In August 1977, Joe Hayden, aged seventeen, tried to set an American record by challenging 180 people to a simultaneous chess display in a shopping centre in Cardiff, New Jersey. Only twenty showed up. His score – eighteen losses (including one to a seven-year-old) and two wins. One win happened because his opponent got tired of waiting and drifted away. Joe's other win was scored against his mum.

♜

In the early years of this century, according to *Chess*, the Viennese master Josef Krejcik got the worst birthday present in chess history. Having reached his twenty-fifth birthday, he took on twenty-five players in a simul. The result was immaculate: 0–25.

♜

The worst claim to a world record: in 1925 José Juncosa of Saragossa in Spain (immortalized through the opening 1. c3) announced he was going to attempt to play thirty-two people simultaneously, blindfold. Only three of the thirty-two he'd invited came to the display and he didn't do too well against them. This didn't stop Juncosa from claiming the record: 'Won twenty-nine (by default), drew one, lost two.'

♜

Daftest use of chess in English literature: the romantic novelist Ouïda, in her novel *Strathmore*, has one of her female characters 'castling her adversary's Queen, and nestling herself in her chaise to await his next move' (disinterred by Norman Knight – see our bibliography).

♜

Another entrant in this category: Gilbert Frankau in *Experiments in Crime* has a character playing 'King's pawn to king one'.

♜

A parallel award for television goes to Anthony Aloysius Hancock, none other. In *The Radio Ham*, the champion of Railway Cuttings sent the following improbable move zinging into the ether: 'King's pawn to queen's bishop three.' His Yugoslavian opponent replied with the equally implausible: 'Queen's pawn to king's rook two, checkmate.' (!)

♜

Most boring tournament performance: grandmaster István Bilek agreed ten short draws out of ten, the games taking a mere nine to seventeen moves each (125 moves in 109 minutes) at Słupsk in 1979.

✗

Worst writer on chess: an easy win for the impenetrable Franklin Knowles Young (1857–1931). For a flavour of his style, here's how Young describes checkmate: 'Given a Geometric Symbol Positive or a combination of Geometric Symbols Positive which is coincident with the Objective Plane; then if the Prime Tactical Factor can be posted at the Point of Command, the adverse King may be checkmated' (*The Grand Tactics of Chess*, 1896). Got it?

✗

The worst opening is called, gaelophobically, the Irish Gambit; it has been dignified by inclusion in Hooper and Whyld's admirable book *The Oxford Companion to Chess*.

It goes (unbelievably):

1. e4 e5   2. Nf3 Nc6   3. Nxe5

The inventor of this opening was asked on his deathbed what possessed him to take the pawn. 'I didn't see it was defended' he gasped, and expired.

✗

The worst advice—'Great players never castle'—was given in *Kort Afhandling* by Königstedt, the oldest Swedish textbook on chess (1784). A subsequent edition improved this to: 'Good players seldom castle.'

✗

Worst equipment in a national event: in a section of the 1946–7 Hastings tournament, one of the competitors complained that his clock was going backwards.

✗

The worst decision by a referee? Up there among the shoals of contenders must be the arbiter supervising Denker v. Reshevsky in an American tournament. Sammy Reshevsky overstepped the time limit. The referee picked up the clock, turned it towards him and in doing so, reversed it. (It's easily done.) So Denker was given a loss instead of Sammy. Uproar: but the result stood.

✗

The worst bit of psycho-analysis: 'To checkmate the opponent's King in chess is equivalent to castrating him and devouring him, becoming one with him in a ritual of symbolic homosexuality and cannibalistic communion, thus responding to the remnants of the infantile Oedipus complex' (from a 1960 paper by Dr Felix Martí Ibañez, and reprinted, courtesy of William Hartston, in *Chess Notes*).

♜

Stuff like this prompted the comment (on Grandmaster Fine's giving up chess for psycho-analysis): 'a great loss for chess, at best a draw for psycho-analysis'.

♜

The worst commentary on a chess game may have happened in London in 1986. It's the first game of the world championship. Kasparov and Karpov are playing a pretty boring Grünfeld Defence and the masters in the commentary box are having a bad time thinking of anything interesting to say to the audience, listening on headphones. Suddenly there's a flurry of exchanges which the masters miss entirely. To the bewilderment of their listeners, they start analysing a totally irrelevant position. By the time they realize their goof the game has moved on too far for them to reconstruct the moves. Their panic is allayed by the arrival of one of the most respected chess pundits in Britain. You can hear the relief as they announce: 'Here is International Master Blank straight from the press room; he'll bring us right up to date. Over to you, Blank.' Blank's reply was memorable: 'I'm so pissed I can't stand up.'

♜

The Tony Blackburn award for naffest chess compère: our vote goes to Tony Bastable of Thames TV, not least for his habit of interrupting Kasparov's fascinating post-mortem analysis with dumb questions.[1] In the words of *The Times*' Andrew Hislop: 'He approaches chess like a Brut salesman at a miners' conference ...'

♜

The most boring games of all time? We turn to the London tournament of 1851, and the interminable encounters between Elijah (the Bristol Sloth) Williams and the deservedly unknown James Mucklow ('a player from the country' says the tournament book sniffily). Elijah introduced the concept of *Sitzkrieg* into chess: he'd sit there, taking two and a half hours or more on a single move until his opponent dropped from boredom. The tournament book records games in excess of twenty hours (one was adjourned after a whole day, at the twenty-ninth move). Mucklow (a much worse player) was no swifter, and when they got

[1] e.g. 'How you think so far ahead?'

together it must have been like watching an oil painting. ('Both players nearly asleep,' recorded a drowsy secretary midway through one mind-grinding marathon.) Howard Staunton's commentary says it all: 'Each...exhibits the same want of depth and inventive power in his combinations, and the same tiresome prolixity in manoeuvring his men. It need hardly be said that the games, from first to last, are remarkable only for their unvarying and unexampled dullness.'[1]

♜

Another contender for the slowest player award might be Louis Paulsen; (according to some editions of *The Guinness Book of Records* he once took *eleven* hours over one move). In mitigation, he was one of the greatest players of the nineteenth century. Still, he's worthy of note if only for an anecdote that made Bobby Fischer laugh for days. He was playing Morphy (one of the quickest players in history), and taking aeons over his move. Many leaden hours of silent cerebration ticked slowly by. Even Morphy, normally the acme of politeness, was constrained to remark: 'Excuse me, but why don't you make a move?' Paulsen came to with a jerk: 'Oh, is it really my move?' No wonder Morphy gave up chess.

♜

The most long-winded notation: that in the fifteenth-century book by Lucena, *Repetición de Amores E Arte de Axedrez*: 'Jugar del peon del rey a IIII casas, que se entiende contando de donde esta el rey.' Nowadays they write e4.

♜

Before we conclude this collection of supergoofs, you may like to have our choice for the all-time rock bottom: the worst blunder of all. There are four contenders for the title, quite different in kind, but each of epic proportions. You choose.

Number one is from the master with the hardest name to pronounce: Przepiórka. He's playing Ahues (Black) in an important tournament (Kecskemét) 1936. This is the position:

---

[1] For even slower games, see Chapter VI.

Black played … Rxd2. After much thought, White picked up Black's rook and *captured his own bishop* (on b2). Ahues, getting the flavour of the thing, carried on by capturing the pawn on a2. Przepiórka had lost three pieces in one and a half moves: a world record. Sadly for our story, the tournament director, a spoilsport, stepped in and made them play the moves again. (P.S. Pronounce it P'shepiorka.)

Number two is what German chess-players call a Fingerfehler. It's what happens when the brain sends out an instruction to the hand – and gets number unobtainable.

The protagonists are Herr Lindemann and Herr Echtermayer, and they're playing in a tournament in Kiel in 1893. On move 3, Lindemann, wishing to move a knight, touches his queen's bishop by mistake. According to the rules of the time, he must move his king. The result is this sparkler:

Lindemann–Echtermayer

1. e4 d5   2. exd5 Qxd5   3. Ke2?? Qe4 mate

Number three is much simpler. It's New York 1963, the last round of the American championship. Bisguier and Fischer are equal first. Fischer doesn't make a move for a long time. Bisguier looks up and sees his opponent is fast asleep. In another half-hour the great Bobby's clock will fall, making Bisguier the champ. That's where we come to the ultimate blunder. In Bisguier's words: 'I made a bad move. I woke up Bobby Fischer.' And of course Bobby, after a couple of yawns, went on to collect his fifth US title.

Our fourth example is the most encouraging of all. Here are two of the greatest masters who ever lived, both missing something we ordinary mortals wouldn't.

It's Rubinstein–Nimzowitsch, San Sebastián, 1912.

Rubinstein is threatening Qxf7+ followed by Qxf8+.

Nimzo 'prevents' it by Bc5?? and Rubinstein plays Bd4?? instead of
... well, you tell us.

IV *The Unacceptable*

You may knock your opponent down with a chess board but that does not prove you are a better player.   *Proverb*

If you ain't cheatin' you ain't tryin'.   *James Coburn*

You should be nice at all times but there is a lot to be said for an elbow in the chops when all else fails. This is forceful psychology.
Bill Russell, basketball star

You can't play chess if you're kind-hearted.   *French proverb*

Sports do not build character; they reveal it.   *Heywood Broun*

A bad bishop

Next time you kick the board over, this is the chapter to make you feel better. It's a monument to sore losers; a collection of the baddest of bad scenes; and an instructive guide by some of the world's leading exponents on how not to behave around a chessboard.

'We are all one people' is the International Chess Federation's peaceful motto;[1] but now and again the agony of losing becomes insupportable (or the craving for victory at any price becomes overwhelming), and the quiet game gets rough. So in this chapter, we unflinchingly present behaviour that would not be out of place in Madison Square Garden – or on the Centre Court at Wimbledon.

It also takes in such side-issues as cheating, bribery, murder, and drunkenness in charge of a chessboard.

Welcome to the Chamber of Horrors.

♘

The Caliph al-Walīd the First, shouting 'Woe be unto you', cracked open a courtier's head for throwing a game in about AD690; not much later another Caliph (al-Ma'mūn) became the first person in history to knock the board over;[2] and a thousand years ago Ibn al-Mu'tazz wrote complaining of chess-players swearing, squabbling, making excuses and generally behaving badly.

♘

Things didn't improve as chess spread to Europe. Swearing, for example (the more delicately nurtured of our readers should skip the next couple of paragraphs):

We have already seen ('The Royals'), the Dauphin of France, after losing a series of games to Prince Henry of England, 'called him the

[1] *Gens Una Sumus*, actually.

[2] But not the last. The long list of people who've sent the chessman flying includes Napoleon, Lenin, Alekhine and the sixteen-year-old Bobby Fischer. Bobby was normally impeccably behaved at the board, but after losing a game to Pachman at Mar del Plata in 1959 he was sufficiently miffed to hit the pieces. And as we go to press, Viktor Korchnoi did it. 'Korchnoi scatters the pieces in chess walkout' said *The Times* headline. In a drawn position he'd touched the wrong piece accidentally, against Karpov (SWIFT Tournament, Brussels 1987). Bam! went the chessmen, and out stormed old Vik.

fonne of a Baftard, and threw the Cheffe in his face'.

This was mild stuff compared to that recorded in *The Noble and Puissant Galyen Rethore*, an ancient tale of chivalry. Galyen having mated his uncle Thibert one evening after supper got the old board-over-the-head treatment; and then, adding ins. to inj. Thibert called the noble and puissant Galyen 'Baftardly fonne of a whore'. (It's no excuse that Uncle Thibert's curse later turned out to have been at least partly true; Galyen's mother was bedded fifteen times in one night by a passing count for a bet – but we digreff).

♞

Our gold medal for cursing, however, goes to an Icelandic priest. Here's Father Stefan Olafsson getting it off his chest after losing a piece circa 1650:

'My malediction I utter – may Steini's men fall in heaps! May my fearful incantation bewitch him, so that peril shall beset two or three of his pieces at once! May the Old One (the queen) lose her life! May the wee pawns grow fewer and fewer on the squares and may he be mated both with the low and high mates!' Nasty.

♞

The Harvey Smith award for silent profanity goes to the ingenious designer of a handcarved chess-set in the Bavarian National Museum in Munich. It's eighteenth century, probably Flemish, and particularly interesting is the bishop. The upper part is decorated with a gay acanthus design; if you lose, you press a button and out pops a little man, baring his bottom at your opponent (see illustration at the beginning of the chapter).

We should, *en passant*, mention a twentieth-century entrant who might have challenged Father Stefan for the gold: woman grandmaster Alla Kushnir of Israel (and ex-USSR). In a famous telegram sent to Viktor Korchnoi after his thirteenth match game against Boris Spassky in 1977, Alla called Boris (who we always thought was Mr Nice Guy) a ****, a ****, and a ****. But since the book of the match[1] refused to translate the asterisks because of the laws of libel, Ms Kushnir's entry must be *hors concours*.

♞

Turning from bad-mouthing to bad sports, we nominate three outstanding contenders for the title of worst loser in chess history.

[1] *Korchnoi vs. Spassky, Chess Crisis*, by Raymond Keene.

In third place, former World Champion Alexander Alekhine, a notoriously temperamental loser. At Vienna in 1922, Alekhine resigned spectacularly against Grünfeld by hurling his king across the room.[1]

In the silver-medal position, another famous loser – a world title contender of the twenties, Aron Nimzowitsch. At a lightning chess tournament in Berlin, he said out loud what all of us have at one time felt. Instead of quietly turning over his king, Nimzo leapt on to his chair and bellowed across the tournament hall: 'Why must I lose to this idiot?' Not nice, but one knows the feeling.

But the gold medal, plus the John McEnroe Award for bad behaviour at a tournament, goes to the lesser-known Danish player (reported in *The Chess Scene*) who lost as a result of a fingerslip involving his queen. Unable to contain his despair, he snuck back into the tournament hall at dead of night, and cut the heads off all the queens.

♘

All of which goes to confirm that depressing chess adage: the pain of losing is greater than the joy of winning. We'd sooner not name him, but in 1977 an American player certainly felt that way. After a particularly hurtful loss he tried to end it all. Unsuccessfully, we're happy to relate.

♘

Murder and chess are, happily, infrequent companions these days, but as you saw in 'The Royals' section, it wasn't always thus. The London Law Rolls contain a couple of thirteenth-century examples (e.g. William of Wendene stabbed his opponent to death during a chesse quarrel in 1254 and had to seek sanctuary in a nearby church); and according to some sources, at least two world-class players met their death by poison: Paolo Boi and Leonardo da Cutri, probably the two best players in the world in 1575.

Boi's life reads like an adventure story from the *Boys' Own Paper*. He travelled to Spain where he carved up the best players of the day at the Spanish court. On his way back to Italy (having netted a life pension from King Philip for his skill) he was captured by Algerian pirates, sold into slavery, and earned his freedom through his chess skill (he made his master a fortune in side-bets). He later travelled to Hungary where he beat the best Turkish players the hard way – on horseback. Paolo ended up in Naples in 1598, poisoned, it is said, by a jealous rival.

[1] Or so it is said. These stories grow in the telling – like the one of Alekhine 'reducing the furniture in his hotel room to matchwood' after a particularly galling loss to Yates.

Leonardo da Cutri's end, according to one source, was straight out of Hammer Films. He, having been thoughtless enough to upset the Borgias, had a terminal interview with a Borgia hit man. Death by forcible poisoning was the verdict; the gruesome part is that when they removed the gag from around his mouth, a pawn was found clenched between Leonardo's teeth.[1]

The next murder at the chessboard is more reliably documented. It's New York City 1960. A seaman goes into a Greenwich Village bar and throws out the challenge that John L. Sullivan made famous: 'I can lick any man in the house.' Unlike the great John L., however, the matelot didn't make it stick: he lost. In the animated post-game debate a spectator, one Clinton Curtis, was struck in the jugular vein with a broken beer bottle. The sailor was lucky: 'accidental death' was the jury's verdict.

And happily for chess, a murder-at-the-board attempt during the last round of the great interzonal tournament at Saltsjöbaden, 1948, failed. The intended victim was one of the outstanding geniuses of modern chess, USSR grandmaster David Bronstein; the assailant, a political nutter, was removed by the local constabulary. David was shaken, but hung on to win the game and the tournament.

Finally, before we leave this macabre section, there is the story of Alekhine's terrible confession. Alekhine, near the end of his life, lonely and sick, but still world champion, told a friend of the amazing happenings at the great St Petersburg tournament of 1914. One night, in mid-tournament, there's a knock on Alekhine's hotel room door. A ragged old Russian peasant demands entrance, saying he has found a chess secret of great importance. Impatiently Alekhine lets him enter. 'I have found a way for white to checkmate in twelve from the starting position,' claims the old man. Alekhine starts to throw him out, but the peasant is insistent. To end matters, Alekhine sets up the board. Twelve moves later, the future world champion, white-faced, turns his king over. 'Do that again,' he says. The old man does. And again. Aghast, Alekhine hustles the old man along the corridor, to the room of his great

[1] The great authority on these matters, Murray, says of the main source for stories about Boi and Da Cutri (Salvio's *Il Puttino*): 'It is not easy to distinguish the basis of truth from the superstructure of fable.'

colleague Capablanca. The same sequence of events happens. Capablanca thinks first it's a bad joke: he ends up beaten again and again in twelve no matter what defence he tries.

As Alekhine concluded his sensational account, the friend leans forward eagerly and asks the question you are now asking yourself: 'Then what did you do?' Alekhine's devastating reply: 'Why, we killed him of course.'

Before you throw this book in the fire in disbelief, we'd better come clean. The above (roughly) is the plot of a terrific short story we read some years ago; annoyingly we couldn't track it down. If you know the source, drop us a line.

⌘

Our next section covers grievous bodily harm i.e. chess acrimony stopping short of actually eliminating your opponent.

Here's a letter from the Revd Sydney Smith, Canon of St Paul's, London, to the Canon of Worcester in 1837, about someone who should have known better:

'I was at school with the Archbishop of Canterbury. Forty-three years ago he knocked me down with a chess-board for checkmating him, and now he is attempting to take away my patronage.'

How different from the life of our own Archbishop Runcie (who, as we've observed, doesn't play chess at all).

⌘

Physical violence around the board seems on the wane in modern chess, although both authors were present at a Thames Valley League match in the seventies when the Richmond board four, in animated discussion with Hammersmith's team captain, threw a right hook that wouldn't have disgraced Mike Tyson.

⌘

At a more elevated level, the most notable bit of aggro in modern chess happened at a London club (Purssell's) in 1867. World champion Steinitz, a pretty irascible character at the best of times, fell out with the great English master, Joseph Henry Blackburne (nicknamed The Black Death). The way Steinitz told it, Blackburne assaulted him, and gave him a black eye – so the world champion spat at him. Other versions have Steinitz spitting first and Blackburne knocking him through a window in retaliation. We shall never know. What we do know is that the same pugnacious pair were at it again in Paris some years later.

♞

Since then, very little physical stuff, although GMs Reshevsky and Najdorf were involved in a post-game scuffle at the Amsterdam tournament of 1950.

♞

The most tension-packed match of modern times was a world title eliminator. Korchnoi–Petrosian (1977) was billed as the Match of Hate; it featured more aggro than the Stretford end on a Saturday afternoon and culminated in the organizers having to put a board under the table to stop the two grandmasters kicking each other.

♞

Petrosian was no stranger to g.b.h. at the chessboard. When he lost his famous match against Fischer in 1971, his wife, noted for her excessive partisanship, slapped the face of grandmaster Alexei Suetin – her husband's second.

Mrs Petrosian also features in our next section – gamesmanship, not to say downright cheating.

♞

Sharp practice at the chessboard has a long and doleful history. Not quite cheating, but teetering on the extreme limits of gamesmanship was Lucena's advice in his famous textbook (1497): 'Try to play after your opponent has eaten or drunk freely' and Ruy López' suggestion that you place the board 'so that the sun is in your opponent's eyes' (unhelpful to modern English club players).

♞

More modern examples of gamesmanship include Lasker and his famous mephitic cigars;[1] Alekhine and his cats (one called 'Chess', another 'Checkmate'), which he used to put on the board before an important game – tough if you were allergic;[2] and a trio of world champions who were not above using music as a weapon. Steinitz would quietly hum *Tannhäuser* during games (Wagner, on receiving this information, expressed the hope that Steinitz' humming ability was better than his own chess ability); Bobby Fischer (in casual games) used to whistle the *Bridge on the River Kwai* theme ('Colonel Bogey') when in a winning position; and Bourdonnais used to sing at the chessboard (and 'swore tolerably round oaths' when things weren't going so well).

---

[1] It is at this point we omit the over-used story of Nimzowitsch complaining that his opponent, Vidmar, was threatening to smoke.
[2] He used this ploy against Euwe in a world-title match.

♘

We draw a veil over some of the more extreme forms of bad behaviour, pausing briefly to mention Mason's spitting and an allegation that a late world champion used the corner of a tournament hall as a urinal during a simul (anticipating the behaviour of TV's most colourful snooker player by several decades) and we move hurriedly on to plain cheating.

♘

The first example of downright crookedness we have is also a leading contender for the all-time bad sportsmanship award. The Sultan Suleiman (Suleiman the Rotter, they should have called him) was playing a blind chap in 1557. Feeling the need for a little extra help, the Sultan nicked a rook from his opponent's side of the board. As the sightless one remarked afterwards – if anyone else had done it, he would have complained to the Sultan.

♘

In modern times, cheating is generally less obvious, but just as appalling.

Take Mrs Petrosian (again). In 1962 she 'won' a world title shot for her husband by organizing a night of grandmaster analysis to help a relative outsider, US grandmaster Benko, find a winning line against Paul Keres (Petrosian's fellow Soviet grandmaster and his main rival for the title shot). The result: Petrosian won the tournament, and eventually the title. Worse, at Zagreb in 1970, Mrs P. is not best pleased to see Bobby Fischer walking away with the tournament. In the middle of Bobby's game against the unfancied Yugoslav Kovačević, her husband and Korchnoi spot a Fischer trap. To Korchnoi's horror, Mrs Petrosian oils across to the game and whispers the news to Kovačević. The result – one of the shocks of the tournament – a rare loss for Fischer.

R. J. Fischer–V. Kovačević, Rovinj/Zagreb, 1970. French Defence

1. e4 e6	9. Ne2 b6	17. Qg5 Rdg8	25. Nf1 Rxg2+
2. d4 d5	10. Bg5 Qe7	18. f3[1] e3	26. Ke1 Qh4+
3. Nc3 Bb4	11. Qh4 Bb7	19. Bxe3 Nf8	27. Kd2 Ng6
4. a3 Bxc3+	12. Ng3 h6	20. Qb5 Nd5	28. Re1 Ngf4
5. bxc3 dxe4	13. Bd2 O-O-O	21. Kf2 a6	29. Bxf4 Nxf4
6. Qg4 Nf6	14. Be2 Nf8	22. Qd3 Rxh2	30. Qe3 Rf2
7. Qxg7 Rg8	15. O-O Ng6	23. Rh1 Qh4	White resigns
8. Qh6 Nbd7	16. Qxh6 Rh8	24. Rxh2 Qxh2	

[1] The trap: black can win the queen by 18. Nh4 but after 19. fxe4 Rxg5 20. Bxg5 white is on top.

There's a happy ending, though. Bobby, despite all, strolled to a great tournament win. Mrs Petrosian's favourite grandmaster finished sixth.

♘

But if Mrs Petrosian has a dodgy form card, how about Yugoslav grandmaster Milan Matulović? Golombek's *Encyclopedia of Chess* accuses him euphemistically of 'extravagant behaviour'. What this means is that Milan has more than once been caught trying to get away with stuff that would get him thrown off any primary-school chess team. Against Bilek at Sousse in 1967 he, not liking his position, *took a move back*, saying as he did so, '*J'adoube*.'[1] Bilek's jaw dropped, but the arbiter hadn't seen the outrage and Matulović went on to win. According to David Levy and Stewart Reuben (*The Chess Scene*) the sneaky Slav repeated the same horror in the same year – against the same opponent. Which is why, for a while, Matulović was known on the tournament circuit as J'adoubovich.[2]

♘

And in 1970, the experts reckon Matulović threw his last-round game to help Taimanov qualify for the next round of world title matches (he arrived fifteen minutes late, and spent most of the game wandering round the tournament room, chatting to spectators). The game was played by M., say Wade and Blackstock in the tournament book, 'at colossal speed'.

For this sad effort, our hero is rumoured to have received $400 under the table. It is some comfort to know that the 'winner', as a result of this game, went on to play Bobby Fischer – and was terminally crushed 6–0.

For more Matulović beastliness see 'The Bizarre'.

♘

The most recent and (if you're English) outrageous bit of cheating happened in November 1986. It's the Chess Olympiad; England, who were silver medallists in 1984, are doing even better – they're leading the field, the unbeatable Soviets are in third place and a sensational upset is on. England are due to play Spain (who are not in the top dozen rated teams) and expect an easy win. But before the match, the Russians lend the Spaniards their precious dossiers on each member of the English team. Now this, while not exactly ethical, isn't crooked either. But

[1] See glossary.
[2] A more eminent practitioner of this tactic may have been a former world champion. Alekhine was accused of having touched a rook *before* saying '*J'adoube*', against Schmidt in 1941.

what followed was: in the middle of the match, Georgadze, the Spanish team trainer (a USSR grandmaster) 'discussed' the Illescas–Nunn game loudly enough for Illescas to hear his suggestion. The result – Nunn lost, and the English team went down 3½–½. England's final result in the Olympiad was a notable silver medal – but half a point more would have meant gold for them instead of USSR.

♘

The best player Brazil ever produced was Henrique Mecking, one of the giants of the seventies. Tragically his career was cut short by illness; but whilst he was around he was a fearsome opponent and not just because of his chess skill. When he played a match with Korchnoi he fidgeted so much the table shook; and during the Hastings tournament of 1971–72 he tried a novel tactic against future Welsh international George Botterill: when they were both in time trouble, Henrique pressed his clock, then kept it pressed down so poor old George couldn't stop *his* ticking. The result – a loss on time for Botterill, and third place for the (if you'll excuse the expression) irrepressible Brazilian.

♘

We leave the best bit of skulduggery to the last.

George Treysman, king of New York coffee-house players was a legendary win-at-all-costs tactician. Playing in the smoke, noise and confusion of New York cafés, he is said to have got away with murder. His most brilliant improvisation was in the heat of a blitz game: Treysman, a rook down, managed successfully to castle with another rook from an adjacent game. He won, collected his dime, and speedily set up the pieces for a fresh game, while three other confused chess-players tried to figure out what had happened.

It is also said – but you don't have to believe it – that Treysman once managed to castle with a salt cellar from the tray of a passing waiter. Treysman never opened a chess book and rarely played outside New York cafés – but on one memorable occasion, in his first major tournament, he finished equal third with grandmaster Fine in the first modern US Championship.

V *The Awesome*

Wait a minute, wait a minute, you ain't heard nothing yet, folks!
Al Jolson

The Philosopher invents the game of chess
William Caxton, *Game and Playe of the Chesse*

Warning: over-indulgence in the material in this section could very easily turn you into the club bore. (On the other hand, judicious use of it could win you quite a few bets down the pub.) It's a collection of somewhat technical facts of the type that are normally preceded by the words 'Not a lot of people know this but . . .'

It's also your opportunity to break a world record. If you have the score of a game played under match conditions which lasted longer than 193 moves, or in which you castled later than the forty-sixth, or if you can better any other of the arcane feats mentioned below, you're in with a chance. Drop us a line, care of Faber and Faber.

♟

One of the many legends about the invention of chess goes like this. Many centuries ago in India there lived a Brahmin called Sissa (or possibly Sassa). The ruler of his province was a tyrant and in order to teach him a lesson the crafty Brahmin invented the game of chess. This demonstrated to the ruler that a king can only succeed with the help of his subjects. Enlightened by this revelation he offered Sissa a reward: anything in the kingdom he asked for would be his. 'I am a humble man,' replied the Brahmin. 'I only want a modest reward. Just give me one grain of rice on the first square of the chessboard, two on the second, double the number, four on the third, and so on up to the sixty-fourth square.' 'Surely you'd like something better than that,' entreated the king. 'Look at all these nubile serving girls, this fine jewellery, gold and diamonds. Whatever you want, it shall be yours.' 'No, no. Just give me the rice,' insisted Sissa. So the king got out the rice sacks. The more mathematically inclined among our readers will already have realized that the total number of grains of rice Sissa asked for was $2^{64}-1$, or 18,446,744,073,709,551,615 grains of rice. This would cover England to a depth of 10 metres, or sow the entire land mass of the planet 76 times. (In some versions of the story, Sissa got his head chopped off for being a smartyboots.)

♟

A few more large numbers. The number of different legal positions on a chessboard is 2×10^{43}. The number of different 40-move games has been estimated at 25×10^{115}. This is considerably larger than the estimated number of electrons in the universe: 10^{79}.

♟

In the starting array, white has a choice of 20 moves, and black a choice of 20 replies, making a total of 400 possible positions after one move by each side. After two moves by each side the number is 71,852. In 232 of these positions white will have the option of making an *en passant* capture, so, theoretically speaking, the number should be 72,084, which may be reached in about 200,000 different ways. After three moves the number of possible positions is somewhere over nine million. If you wanted to reach every possible position after four moves, taking one minute for each one, it would take you a matter of 600,000 years.

♟

The longest possible game, applying the 50-move rule, would conclude on white's 5,949th move. FIDE has decreed that in certain positions 100 moves, rather than 50, are allowed on each side. It is only possible to reach one of these positions in a game, so the figure for the longest possible legal game can be raised to 5,999.

♟

The longest game actually played (excluding deliberate record-creating attempts)was Stepak–Mashian, played in Israel in 1980. The game lasted 24 hours 30 minutes, black resigning on move 193. Sadly, Mashian blundered on move 186, otherwise, the game would probably have gone on to about move 210. White's c-pawn in this game also has a record all to itself. It moved to c4 on move 2, remaining there until being captured on move 173, a record 172 moves. For the masochists among you who would like to play through the game, here it is (actually it's rather interesting):

The Monster

Stepak–Mashian, Israel, 1980. Queen's Indian Defence

1. d4 Nf6	6. Nc3 Ne4	11. Qc2 Nd7	16. d5 Bf8
2. c4 e6	7. Qc2 Nxc3	12. e4 Qc7	17. Re2 g6
3. Nf3 b6	8. Qxc3 O–O	13. b3 Rfe8	18. Bc1 Bg7
4. g3 Bb7	9. O–O c5	14. Bb2 Rad8	19. Bg5 f6
5. Bg2 Be7	10. Rd1 d6	15. Rd2 e5	20. Bd2 Bc8

21. Nh4 Nf8	65. Be3 Bd8	109. Ke3 Kf7	153. Kh5 Bc1
22. h3 Bd7	66. b4 axb4	110. Ba4 Bh6	154. Kg4 Bd2
23. a4 Qc8	67. Kd3 Kf8	111. Kf3 Bf8	155. Kf3 Bc1
24. Kh2 a5	68. Bc1 Ke7	112. Kg4 Be7	156. Ke2 Bg5
25. Rf1 Qc7	69. Bb2 Kf8	113. Kh5 Kg7	157. Be1 Kf7
26. Qd3 g5	70. Kc2 Ke7	114. Bf2 Bf8	158. Bb1 Bf4
27. Nf5 Bxf5	71. Kb3 Kd7	115. Bh4 Be7	159. Bd2 Be5
28. exf5 Qf7	72. Bh5 Ke7	116. Bg5 Bd8	160. Bc2 Ke7
29. Re4 Nd7	73. Bc1 Kd7	117. Bd1 Be7	161. Kf3 Kf7
30. Qe2 Kh8	74. Bd2 Ke7	118. Bh6+ Kf7	162. Kg4 Kg7
31. Bf3 Rg8	75. Be1 Kd7	119. Kh4 Kg8	163. Bf4 Bxf4
32. Bh5 Qe7	76. Bd1 Kc7	120. Ba4 Kf7	164. Kxf4 Kh6
33. Kg2 Bh6	77. Kc2 Kd7	121. Kg4 Bd8	165. Ke3 Kg5
34. Rh1 Rg7	78. Kd3 Ke7	122. Bg5 Be7	166. Kd2 Kf4
35. h4 Rdg8	79. Bh4 Kd7	123. Kh5 Kg7	167. Kc1 Ke3
36. Kf1 Nf8	80. Kc2 Kc7	124. Bh4 Bf8	168. Kb2 Kd2
37. Rg4 Qd7	81. Kb3 Kb7	125. Be8 Be7	169. Kb3 Kc1
38. Qc4 Qc8	82. Bh5 Be7	126. Kg4 Kf8	170. Be4 Kd2
39. Ke2 Qd7	83. Be8 Kc7	127. Bd7 Kf7	171. Ka4 Kc3
40. Rh2 Qc8	84. Kc2 Kd8	128. Kf3 Bf8	172. Kb5 b3
41. Kd3 Qd7	85. a5 bxa5	129. Ke4 Bg7	173. Kc6 Kxc4
42. Kc2 Qe7	86. Ba4 Kc7	130. Bc6 Bh6	174. Kxd6 Kd4
43. Kb2 Qd7	87. Kd3 Kc8	131. Kd3 Bxf4	175. Bb1 c4
44. hxg5 Bxg5	88. Ke3 Kd8	132. Kc2 Ke7	176. Ke6 c3
45. f4 exf4	89. Kf3 h5	133. Kb3 Be5	177. d6 c2
46. gxf4 Bh6	90. Kg2 Kc7	134. Be1 Kd8	178. Bxc2 bxc2
47. Rxg7 Bxg7	91. Kh3 Kd8	135. Ka4 Kc7	179. d7 c1=Q
48. Bc3 h6	92. Bg3 Bf8	136. Kxa5 Bf4	180. d8=Q+ Ke4
49. Re2 Nh7	93. Kh4 Ke7	137. Ba4 Be5	181. Qd5+ Kf4
50. Qe6 Nf8	94. Kxh5 Kf7	138. Ka6 Bf4	182. Qd4+ Kg3
51. Qxd7 Nxd7	95. Kg4 Bg7	139. Bh4 Be5	183. Kf7 Qc2
52. Re6 Bf8	96. Kf3 Ke7	140. Bd1 Bd4	184. Qxf6 Kf4
53. Be8 Rg2+	97. Bh4 Kf7	141. Bg3 Be3	185. Qd6+ Kg4
54. Kc1 Rg1+	98. Ke4 Bf8	142. Kb5 Bh6	186. f6 Qh7+
55. Kd2 Rg2+	99. Kd3 Bg7	143. Ka4 Kd7	187. Kf8 Qh8+
56. Re2 Rxe2+	100. Kc2 Ke7	144. Kb3 Ke7	188. Ke7 Kf5
57. Kxe2 Kg7	101. Kb3 Kd8	145. Kc2 Bg5	189. Qe6+ Kf4
58. Bxd7 Be7	102. Bb5 Kc7	146. Kd3 Bc1	190. f7 Qh7
59. Be8 Bd8	103. Ka4 Kb6	147. Ke4 Bd2	191. Qe2 Kg3
60. Bh5 Kf8	104. Be8 Ka6	148. Kf3 Bc1	192. Qe5+ Kf2
61. Kd3 Ke7	105. Bb5+ Kb6	149. Kg4 Bd2	193 Ke6 Black
62. Ke4 Kf8	106. Kb3 Kc7	150. Kh5 Be3	resigns.
63. Bg6 Kg7	107. Kc2 Kd8	151. Kg6 Bg5	Phew!
64. Bd2 Be7	108. Kd2 Ke7	152. Bc2 Bd2	

A close runner-up, and the longest drawn game is Pilnik–Czerniak (Mar del Plata 1950), a mere 191 moves and 23 hours long.

As a British national record we suggest the game Miller–Uber, Cheltenham, 1913, which lasted 168 moves.

♟

We award a special prize for *Sitzfleisch* to the Romanian international master Drimer. The only titled player at Whitby, 1967, he duly won with 10 out of 11. What makes his performance remarkable was that three of his games, including his two draws, exceeded 100 moves (one lasting 132 moves and another 125 moves). See Chapter II for his horrible fate against a little girl.

♟

Also worth a mention is the longest game in a world championship match. This is Korchnoi–Karpov, the fifth game of their 1978 match, where White delivered stalemate on move 124. It was, incidentally, the only world championship game to have ended in stalemate.

♟

For the longest game without a capture (and a candidate for the most boring game of all time) we offer Filipowicz–Smederavac. This was a 70-move game in which White claimed a draw by the 50-move rule, having had several previous draw offers turned down. Here's their narcoleptic effort.

Filipowicz–Smederavac, Polanica Zdrój, 1966. French Defence

1. e4 e6	19. Nf3 Be7	37. Qg1 Bb7	55. Ree1 Ra6
2. d3 Ne7	20. h4 h5	38. Nb5 Raa8	56. Re2 Rba8
3. g3 c5	21. Qe2 Ncb4	39. Na3 Ba6	57. Ree1 R8a7
4. Bg2 Nbc6	22. Rfc1 Bb7	40. Qf1 Rab8	58. Na3 Ra8
5. Be3 b6	23. Kh2 Bc6	41. Nc4 Bd8	59. Nc4 Nh6
6. Ne2 d5	24. Na3 Ra8	42. Qd1 Ne7	60. Na3 Nf7
7. 0-0 d4	25. Qe1 Rdb8	43. Nd6 Bc7	61. Nf2 Rd8
8. Bc1 g6	26. Qg1 Qb7	44. Qe2 Ng8	62. Nc4 Rb8
9. Nd2 Bg7	27. Qf1 Kg7	45. Ng5 Nh6	63. Nh3 Bd8
10. f4 f5	28. Qh1 Qd7	46. Bf3 Bd8	64. Na3 Ra7
11. a3 O–O	29. Ne1 Ra7	47. Nh3 Ng4+	65. Qh1 Nh6
12. e5 a5	30. Nf3 Rba8	48. Kg1 Be7	68. Ng5 Nf7
13. a4 Ba6	31. Ne1 Bd8	49. Nc4 Nd5	69. Nh3 Qe8
14. b3 Rb8	32. Nf3 Rb8	50. Nf2 Bb7	70. Kh2 Rd7
15. Nc4 Qc7	33. Ne1 Bc7	51. Nh3 Bc6	Drawn by the
16. Kh1 Nd5	34. Nf3 Rh8	52. Qg2 Rhc8	50-move rule
17. Bd2 Rfd8	35. Ng5 Bd8	53. Re1 Rc7	(Zzzzzzzz)
18. Ng1 Bf8	36. Nf3 Be7	54. Re2 Ra7	

♟

Soviet grandmaster David Bronstein was in the habit of thinking half an hour or more over his first move. In a game played in 1982 Viktor Korchnoi thought for well over an hour and a half on his sixth move in a Ruy López opening. But the record 'longest think' since the introduction of chess clocks currently belongs to Brazilian IM Trois, who, against Santos at Vigo 1980, thought for two hours twenty minutes over his seventh move! The time limit for the tournament was (presumably) 40 moves in two and a half hours. The opening was 1. c4 e5 2. Nc3 Nf6 3. Nf3 Nc6 4. e4 Bc5 5. Nxe5 Bxf2+ 6. Kxf2 Nxe5 7. d4 and ... eventually ... Ng6.

♟

The records for latest castling have been tabulated, like much else in this section, by the indefatigable Tim Krabbé and published in *New In Chess* (a terrific English-language magazine for the real enthusiast) and his wonderful book *Chess Curiosities*. The record-holders at the time of writing look like this:

–Latest castling: Bobotsov–Ivkov, Beverwijk, 1966 (46. O–O).

–Latest castling by black: Soeterboek–Van der Heijden, Netherlands, 1981 (44. ... O–O).

–Latest queen-side castling: Popovych–Ivanov, New York, 1983 (43. ... O–O–O).

–Latest queen-side castling by white: Pupols–Myers, Lone Pine, 1976 (40. O–O–O). This game also holds the record for castling with the fewest pieces on the board – eight.

–Latest castling as sealed move: Magrin–Rosenblatt, Biel, 1972 (42. O–O), just half a move better than the previous, hitherto unpublished, record, James–Mozoomdar, Twickenham, 1971 (41. ... O–O). As this game was won by black, we shan't give the score.

–The record total of castling move numbers in one game is still held by Yates–Alekhine, San Remo, 1930, with a total of 60 (24. ... O–O, 36. O–O). This looks very beatable to us.

♟

The greatest number of queens on the board at once – a controversial one, this. The well-known five-queens 'game', Alekhine–Grigoriev, is actually only Alekhine's analysis of a Grigoriev–A. game. (Alekhine was also notorious for doctoring the finishes to his games to make them look more brilliant than they really were.) Hoax games with six and seven queens on the board have also been published. But the only genuine game with five queens on the board at once remains Tresling–Benima (Winschoten, 1896) – see below. Black had three queens against one in Williams–Ginsburg, New York, 1982–3 and in Dely–F. Portisch (Budapest, 1968) black resigned on seeing White's third queen appear on the board. (This record excludes the many thousands of games in kiddie tournaments where one player tries to queen as many pawns as possible, so don't write and tell us that your seven-year-old son got five queens in a school game.) The greatest number of queens to appear at any time in one game is seven, this record standing to Konopleva–Schmidke (1968): black scoring four queens to three and winning the game.

Tresling–Benima, Winschoten, 1896. Ruy López

1. e4 e5	13. axb3 e4	25. Qd1 c5	37. Be5 Bxe5
2. Nf3 Nc6	14. Nd2 O–O	26. dxc5 Bxb2	38. Qxe5 a2
3. Bb5 a6	15. c4 Rfe8	27. Rf4 Qe7	39. d7 Qa3
4. Ba4 Nf6	16. Nxe4 Nxe4	28. Qxh5 Bf6	40. c7 b3
5. Nc3 Be7	17. Qxe4 Bf6	29. cxd6 Qxd6	41. d8=Q b2
6. O–O b5	18. Qd3 Qg4	30. Qf3 Re5	42. c8=Q b1=Q
7. Bb3 d6	19. Be3 b4	31. Re4 Rxe4	(and there we
8. d3 Be6	20. f4 h5	32. Qxe4 Qg3	are – five
9. Qe2 Qd7	21. h3 Qd7	33. Bf4 Qxb3	queens)
10. Nd5 Bxd5	22. f5 Qe7	34. d6 Rf8	
11. exd5 Na5	23. Rae1 a5	35. c5 a4	
12. d4 Nxb3	24. Kh1 Qe4	36. c6 a3	

Position after black's 47th move.

43. Qxf8+ Qxf8 44. Qxf8+ Kxf8 45. Qe8 mate

We also have one game with five knights on the board at once – Szabó–Ivkov, Belgrade, 1964. Black's three horsepower proved better than white's two and he triumphed in 93 moves. Underpromotion to a knight is relatively common as the knight has properties denied to a queen, but a unique case arose in the Yogoslav Ladies' Championship in 1985 where white had to promote to a knight to avoid a fork, leaving the first practical example of an ending with three knights against one (a win for the three knights as it happens).

Forced underpromotions (that is excluding trivial or facetious examples) to rook or bishop are very rare: Tim Krabbé only gives six examples. We are still awaiting the first game in which one player has three rooks or bishops on the board at once.

♟

The record for the piece making the longest series of moves goes to the Black queen belonging to James Mason, which made 73 consecutive moves (from move 72 to 144) before the point was shared in the second match game Mackenzie–Mason, London, 1882. This game also holds two other records: black's f and h pawns never moved during the whole game, and black's king reached g8 on move 8, remaining there for the game's remaining 136 moves.

♟

In Westerinen–Keres, Tallinn, 1969, black made 38 checks in succession, another record.

♟

In a game Clawson–Fletcher, USA, 1983, black made nine successive captures, which he claims as a record.

♟

The record for the longest series of mutual captures is 13, shared between Heidenfeld–Littleton, Dublin, 1964 and Suttles–Yepez, Nice Olympiad, 1974.

Heidenfeld–Littleton, Dublin, 1964. Bird's Opening

1. f4 Nf6	11. Qh4 e6	goes)... Nxc2	29. h3 Ke7
2. Nf3 g6	12. Ng5 h6	21. dxe4 Nxe3	30. b4 Kd6
3. b3 Bg7	13. Nf3 Nb4	22. Rxd6 Rxd6	31. Kf3 Rc4
4. Bb2 O–O	14. Rad1 Ne4	23. Nxd6 Rxe2	32. Ke3 f5
5. e3 b6	15. Qxd8 Rfxd8	24. Nxb7 Nxf1	Draw agreed
6. Be2 Bb7	16. Bxg7 Kxg7	25. Kxf1 Rxe4	
7. O–O c5	17. Ne1 b5	26. Nxc5 Rxf4+	
8. a4 a6	18. axb5 axb5	(end of sequence)	
9. Na3 d6	19. Nxb5 Ra2	27. Ke2 Kf6	
10. Qe1 Nc6	20. d3 (and here	28. Ned3 Rh4	

Suttles–Yepez, Nice Olympiad, 1974. English Opening

1. d3 e5	12. Nd4 d5	21. Qxe4 Qxe4	32. Re2 Rf7
2. c4 d6	13. bxc6 bxc6	22. Nxe4 Bb7	33. Re3 Rd2+
3. Nc3 f5	14. cxd5 cxd5	23. Re5 Bxe4	34. Kf3 Rdd7
4. g3 Nf6	15. Rb5 Ne6	24. Rxe4 Rab8	35. Rea3 Rc7
5. Bg2 c6	(Here we go	25. Ra4 Rf7	36. Kg4 Rb7
6. Nf3 Be7	again)	26. Rc1 g6	37. h5 Rbe7
7. O–O Na6	16. Bxe7 Nxd4	27. Rc2 Rbb7	38. hxg6 hxg6
8. Rb1 O–O	17. Rxd5 Nxe2+	28. Ra6 Kg7	39. R3a5 Kh7
9. b4 Qe8	18. Qxe2 Qxe7	29. h4 Rf5	40. Kg5
10. b5 Nc5	19. dxe4 fxe4	30. f4 Rd5	Black resigns
11. Ba3 e4	20. Bxe4 Nxe4	31. Kf2 Rd3	

♟

One other possible record that deserves mention if only for the stratospheric nature of both the contestants and circumstances was provided by the 32nd game of the notorious 1984 Karpov–Kasparov match. In this game both kings remained unmoved until White's 34th move, at which point there were only eleven pieces left on the board.

♟

The 1984 K–K match, of course, holds a number of other records. The longest world championship match (forty-eight games), the highest number of draws in a match (forty), the most consecutive draws in a match (seventeen), the only world championship match to be abandoned without a result. It is a little-known fact, however, that the dreaded Campo considered abandoning the 1978 Karpov–Korchnoi match in similar circumstances, at the point when Viktor was catching up on his rival. (This was reported in the Filipino book of the match.)

♟

The longest master tournament concerns our friends Mason and Mackenzie. In New York, January 1869, the forty-eight competitors had to meet each other twice. Unsurprisingly, not all the games were completed, the leading scores being Mackenzie (+82. −8). Delmar (+69 −13) and Mason (+69 −17).

♟

The esoteric field of chess problems has its own records. Lack of space prevents more than a brief mention of one of the longest direct mate problems. This effort, published back in 1889 by Ottó Bláthy, requires white to force mate in 290 moves. One of the black bishops is a promoted pawn. The solution starts with 1. Rd1+ Bd4 2. c4+ Kd6 3. Rxg1, and involves a 16-move manoeuvre repeated 17 times.

Vielzügige Schachaufgaben 1889

The Bláthy problem is, of course, illegal (look at the pawns and white bishops). The longest direct mate problem in a legal position is shown in the second diagram, composed by one of the most remarkable of contemporary composers, Nenad Petrović (Yugoslavia), in 1969. White is to play and mate in 270 moves. Again there is a promoted bishop on the board. The solution runs

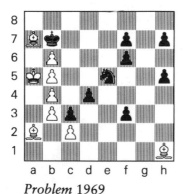

Problem 1969

1. Bb1 h4	2. Ka4 Ka8	(from here

to move 231 the black king moves between b7 and a8 except when he moves a pawn)

3. Ka3	11. Bb1	19. Ka1
4. Ka2	12. Kf1	20. Bb1
5. Ka1	13. Kf2	21. Ka2
6. Ba2	14. Ke1	22. Ka3
7. Kb1	15. Kd1	23. Ka4
8. Kc1	16. Kc1	Kb7
9. Kd1	17. Ba2	24. Ka5
10. Ke1	18. Kb1	f5

White now repeats moves 2 to 4 nine times, with black moving a pawn at the end. viz.

47. ... f4	208. ... h4	257. b8=Q f1=Q	264. Bxf4 Ke2
70. ... f6	231. ... h3	258. Qxe5 Qxh1	265. b6 d3
93. ... f5	and then	259. Qg7+ Ke6	266. cxd3 Kf2
116. ... h3	we reach	260. Qg6+ Ke5	267. Bc2 Ke2
139. ... h2	254. Ka5 Kc8	261. Bb8+ Ke4	268. Bd1+ Kf2
162. ... h6	255. Ka6 f2	262. Qc6+ Ke3	269. Qf3+ Kg1
185. ... h5	256. b7+ Kd7	263. Qxh1 Kf2	270. Be3 mate.

173

Our next diagram is a composition by J.N. Babson, dated 1882. White is to mate in 1220(!) moves, with the condition that the black knight makes three successive complete tours of the board. The authors regret that they do not have the solution to this problem. You may nevertheless try to solve it. Lots of luck.

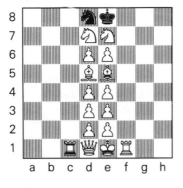

The award for the longest announced mate goes to Liverpool Chess Club, who, in the appended diagram from a correspondence game against Edinburgh Chess Club in 1901 announced mate in 45 moves.

The analysis starts

53. ... Bxf4	56. Kd4 c5+	60. Kb5 Kd6	64. cxb5 c4
(best)	57. Kc3 Kd7	61. f7 Ke7	65. b6
54. Kxf4 Kd6	58. Kb3 Kd6	62. Kc6 Kxf7	
55. Ke4 Ke6	59. Ka4 Kd7	63. Kb7 b5	

when White queens first and apparently mates on move 98.

Mrs Ellen Gilbert, an American correspondence player, certainly deserves an honourable mention here. In 1879 she played in a correspondence match between Britain and the USA against the egregious and hapless George Gossip, whom we met in Chapter III. In one game she announced mate in 21 moves, and in another mate in 35. From the diagrammed position in the latter game she analysed

42. .... g5	51. Kc3 g1=Q	60. Kc4 Ke5	69. Kxc6 a1=Q
43. hxg5 hxg5	52. Bxg1 Kxg1	61. Kc3 Ke4	70. Kd7 Ka3
44. Bd8 Kf4	53. Kd3 Kf2	62. Kc4 Ke3	71. c6 b2
45. e5 g4	54. Kd2 Kf3	63. Kc3 Ke2	72. c7 b1=Q
46. Bxc7 g3	55. Kd3 Kf4	64. Kb4 Kd2	73. c8=Q Qd4+
47. e6+ Kf3	56. Kc4 Ke5	65. Ka3 Kc2	74. Ke7 Qh7+
48. Be5 g2	57. Kb4 Ke6	66. Kb4 Kxb2	75. Ke6 Qg6+
49. Bd4 Ke2	58. Kc4 Kxe7	67. Ka5 a3	76. Ke7 Qdd6
50. e7 Kf1	59. Kb4 Ke6	68. Kb6 a2	mate

This diagram shows a position in which Blackburne announced mate in 16 as follows:

175

1. Rxe6+ Kh7	5. Be6+ Kf8	9. Rxa7+ Kb8	13. Rf7+ Kd8
2. Qd3+ Rg6	6. Rf7+ Ke8	10. Nd7+ Kc8	14. Nb7+ Ke8
3. Qxg6+ fxg6	7. Nf6+ Kd8	11. Nc5+ Kd8	15. Nxd6+ Kd8
4. Re7+ Kg8	8. Rd7+ Kc8	12. Rd7+ Kc8	16. Bb6 mate.

Alternatives throughout lead to quicker mates. Nothing so remarkable about that, you may think; but no, it wasn't a correspondence game, and yes, this was one of eight games played simultaneously blindfold.

♟

Finally we present the oldest recorded game of modern chess. (For the oldest recorded game of any form of chess see chapter VII.) It comes from an allegorical poem published in Spain towards the end of the fifteenth century, shortly after the moves of the queen and bishop were changed. According to Murray it may well have been played over the board. Francisco de Castellvi took the red pieces and Narciso Viñoles the green.

F. de Castellvi–N. Viñoles, c.1475. Scandinavian Defence.

1. e4 d5	7. Qxf3 e6	13. Bb5+ Nxb5	19. Bf4 Bxf4
2. exd5 Qxd5	8. Qxb7 Nbd7	14. Qxb5+ Nd7	20. Qxd7+ Kf8
3. Nc3 Qd8	9. Nb5 Rc8	15. d5 exd5	21. Qd8 mate
4. Bc4 Nf6	10. Nxa7 Nb6	16. Be3 Bd6	
5. Nf3 Bg4	11. Nxc8 Nxc8	17. Rd1 Qf6	
6. h3 Bxf3	12. d4 Nd6	18. Rxd5 Qg6	

♟

VI *The Bizarre*

We are all born mad. Some remain so. *Samuel Beckett*

A useful invention   *P.H. Williams* 1909

You're not going to believe this, but a dog once played on board eight for Brighton third team. Honest. The details are in this chapter, together with the chess-playing monkey, the revolting habits of certain Indians, the exploits of the Mad Parson, and what your favourite chessmasters do when they aren't playing chess.

If you're a Trivial Pursuits addict, or if you find unputdownable all those mind-numbing collections of useless information that regularly appear in the *Sun* newspaper ('Twenty things you didn't know about Prince Charles's bald patch') you'll love what follows.

♖

Up to a few years ago the annual Hastings Christmas Congress took place beneath a concert hall which was staging a pantomime. As reported by Ray Keene in the *Spectator*, one of the players sent a spy to watch the panto. At one point a clown asked the children to stamp their feet loudly on the floor to disturb the chess-players below. Later, they were encouraged to stamp especially loudly because a Russian was winning the tournament.

♖

The 1876 Customs Act was introduced to prevent the import of indecent chess-pieces which were being sent to a girls' boarding school.

♖

The Dutch for 'resigns' is '*Geef het op*' and the Swedish is '*Upgivvet*'. The Swedish for 'good move' is '*bra drag*'.

♖

If you're sufficiently desperate for a reason to believe in the superiority of homo sapiens over other animals you may alight on the fact that only humans can play chess. But wait. Here's Baldasare Castiglione, the early sixteenth-century Italian author of a perfectly serious tome entitled *The Book of the Courtier*. Doubtless a man whose veracity is to be trusted. He tells us how the Portuguese brought a chess-playing ape back with them from the Indies. On one occasion the ape played the fellow who brought her back with him. The ape, needless to say, soon

179

forced checkmate, whereupon her victim, understandably miffed by this development, took the king and cuffed her about the ear with it. He then demanded his revenge and the ape, reluctantly, agreed. As the ape was about to play the winning move she took a cushion from under her opponent's arm and held it against her head with one hand while delivering checkmate with the other.

♖

Among the members of Brighton Chess Club in the 1930s was Mrs Sidney, an aristocratic old lady whose inseparable companion was her dog, Mick. At that time the club met in the splendid Royal Pavilion, built for George IV when he was Prince Regent. There was a strict rule: No Dogs Allowed, but the club secretary, not wishing to incur the fearsome old crone's wrath, pretended not to notice her canine companion. Then a new club secretary was appointed, who asked Mrs S. not to bring her dog in future. A tirade of angry words from Mrs S. and eventually a compromise was reached. Mick was to be elected a full member of the club, his owner paying the subscription. Some time later, the third team played a friendly match. The team captain, noticing a new name on the Members' List, decided that he should be given some match experience, so the name of Mr Mick went on to the match sheet. The result? He lost on time. Persistent rumour has it that the opening was the Collie System. (Unless he was a paw to king four player.)

♖

Chess magazine, in 1976, reviewed a volume entitled *Sex Mates of a Chess Mistress*. Quite apart from the rather dubious delights you might expect from the title ('nauseating to the point of hilarity') it features a chess-playing kangaroo. 'NOT available from stock,' they added. (This was not the first example of soft pawn. A pornographic novel published in 1968 called *The Pushers*,[1] whose author hid under the alias of Kenneth Harding, featured lookalikes of leading contemporary players.) players.)

♖

Chess Openings and Variations with Zoological Names
-Bird's Opening (1. f4, also known as Bird's Bastard)

-Orang-Utan Opening (1. b4)

-Döry Defence (1. d4 Nf6 2. c4 e6 3. Nf3 Ne4)

[1] No connection with Haroun al Rashid (see Chapter I).

-Dragon Variation (Sicilian Defence with Black Bishop on g7)

-Pelikán Variation (Another variation of The Sicilian)

-The Rat (Canadian name for 1...g6 2...Bg7)

-The Hippopotamus (Putting most of your pawns on the 3rd rank)[1]

-The Krazy Kat (American version of The Hippo)

-The Hedgehog (More sophisticated modern form of Hippo)

-The Monkey's Bum (1. e4 g6 2. Bc4 Bg7 3. Qf3)

-The Vulture (1. d4 Nf6 2. c4 c5 3. d5 Ne4)

-The Pterodactyl (Canadian name for The Rat with 3...c5)

The Monkey's Bum was analysed and practised by members of Streatham Chess Club in London in the mid-seventies. When one of them was shown the idea his first reaction was 'If that works, then I'm a monkey's bum!'

Other chess openings with strange names

-Fried Liver Attack (Variation of Two Knights Defence)

-Long Whip Variation (Variation of King's Gambit)

-Horny Defence (Another variation of King's Gambit)

-Stone-Ware Defence (Variation of Evans Gambit)

-Corkscrew Counter-Gambit (Variation of Greco Counter-Gambit)

-The Spike (Another name for Grob's Opening, 1. g4)

-Bayonet Attack (Line in Giuoco Piano)

-Siesta Variation (Variation of Ruy López)

-Meadow Hay Opening (1. a4)

-The Corn Stalk Defence (1. ... a5)

-Lolli Gambit (Another King's Gambit line)

-Fingerslip Variation (French Defence line accidentally played by Alekhine)

-Frankenstein-Dracula Variation (Variation of Vienna Opening)

---

[1] The most persistent devotee of this opening, J.C. Thompson, was famous for wearing boots and no socks.

-The Fred (1. e4 f5 2. exf5 Kf7)

-The Woozle (1. d4 c5 2. d5 Nf6 3. Nc3 Qa5)

-The Gotcha[1] (1. d4 c5 2. d5 Nf6 3. Nf3 c4)

♖

The names of chess openings may seem strange to non-aficionados. What, for instance, would the man on the Clapham omnibus make of books with titles like *Sicilian–Accelerated Dragons*, *Play the Bogo-Indian* or the sadistic *Beating the Sicilian*?

♖

Bruce Hayden, in *Cabbage Heads and Chess Kings* (the source of several items in this chapter) tells what happened when his friend Daniel Castello played against the Mad Parson. Castello played a strong game, his opponent beaming with pleasure at such fine play. After a particularly strong move the cranky cleric got up and stood behind Castello's chair to study the board. Castello pondered his next move. Suddenly, an awful sensation. He felt a pair of hands patting and stroking his hair. There was only one solution. He had to play a move quickly. Any move. Alas, the move he played was an outright lemon. But at least the raving reverend returned to his seat. Now frowning, he could be heard murmuring quietly to himself. 'Mentally deficient. Fellow must be mentally deficient.'

♖

Especially revolting were the habits of certain Indians as reported by one al-Maṣ'ūdī, an Arabian historian, in about AD 950. It seems that they wagered parts of the body on the result of chess games. After a defeat they would cut a finger with a dagger, cauterizing the wound with a reddish ointment boiled over a fire. When they ran out of fingers they moved on to hands, forearms, elbows and 'other parts of the body'. At which point it must have been rather difficult for them to move the pieces.

♖

A continental tournament shortly after the Second World War was interrupted when one of the spectators, overcome by the excitement of the moment, started to remove all his clothes. The clocks were stopped while he was hustled out into the next room. But shortly afterwards he was back again doing the same thing. Again play was halted, and this

[1] Our translation from the German.

time he was forcibly dragged back to his hotel room, while the local constabulary was called. A few minutes later he could be seen again, performing in his hotel window. At this point Dr Tartakower, the wittiest of grandmasters, claimed a draw by threefold repetition.

♖

Back in 1961 the hearts of all sex-starved American chess players were set a-flutter when luscious Lisa Lane won the US Ladies' Championship. Lisa (Mrs, alas) hit the headlines, not just for her play, but also for the daringly low-cut dresses she wore. Hastings, 1961–2, and good news for British players: the lovely LL is due to take part. Even better news, she's just been divorced. She arrives to find herself in a morning tournament. The tournament director and her opponents generously agree to let her play in the afternoon ('Just couldn't get up at nine o'clock in the morning'). She draws her first game, loses the next two, fails to turn up for rounds 4 and 5, and announces her withdrawal from the tournament, revealing to a press conference that she is unable to concentrate because she is in love. Hotly pursued by the paparazzi she hurriedly disappears from Hastings, and, after a few years, from the chess scene.

♖

A strong candidate for the least successful simul-giver of all time (his rivals may be found in Chapter III) is one Leon Roper. Claiming to be an international player, he gave a simultaneous display at Dane Court School, Broadstairs, Kent. Against seven young boys he lost five games and drew two. His £20 fee was refused. Dover College, where he had arranged to give a talk on 'the finer points of the game', was warned, and his lecture was cancelled. It was later revealed in court that Roper had previous convictions for theft, burglary, assault and attempted fraud, and that he lived with a woman named Countess Racquel von Kruger (né Christopher Collins) .

♖

Oscar Tenner, for many years a well-known figure on the American chess scene, was at one time in the habit of eating his chess pieces. As a prisoner during the First World War he did not have access to a chess-set, so pieces were constructed out of the daily bread ration. (Dr B. in Stefan Zweig's famous short story 'The Royal Game' ate his chess-pieces for the same reason.)

♖

The most extraordinary World Championship Match was undoubtedly that between Karpov and Korchnoi held in Baguio City in 1978. During the second game Karpov had a yoghurt delivered. This triggered off the Great Yoghurt Controversy. The Korchnoi camp, including English GMs Ray Keene and Michael Stean, protested that this could constitute a coded message. 'Thus a yoghurt after move 20 could signify "we instruct you to offer a draw"; or a sliced mango could mean "we order you to decline a draw". A dish of marinated quails' eggs could mean "play Ng5 at once", and so on.' This was intended as a parody of previous protests but was taken seriously at the time. Eventually it was agreed that Karpov could be served with a bilberry yoghurt at a specific time by a specific waiter. Later diversions included the mysterious Soviet hypnotist (or whatever) Dr Zhukar and assorted parapsychologists, mystics and gurus. These included Dada and Didi, a.k.a. Stephen Dwyer and Victoria Shepherd, two members of a mystical sect called Ananda Marga who had apparently been convicted of attempted assassination. These two characters joined the Korchnoi camp and soon had Viktor and his colleagues standing on their heads, meditating and chanting mantras.

♖

In 1982 Batsford's published a book called *The Amazing Adventures of Dan the Pawn*, by Simon Garrow. It aimed to teach the moves of chess to young children by weaving a story around a short game, which, as it happened, was won by white. The editor of the official magazine of the National Union of Teachers wrote: 'It would have been more symbolically exciting if the blacks had been allowed to win. Racist stereotypes and assumptions permeate our culture in many subtle ways.'

♖

The only good chess joke we know goes like this. Two scientists, one at the North Pole, the other at the South Pole, were engaged in a game of correspondence chess. Every four months one or the other would receive a move, borne by a sledge drawn by a dog across the ice. The game had been in progress for several years and a critical position had been reached in the early middle-game of a Sicilian Defence Poisoned Pawn Variation. North, playing black, was eagerly awaiting South's next move. But after four months he had heard nothing. The fifth month elapsed, then the sixth month. Still no sign of a move. The days, weeks and months passed and the tension was increasing daily. Then, one day, after nine months, he heard the distant sounds of the husky's paws and the runners of the sledge crunching the ice. Soon it came into view, and eventually reached him. With hands trembling and heart pounding he reached for the envelope containing South's next move. The suspense was unbearable. Finally, he managed to open the envelope and read the message inside. *'J'adoube.'*

♖

The life expectancy of leading chess players (from Philidor to Alekhine) has been calculated at 60, according to a Pittsburgh University study, while that of 24 other occupations comes out between 64 (British authors) and 71 (US presidential advisers). Another American study has estimated that the strain of a five-hour game of tournament chess is equivalent to ten rounds of boxing or five sets of tennis. Capablanca lost eleven pounds in weight in winning the world championship from Lasker; and Petrosian nearly a stone (fourteen pounds) in winning the title from Botvinnik.

♖

Some chess players have met their end in bizarre fashion. Here are three.
    Alonzo Morphy, father of the legendary Paul, was killed by a Panama hat. A cut above the eye from a Panama hat worn by a friend led to congestion of the brain, causing Judge Morphy's untimely end.

♖

W.R. Henry (William Henry Russ) (1833–66), was a pioneer American chess archivist. When his girl-friend declined his hand in marriage he shot her four times in the head and jumped off the nearest bridge into the river. Alas for his calculations, the tide was out, so he climbed out and shot himself twice in the head. Again he failed to end it all, was arrested and taken to hospital. But, broken-hearted from the loss of his beloved, he lacked the will to live and died ten days later. He was evidently not a very good shot. His girl-friend survived.

♖

Thomas Barnes, one of the leading English players of the same era, was the Cyril Smith of chess. He dieted so successfully that he lost 130 pounds in less than a year. Too successfully, as it turned out. His body was unable to accept the sudden change and he died.

♖

From the dead to the quick, and US master Sidney Bernstein who, in 1931, turned up one hour 59½ minutes late for a match. This left him just 30 seconds for 40 moves, which he negotiated successfully, drawing the game. This was, however, the only half-point dropped by his college team all season (Reuben Fine was on top board).

185

♖

At the opposite extreme are Glaswegian Lawrence B. Grant and Dr J. Munro MacLennan from Ottawa. When last heard of in 1975 they had been playing a correspondence game for forty-nine years at the rate of about one move a year. As Mr Grant said, 'Ye cannae hurry these things.'[1]

♖

Chess Players with Impressive Names
Abu'l Faraj bin al-Muzaffar bin Sa'-īd al-Lajlāj ('The Stammerer')[2]
Don Scipione del Grotto
Prince Dadian of Mingrelia[3]
Count Alberic O'Kelly de Galway
Marquis Stefano Rosselli del Turco
Count Jean de Villeneuve Esclapon
Baron Tassilo von Heydebrand und der Lasa
Alexander Markovich Konstantinopolsky
Alexander Feodorovich Iljin-Genevsky
Mikhail Alexandrovich Bonch-Osmolovsky
Feodor Ivanovich Duz-Khotimirsky
Eugene Alexandrovich Znosko-Borovsky
Roman Jakovlevich Dzindzikhashvili
Octavio Siqueiro F. Trompowsky de Almeida
K.D. Mulder van Leens Dijkstra
Conel Hugh O'Donel Alexander
Wellington Pulling
Lionel Adelberto Bagration Felix Kieseritzky[4]

♖

David Spanier tells a haunting story in his fascinating book *Total Chess*. Björn Palsson Kalman, a schoolboy chess prodigy in Iceland in the early years of the century, was, because of his chess prowess, invited to study at Harvard University. On the boat crossing the Atlantic he beat two

---

[1] B.H. Wood and W. Ritson Morry engaged in a consultation correspondence game with two Londoners that dragged on from the mid-thirties to the mid-fifties.
[2] See chapter II.
[3] He used to pay chess masters to lose brilliancies to him.
[4] For our schoolboy readers we have an Austrian called Tits, a Dutchman called Messemaker, a Pole called Fux and a Yugoslav called Manić. Also Karl Willy.

chessmasters simultaneously blindfold. But on reaching Harvard he discovered to his chagrin that he was not allowed to play for the university until he had been in residence a year. To console himself he immersed himself totally in chess until he feared he was going mad. He gave up chess, dropped out of university, and eventually surfaced in Winnipeg, working as a bricklayer. Several years later he was persuaded to play in a simul against Frank Marshall, the leading American player of the time. He won and was challenged to a return game, but declined and was never heard from again.

♖

Some Bobby Fischer quotes (mainly from his notorious 1961 interview with Ralph Ginzburg)[1]

On women: 'They're all weak, all women. They're stupid compared to men. They shouldn't play chess, you know. They're like beginners. They lose every single game against a man.'

On chess clubs: 'When they used to have the clubs, like no women were allowed and everybody went in dressed in a suit, a tie, like gentlemen, you know. Now, kids come running in in their sneakers – even in the best chess club – and they got women in there.'

On Jews: 'Yeh, there are too many Jews in chess. They seem to have taken away the class of the game. They don't seem to dress so nicely, you know.'

On school: 'You don't learn anything in school.' 'You shouldn't be doing homework.' 'The teachers are stupid. They shouldn't have any women in there. They don't know how to teach. And they shouldn't make anyone go to school.'

On his mother: 'She keeps in my hair and I don't like people in my hair you know so I had to get rid of her.'

On Kennedy: 'Besides, he doesn't have any class. He puts his hands in his coat pockets. God, that's horrible.'

On becoming World Champion: 'First of all, I'll make a tour of the whole world giving exhibitions.' 'I'll have my own club. The Bobby

---

[1] To be fair to the strongest player who ever lived, Bobby later denied having said some of the things attributed to him by Ginzburg.

Fischer... uh, the Robert J. Fischer Chess Club. It'll be class. Tournaments in full dress. No bums in there. You're gonna have to be over eighteen to get in, unless like you have special permission because you have like special talent.' 'I got strong ideas about my house. I'm going to hire the best architect and have him build it in the shape of a rook. Yeh, that's for me. Class. Spiral staircases, parapets, everything. I want to live the rest of my life in a house built exactly like a rook.'

Fischer again from another 1961 interview: 'I would not marry an American girl. With a foreigner would be much better. First you get her without customs, second, if you don't like her you can send her back home.'

And again, on the same subject: 'Chess is better.'

And, it seems, a lifetime ago: 'All I want to do, ever, is play chess.' Alas.

Since winning the World Championship Bobby has not pushed a pawn in anger.[1] He now lives in Pasadena, California, moving from one cheap hotel to another, hiding behind a red beard and the alias of Robert D. James. He leads a strange, nocturnal life, reportedly collecting Nazi memorabilia and distributing religious tracts under the windscreens of cars. His religious inclinations: fundamentalist; his political views: extreme right wing, still paranoid about Russians and Jews.[2]

♖

Another World Champion who may have shared Fischer's anti-semitism was Alexander Alekhine. In 1941 a series of articles was published under his name claiming the superiority of Aryan attacking chess to Jewish defensive chess. Alekhine later denied authorship, but the original manuscript in his handwriting was found after his wife's death.

♖

Alekhine holds the record for the World Champion with the most wives. He was married four times, and three of his wives were much

---

[1] He's played friendly games against Campomanes, ex-President Marcos and MAC HACK (see Chapter VIII); and around 1981, one of the authors, in the Manhattan Chess Club, heard a fascinating story that Bobby had that year played around a hundred blitz games with Canadian GM Peter Biyiasis. Fischer drew one and won the rest.

[2] An astonishing (and ridiculous) footnote to the Fischer saga: on 13 March 1986 the United States House of Representatives passed a resolution recognizing Bobby Fischer as still the official World Chess Champion.

older than him. But, unlike Capablanca, he was much more interested in chess than women. During the London Tournament in 1922 he and Capa were taken to a show. It was reported that Alekhine never took his eyes off his pocket chess-set, while Capa never took his eyes off the chorus line.

♖

Runner up to Alekhine in the marriage stakes is Boris Spassky, who has so far been married three times. After divorcing his first wife he described their relationship as 'like bishops of opposite colours'.

♖

Gary Kasparov seems to share Alekhine's preference for older women. His current belle is an actress in her late thirties. His great rival, Karpov, married an attractive young secretary several years ago. A few months later she produced a son; shortly afterwards they were divorced.

♖

For the chess groupies amongst our readers we have two suggestions. Filipino GM Eugenio Torre was once voted one of the ten sexiest sportsmen in the Philippines, and featured in a film entitled *Basta't Isipin Mong Mahal Kita* (Always Remember That I Love You) along with a couple of local starlets. Or you may prefer US Number One Yasser (Yaz) Seirawan, who, after being featured as *Cosmopolitan* magazine's Bachelor of the Month ('I love snorkelling, tennis, dancing till dawn. Also women with lustrous hair and twinkling honest eyes – a direct gaze is *all*') was inundated with marriage proposals.

♖

A romance that never blossomed was that between Bobby Fischer and Barbra Streisand. Yes, really. Bobby and Barbra were fellow students at Erasmus High, Brooklyn. Imagine being the teacher in charge of those two gigantic egos. They used to swap *MAD* comics, and, it is reported, Barbra had a crush on the future champion. Friends said they looked good together: even their noses matched. (A few years later, in the 1959 Candidates' Tournament, Bent Larsen's main duty as Bobby's second was to read him Tarzan stories.)

♖

Other leading players have had more healthy interests. Botvinnik, for example, was good at skittles and reached championship standard at dancing the Charleston and foxtrot.[1] Spassky, in his youth, was a 5′

---

[1] He also won an award for designing a trench mortar.

11¾" high-jumper. Euwe was a boxer, Capablanca was good at baseball and basketball, Keres excelled at tennis and Reshevsky at table-tennis. Alekhine listed canoeing among his interests. The Graeco-Russo-Franco-American GM Nicolas Rossolimo was a brown belt at judo.

♖

Just as many musicians, as we have seen, are keen on chess, so many chess-players have an interest in music. Most notably, Philidor. Smyslov has a fine baritone voice and in 1950 just missed a place in the Bolshoi Opera. During tournaments he frequently gave recitals, often accompanied by fellow grandmaster Taimanov, a concert pianist. Julius du Mont, a prominent chess author and editor of the *British Chess Magazine* was also a concert pianist. Rudolf Loman, a Dutch master, was organist of the Dutch Church in London for many years. On the other hand, the versatile Rossolimo played the concertina and made a record of Russian folk songs. Fischer once considered a career as a pop singer. Korchnoi sang a heavily accented version of 'There is a Tavern in the Town' at a banquet during one of his matches with Karpov. Nigel Short was a member of a group called The Urge which appeared on BBC TV's popular children's show *Blue Peter*. (He had originally wanted to call his band Pelvic Thrust but this was vetoed by the other members. Probably just as well.)

♖

Other masters have also had artistic leanings. Alekhine was a pupil at Moscow's first school for film actors, but failed. Howard Staunton, the Englishman who was unofficial World Champion between 1843 and 1851 was, before he took up chess, an actor who appeared alongside Edmund Kean, and later edited the works of Shakespeare. Max Harmonist, a minor Berlin master in the late 1880s, was a dancer in the Royal Ballet. The Swiss international master Henry Grob, who gave his name to the eccentric début 1. g4, was a celebrated portrait painter.

♖

It is only to be expected that many chess-players also have an interest in bridge. Capablanca and Alekhine played. Emanuel Lasker was good enough to represent Germany.[1] The Swedish grandmaster Ståhlberg was a very strong player. The Soviet woman grandmaster Irina Levitina

---

[1] But opinions differ on how good he was. Gerald Abrahams, an authority, says he wasn't so hot.

won an award in 1986 for the best-played hand of the year. Karpov and Korchnoi are also amongst the many contemporary stars who play (sometimes as partners!).

♖

Nearly as many masters were addicted to gambling, notably Tartakower, Janowski and Marshall. At one tournament, held in a casino, the craving overcame Tartakower to such an extent that he was seen placing bets at roulette between moves. Janowski regularly lost his prize money at the gaming tables. In his later years Marshall became addicted to, of all things, bingo.

♖

The most boring World Champion must surely be Anatoly Karpov. On one occasion he gave his interests as 'stamp-collecting and Marxism'. Later, he admitted to reading the detective novels of Dame Agatha Christie; and in 'The Sportsmen' section you can read of his unlikely relationship with snooker champion Steve Davis, who has also been (unkindly) called boring.

♖

One of the most versatile chess masters was Alexandre Louis Honoré Lebreton Deschapelles, perhaps the world's strongest player between Philidor and Bourdonnais. He learned, so he said, all he needed to know about chess in three days, and soon became the best player in France, giving odds of at least pawn and two moves to even his strongest rivals. Finding no serious opposition he took up whist instead, rapidly becoming expert at that game as well. (He is remembered among bridge-players even today as the originator of the Deschapelles Coup – perhaps he should be board one for our Sportsmen's team.) He was also an expert billiards player, using the stump of his right arm which he had lost fighting for Napoleon, and grew the best melons in Paris.

♖

Even Deschapelles would have seemed modest compared with Johannes Zukertort, the loser of the first official World Championship Match. He claimed fluency in nine languages, had studied theology, philology and social science, was an expert swordsman, domino-player, whist-player and pistol shot, a musician and music critic, a military veteran of over a dozen battles, twice dangerously wounded and once left for dead, entitled to wear seven medals, the orders of the Red Eagle and the Iron Cross, a student of chemistry (under Prof. Bunsen) and physiology to degree level, and editor of a political journal. To the best of our knowledge, no one believed him.

♖

Alexander Iljin-Genevsky played a major part in the shaping of modern chess. One of the leading early Soviet players, he was also a friend of Lenin, doing much to popularize chess in the Soviet Union. The remarkable thing about I-G was that he had to learn chess twice. Shell-shocked during the First World War, he suffered amnesia as a result and had to learn again how to play chess.

♖

Margaret Pugh of Edgbaston, the chess benefactor (she was donor of the Oxford-Cambridge cup) wished to donate a trophy to the public school, Oundle. She was told that school trophies matched in height the status of their particular sport; so the chess trophy should not be more than four inches high. The trophy she gave is indeed four inches high, 'and about a yard wide' said B.H. Wood, to whom we are indebted for this information.

Drink Like A Grandmaster

Chess and alcohol, we find, go very well together.[1] Provided, that is, you exercise a certain degree of restraint. We certainly don't recommend downing six pints of Old Peculier just before your decisive last-round game in the club championship. Here are some players noted for their fondness for the bottle:

1. *Alexander Alekhine*, whose penchant for drink cost him his World Championship title to Max Euwe in 1935. His Dutch hosts thoughtfully provided him with free champagne. Stunned by his defeat he renounced alcohol in favour of milk, and, two years later, regained his title.

2. *Joseph Blackburne*. Fond of the Scotch Game, and also the Scotch bottle, which he placed at strategic locations while giving simuls, frequently with amusing consequences,[2] though it didn't seem to affect his results. He even penned a testimonial to the powers of whisky for a trade journal, much to the chagrin of The Temperance Society.

3. *James Mason*, one of the leading players of his day, who, it is claimed, frequently lost games in a 'hilarious condition'. During a game in the

---

[1] 'Chess and wine are born brothers.' (Russian proverb)
[2] We omit here the oft-told tale of Blackburne taking his opponent's glass of whisky *en passant*.

London Tournament, 1899, he was discovered asleep in the fireplace.

4. *Charles Stanley*, American Champion before Morphy, was an incurable alcoholic who was confined to an institution for his last twenty years. Morphy played a match against him, sending his winnings to Mrs Stanley.

5. *Jacques-François Mouret*, one of the operators of The Turk (see Chapter VIII), a great-nephew of Philidor. Another alcoholic, in 1834 he sold the secret of how the automaton worked to keep himself in drink.

6. *Georg Marco*, a Viennese master rated one of the best annotators of all time. During a tournament he complained to Frank Marshall, a fellow competitor, of stomach-ache. Marshall poured him a drink and took one himself. Marco felt no better so they had another. And another. And another. The next day they played in the tournament. 'He beat me like a child,' said Frank, ruefully.

7. *Efim Bogoljubow*. Originally Russian but later a naturalized German, he developed a taste for beer. It is said that 'beer' was the only word of English he knew. Once he gave a blindfold simul in a small town in Spain. The local press photographer came along to record the event for posterity, but when the picture appeared Bogol wasn't there. 'Oh, you mean the fat little fellow with the glass of beer? I took him out of the photo: he didn't seem to fit in,' he explained.

8. *Mikhail Chigorin*, founder of the Russian school of chess, was particularly fond of drink. During his World Championship matches with Steinitz a sponsor provided him with free brandy (while Steinitz preferred champagne).

9. *Cecil De Vere*, first British Champion in 1886 at the age of twenty-one but dead of tuberculosis before his thirtieth birthday. He turned to drink on learning of what was to be his fatal disease, never approaching the fulfilment of his tremendous natural talent.

10. *Frank Marshall*, a couple of years before his death, played a series of ten lightning games against Reuben Fine, one of the best players in the world at that time. Frank was drunk, Reuben sober. The result: 10–0 in Marshall's favour.

At the concluding banquet of an International Team Tournament, says Fine, Frank was so overcome with emotion that when he was asked to make a speech on behalf of the victorious Americans, he could only wave the Stars and Stripes and shout 'Hip-hip-hoorah!'

193

11. *Florencio Campomanes*. Yes, the man who aborted the first K–K match. A surprising entrant perhaps, but US master Tony Santasiere tells how he once played Campo in New York State Championship. Campo 'arrived fifteen minutes late, and rather intoxicated, carrying six bottles of beer which he put carefully on the floor. After play began, he suddenly burst into tears, and nursed this outburst by consuming bottle after bottle of the beer, all the while making some very good chess moves.' The game was drawn. (*Essay on Chess*)

12. *Mikhail Tal*, who, on being told that the Soviet state was launching a campaign against alcoholism, commented, 'The state against vodka? I'll be on the side of vodka.' We'll drink to that.

We have one example of an alternative approach. Canadian IM Lawrence Day played in the 1972 Toronto Championship while stoned on grass. 'Really it was a disaster, result-wise,' he says.

Clink For A Grandmaster
From masters who like propping up bars to those who have spent time behind bars. Some for a variety of crimes, but others on matters of principle, or as victims of oppressive regimes. (We exclude from this list wartime internees.)

1. *Norman Whitaker*. American international master and professional confidence trickster, whose exploits are recounted in Chapter I.

2. *Raymond Weinstein*. American international master and murderer, another refugee from our Sinners' team in Chapter I.

3. *Milan Matulović*, star of Chapter IV got nine months porridge after a car crash in which a woman was killed. 'The sentence was too long,' complained the errant grandmaster, 'she was only a Bosnian.' Perhaps he should have shouted '*J'adoube*' first.

4. *William Winter*, an English International Master of bohemian out-look and communist sympathies, and a nephew of J.M. Barrie. He served a six-month sentence, which, he said, he rather enjoyed, for sedition in 1921.[1] Winter was responsible for what must have been one

---

[1] Willie once set up a provisional communist government of Britain in Bristol. It was rather less popular than Screaming Lord Sutch's Official Monster Raving Loony Party is now.

of the most hilarious simuls of all time, against Winchester Conservative Club. No doubt Willie tried extra hard in this display, winning all fifteen games.

5. *Alexandre Deschapelles*, who was incarcerated for his part in the insurrection of June 1832. Despite his well-known republican sympathies he pleaded with the king for his release on the grounds that he was too old, too ill, and innocent.

6. *James Mortimer*, a late-nineteenth-century rabbit who usually managed to finish just above our friend Mr Gossip, but at the age of seventy-four was still able to beat the likes of Tartakower and Blackburne. He was by profession a playwright, who wrote a successful series of farces, and a newspaper editor. His crime, for which he was imprisoned, was to refuse to reveal the author of an article which was sued for libel. While inside he taught his fellow inmates how to play chess.

7. *Ludek Pachman*, Czech-born grandmaster and author, was a supporter of the Dubček regime during the 'Prague Spring' of 1968. After the Russian tanks had moved in he was gaoled twice between 1969 and 1970 and again in 1972. He was then granted permission to leave his country and settled in West Germany.

8. *Alexander Alekhine*, who told Reuben Fine that he spent some time in prison during the Russian Revolution accused of passing on secret information.

And a couple of World Champions who were victims of false allegations.

1. *Wilhelm Steinitz*, who was arrested and accused of spying when the moves of some correspondence games against Chigorin were intercepted. The authorities suspected that the moves were coded military secrets (c.f. Graham Mitchell, Chapter I).

2. *Bobby Fischer* was arrested in Pasadena in May 1981 under suspicion of being a bank robber. Two years later he published a pamphlet entitled 'I was tortured in the Pasadena Jailhouse', in which he claims he was held for two days, the first twenty-four hours without food or drink, stripped and beaten up before being released on bail. He was later charged with damaging gaol property: to wit one mattress.

Perchance to Dream

What do chess-players dream about? Why, chess, of course. Some players even dream complete games, and problemists compose problems in their sleep.

This game was dreamed up by David Bronstein in 1961, and an instructive and entertaining one it is too:

Nimzo–Indian Defence

1. d4 Nf6	6. Nf3 d6	11. dxc6 O–O	16. Qb3 Be6
2. c4 e6	7. Qa4+ Nc6	12. a3 Ng4	17. Qa3 Ne3+
3. Nc3 Bb4	8. d5 exd5	13. g3 Qf6	18. Kc1 Qe1+
4. Bg5 h6	9. cxd5 Qe4	14. axb4 Qxf2+	19. Nd1 Qxd1
5. Bh4 Qe7	10. Nd2 Qxh4	15. Kd1 b5	mate

And, twenty years later, a contribution from American IM Anthony Saidy:

French Defence (by transposition)

1. Nf3 Nf6	6. e5 Nfd7	11. exf6 Qxf4	16. Nc7+ Kd8
2. Nc3 d5	7. Bd3 Nc6	12. fxg7 Rg8	17. Ngxe6 mate
3. d4 c5	8. Qe2 a6	13. Qxe6+ Ne7	
4. dxc5 e6	9. O–O Qc7	14. Nxd5 Qd6	
5. e4 Bxc5	10. Bf4 f6	15. Ng5 Qxe6	

♖

This dream chess problem was composed by US problemist William Spackman. It's pretty easy. You should be able to solve it with your eyes closed.

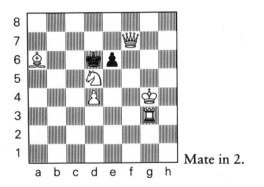

Mate in 2.

The game that never was

Alas, the famous and astonishing Adams-Torre game, with its witty offer of a queen sacrifice on six consecutive moves, is now widely believed to have been a paste diamond. It was partly manufactured by Torre, says Dale Brandreth, as a present for Torre's friend E.Z. Adams. Still, it's well worth a look:

E.Z. Adams (?)–C. Torre (?), New Orleans 1925 (?) Philidor's Defence. Defence.

1. e4 e5	7. Nc3 Nf6	13. cxd5 Re8	19. Qc4! Qd7
2. Nf3 d6	8. O–O Be7	14. Rfe1 a5	20. Qc7! Qb5
3. d4 exd4	9. Nd5 Bxd5	15. Re2 Rc8	21. a4! Qxa4
4. Qxd4 Nc6	10. exd5 O–O	16. Rae1 Qd7	22. Re4! Qb5
5. Bb5 Bd7	11. Bg5 c6	17. Bxf6 Bxf6	23. Qxb7
6. Bxc6 Bxc6	12. c4 cxd5	18. Qg4! Qb5	Black resigns

For other mythical games, see pp. 67, 133, and 169.

The stars' stars

We conducted a survey into the birth signs of 851 prominent chess-players. The results look something like this:

Capricorn	63	(Lasker, Keres, Chiburdanidze)
Aquarius	79	(Spassky, Bronstein)
Pisces	101	(Fischer, Tarrasch, Geller, Larsen)
Aries	76	(Smyslov, Kasparov, Korchnoi, Portisch)
Taurus	77	(Miles, Nunn, Steinitz)
Gemini	67	(Petrosian, Karpov, Short, Euwe)
Cancer	54	(Morphy, Anderssen)
Leo	67	(Botvinnik)
Virgo	63	(Philidor)
Libra	69	(Rubinstein, Fine)
Scorpio	71	(Capablanca, Alekhine, Nimzowitsch, Tal)
Sagittarius	64	(Reshevsky, Pillsbury)

So players born under Pisces are clearly no fish. And it seems that the best time of year for chess-players to be born is in the spring. Interestingly, astrologers claim that those born under the sign of Pisces have no interest in things logical or rational, whereas those born under Cancer, the worst sign on our survey, are just the opposite. What this proves we're not quite sure.

Postscript

The largest chess piece in the world is reputed to be the giant knight guarding the entrance to the Dubai Trade Centre for the 1986 Chess Olympiad. It is ten metres high. For the smallest, see 'The Entertainers'.

Dream solution: Kf3

VII *The Unorthodox*

'Well, I sort of made it up,' said Pooh ... 'it comes to me sometimes.'
A.A. Milne

'At chess, before gunpowder, The Queen took only Diagonal steps.'
W.H. Auden

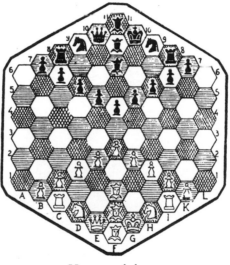

Hexagonal chess

What kind of chess did Aladdin play? You'll find it here, along with the enchanting games of Kriegspiel, Alice chess, snooker chess, alcoholic chess, and even chess as played on Mars.

It's a therapy session for those poor souls who've become bored with chess: a collection of the other games playable on a chess board (and a few, including two of the best, that aren't).

To give the rules of each one would be too space-consuming – but if you want to pursue the matter, you'll find help in our bibliography.

Shaṭranj (or Arabian Chess)

The form of chess played by Aladdin, and an excellent game, if rather slower than the modern variety. The queen is replaced by a *firzān*, which moves one square at a time diagonally. The bishops are replaced by *fīls* (or *alfīls*), which can jump two squares diagonally (e.g. from f1 to h3). Pawns move one square at a time only and may only be promoted to *firzāns*. Castling is not permitted. A player can win by checkmate, baring the enemy king or stalemating the enemy king. The problem attributed to Aladdin in our frontispiece follows these rules.[1]

Here's a reconstructed game of Shaṭranj, dating from the tenth century. The position after White's 24th move was published by as-Sūlī, the greatest player of his time, and may have arisen from one of his games. We use the letters F for *firzān* and A for *fīl*. Black has the first move:

1. ... f6	9. Fe2 Ah6	17. dxe4 d5	25. Nd1 Nxe4
2. f3 f5	10. g3 Kf7	18. Fd3 c4	26. N1c3 Rxd3
3. f4 Nf6	11. Nf3 Rd8	19. bxc4 dxc4	27. Axd3 Nxd3+
4. Nf3 c6	12. Ne5+ Kg8	20. Fxc4 Aa6	28. Kf1 Rf2+
5. e3 c5	13. Nd3 d6	21. Fd3 Rac8	29. Kg1 Nd2
6. Ah3 g6	14. Nf2 Nc6	22. Nc3 Nb4	30. any Nf3
7. Nh4 e6	15. d3 b6	23. Na4 Rxc2	mate
8. b3 Fe7	16. e4 fxe4	24. Af1 Ac4	

[1] The Aladdin problem (frontispiece) is Shaṭranj: White to play and win.

Solution: 1. Rg7+ Kd6 2. c5+Kd5 3. Rd7+ Ke4 4. Re3+! Kxe3 5. Ac1+ Ke4 6. Fd3+ Kxf5 7. Ng7 mate. Or 4. ... dxc3 5. Fd3+ Kxf5 7. Ng7 mate. Or 4. ... Kxf5 5. Ng7 mate.

And now part of a game between as-Sūlī (White) and his pupil al-Lajlāj (The Stammerer), again from the first half of the tenth century. This is the oldest recorded game of chess:

1. f3 f6	10. fxg5 hxg5	19. Nd2 Nd7	28. Axc5+ Ke8
2. f4 f5	11. d3 d6	20. Fc2 Fc7	29. dxe5 Nxe5
3. Nf3 Nf6	12. e4 e5	21. Fd3 Fd6	30. Nxe6 Rxg1
4. g3 g6	13. Ae3 Ae6	22. Ndf3 Ndf6	31. Rxg1 Nxf3
5. Rg1 Rg8	14. Nxg5 Ke7	23. Ah3 Ah6	32. Kxf3 with
6. h3 h6	15. c3 Nxg4	24. Af5 Af4	advantage to
7. e3 e6	16. Ke2 c6	25. Rac1 a6	White
8. g4 fxg4	17. d4 d5	26. c4 Rac8	
9. hxg4 g5	18. b3 b6	27. c5 bxc5	

Great Chess

Innumerable other versions of chess can be played simply by assigning new powers to existing pieces. Forms of chess played on larger boards with extra pieces are known as 'Great Chess'. Among the most famous devotees have been Aladdin and Tamerlane (see Chapter I), and the third Duke of Rutland, whose variant was played by Philidor and his circle. An eighteenth-century Duke of Brunswick played a mind-boggling version called Helwig Chess on a board of 1414 squares. And, even more boggling, the Count of Firmis-Periés invented a game of Military Chess on a board of 2640 squares with 940 men a side! (Paris *c*.1815).

Fairy Chess

Here are some examples of pieces which have been used in various forms of chess in the past, or have been invented by chess problemists. These are known in problem circles as 'fairy pieces':

Amazon (or Terror)—combined queen and knight.

Empress (or Chancellor)—combined rook and knight.

Princess (or Cardinal)—combined bishop and knight.

(A version of chess played on a 10×8 board with the addition of the Chancellor and Cardinal was invented by Bird in the nineteenth century and reinvented by Capablanca fifty years later. Bird placed the new pieces next to the king and queen, while Capa placed them between the bishops and knights, the Chancellor on the K-side and the Cardinal on the Q-side. The Cuban maestro considered the game vastly superior to chess and noted that games seldom lasted beyond 30 moves.)

Mann—moves like a king but is captured not mated.

Dabbaba—a 2×0 leaper (compare the knight, a 2×1 leaper, or the Fīl, a 2×2 leaper).

Camel—a 3×1 leaper.

Zebra—a 3×2 leaper.

Giraffe—a 4×1 leaper.

Wazir (or *Vizier*)—moves one square orthogonally. (A Mann is a combined Wazir and Firzān.)

Nightrider—moves like a knight but may make a sequence of moves in the same geometrical direction.

Mao—a non-jumping knight, moving one square orthogonally followed by one square diagonally.

Berolina pawn—moves one square diagonally forwards (or two on its first move). Captures by moving one square forwards. A game played using Berolina pawns:

C.F. Snooks–K.M. Oliff, Correspondence, 1957

1. c2–e4 f7–d5	6. Qxd8+ Kxd8	11. h2–g3 Bf5	16. e2–g4 c4–d3
2. Nf3 Nc6	7. Nbd4 Nxd4	12. f2–e3 c5–d4	17. Ke1 c3–d2
3. Nc3 d5–c4	8. Nxd4 f5xf4	13. Ng5 Bb4+	18. Rc1 d3–c2
4. Nb5 d7–f5	9. Bxf4 b7–d5	14. Kd1 d4–c3	White resigns
5. d2–f4 a7–b6	10. Nf3 e7–c5	15. e3–d4 d5xd4	

Barasi Chess

This leads us to Barasi Chess, named after David Barasi, a friend of one of the authors. Pawns are Berolina pawns, but may also move and capture backwards. They are barred from the back ranks and may always move two squares between their own second and fourth ranks (or vice versa). Pieces, on the other hand, can only move forwards. A bishop or knight on the back rank is dead, and a king, queen or rook may only move along the back rank.

Progressive (or Scottish) Chess

White makes one move, Black replies with two moves, then White plays three moves, and so on. A check at any point concludes a sequence of moves, and a player must move out of check on the first move of his next sequence. An excellent quick game.

A few games:

J. Boyer–A. Verse, Correspondence, 1957

1. d4; d5,Na6	3. Bxa6,Bxb7,	4. Ke2,Rc1,Rxc6,
2. Bg5,Bxe7,	Nc3,Nxd5,	Kf3,Rxc7,
Bxd8; Bg4,	Bc6+; Rd7,	Rxa7,g4; Bd2,
Bxe2,Bxd1,	Bxc2,Bb3,	Rxd4,Rxg4,
Rxd8	Bxd5,Bxc6,	h5,Ne7,Nc6,
	Bb4+	Nd4 mate

A. Verse–J. Boyer, Correspondence, 1957

1. Nh3; d6,	3. Kxd1,gxh3,	4. Ke2,Rf1,
Bxh3	Nc3,Nd5,	Rxf2,Rxf7,Rxg7,
2. e4,d4,Bb5+;	Nxc7+; Kd7,	Rxh7,Rxh8;
c6,Qd7,	Kxc7,cxb5,	Bh6,Bxc1,
Qg4,Qxd1+	Nf6,Nxe4,	Bxb2,Bxa1,
	Nxf2+	Bxd4,Bxh8,
		b6,a5 White
		resigns

J. Ford–P.Coast, Correspondence, 1959

1. e4; d5,dxe4	2. d3,dxe4,	3. Nc3,Bd2
	Qxd8+; Kxd8,	Bb5,O–O–O,
	e5,h5,Bb4+	Bg5 mate

J. Ford–C. Duffield, Correspondence, 1959

1. e4; e6,Be7	3. Kxd1,h4,Nc3,	4. Kd2,Ne2,h5,	5. Kxc3,Kb4,
2. d4,Bg5,Bxe7;	Nb5,Nxc7+;	h6,hxg7,	Kb5,a4,a5,
Qxe7,Qd6,	Kd8,Kxc7,b6,	gxh8=Q,Qc3+;	axb6,Ng3,
Qxd4,	Ba6,Bxf1,Bxg2	Kb7,Bxh1,a5,	Nf5,Nd6
Qxd1+		a4,a3,axb2,	mate
		bxa1=Q,	
		Qxc3+	

Marseillaise (or Double-move) Chess

Each player makes two moves on his turn. (In another version White starts with one move only.) Check may only be given on the second of two moves. A player must move out of check on the first move of his pair. Alekhine once played Three-move Chess. He considered that White should always win. Here he is, playing the Marseillaise version:

A. Fortis–A. Alekhine 1925

1. b3,Bb2	6. Bxe5,Ng5	11. Rg1,Re1+	16. Kxe1,Rd2
b6, Bb7	Ng4,Nxf2	Kd8,Bf3+	Rc8,Rc6
2. e4,Be2	7. Kxf2,d4	12. Kd2,Kd3	17. Rf2,Kd2
Bxe4,Bc6	Qxg5,Qf5+	Bg2,f3	g5,Rd6+
3. a4,a5	8. Ke1,Bd3	13. Ke3,Kf2	18. Ke3,c3
a6,b5	Qxd3,Qxd1+	Nc6,Nxd4	h5,Re6+
4. Bxb5,Be2	9. Kxd1 Bg3	14. Ne2,Nxd4	White resigns
Bxg2,Bc6	Bd6,Bxg3	c5,cxd4	
5. Nh3,Rg1	10. Rxg3,Nc3	15. Rad1,Rxd4	
e5,Nf6	f5,f4	Re8,Rxe1	

Cylindrical Chess

The board is considered to be a cylinder joined at the a and h files. Thus 1. e4 f6 2. Nf3 g5 3. c3 is checkmate.

Snooker Chess

Line-pieces may bounce off the side of the board at an angle of 90°. For example. 1. e4 e5 2. Bc4 Nf6 3. Qd1xf7 (via h5) is checkmate. Also known as Billiards Chess, but we prefer snooker. The pieces are sometimes referred to as reflecting bishops etc.

Grid Chess

The board is assumed to be divided by a grid into quadrangles, each consisting of four squares, as in the diagram. On each move a piece must cross one of the grid-lines. If the previous example were Snooker-Grid Chess (!) Qxf7 would be neither check nor mate as neither White Queen nor Black King may move between f7 and e8.

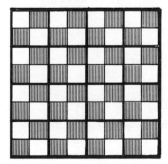

The board is assumed to be divided by a grid into quadrangles, each consisting of four squares, as in the diagram. On each move a piece must cross one of the grid-lines. If the previous example were Snooker-Grid Chess (!) Qxf7 would be neither check nor mate as neither White Queen nor Black King may move between f7 and e8.

Reverso

The simplest variant of all. The positions of the bishops and knights are reversed. Apart from this, proceed as normal. The advantage, of course, is that all opening theory is thrown out of the window. Try it against your club theoretician and watch him flounder! Several tournaments under these rules were held in the late nineteenth century. During the forties, Lord Brabazon (see Chapter I), in the interests of brighter chess, proposed reversing the position of White's king and queen in the initial set-up.

Varied Baseline Chess

There are two versions of this.

i) White chooses a random piece and places it on a1. Black places a similar piece on a8. White chooses a random piece for b1, and so on, with the provision that the bishops must start on opposite coloured squares. This is also known as 'Randomized Chess'. There are 2,880 possible starting positions.

A game from a 1953 match between Combined Universities and Hampstead featuring two strong players. (The other games in the match were of orthodox chess.)

I.J. Good–M. Blaine, 1953
White baseline: Na1, Rb1, Kc1, Bd1, Be1, Nf1, Rg1, Qh1
Black baseline: Na8, Rb8, Kc8, Bd8, Be8, Nf8, Rg8, Qh8

1. e4 e5	6. Nxe8+ Rxe8	11. Be2 Nb6	16. Ra1 Qxb3+
2. Ne3 c6	7. Nb3 Bg5	12. Kc2 a5	17. Kb1 Nba4
3. Nf5 Ne6	8. Bg4 Rbd8	13. a4 Qb4	18. Ra3 Nxc3+
4. g3 g6	9. c4 Qf8	14. d3 Qxa4	19. Ka1 Qa2+
5. Nd6+ Kc7	10. h4 Bh6	15. Bc3 Nc5	White resigns

ii) A screen is placed across the board while the players arrange their back rank pieces. A tournament under these rules was held in Brighton in 1976. Also known as 'Screen Chess'. Here's a game between two players of county strength:

T.J. Gluckman–G.H. James, Brighton, 1976
White baseline: Ra1, Bb1, Bc1, Qd1, Ke1, Nf1, Ng1, Rh1
Black baseline: Qa8, Bb8, Rc8, Rd8, Be8, Nf8, Ng8, Kh8

1. c4 c5	5. Ne3 Qb7	9. Nh4 Nh6	13. d3 e5
2. Nf3 b6	6. Bb2 f6	10. f3 Bg3+	14. Qc2 Ne6
3. b3 d5	7. h4 Bg6	11. Kf1 Bxb1	15. Rh3 Bf4
4. cxd5 Qxd5	8. h5 Be4	12. Rxb1 Qd7	16. Nd1 b5

17. Nf2 Nd4	21. g4 Be3	25. fxg4 Qxg4+	29. Qxb4 Rxe2+
18. Bxd4 cxd4	22. Kg2 Rc2	26. Ng3 Bd2	White resigns
19. Qb2 Rc6	23. Re1 a5	27. Reh1 Bb4	
20. Qa3 Rdc8	24. Ne4 Nxg4	28. Ng6+ Kg8	

Losing Chess

The object of the game is to lose all your pieces or to be stalemated. A player who can make a capture must do so. If he has more than one capture he may choose which one to make. The king has no royal powers and may be captured just as any other piece.

Rifle Chess

When a capture is made, the capturing piece does not actually move. For example, after 1. e4 e5 2. Nf3, Nc6 does not defend the e-pawn as after Nxe5 the white knight remains on f3.

Pocket Knight Chess

Each player has a spare knight which, on any occasion during the game, he may place on the board instead of making a move. In this Pocket Knight game played by post, Black is a grandmaster of correspondence chess.

G. Buckley–K.B. Richardson, Ruy López

1. e4 e5	8. c4 Nf6	15. Kf1 Bh3+	22. Rf1 Nf4
2. Nf3 Nc6	9. g3 Nd7	16. Kg1 hxg6	White resigns
3. Bb5 f5	10. PNe6 Qg6	17. Nxa8 PNe5	(PN = Pocket
4. Nc3 fxe4	11. Nxc7+ Kf7	18. b4 Bxb4	Knight.)
5. Nxe4 d5	12. Ne5+ Nxe5	19. Bb2 Bc5	
6. Nxe5 dxe4	13. Be8+ Kg8	20. Qe2 Nf3+	
7. Nxc6 Qg5	14. Bxg6 Nd3+	21. Qxf3 exf3	

Rejection Chess

At any move a player may reject his opponent's move. He must accept the alternative chosen by his opponent.

Endgame Chess

As played by Russian schoolboys in their break. Pawns and kings only. Put them on their original squares and away you go. Does wonders for your endgame.

Canadian (or Madhouse) Chess
When a player makes a capture he must replace the captured piece on the board, on any square he chooses. Pawns may not be replaced on the back rank.

Circe Chess
When a piece is captured it is reborn on its assumed square of origin as follows: pawns on the file on which they were captured, rook, bishop and knight to a square of the colour of that on which they were captured, queens to d1 or d8. If this is not possible the captured piece is removed from the board.

Alice Chess
Invented in 1954 by an Englishman called V.R. Parton and named after Lewis Carroll's eponymous heroine. Two boards and one set of pieces are required. The game starts with all the pieces on one board. When a piece is moved it is transferred 'through the looking-glass' on to the other board. A move has to be legal only on the board on which the piece starts its move. Pieces on the other board may not be captured. An example: 1. e4 d5 2. Be2 dxe4 3. Bb5 mate. The bishop has reappeared on the first board. The black king has no legal move and any piece that tries to interpose disappears at once on to the second board. A very confusing game.

Abbott's Ultima
There is a game from Madagascar called Fanorona in which the pieces take by moving *away* from the enemy. Robert Abbott used this idea in a strange chessboard game called Ultima. Very playable. It's in a unique book: *Abbott's New Card Games* (Stein and Day, New York, 1983).

Lord Dunsany's Chess
White has thirty-two pawns on his half of the board. Black just eight pieces placed on the back rank in the normal way. Black moves first and wins by capturing all the white pawns. White wins by checkmating Black.

Kriegspiel
One of the best and best-known variants. Three sets and boards are required, two players and one umpire. The rules that follow are the

house rules used by Richmond Junior Chess Club: various minor amendments are possible.

The players sit back to back at separate boards and move as in chess. The umpire, who can see both games, has another board placed between the players so that they cannot see it. The basic idea is that neither player knows what his opponent is doing. The umpire monitors the game and announces when a player has made a move. He also announces when a capture has been made, and on which square ('white has captured on e5'). Checks are announced as being on the rank, file, long diagonal, short diagonal or from a knight. He also informs a player if he tries to make an impossible move. On any turn a player may ask if there are any pawn captures ('Any?'). If there are, the umpire replies 'Try'. In our version a player may make three attempts to find the pawn capture, but this rule is not standard. If he is unsuccessful he must make another move. The game is tremendous fun, especially for the umpire.

Jetan

Edgar Rice Burroughs, in *The Chessmen of Mars*, describes a chess variant he calls 'Jetan' or 'Martian Chess' played on a 10×10 board. The game is playable but complex. We refer readers to our bibliography for further information.

Exchange Chess

A very popular pastime among young players. Four players in teams of two, and two boards. The partners sit next to each other, one playing white, the other black. Checkmate on one board ends the game. When a player captures a piece he passes it to his partner. The player to move may, instead of moving a piece, place a man captured by his partner on the board. A captured piece may not be placed so as to put the opponent in check, and pawns may not be placed on the first or eighth ranks. When a pawn queens it is placed on its side, and, on capture, reverts to being a pawn. The game is best played with a clock at a fast time limit (usually five minutes per player) to prevent stalling.

Alcoholic Chess

Each piece contains an alcoholic drink, the strength of which corresponds to the strength of the piece. Lasker (it is said) once played

Alcoholic Chess, winning by sacrificing his queen at an early stage. Also known as Spirited Chess.[1]

Lack of space forbids more than a brief mention of the existence of various forms of three- and four-handed chess, three-dimensional chess and hexagonal chess. A four-handed chess club was in existence for about fifty years up to the Second World War. Kieseritzky invented Baltic four-handed chess, played on a board shaped like an eight-pointed star, and is supposed to have shown Anderssen a form of 3-D chess in 1851.[2] One of the authors has a dim memory of Batman sitting at a 3-D chess-board. Robin comes in, sees him and exclaims, 'Holy Reshevsky, Batman! Two-dimensional chess is hard enough for me!', or words to that effect. Can any reader verify this? A variation of hexagonal chess invented by a London-based Pole named Wladyslaw Glinski has recently become sufficiently popular for World Championships to be held.

We have omitted from this necessarily brief survey games played on a chessboard with non-chess pieces, such as draughts and reversi (or Othello, not to be confused with Reverso). We have also omitted Chinese Chess and Shogi (Japanese Chess), claimed by its devotees to be even better then chess. In one version of Shogi the pieces include a Drunk Elephant and a Horrible Panther. Regretfully, we have also had to leave out the superb Japanese game of Go,[3] perhaps the most subtle and difficult of all board games, and Mancala,[4] a most delightful and demanding board game played throughout Africa.

---

[1] A San Francisco liquor store used to, and maybe still does, sell hollow glass chess-sets which you fill with red or white wine.

[2] A 3-D chess game was on sale in New York in the seventies.

[3] Try any Japanese shop.

[4] or Wari. Spear's Games used to sell Mancala. Maybe still do.

VIII Adjournment: *Desert Island Chess*

It is a riddle wrapped in a mystery inside an enigma: but perhaps there is a key.

W.S. Churchill

Hell, says Sartre, is other people. If he'd been a chess-player,[1] he would have known better. Hell is being stuck somewhere with a chessboard and men, and no opponent. Should this ever happen to you, the next section will serve as a pain-killer. It's a collection of solitary pursuits you can enjoy on a chess-board.

Some of them shouldn't tax the intelligence of the average vole; most of the remainder will detain you for not more than a couple of hours; but for those of our readers who are in Antarctic research stations, or Wormwood Scrubs, or lost up the Amazon, we've put in a few killer-dillers that should make the time race past.

Answers, where necessary, are at the end of this section.

1. The knight's tour

A most ancient puzzle. A thousand years ago the Hindu Rudraṭa was writing about it. Stick the knight on any square, and then tour the board, touching each square once only.

There are billions of solutions. Many of them make pretty patterns.

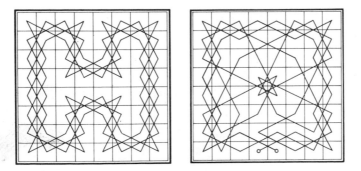

[1]Maybe he was. Before the twentieth game of the 1978 Karpov–Korchnoi match a telegram ('Avec vous en coeur') arrived, addressed to Korchnoi, and bearing the names of four literary eminences—Sartre, Beckett, Arrabal and Ionesco.

The next one is a re-entrant (the knight is able to reach the first square after its 64th move). There are 122 million like that.

This version (expressed in figures) was invented by Euler, the great mathematician. It almost makes a magic square: each rank and file adds up to 260.

63	14	37	24	51	26	35	10
22	39	62	13	36	11	50	27
15	64	23	38	25	52	09	34
40	21	16	61	12	33	28	49
17	60	01	44	29	48	53	08
02	41	20	57	06	55	32	47
59	18	43	04	45	30	07	54
42	03	58	19	56	05	46	31

Now you try.

2. The eight queens
Put eight queens on the board, so that none commands a square occupied by another.

This problem fascinated the prince of mathematicians, Karl Gauss. He demonstrated that there are only 12 basic solutions. With rotations of the board, this gives 92 possible ways of doing it (and, roughly, four and a half thousand million ways of doing it wrong).

3. The five queens
Place five queens so that they control all 64 squares (there are 4,860 ways of doing this).

4. The eight chess pieces
Place the eight white chess pieces on the board (keeping the bishops on opposite coloured squares) so that

i)   the maximum number of squares are guarded
ii) the minimum number of squares are guarded

5. The student's breakthrough
i)   Every Russian schoolboy knows it.

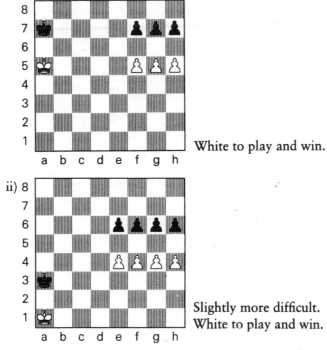

White to play and win.

ii)

Slightly more difficult.
White to play and win.

6. Constructions
i) Construct a game in which Black delivers mate by discovered check
on move 4; (S. Loyd, Le Sphinx, 1866)

ii)

construct a game to reach this
position after Black's fourth move;
(Mortimer)

iii) construct a game to reach this position after white's sixteenth move.

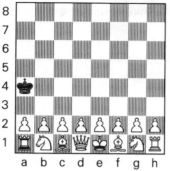

(K. Fabel)

7. Reconstruction

White's king has fallen off the board. On which square must it be replaced?

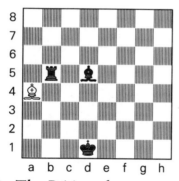

R. Smullyan,
Manchester Guardian, 1957

8. The Réti study

This seeming impossibility gets our vote as the bestest, simplest chess composition of all. Richard Réti created it in 1922.

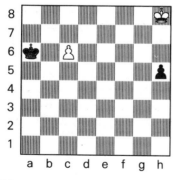

R. Réti, *Kagans Neueste Schachnachrichten*, 1922

White to play and draw.

9. The Saavedra position

The most famous chess study of all (and one of the most elegant) was named after a Spanish priest living in Glasgow in 1895. Maybe he should be in the holy team. Fernando de Saavedra was a duff chess-player, but found immortality when he spotted a win in a position that was thought to be a draw. The result, this gem (composed by Barbier, improved by Saavedra):

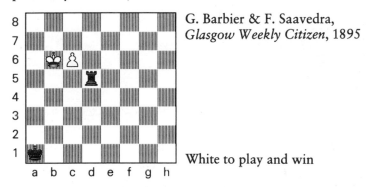

G. Barbier & F. Saavedra,
Glasgow Weekly Citizen, 1895

White to play and win

10. The ten-move stalemate

A genius called Sam Loyd invented this. From the starting position, reach a stalemate in just ten moves. This could take you years. Unless you're on a desert island, consult the solution immediately.

11. Just how good are you?

Older, less talented, players may find this depressing. It was used by the Czechs as a test of young chess talent. You need a stop-watch, and a friend to time you.

You put black pawns on c3, f3, c6 and f6. You put a white knight on a1, then you move to b1 (via c2, a3) c1 and through to h1 and then h2, and so on to a8 — without going to a square occupied by or attackd by a pawn (ten seconds penalty each time you do).

According to C.H.O'D. Alexander, ten to fifteen minutes is respectable, under seven minutes is good, and below two minutes is young grandmaster standard. One of us took six and a half minutes. If you care to try a second time, a 25 per cent improvement means you have good learning ability. We got worse.

12. *Eight more studies*

You've already (8 and 9 above) seen two of the most famous studies; here are eight more well known ones:

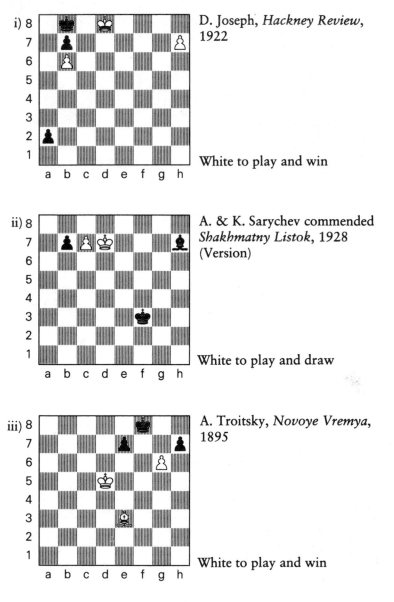

i) D. Joseph, *Hackney Review*, 1922

White to play and win

ii) A. & K. Sarychev commended *Shakhmatny Listok*, 1928 (Version)

White to play and draw

iii) A. Troitsky, *Novoye Vremya*, 1895

White to play and win

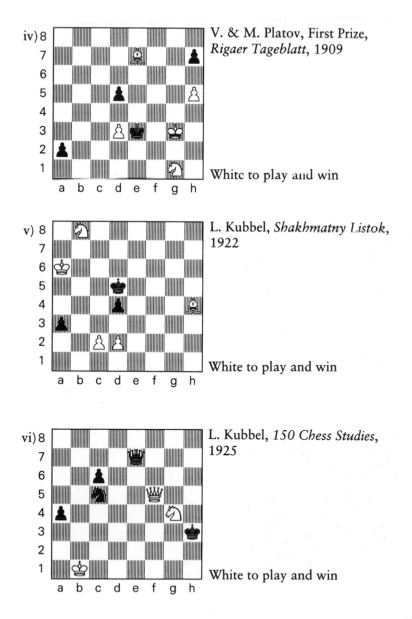

iv)

V. & M. Platov, First Prize,
Rigaer Tageblatt, 1909

White to play and win

v)

L. Kubbel, *Shakhmatny Listok*,
1922

White to play and win

vi)

L. Kubbel, *150 Chess Studies*,
1925

White to play and win

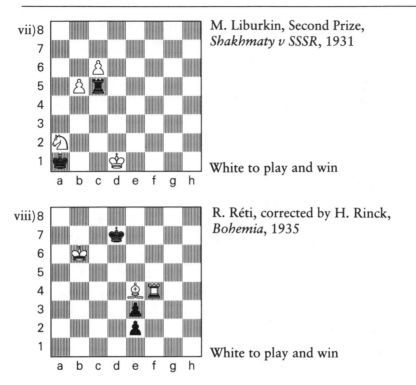

vii) M. Liburkin, Second Prize, *Shakhmaty v SSSR*, 1931

White to play and win

viii) R. Réti, corrected by H. Rinck, *Bohemia*, 1935

White to play and win

13. And ten problems

In case you're wondering, a *study* has no fixed limit of moves attached to it, and generally looks like something that might happen in a game. A *problem* has a fixed number of moves as a condition, and is often artificial in its appearance. We're no experts, but here are ten of the most famous:

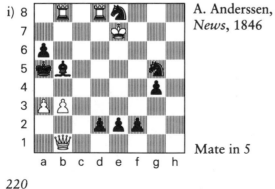

i) A. Anderssen, *Illustrated London News*, 1846

Mate in 5

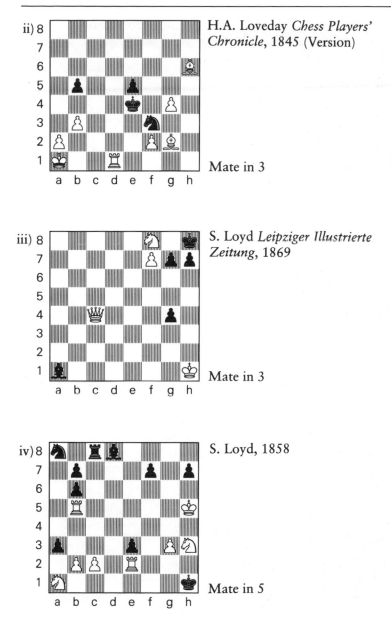

ii) H.A. Loveday *Chess Players' Chronicle*, 1845 (Version)

Mate in 3

iii) S. Loyd *Leipziger Illustrierte Zeitung*, 1869

Mate in 3

iv) S. Loyd, 1858

Mate in 5

v)

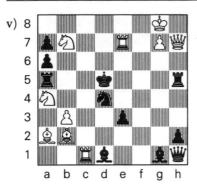

G. Heathcote, First Prize
Hampstead and Highgate Express,
1905

Mate in 2

vi)

C. Mansfield, First Prize *Good
Companions,* March 1917

Mate in 2

vii)

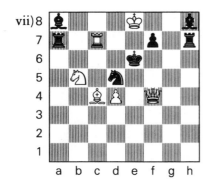

L. Loshinsky, Commended
Tijdschrift v.d. N.S.B., 1930

Mate in 2

222

viii)

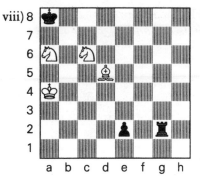

C.S. Kipping, *Manchester City News*, 1911

Mate in 3

ix)

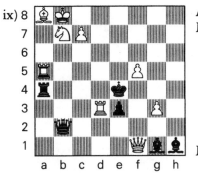

A. Ellerman, First Prize Guidelli Memorial Tourney, 1925

Mate in 2

x)

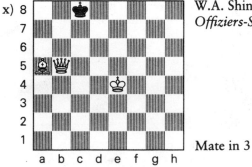

W.A. Shinkman *Offiziers-Schachzeitung*, 1905

Mate in 3

14. Three jokes

i)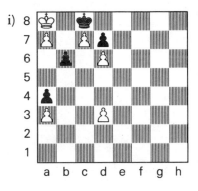

The easiest problem of all.

Find someone who claims to be no good at chess problems. Bet him he can solve this one no matter how hard he doesn't try: (Ropke)

Mate in 6

ii)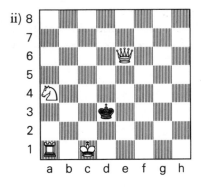

Deliver mate in half a move

iii)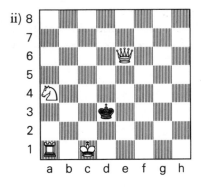

Deliver mate in no moves

15. The most difficult position of all

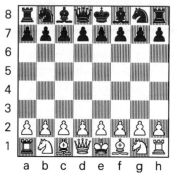

White to play, what result?

16. The Dudeney problem

This, invented by the English genius Henry Ernest Dudeney, has been called the best puzzle ever devised. You don't need to know the rules of chess to tackle it.

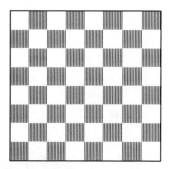

Two people have a perfectly constructed chessboard, and an unlimited supply of white pawns of exactly the same dimensions. The first person places a pawn anywhere on the board (not necessarily in the middle of a square – *anywhere*); the second does the same. And so on until one person can't fit another pawn on the board. He's the loser.

With perfect play, who wins?

Solutions

1 James Mason (*Elements of Chess*) says where two apparently equal routes lie open choose that which leads the furthest outward, or to the square whence the knight will have less scope for action.

2 One answer is: a6, b4, c1, d5, e8, f2, g7, h3

3 One answer is: h1, f3, e4, d5, b7

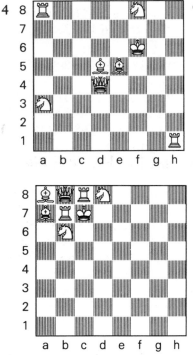

4 63 squares controlled (all except e2. This is one of over 80 solutions)

16 squares controlled (including the ones on which the pieces stand)

5   i) g6 fxg6 2. h6 gxh6 3. f6 and wins, or 1. ... hxg6 2. f6 gxf6 3. h6.

   ii) h5 gxh5 2. e5 fxe5 3. f5 and white promotes with check.

6   i) 1. f3 e5 2. Kf2 h5 3. Kg3 h4+ 4. Kg4 d5 mate.
   ii) 1. Nf3 d5 2. Ne5 Nf6 3. Nc6 Nfd7 4. Nxb8 Nxb8
  iii) 1. Nc3 b5 2. Nxb5 Nf6 3. Nxa7 Ne4 4. Nxc8 Nc3 5. Nxe7 c6 6. Nxc6 Nb1 7. Nxb8 Ra3 8. Nxd7 g5 9. Nxf8 Qd6 10. Nxh7 Kd7 11. Nxg5 Rh4 12. Nxf7 Rc4 13. Nxd6 Kc6 14. Nxc4 Kb5 15. Nxa3+ Ka4 16. Nxb1.

7   K on c3. (−1. c2-c4 b4xc3 e.p. 0. Kxc3 must have been the previous moves)

8   1. Kg7 h4 2. Kf6 Kb6 3. Ke5 Kxc6 4. Kf4 and draws

9   1. c7 Rd6+ 2. Kb5 Rd5+ 3. Kb4 Rd4+ 4. Kb3 Rd3+ 5. Kc2 Rd4 6. c8=R Ra4 7. Kb3 and wins

10   1. e3 a5 2. Qh5 Ra6 3. Qxa5 h5 4. Qxc7 Rh6 5. h4 f6 6. Qxd7+ Kf7 7. Qxb7 Qa3 8. Qxb8 Qh7 9. Qxc8 Kg6 10. Qe6.

12   i) 1. h8=Q a1=Q 2. Qg8 Qa2 3. Qe8 Qa4 4. Qe5+ Ka8 5. Qh8 and wins

    ii) 1. Kc8 b5 2. Kd7 Bf5+ 3. Kd6 b4 4. Ke5 Kg4 5. Kd4 and draws

   iii) 1. Bh6+ Kg8 2. g7 Kf7 3. g8=Q+ Kxg8 4. Ke6 Kh8 5. Kf7 e5 6. Bg7 mate (or 2. ... e6+ 3. Kd6 Kf7 4. Ke5 Kg8 5. Kf6 and wins, or 2. ... e5 3. Ke6 e4 4. Kf6 and wins)

   iv) 1. Bf6 d4 2. Ne2 a1=Q 3. Nc1 Qa5 4. Bxd4+ and 5. Nb3+ wins (or 3. ... h6 4. Be5 wins)

    v) 1. Nc6 Kxc6 2. Bf6 Kd5 3. d3 a2 4. c4+ Kc5 5. Kb7 a1=Q 6. Be7 mate

   vi) 1. Ne3+ Kg3 2. Qg4+ Kf2 3. Qf4+ Ke2 4. Qf1+ Kd2 5. Qd1+ Kc3 6. Qc2+ Kb4 7. Qb2+ Nb3 8. Qa3+ Kxa3 9. Nc2 mate

  vii) 1. Nc1 Rxb5 2. c7 Rd5+ 3. Nd3 Rxd3+ 4. Kc2 Rd4 5. c8=R Ra4 6. Kb3 and wins (cf 9) (or 1. ... Rd5+ 2. Kc2 Rc5+ 3. Kd3 Rxb5 4. c7 Rb8 5. cxb8=B and wins)

 viii) 1. Bf5+ Kd6 2. Rd4+ Ke7 3. Re4+ Kd8 4. Bd7 e1=Q 5. Bb5 and 6. Re8 mate

13   i) 1. Qe1 dxe1=Q 2. Rd4 f1=Q 3. Ra4+ Bxa4 4. b4+ Qxb4 5. axb4 mate

    ii) 1. Bc1 b4 2. Rd2 Kf4 3. Rd4 mate

   iii) 1. Qf1 Bb2 2. Qb1 and mate next move, or if 1. ... Bc3 or Bd4, 2. Qd3, or if 1. Be5 or Bf6, 2. Qf5, or if 1. ... g6 2. Ng6+

   iv) 1. b4 Rc5+ 2. bxc5 a2 3. c6 Bc7 4. cxb7 any 5. bxa8=Q mate

    v) 1. Rcc7 threatening Nc3 mate. After every move of the black knight on d4 a different mate occurs.

   vi) 1. Be4 threatening Nxc4 mate. If 1. ... Ne5, Rd3 mate, or 1. ... Nxd6+ Bd3 mate, or 1. ... Nxe3+ 2. Nb5 mate, or 1. ... Nd2+ Nc4 mate

vii) 1. Bb3, no threat. All twenty-three of black's replies allow mate. Note the interferences on b7, g7 and f6.

viii) 1. Ka5 d1=Q+ 2. Kb6 and mate next move. Or 1. ... Rg8 2. Nd4+ Ka7 3. Nb5 mate, or 1. ... Kb7 2. Ne7+ Ka7 3. Nc8 mate. But not 1. Kb5 because of Rg8.

ix) 1. Rd7 threatening Qf4. If 1. ... Qd4, 2. Nd6, or if 1. ... Qe5, 2. Nc5, or if 1. ... Qh8+, 2. Nc8, or if 1. ... Bf2, Qxh1, or if 1. ... Bf3, 2. Qd3, or if 1. ... Rd4, 2. Re7

x) 1. Qb2 Kd7 2. Qe5 Kc8 3. Qc7 mate or 2. ... Kc6 Qd5 mate

14 i) If you can't solve this, you really do have a problem.

ii) Rd1 (i.e. white completes the second half of castling queen side. He's already played the other half: Kc1)

iii) Just turn the board round. Now the white pawn is giving mate.

15 Crack this one and you'll become immortal (and rich)

16 The first player. He puts a pawn in the exact geometric centre of the board; then whatever move his opponent makes, he matches it symmetrically, until there are no more spaces left for the second player. (As far as we recall this problem was originally set with cigars and a large table as the props – but it has appeared in many guises.)

IX *The End?*

'The Eighth Square at last!' she cried... 'Oh how glad I am to get here!
And what *is* this on my head?'

Lewis Carroll, Through the Looking Glass

The Turk

Since 1968, David Levy, a Scottish international master, has been making and winning bets that he can beat any chess computer in the world. Round about now, he's going to have to stop doing it. The machines have caught up with him. Whether computers will make it all the way to Bobby Fischer level in our lifetime is debatable – but it looks like just a matter of time before they start thrashing your run-of-the-mill grandmasters. What effect this will have on the game that Voltaire said 'reflects most honour on human wit' is unknowable.

What we do know is that chess machines have a very long history. The first chess automaton was built as long ago as 1769. It revolutionized the world of magic, inspired the invention of Cartwright's power mill and indirectly furthered the career of Edgar Allan Poe. The astounding history of The Turk and its successors is related in this chapter.

Read also about the world's first genuine chess-playing machine, created, would you believe it, back in 1890, and about how Britain's leading chess-players helped win the Second World War and, in so doing, helped sow the seeds of the computer revolution.

Finally, we feature the triumphs and disasters of today's silicon superstars, from programs running on the world's most powerful computers to those micro marvels without which any civilized home is assuredly incomplete.

♚

The first chess automaton, known as The Turk, was designed by the Hungarian inventor and engineer Wolfgang von Kempelen in 1769 to entertain the Empress Maria Theresa. The empress and her court saw a figure dressed in Turkish costume, slightly larger than life, seated at a wooden cabinet. The figure would take on all-comers at chess, and beat them, perform the knight's tour starting from any square designated by one of the audience, and finally answer questions by pointing to letters on a board. The Turk was the first of the great cabinet illusions which have delighted audiences at magic shows for the past two hundred years.

♚

Between 1781 and 1838 The Turk toured Europe and then, in the ownership of Johann Nepomuk Maelzel, of metronome fame, America, amazing and delighting its opponents, who included many celebrities.

♚

Ben Franklin played The Turk at the Café de la Régence in Paris. According to his grandson he was 'pleased with the Automaton'.

♚

The Revd Edmund Cartwright, an obscure country clergyman and poet, visited The Turk in London. Inspired by the thought that, if it were possible to construct a machine to play chess, a weaving mill would present few problems, he set about creating his power loom, changing the face of the clothing industry and playing a major part in the Industrial Revolution.

♚

Napoleon played against The Turk in 1809. As we have seen in Chapter I, the general was one of the world's worst losers, and, true to form, he tried to cheat the machine by making illegal moves. According to some versions of the story he also tried the effect of placing an enormous magnet on the board, or covering the android's head with a shawl. Despite these efforts he was still soundly beaten, and, it is reported, threw the chessmen off the board and stormed out of the room shouting 'Bagatelle.'

♚

Amongst The Turk's visitors in America was a young journalist named Edgar Allan Poe who in 1836 published an essay speculating, for the most part correctly, on how the machine worked.[1] This has been claimed by his biographers to be the first example in Poe's writings of purely logical reasoning, and may have encouraged his later forays into detective fiction.

♚

The Turk was finally retired to the Chinese Museum in Philadelphia, where it perished in a fire in 1854.

♚

The next celebrated chess automaton was built by an Englishman, Charles Alfred Hooper, in the 1860s, and was later to be known as Ajeeb. It was first exhibited in 1868 at the Polytechnic in Regent Street.

♚

---

[1] If you haven't already guessed: it had a man inside.

A few months later the Automaton was moved to Crystal Palace, where it remained for another seven years. It was operated either by Hooper or his son. The son, who had aspirations to become a chessmaster, had to give up operating the Automaton when he became too fat to enter the machine.

♟

One of the Crystal Palace Automaton's most persistent opponents was the artist and critic John Ruskin, who wrote to a friend in 1874: 'I shall play some games of chess with the automaton chessplayer. I get quite fond of him, and he gives me the most lovely lessons in chess. I say I shall play him some games, for I never keep him waiting for moves and he crushes me down steadily.'

♟

In January 1876 the Automaton moved to the Royal Aquarium in Westminster, London. Among its visitors there were the Prince (later King Edward VII) and Princess of Wales, and Prince Leopold, who, the previous year, had been President of the Oxford University Chess Club.

♟

For thirty years from 1885 to 1915 the original Crystal Palace Ajeeb (there was by now at least one imitation) was exhibited at the Eden Musée, New York's answer to Madame Tussaud's. In 1889 Hooper decided to hire masters to operate his automaton. The most famous of these was the brilliant and tragic Harry Nelson Pillsbury. It has often been speculated whether operating Ajeeb contributed to Pillsbury's early death.

♟

One of Ajeeb's New York operators, Peter J. Hill, was twice attacked by dissatisfied customers. On one occasion Ajeeb was stabbed by a lady with a hatpin, who was clearly upset at just having had her bishop taken. Even more painful: when an angry Westerner with a six-gun shot the automaton, wounding Hill in the shoulder.

♟

Another operator had the habit of falling asleep during games. When this happened a flunkey from the museum was called in to make repairs. This consisted of banging loudly until the operator woke up again.

♟

Among the celebrities who played Ajeeb at the Eden Musée were Admiral Dewey, Teddy Roosevelt, Houdini, Sarah Bernhardt and O. Henry.

♛

Twenty years after the closure of the Eden Musée Ajeeb was bought by Frank Frain and Jesse Hanson, who had been its last draughts operator at the museum; and it toured the country playing draughts. The following year they signed a contract with RCA to advertise Magic Brain radios, and Ajeeb's turbaned head was transformed into a Magic Brain.

♛

Ajeeb was last heard of dumped in a Cadillac in a parking lot in 1943.

♛

The third of the famous chess automata (there were many others), called Mephisto, was constructed by Charles Godfrey Gumpel, a manufacturer of artificial limbs and surgical appliances, and first exhibited in 1878. Unlike Ajeeb and The Turk, the operator was not hidden inside the machine but in an adjacent room. The moves were transmitted to the operator electro-mechanically. The operator when it was displayed in London was Isidor Gunsberg, a young Hungarian who was later to put up a good show in a World Championship match against Wilhelm Steinitz.

♛

In August 1878 Mephisto entered the Counties Chess Association Knock-out Handicap Tournament. In the first round it was paired against the Revd George Alcock MacDonnell,[1] who promptly withdrew from the event in protest—not because he refused to play against the Devil, but for more practical reasons. There was no guarantee that the operator could not consult books or move the pieces around, or indeed that he would be the same player in every game. Mephisto had no difficulty in winning the tournament, our favourite rabbit G.H.D. Gossip being amongst the also-rans.

♛

In 1879 Mephisto founded his own chess club, and from 1881 to 1890 edited a chess column in a popular scientific magazine called *Knowledge*.

♛

Mephisto was exhibited in London and Brighton sporadically for ten years after its construction, but public interest gradually waned. Although it was a much more impressive device than The Turk or Ajeeb,

---

[1] See 'The Holy'.

Gumpel was not so much of a showman as Maelzel or Hooper. It made its last appearance at the 1889 Paris Exposition, when the operator was the Franco-Polish master Jean Taubenhaus.

♚

The concept of a chess-playing machine has always proved fascinating to those in the forefront of computer development. In 1864 the computer pioneer Charles Babbage considered using his Analytical Engine, a prototype computer which, sadly, he was never able to develop very far, to play chess.

♚

The first genuine chess-playing robot was invented, believe it or not, back in 1890. This was a machine designed to play the ending of king and rook against king, and was invented, appropriately, by a Spaniard named Leonardo Torres y Quevedo (*torre* is the Spanish word for rook). Among his other inventions were a machine for solving algebraic equations and the Astro-Torres airship, which was used by France in the First World War. The Torres machine, of course, pre-dated the electrical age and consisted of a series of pulleys, weights and wires, which caused moves to be made on a small chessboard according to a simple algorithm. It was first demonstrated to the public at the Sorbonne in 1915 and can be seen today, still in working order, at the Polytechnic Museum in Madrid.

♚

In the early months of the Second World War the Government Code and Cipher School was set up at Bletchley Park to break the machine-generated German Enigma codes. Many of the best brains in the country were recruited, including the best young British chess-players. Two of the earliest recruits were the late Hugh Alexander and Stuart (now Sir Stuart) Milner-Barry, and they were later to be joined by Harry Golombek. Among the mathematicians at Bletchley Park were Donald Michie, whom we shall meet again later in the chapter, and Alan Turing. Turing, who was to die tragically and far too young, was the most brilliant of the lot. He could well be described as the father of the modern electronic computer, as the machine he designed to break the Enigma codes was in effect the prototype of the computers we know and love today. But, genius though he was, Turing was, as we have seen in Chapter I, a complete rabbit at chess. The success of the Bletchley Park team was recognized by no less a person than Churchill himself, who maintained that they played a major part in winning the war.

In the late 1940s both Alan Turing and Donald Michie produced sets of instructions which simulated computer chess, called respectively TUROCHAMP and MACHIAVELLI. Turing started to program both TUROCHAMP and MACHIAVELLI but never completed the task. In 1951, though, TUROCHAMP 'played' a game against a weak human opponent, with Turing carrying out manually the calculations necessary to produce each move. TUROCHAMP had White and was doing well until blundering on move 29.

TUROCHAMP–Human, Manchester, 1951

1. e4 e5	9. gxf3 Bh5	17. Bb5 Nxb7	25. Bb3 Qa6
2. Nc3 Nf6	10. Bb5+ c6	18. O–O–O Nc5	26. Bc4 Bh5
3. d4 Bb4	11. dxc6 O–O	19. Bc6 Rfc8	27. Rg3 Qa4
4. Nf3 d6	12. cxb7 Rb8	20. Bd5 Bxc3	28. Bxb5 Qxb5
5. Bd2 Nc6	13. Ba6 Qa5	21. Bxc3 Qxa4	29. Qxd6? Rd8
6. d5 Nd4	14. Qe2 Nd7	22. Kd2 Ne6	White resigns
7. h4 Bg4	15. Rg1 Nc5	23. Rg4 Nd4	
8. a4 Nxf3+	16. Rg5 Bg6	24. Qd3 Nb5	

The boffins at the Los Alamos Scientific Laboratory in New Mexico spent most of their time developing the atomic bomb, but in 1956 they came up with a rather more constructive project. They programmed their MANIAC computer (not an inappropriate name considering its main function) to play a game of mini-chess with no bishops on a 6×6 board. A strong player gave it queen odds and won but a young woman who had just been taught chess contrived to lose to it, thus going down in history as the first human to lose to a computer at chess.

The first genuine chess-playing program was written in 1958 by an American named Alex Bernstein. Here it takes on a strongish human opponent and soon runs into trouble, dropping its queen.

IBM 704 (Bernstein's program)–Human

1. e4 e5	7. O–O d5	13. Ng5 Qg6	19. g3 exd1=Q
2. Bc4 b6	8. exd5 cxd5	14. Nh3 e3	20. Nxd1 Qc2
3. d3 Nf6	9. Bb5+ Nc6	15. f3 Bc5	21. b3 Rad8
4. Bg5 Bb7	10. c4 dxc4	16. Re1 O–O	22. h4? Rxd1
5. Bxf6 Qxf6	11. Bxc6+ Qxc6	17. Nc3? e2+	White resigns
6. Nf3 c6	12. dxc4 e4	18. Nf2 Bxf3	

In 1966–7 a four-game match was played between Russian and American computers. The Soviet program won two games and conceded draws in favourable positions in the others. Here's one of the wins:

USSR Program–USA Program. Three Knights Defence

1. e4 e5	6. dxe5 Bxe5	11. Qd5 Ne6	16. Rxg7 c6
2. Nf3 Nc6	7. f4 Bxc3+	12. f5 Ng5	17. Qd6 Rxf5
3. Nc3 Bc5	8. bxc3 Nf6	13. h4 f6	18. Rg8+ Rf8
4. Nxe5 Nxe5	9. e5 Ne4	14. hxg5 fxg5	19. Qxf8 mate
5. d4 Bd6	10. Qd3 Nc5	15. Rxh7 Rf8	

♛

The first computer to enter a tournament was MAC HACK VI, programmed by Richard Greenblatt, a student at Massachusetts Institute of Technology. Its first tournament was in February 1967, where it scored one draw from five games. The following month it managed one win from five games, scoring its first victory with a queen sacrifice in the style of Morphy.

MAC HACK VI–Human, Massachusetts State Championship, 1967. Sicilian Defence

1. e4 c5	7. Bf4 e5	13. Bh4 Bg7	19. Nxe5 Be6
2. d4 cxd4	8. Bg3 a6	14. Nd5 Nxe4	20. Qxc6+ Rxc6
3. Qxd4 Nc6	9. O-O-O b5	15. Nc7+ Qxc7	21. Rd8 mate
4. Qd3 Nf6	10. a4 Bh6+	16. Qxc7 Nc5	
5. Nc3 g6	11. Kb1 b4	17. Qd6 Bf8	
6. Nf3 d6	12. Qxd6 Bd7	18. Qd5 Rc8	

Mac continued to play in tournaments and hacked quite a few more opponents before retiring from competitive chess in the early 1970s. A few years later he provided the opposition for Bobby Fischer's last published games, which show how an early computer program compared with a galactic megastar of the (almost) human variety.

Fischer–MAC HACK. King's Gambit

1. e4 e5	7. O-O Nxd5	13. dxe5 c6	19. Rc1 Kg7
2. f4 exf4	8. Nxd5 Bd6	14. Bxf4 Qg7	20. Rg3 Rh8
3. Bc4 d5	9. d4 g5	15. Nf6+ Kh8	21. Qh6 mate
4. Bxd5 Nf6	10. Nxg5 Qxg5	16. Qh5 Rd8	
5. Nc3 Bb4	11. e5 Bh3	17. Qxh3 Na6	
6. Nf3 O-O	12. Rf2 Bxe5	18. Rf3 Qg6	

♚

'COMPUTER LOSES GAME IN KING-SIZE BLUNDER' trumpeted the *New York Times* after the first round of the first-ever computer chess tournament in 1970. One of the programs, named MARSLAND after its programmer, had developed a bug which caused it to choose fairly randomly between its best and worst moves. Its opponent in this game was J. BIIT (Just Because It Is There), programmed by Hans Berliner, a man destined to play a large part in the history of computer chess.

MARSLAND–J. BIIT, New York, 1970

1. c4 Nf6	4. Nf3 d5	7. Bd2 Bxd2+	9. Qc5??? Ne4+
2. d4 e6	5. Ne5 dxc4	8. Kxd2?? Nxe5	White resigns
3. Qd3 Nc6	6. Qxc4 Bb4+		

♚

The 1971 United States Computer Championship witnessed what USCF Computer Chess Committee Chairman David Welsh has described as an 'all-time classic of computer ineptitude'. Strangely enough, it also showed how far ahead some of the early programs were capable of calculating. On the morning of this game, Ed Kozdrowicki of Bell Telephone Laboratories had joined the consortium betting that David Levy would lose to a computer by 1978.

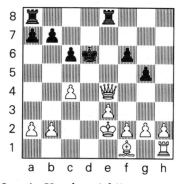

Here is Kozdrowicki's program, COKO III a queen up after twenty-seven moves against GENIE COKO has seen a forced mate so kicks off with ...

28. c5+ Kxc5 29. Qd4+ Kb5 30. Kd1+ Ka5 31. b4+ Ka4 32. Qc3 Red8+ 33. Kc2 Rd2+

GENIE sacs its rooks to delay the inevitable. 34. Kxd2 Rd8+ 35. Kc2 Rd2+ 36. Qxd2 Ka3 37. Qc3+ Kxa2. White has a choice of two mates in one but now COKO starts clowning around. 38. Kc1? f5 39. Kc2?? f4 40. Kc1??? g4 41. Kc2???? f3 42. Kc1????? fxg2 43. Kc2?????? gxh1=Q COKO's last chance for mate. 44. Kc1??????? Qxf1+ 45. Kd2 Qxf2+ 46. Kc1 Qg1+ 47. Kc2 Qxh2+ 48. Kc1 Qh1+ 49. Kc2 Qb1+ 50. Kd2 g3 51. Qc4+ Qb3 52. Qxb3+ Kxb3 53. e4 Kxb4 54. e5 g2. Aladdin rubs his magic lamp and GENIE produces a new Queen. COKO's masters had had enough and resigned on its behalf at this point. Observers reported that Kozdrowicki was heard mumbling something about a 'dam' fool bet'[1] after the game.

♚

You remember what happened to poor Vlastimil Hort in his Candidates' Match against Spassky? In a winning position he 'froze' and lost on time. You might think that this couldn't happen to a computer, but you'd be wrong.

Here's TECH II with White against something called RIBBIT, again in the 1974 US Computer Championship. TECH II has forty-five minutes to go to the time control and, amongst other goodies, a simple mate in two. But TECH II fell asleep and RIBBIT unsportingly claimed a win on time.

♚

The First European Computer Chess Championship, held in Amsterdam in 1976, matched ORWELL, from England, against TELL, from Switzerland. ORWELL, two rooks up, pushed a pawn to the end of the board and. . . left it there. TELL had no objection to this so arbiter David Levy decided that the game should continue. George pushed another

---

[1] See page 243 for how Kozdrowicki lost his bet. Last time we heard, he hadn't paid up.

pawn to the eighth rank, again left it there, and finally mated William with his two rooks.

♟

The first computer to play in the US Open was one SNEAKY PETE, in 1977. It played very weakly and was annihilated in the first few rounds. Then it came up against an inexperienced young woman player. The word soon spread that SNEAKY PETE was winning and crowds gathered at the board. His opponent, in desperation, set a trap. Pete fell headlong into it and his victorious opponent slammed down the winning move shouting, 'Games for people, not machines! Games for people, not machines!'

♟

Playing against human opposition in the 1982 US Open, CHAOS made a valiant attempt to emulate grandmaster Sämisch,[1] losing four games on time, one of them on move 15. The time control was fifty moves in two hours so it had another thirty-six moves to go.

♟

OK, it's time to stop sniggering and look at some of the successes of the silicon stars of the sixties and seventies.

In the first diagram old MAC HACK VI, in one of its early tournaments, found a winning combination which some watching US masters apparently failed to spot. Can you find the winning move for black?

The second diagram is from a 1974 World Championship game between CHAOS and CHESS 4.0. Here, white unleashed the first ever positional sacrifice played by a computer. Over to you, maestro.

---

[1] See Chapter III

Finally, here's a position from the Second World Computer Chess Championship, held in Toronto in 1977. The Soviet program KAISSA, black against DUCHESS, from Duke University, caused a sensation by giving up a rook with Re8. What had it seen that had been missed by the masters in the audience?

Don't be outwitted by a computer. Work out your own solutions before looking up the answers at the end of the chapter.

♚

In February 1977, CHESS 4.5 became the first machine (discounting Mephisto) to win a tournament against humans when it took the Minnesota Open with five wins and one loss. How it spent its prize money is not recorded. Later in 1977, CHESS 4.6 became the first computer to beat a grandmaster when taking a five-minute game off English grandmaster Michael Stean.

CHESS 4.6–Stean, Blitz Game, 1977. Owen's Defence

1. e4 b6	11. Rad1 Rd8	22. Ncxe4 Rxf2	33. Qg4 Bxe4
2. d4 Bb7	12. Qc4 Ng6	23. Rxd6[1] Qxd6	34. Qxe6+ Kh8
3. Nc3 c5	13. Rfe1 Be7	24. Nxd6 Rxg2	35. Qxe4 Rf6
4. dxc5 bxc5	14. Qb3 Qc6	25. Nge4 Rg4	36. Qe5 Rb6
5. Be3 d6	15. Kh1 O–O	26. c4 Nf5	37. Qxc5 Rxb3
6. Bb5+ Nd7	16. Bg5 Ba8	27. h3 Ng3+	38. Qc8+ Kh7
7. Nf3 e6	17. Bxe7 Nxe7	28. Kh2 Rxe4	and Black
8. O–O a6	18. a4 Rb8	29. Qf2 h6	resigns
9. Bxd7+	19. Qa2 Rb4	30. Nxe4 Nxe4	
Qxd7	20. b3 f5	31. Qf3 Rb8	
10. Qd3 Ne7	21. Ng5 fxe4	32. Rxe4 Rf8	

In deference to grandmaster Michael Stean, we must point out that his opponent was, relatively speaking, a very much stronger player at blitz speed than at tournament speed.

The following year, CHESS 4.6 took the Twin City Open with 5/5, and followed up with a win in a simul against grandmaster Walter Browne.

♚

1978 saw the famous challenge match between CHESS 4.7, as it had now become, and international master David Levy. This was the culmination of the first stage of the 'Levy bet', among the academics on the side of the machines being Donald Michie, whom you will remember from Bletchley Park days. In the first game Levy weakened his king's side, allowing CHESS 4.7 a stunning sacrifice. Defending desperately, Levy managed to reach an ending three pawns down, which he came close to winning! In the next two games, the human representative took no chances but then , convinced that he could win whenever he wanted, tried a risky opening in game 4. This is what happened:

CHESS 4.7–Levy, Challenge Match, 1978. Greco Counter Gambit

1. e4 e5	8. Qxf7+	16. Na4 Bd4	25. Re2 Bc8
2. Nf3 f5	Kxf7	17. Be3 Be5	26. Kg2 Bd6
3. exf5 e4	9. Nc3 c6	18. d4 Bd6	27. Bg1 Rh3
4. Ne5 Nf6	10. d3 exd3	19. h3 b6	28. Rae1 Rg3+
5. Ng4 d5	11. Bxd3 Nd7	20. Rfe1 Bd7	29. Kf2 Rhh3
6. Nxf6+	12. Bf4 Nc5	21. Nc3 hxg4	30. Re3 Ba6
Qxf6	13. g4 Nxd3+	22. hxg4 Rh4	31. Ne2 Bxe2
7. Qh5+	14. cxd3 Bc5	23. f3 Rah8	32. R1xe2 c5
Qf7	15. O–O h5	24. Kf1 Bg3	33. f4 Rxe3

[1] 'Bloody iron monster!' exclaimed the normally equable Stean at this point.

34. Rxe3 Rh4	40. Kg2 Bc5	46. Kf3 Bc5	52. f5 Ra3+
35. Kg3 Rh1	41. Rxd5 Rd2	47. Rd8+ Ke7	53. Kg4 Ra4+
36. Bf2 Rd1	42. b4 Bxb4	48. Bh4+ Kf7	54. Kh5 Rd4
37. Ra3 cxd4	43. Rd8+ Kf7	49. g5 g6	55. Rc7 Be7
38. Rxa7+ Kf8	44. Rd7+ Kf8	50. Rd7+ Kf8	56. f6 Black
39. Rd7 Rd3+	45. Rxd4 Rb2	51. fxg6 Rxa2	resigns

Levy upheld the honour of the human race by winning the fifth game to clinch his bet.

♚

The first of the 1980s superstars was BELLE, from Bell Telephone Laboratories. Running on specially designed hardware it became computer World Champion in 1980, shared second place in the 1982 US Speed Chess Championship and defeated several masters in the 1983 US Open. Here's one of the games from that event. Black had a USCF rating of 2321 (about a 209 BCF grading).

BELLE–Radke, US Open, Pasadena, 1983. Pirc Defence

1. e4 d6	6. e5 Ng4	11. Ne4 f5	16. O–O–O bxc5
2. d4 Nf6	7. dxc5 dxe5	12. exf6 exf6	17. Bb5 Ne5
3. Nc3 g6	8. Qxd8+ Kxd8	13. Nd6 Ke7	18. Nxe5 fxe5
4. f4 Bg7	9. h3 Nh6	14. Be3 b6	19. Rhf1 Black
5. Nf3 c5	10. fxe5 Nd7	15. Bc4 g5	resigns

♚

According to Reuben Fine's authoritative volume *Basic Chess Endings*, queen against two bishops or two knights is a draw. Not any more it isn't. BELLE has demonstrated that the queen wins. Not only that, she(?) will also tell you the number of moves required to win with best play from any starting position. For instance, the longest win with queen against two bishops is seventy moves, which will necessitate the rewriting of the rules of chess (providing exceptions to the fifty-move rule) as well as endgame textbooks. BELLE has also proved that two bishops beat a knight, and provided perfect analysis of the horrendous queen and knight's pawn versus queen endgame. If you've got a spare year or two, try that one yourself sometime.

♚

In 1983 BELLE lost its World Champion title to CRAY BLITZ, running on what was then the world's fastest computer. CRAY BLITZ had already won the Mississippi State Closed Championship with a score of 5/5, achieving a provisional master rating.

♚

The latest cybernetic candidate to attempt to conquer humankind over the chess-board was launched in 1985. Named HITECH, it emanates from Carnegie-Mellon University, where its programming team is led by Dr Hans Berliner, and is currently rated at about 2350, close to international master standard. Berliner, a former World Correspondence Chess Champion, had previously written programs called J. BIIT, which we have met before, and PATSOC (Plays A Terrible Sort Of Chess). In its first tournament against human opposition it beat two masters and drew with a grandmaster. It won the 1985 American Chess Computer Championship with 4/4, CRAY BLITZ only scoring 2/4. But in the 1986 World Computer Chess Championship it was surprisingly beaten by CRAY BLITZ in the last round. This left a four-way tie for first place, with CRAY BLITZ retaining its title on tie-break. Here's HITECH demolishing one of the German representatives with a sacrificial attack.

HITECH–SCHACH, Cologne, 1986. Sicilian Defence

1. e4 c5	8. Qd2 Ne5	15. Bh6 g6	22. Bxg5 fxg5
2. Nf3 d6	9. Be2 O–O	16. Bg5 Qc5	23. Rxg5+ Kh8
3. Bc4 e6	10. h3 Bd7	17. Qf4 Nh5	24. Rdg1 Black
4. d4 cxd4	11. Nf3 Nxf3+	18. Qh4 f6	resigns
5. Nxd4 Nf6	12. gxf3 Qa5	19. Be3 Qa5	
6. Nc3 Be7	13. O–O–O Rac8	20. Bb5 Bxb5	
7. Be3 Nbd7	14. Rhg1 Rfe8	21. Qxh5 g5	

The winning threat is Qxh7+, followed by Rh5 mate.

♛

In June 1986 HITECH took on international woman grandmaster Dr Jana Miles in a charity match. The mighty monster had little difficulty in winning both games.

HITECH–Miles, London, 1986. Caro-Kann Defence

1. e4 c6	10. Nxd5 Bxb5	19. Rad1 Qf6	28. Red1 b6
2. d4 d5	11. Qxb5 Nc6	20. d5 Bd6	29. Qxb6 Nh4
3. Nc3 g6	12. c3 a6	21. b4 a5	30. Nxh4 Qh2+
4. h3 Bg7	13. Qc5 Rc8	22. Qxa5 Qc3	31. Kf1 Qh1+
5. Nf3 Nh6	14. O–O e6	23. a3 exd5	32. Ke2 Re8+
6. exd5 cxd5	15. Nb6 Rc7	24. Nxd5 Qxc4	33. Kf3 Qh2
7. Bb5+ Bd7	16. Qa3 Bf4	25. Nxc7 Bxc7	34. Qf6 Black
8. Bxh6 Bxh6	17. Rfe1 Ne7	26. Qc5 Qf4	resigns
9. Qe2 O–O	18. c4 Nf5	27. Rd7 Bb8	

♛

Today chess computers, which will give all but the very strongest players a good game, are available for a few hundred pounds and machines suitable for beginners can be brought for very much less. We conclude with tournament games by two of the best on the market at the time of writing.

First, the PAR EXCELLENCE, from the Fidelity stable, in action in the Major Open of the British Championships in 1986. Its opponent had a grade of 184 (ELO 2072).

Escott–PAR EXCELLENCE. King's Gambit

1. e4 e5	9. Bc5 Qe3+	17. Nf3 Qxg3	25. Bd2 Qh2
2. f4 Qh4+	10. Be2 Qxe4	18. Rg1 Qh3	26. Qf1 Nf4
3. g3 Qe7	11. Bxd4 Qxh1	19. Bf1 Qh6+	27. Nf3 Ne2+
4. fxe5 d6	12. Bf2 Nf6	20. Be3 Qh5	28. Qxe2 Bxf3
5. b3 Nc6	13. Nc3 Qxh2	21. Ng5 Bg4	29. Qf2 Bxc4
6. d4 dxe5	14. Qd3 a6	22. Bg2 Rad8	White resigns
7. Ba3 Qg5	15. O–O–O O–O	23. Qc4 c6	
8. Bxf8 Nxd4	16. Bc5 Re8	24. Nce4 Nd5	

Finally, the Novag CONSTELLATION FORTE tricking an opponent from Bangladesh rated 2195 in 1986 Commonwealth Championship.

CONSTELLATION FORTE–Sohel. Queen's Gambit Declined.

1. d4 Nf6	16. a3 Bb7	31. Rc5 Kd6	46. Rf4 Ra3
2. c4 e6	17. b4 c5	32. Ra5 Bxc6	47. Rxf6 e5
3. Nc3 d5	18. Bxf6 gxf6	33. Ra6 f6	48. Kh3 e4
4. Bg5 Be7	19. dxc5 f5	34. Bxc6 Rxc6	49. g4+ Kh6
5. e3 O–O	20. Nd6 Bxd6	35. Rxa7 Ke5	50. h5 Ra2
6. Rc1 c6	21. cxd6 Qxd6	36. a4 f4	51. Rxg6+ Kh7
7. Nf3 Nbd7	22. c5 bxc5	37. a5 Kf5	52. Kg3 Ra1
8. Bd3 Re8	23. Bb5 Qxd1	38. Ra8 Kg4	53. Re6 Rg1+
9. O–O Bd6	24. Rfxd1 Red8	39. a6 Rc1+	54. Kf4 Rg2
10. e4 dxe4	25. bxc5 Rxd1+	40. Kh2 Ra1	55. Re7+ Kh6
11. Nxe4 Be7	26. Rxd1 Bd5	41. a7 Kf5	56. Rd7 Rxf2
12. Bf4 Nf8	27. c6 Rc8	42. g3 f3	57. g5+ Kxh5
13. Ne5 Ng6	28. Rc1 Rc7	43. Rd8 Rxa7	58. Rd6 Black
14. Nxg6 hxg6	29. h4 Kf8	44. Rd3 Kg4	resigns
15. Be5 b6	30. Ba4 Ke7	45. Rd4+ Kh5	

Answers

1. MAC HACK played 1...Rxf2+, and if 2. Rxf2 Nh2+ 3. Ke2 Qb2+ 4. Kd1 Qb1+ 5. Ke2 Rb2 mate. White instead tried 2. Kg1 and resigned a couple of moves later.

2. White played 1. Nxe6+, and after 1...fxe6 2. Qxe6+ Be7 3. Re1 CHAOS had an overwhelming position.

3. KAISSA had seen that after Kg7 DUCHESS had a forced mate with the startling 1. Qf8+ Kxf8 2. Bh6+ Kg8 (or Bg7) 3. Rc8+ Qd8 4. Rxd8+ Re8 5. Rxe8 mate.

♚

It's only tenuously related to chess, but since our book is largely for entertainment, we couldn't resist concluding with this story. We found it in an advertisement for Epson computers, so it must be true: Gilbert Bohuslav, a computer wizard from Houston, Texas, programmed his computer (DEC 11/70) to play chess. He was so pleased with its prowess that he decided to introduce DEC 11/70 to the world of literature. He fed into it all the most used words in every Western movie he'd ever seen. Here is the result:

'Tex Doe, the marshal of Harry City, rode into town. He sat hungrily in the saddle, ready for trouble. He knew that his sexy enemy, Alphonse the Kid, was in town.

'The Kid was in love with Texas Horse Marion. Suddenly the Kid came out of the upended Nugget Saloon. "Draw, Tex," he yelled madly. Tex reached for his girl, but before he could get it out of his car, the Kid fired, hitting Tex in the elephant and the tundra.

'As Tex fell, he pulled out his own chess board and shot the Kid 35 times in the King. The Kid dropped in a pool of whisky. "Aha," Tex said, "I hated to do it but he was on the wrong side of the Queen." '

Bibliography

A much earlier labourer in the same vineyard, Richard Twiss, eighteenth-century collector of chess anecdotes, had this to say: 'It is unnecessary to particularize the number of books, many of them tedious and disgusting, I have waded through, swallowing and exccrating to the end.' Here are some of those we consulted that were a pleasure to read.

Magazines

British Chess Magazine (St Leonards-on-Sea), *passim*
Chess (Sutton Coldfield), *passim*
Chess Notes (Geneva) *passim*
Also various issues of *New in Chess* (Amsterdam), *Chess Life and Review* (Published by USCF), *Kingpin* (Ilford), *Myers Opening Bulletin* (Davenport, Iowa), and other periodicals.

Reference Books

The Oxford Companion To Chess (Hooper and Whyld), OUP, 1984
Chess: The Records (Whyld), Guinness Books, 1986
The Encyclopedia of Chess (ed. Golombek), Batsford, 1977
The Encyclopaedia of Chess (Sunnucks), Robert Hale, 1970
A Catalog of Chess players and Problemists (Gaige) Privately published 1971
Hundert Jahre Schachturniere 1851–1950 (Feenstra Kuiper) W. Ten Have, Amsterdam

Chess History

A History of Chess (Murray), OUP, 1913; reprinted Benjamin Press, n.d.
A History of Chess (Golombek), Routledge and Kegan Paul, 1976
Chess: The History of a Game (Eales), Batsford, 1985
History of Chess (Gizycki, ed. Wood), The Abbey Library, 1972; rev. 1977
Grandmasters of Chess (Schonberg), Fontana, 1975

The Kings of Chess (Hartston), Pavilion, 1985
A Century of British Chess (Sergeant), Hutchinson, 1934
The 1851 Chess Tournament (Stanton), Batsford, 1986

Chess and Literature–Compilations

Chess Pieces (Knight), Sampson Low, 1949
King, Queen, Knight (Knight and Guy), Batsford, 1975
Chess (Twiss), 1787
Caissa's Web: The Chess Bedside Book (Harwood), Latimer, 1975
The Poetry of Chess (Waterman), Anvil Press, 1981

Games Collections

Oxford Encyclopaedia of Chess Games, Volume I, (ed. Levy and
    O'Connell), OUP, 1981
The Golden Dozen (Chernev), OUP, 1976
The Golden Treasury of Chess (Wellmuth), Arco, 1958
Die Hypermoderne Schachpartie (Tartakower), Olms, 1981
500 Master Games of Modern Chess (Tartakower and du Mont) Dover,
    1975

Computer Chess

Chess: Man vs Machine (Ewart), Barnes/Tantivy, 1980
Chess and Computers (Levy), Batsford, 1976

Endgame Studies and Problems

Test Tube Chess (Roycroft), Faber and Faber, 1972
An ABC of Chess Problems (Rice) Faber and Faber, 1970
Solving in Style (Nunn), Allen and Unwin, 1985

Chess Variants

100 Other Games to Play on a Chessboard (Addison), Peter Owen,
    1983
Chess Variations (Gollon), Tuttle, 1968

Miscellaneous

The World of Chess (Saidy and Lessing), Collins, 1974
Wonders and Curiosities of Chess (Chernev), Dover, 1974

The Chess Companion (Chernev), Faber and Faber, 1970

The Book of Chess Lists (Soltis), David McKay, 1984

Chess Curiosities (Krabbé), George Allen and Unwin, 1985

Total Chess (Spanier) Secker and Warburg, 1984

The Chess Scene (Levy and Reuben), Faber and Faber, 1974

Cabbage Heads and Chess Kings (Hayden), Arco, 1960

Chess Panorama (Lombardy and Daniels), Chilton, 1975

The Adventure of Chess (Edward Lasker), Dover, 1959

Chess and its Stars (Harley), Whitehead and Miller, 1936

The Soviet Chess School (Kotov and Yudovich), Moscow, 1984

The Ratings of Chess Players Past and Present (Elo), Batsford, 1978

Idle Passion: Chess and the Dance of Death (Cockburn), Weidenfeld
    and Nicolson, 1975

Chessmen for Collectors (Keats), Batsford, 1985.

The Chess Beat (Evans), Pergamon, 1980

Confessions of Aleister Crowley (Symonds & Grant), Routledge and
    Kegan Paul, 1979

The Prostitutes' Padre (Cullen), Bodley Head, 1975.

If you've enjoyed this book why not join your local chess club?

To find out the address of your nearest club contact:

The General Secretary, British Chess Federation,
9a Grand Parade, St Leonards-on-Sea, East Sussex, TN38 0DD
Phone: 0424 442500

If you're interested in correspondence chess contact:

M. C. Peltz, Hon. Secretary, British Postal Chess Federation,
14 Linden End, Aylesbury, Bucks., HP21 7NA

For chess problems:

C. A. H. Russ, Hon. Secretary, British Chess Problem Society,
Darwin College, University of Kent, Canterbury, CT2 7NY

For endgame studies:

A. J. Roycroft, Chess Endgame Study Circle, 17 New Way Road,
London, NW9 6PL

Finally, and most important of all: teach your children to play chess (see p.78).

Le tout ensemble

'... all the men and women* merely players'
(As You Like It. II viii)*

* and machines, and animals.

263

Post-script:

Since the text was completed, we have come across: Alan Ball, Rodney Marsh, George Cole, George Orwell, André Deutsch, Thomas Hardy and Edwin Lutyens; if you know of, or are, a chess-playing celebrity we've missed, drop us a line c/o Faber and Faber.